C.J. WEISS

SECRETS GNAW AT THE FLESH

Thank you to the bookstores, readers, and hype people who support independent authors.

INTRODUCTION

There is a glossary at the end of the book with specific terms used throughout the novel. I would recommend you not reference any definitions unless you have seen the term prior. Doing otherwise may spoil parts of the novel.

Secrets Gnaw at the Flesh is the second book written in the Virulent Nightmare Origins quartet. These books can be read as standalone novels and in any order. However, if you enjoy the story, I recommend reading my first book next: *A Broken Clock Never Boils*. The plots across the quartet are not directly related but do occur in the same universe. I won't say more about that until the time comes, but I look forward to shaping this world alongside you.

Additional information regarding any concerns about the book's content may be found at https://cjweiss.com/secrets-gnaw-at-the-flesh. With all of that out of the way, I hope you enjoy *Secrets Gnaw at the Flesh*.

1. Proposals

Garrett Mueller knelt before his would-be wife, proffering a modest diamond ring in a small box. Marie laughed sweetly, heartfelt tears already flowing. They had their special picnic bench to themselves, surrounded by a grove of birch and oak trees. Nature enveloped them for miles in the state park, and a breeze rustled the leaves in tranquil harmony. The scene was perfect.

Until Marie shook her head, her black bob swaying in front of her face.

"I'm sorry." She dabbed her eyes. "No." She averted her gaze and carried on joyfully crying as most fiancés did when agreeing to a proposal, not rejecting it. Her normally soothing serenade of laughter raked Garrett's ears. Like Beethoven playing the piano out of tune. He didn't know what to make of her reaction.

A week ago, she'd told him they should break up prior to a lengthy upcoming family retreat of hers. Let fate decide whether they belonged together.

But fate made a fickle mistress for such a perfect couple. Splitting apart due to a temporary absence made no sense. An engagement bound them for the future and demonstrated he'd still love her after she returned to Boston. Garrett had believed she wanted that promise. He evidently erred, but in his embarrassment, another feeling matured.

Resolve.

Garrett stood from the earth, brushing off dirt and stick fragments clinging to his chinos. True commitment didn't falter at a single setback, and he was devoted to the woman he loved. He would ask questions. Listen. Salvage his blunder or, at bare minimum, understand the real reason for breaking up. They'd shared too many intimate conversations for him not to recognize when she hid something. He closed the ring box and slid it into his pocket, then sat next to her.

Marie snapped out of her state and jerked her head up, her eyes wide. She briefly covered her mouth. "Oh, God, Gare, I'm sorry. You must've thought I was laughing at you." She rubbed her hands together, warming them before caressing his cheeks. "That couldn't be further from the truth. I got caught up in the moment, in the idea. I love you, and I love spending time with you. I want to say yes, but you don't know a thing about my family. Marrying a Renault is more trouble than it's worth."

"Then tell me what it's like. I can handle crazy in-laws." Racist, angry, or rude too. His half-Chinese, half-German descent meant he'd dealt with those kinds before, though he doubted someone like that had raised Marie.

"They're not crazy." She chuckled and tilted her head down, hiding her hazel eyes. "They're amazing." She wore suede hiking shoes and ripstop shorts down to her mid-thigh. A plain long-sleeved shirt accentuated the straight angles of her boyish figure. The typical outdoors outfit comforted Garrett, but he loved her in whatever she wore.

Marie recomposed herself with a soft expression and intertwined her fingers with Garrett's. "It's not the family members. It's the family itself. We have obligations you can't imagine. You know who I am, but that's different from knowing *who* I am. I don't ever expect to marry, and I'd rather laugh over it than cry. Not that I can always help it." She lifted her shoulder to brush a tear from her cheek.

She never expected to marry? It almost sounded like she was protecting him. Giving up her happiness for another's fit her to a T, but he couldn't imagine what she believed he couldn't handle. Maybe he'd pushed too hard with marriage. At twenty-nine, Garrett might've discounted the maturity his three years on her afforded him. He placed his other hand on top of hers. Marie reciprocated. Four hands all atop one another on a cold wooden board. Their aptly named hand stack—their symbol for stronger together than apart.

Confidence swelled within Garrett, lightening his load. "We don't have to get married to stay together. My mom won't like it, but my dad can help her come around."

"I'm leaving next weekend for four months. Can you make that kind of commitment when we've barely dated twice that long? Surely a big shot like you can find another girl."

"Not like you." His mom had offered a single piece of relationship advice: find someone he trusted who trusted him. He'd ignored it for far too long with his ex, trying to shoehorn the wrong woman into his life. "Forget I proposed. I'll focus on finishing school while you're gone, and we'll pick up where we left off when you return."

"We've gone over this." She fidgeted within their hand stack.

"I don't get it." He regretted not pleading his case harder last week.

"Marrying me, or whatever"—she started bouncing her legs—"staying together long-term involves a commitment I can't ask of you. Can we walk? It's getting cold."

"Sure." They stood together, Garrett's chin level with the top of Marie's head. He grabbed the backpack from the table and slung it over his shoulders. He tapped the ring box in his pocket, renewing his determination. They started down the wide dirt path. He rubbed her back, inviting her to lean into him.

She smiled sadly, remaining at arm's length.

"Marriage is a commitment. That's the point," Garrett said. A considerate touch from Marie could wash away worries that used to wear him down. With her, everything felt right. He wouldn't relinquish that without a fight. "I'm confused. You've got a normal family, you don't want to ask too much of me, and you think I'm a big shot. Sounds great. What am I missing?"

"I said my family is amazing, not normal. And I do want to ask too much, but I've been selfish enough. I held onto the fantasy of us staying together as long as I could. You deserve more. A collegiate baseball player closing in on a Harvard MBA? You'll go far. With me, you won't. Can't."

"Stop beating around the bush." He unleashed his words faster than intended. "Sorry. Whatever it is, I can take it."

"I want to believe that."

"I feel about you how you feel about me. Isn't that what matters?"

Marie looked up at the canopy of trees, falling into silent reverie.

The trail split in three directions. A wide paved road one way, three guys walking down a dirt road parallel to the first, and to the right, their best chance at avoiding interruption. Garrett guided her down the secluded path of tall bushes and low-hanging trees. He pushed a branch out of her way just before she spun on him.

"Okay, Gare." Marie poked his arm. "Let's start small. Pretend we get married. Can you put your life on hold for a few months every several years? Find a way out of work, drop every obligation, then return as if nothing 'appened?" She dropped the H in happened, a rare display of her Louisiana upbringing.

"Like a beach vacation?"

"Sure. But without a beach. Probably."

"Probably?"

"It's complicated. And not the point. If you want to be part of my family, you have to give up everything, no questions asked, with limited warning, only going back to normal at a time out of your control. That's why I didn't tell you about the retreat until last week. I didn't know about it until the day before. It's frustrating, and it sucks. You think you want to spend the rest of your life with me, but you don't understand what that means. Picture prepping for best man duties one week, then telling the groom you can't make the wedding at all. Follow that up by informing your boss of another family emergency. It's hard.

Really hard. This is my life, and it would be yours too."

Garrett withdrew from her and stuffed his hands in his pockets. He fiddled with the ring box. Marie never spoke so glumly, but she trusted him enough to hint at her secret. He had to prove himself worthy of more.

"I love you," Garrett said. "I'm committed to you."

"I know that. My memory might be bad, but your kneeling is fresh in my mind."

Stay with it. "Then I'll say it differently. Whatever you need from me, I'm willing to give it a try. Willing to try anything. For you."

Marie studied him with an unreadable expression. He considered what angle to take next, which path to walk to buy more time, whether she'd accept his touch again. That all fled when she threw herself at him.

Garrett caught her. Despite her petite size, the sudden momentum almost bowled him over. He dug his foot into the dirt trail, bracing against falling. She clasped his cheeks, her elbows bent wide, and planted her lips on his. He slid his arms around her lower back and drew her in. She pressed her body against him as much as her arms allowed. Their mouths and tongues played in perfect harmony, kissing until they labored to breathe. Then she pulled away, a single hand keeping contact with his face, and laughed. Not the painful laughter of rejection, but the tittering of a free spirit.

"Thanks for shaving today," Marie said. "A scraggly beard would've ruined the moment."

Garrett smiled. This was why he loved her—her spontaneity kept his head out of the weeds and focused on the world's beauty. Her sense of adventure matched his planning skills and took them to new heights, like hiking. Neither of them had cared much for the hobby before meeting. That still didn't explain why she'd jumped him.

"What was that?" he asked.

"Our last kiss." She stroked his cheekbone. "Or the first of many more. I hope this works. You've offered more than I ever expected, but I have to call my dad first. I'll tell him we're serious but leave out the proposal bit. If he lets me, I'll explain some now, and the rest"—she shrugged—"we'll see. His blessing means everything to me, so if he says no, then it's a no, okay?"

"Okay," he hesitated, not wanting to leave his love life up to another individual any more than he wanted to leave it up to fate.

"Schwaz! Give me my phone. I'll make the call."

"That's still not a word." Garrett sloughed a backpack strap, dug out her phone, and handed it over.

"Thanks. And it is if I say it is." She dialed, then raised the phone to her ear. A moment later, "Hi, Dad. One sec." She mouthed, *Be right back*, and skipped away like a little girl. She stayed in eyesight, pacing behind a tree but whispering out of earshot.

Garrett checked the signal on his phone. Nothing. He switched airplane mode on and off. Rebooted. Still nothing. They were in the middle of the woods, and she never worried about her connection. She merely hinted at her family's money in moments like these. Probably what allowed her to shirk responsibilities at a moment's notice. He couldn't though. Was he setting himself up to rely on her?

One step at a time.

Marie paced in a circle. Leaves rustled beneath her feet. She slowed to a halt, gripping her phone-holding wrist. Standing there, she nodded her head, faster and faster. Her words were faint murmurs until she squealed. She bolted back through the trail and jumped up at him.

This time, he steadied himself and caught her by the rear. She wrapped her legs around his waist. After a peck on the lips, he let her down.

"He said yes!"

"That's great." He realized he'd been clutching his phone tight enough to crush an aluminum can. He slackened his grip, stowed his and Marie's phones away. "So dating's okay?" He shook out the cramp.

"We don't need to break up when you go"—he gestured off in the distance—"to your thing?"

"Not exactly. Let's keep going. You take big news better on the move." She didn't wait for a response to start walking.

Garrett shrugged, keeping pace.

"The retreat is at my family estate in Louisiana. Blah. Family estate. So pretentious." Marie tousled her hair. "It's in a small town called Ajaccio. You'll never find it on a map unless you scroll and zoom just right." She took a deep breath, as if every reveal exerted intense effort. "My family's a big part of the community, but they stay pretty insular. Some live their whole lives there. Most leave and return for these retreats. We're particular about who's allowed in the house. It was touch and go convincing Dad. I spent like half the convo rephrasing how much I love you, but I think your agnosticism is what tipped the scales."

"How would that help?" Garrett asked. "Wait, hold on. You want me to visit your estate? I assumed you were hiding that we were dating, that you needed permission for us to get serious. I didn't think I'd be meeting your family. I still have a couple of months in the semester. And you said . . ."

Her trip would last four months. It'd eat into next semester too. He'd drop everything for her in the future, once he established himself. But delaying school delayed everything else.

"I told you. You have to drop everything on a whim for this to work. Including now." Her raised hand halted his response. "My dad said to explain it as bluntly as possible. So," she affected a gruff voice, "let me channel him, and you just listen up, Gare."

"Okay." What else was there to say?

Marie wiggled her whole body, straightened her spine, and adjusted a fake tie at her neck, all without breaking her gait. "Every so often, my family and I are called back home. It's been two years since I've been back. Then four before that, though I was just homesick then. The last time an official call was made before that . . ." She glanced up. Her cheeks crinkled and dimples widened. That, combined with the goofiness of her voice, made resisting the temptation to kiss her as great a challenge as guessing where this was heading. "Ten years ago. I was still living at home. Whenever the call is made, everyone bound by blood or oath returns, which means spouses and children. Death is preferable to not showing up.

"We stay for a few months, until the house lets us leave. Four months is a safe bet, but my grandpa had to last a year once. Marrying me isn't just marrying my family. It's marrying that house. And that house is haunted." Her voice returned to her normal soprano. "There. That *was* simple."

The path narrowed to shoulder-width. Garrett took the lead, feeling claustrophobic and thankful to face away. He massaged his temples, searching for reason in Marie's absurd claim, finding it with a memory.

For Garrett's birthday, she had printed out two fake tickets to an opera he didn't want to see, talked it up all day, then surprised him by driving them to the train station that night. They ended up spending the weekend in New York.

This was another of her pranks.

"Simple?" He fought to keep his voice from betraying his suspicions. "Your family lives in a haunted house? I don't know where to begin."

"How about 'whatever it is, I'm willing to give it a try'. That'd be good."

Garrett dismissed the fledgling idea of a hidden craziness. Her eyes gleamed with warmth, and her behavior in their eight months shouted exuberance, not madness. "What about school? I'd have to drop out."

"That's why I didn't want to ask too much of you. I didn't want to get my hopes up, but you have to decide: is this a life you could live or not?"

Garrett sealed his lips until he regained some semblance of composure. He picked up speed, then slowed, reassuring himself that Marie crafted an epic gag. "A haunted house? Really? People in horror movies spend weeks denying ghosts exist, and once they finally accept it, they can't escape. You come and go as you please."

"Except for the four months or so it traps us. Once you meet every—"

"Sorry, hold on. If it's haunted, why do you go back? Why does anyone?"

"Well," she stretched out the word. "Because if we don't, the world ends." She continued walking as if she'd given a reasonable answer.

She'll crack any moment here.

"The world"—he scratched his nose—"ends?"

"Not right away. It's not like the ghosts will sneak out a batch of supernatural nukes." She playfully nudged Garrett, and he stiffened. However much his rational brain screamed, *Joke!,* his emotions started responding to, *What if?* "You'll have to cut out that jumpiness. Ghosts are real. Demons too, more or less. I could tell you more, but this is dragging into 'easier to show than tell' territory."

Garrett exited the clearing onto the rocky beach of the Aaron River Reservoir and halted. *Demons too? Come on.* Marie hopped out next to him. Two strangers walked wide of them, appearing from the trees as they had, and hurried away. Joke or no, she *had* been ready to break up with him.

"Is this a test?" Garrett rubbed behind his ear. "Can't I join you next time?"

"Nope, sorry. I'm not testing you. That'd be crappy since I already laughed at your proposal." She tugged on his wrist, waiting until he looked up. She intertwined her fingers in his, placed her other hand on top. He reciprocated with the briefest hesitation. "We can't have loose ends. If the real you isn't there, they'll use you against me. I won't be able to tell the difference."

"Who is they? The ghosts? The demons?"

"Both. In different ways. However earnest you are in saying you'll wait for me, I can't erase every shred of doubt. My brain doesn't work that way. The tiniest uncertainty is dangerous for me." She stared beyond him, at someone who seemed far away. "And my family."

A breeze blew in. Garrett shifted to block it from striking Marie. Water lapped at the rocky shore. Cool wind pelted his back as he faced her. In spite of her wild claim, perhaps somewhat because of it, he remained committed to her. Marie crafted this elaborate tale with sincerity.

"If this is so important, why isn't this common knowledge?" he asked.

"Nothing good comes from telling people we live in a haunted house. Skeptics think we're crazy. Believers are worse. They'll convince their friends to explore the house like it's a game. And they'll die through some tragic string of events, the police will investigate my family for murder, and maybe lock us all up. Then, the world ends."

"Back to the world ending. Are you serious?"

"As serious as the world ending. Which in my astute opinion, is quite serious."

Still in their hand stack, Garrett's thumb caressed Marie's knuckles. "This is a lot."

"If you can't drop everything for a week, how can you handle months at a time?"

"A week? I thought I was signing on for four months." Garrett suppressed a grin. The first crack had formed in her story.

"Like I said: easier to show than tell. Skip school for a week. Bring your laptop. Work from the house. The real show doesn't start 'til next week. Before you decide, there's one more thing." Marie squeezed his hands. "Staying past the week means more than me accepting your proposal. It means we're getting married then and there. When I said spouses and children return to the house, I also meant we keep out anyone who isn't one or the other. It's not safe. I could try to cover why in an afternoon, but my sister and dad are way better with explanations."

That suppressed grin turned into a face of open confusion. *Married next week?* He'd spent the afternoon trying to convince her he was ready to marry her. Now, she tossed it out like no big deal. Like they'd overcome the giant hurdle holding her back, a hurdle as big as . . . a haunted house. Except that couldn't be right.

"What about my parents?" he managed.

"Just a private ceremony. We can do the big thing later. You think I'm gonna miss that? For now, let's focus on the present. I was delaying my return so we could spend more time together, but now that you know, we can leave tomorrow. Take the next week to decide if you really want to marry me, with everything that comes attached. Low risk and a pretty good reward, I'd say." With a grin, Marie poked Garrett square in the chest. He barely felt it.

"Low risk? It's a haunted house," he said, but the tangible plan of action emboldened him.

"Well, yeah, but this week is like a good movie trailer. None of the big stuff. Now stop stalling. It's answer time." She wiggled her forefinger. "I'm ready to head back to the car."

Curiosity compelled him as much as love. *What if she's telling the truth?* A stupid thought. *So, what sort of surprise warrants this much of a cover-up?* Either way, every indication pointed at his lightest load of the semester next week. Five days of remote school wouldn't hurt him much.

Marie expectantly shifted her head from side to side in exaggerated, silly motions. He stared at her adorable face lurching left and right. Questions and concerns scrapped for attention, swirling chaotically in his brain. Only one mattered in the end. Either go along with Marie's claims and live in a supposed haunted house for a week, or lose her here and now, forever.

"Show me this haunted house of yours."

2. Travel

Cars passed through the airport pickup area at a steady trickle. With a broad smile, Marie watched each of them drive by where she and Garrett stood. When a shiny silver Mercedes pulled up to the curb, she started bouncing, tipping over a large, checked bag. Garrett caught it halfway to the cement, examining the tag wrapped around the handle.

Alexandria, Louisiana.

"Oops. Thanks, Gare." Marie's full-body bounces eased into small heel lifts. Like yesterday, she wore shorts, sneakers, and a long-sleeved shirt—plus a light jacket left over from a chilly Boston morning. It wasn't much warmer here.

"No problem." Garrett readjusted his backpack. Alexandria wasn't a likely candidate for his first vacation since high school, but the city came with a tantalizing reward: answers.

He had agreed to no more questions until 'butts in seats', but he'd compiled them with every silent moment and sleepless hour. Marie may have been pulling his leg in epic fashion, but he resolved to treat it seriously. First impressions didn't allow for second chances.

The sedan slowed to a stop. Two brunettes, a male and a female, exited from the front. Marie's older twin siblings—Claude and Julie—assuming nobody had changed the pickup plans. Garrett had dedicated the first half of the flight to memorizing the Renaults' names. Now he had a face for two of them.

As soon as Julie stepped on the sidewalk, Marie embraced her.

"You didn't have to dress up for me," Marie said.

"I didn't." Julie resembled one of Garrett's university librarians.

Thick-rimmed glasses, messy hair bun, a cardigan, and a wool knee-length skirt. She wore minimal makeup and, along with Claude, stood close to Garrett's height. "We ate brunch in Alexandria. I wanted an excuse to get out of sweats. Dad and Grandpa never give me a reason to, and the food in Ajaccio hasn't changed in thirty years."

Beaming, Marie squeezed her sister's forearm. "I can't believe it's been two years."

"I can't believe you brought a boy." She extended a stiff hand forward. Garrett accepted her professional handshake. "I'm Julie."

"Garrett. Glad to meet you."

"You say that now." Straight-faced and serious.

"Jules!" Marie shouted.

"Don't get me wrong," Julie said. "We're eager to have you. More help is welcome. It's that I don't think *you*'ll be glad soon. For Marie's sake, I hope I'm wrong."

"I'm sure I can handle it." He believed his words, but how else could he respond to her pessimism?

Julie snorted, crossing her arms. Forehead wrinkles and the start of crow's feet made her look a tad older than the ten years she had on Marie.

"Play nice." Marie brushed past her sister and leaned on the car's front hood, scanning around. "Where'd Claude go?"

Her brother crouched near the trunk, his forefinger over his lips as he crept forward. He seemed to have stolen a couple of years from Julie. With a leap to the sidewalk, he grabbed Marie from behind and lifted her up.

Her legs flailed in the air. "Put me down and give me a real hug."

"You got it, sis." He set her down as if she were too drunk to stand on her own. Marie turned and hugged him with the same joy she hugged her sister. Jealousy nipped at Garrett. He'd always wanted siblings. Always wanted to experience this level of familial camaraderie.

"Nice one." Claude tapped Marie's wrist. Rainbow threads peeked out from her sleeve. She collected friendship bracelets and picked this one up at Logan Airport.

"Thanks." Marie pushed the bracelet back up her forearm. "Gare bought it for me."

"Did he now? I like him already." Claude leaned his shoulder in toward Garrett for a handshake of his own. Much warmer and congenial than his twin sister. "Good to meet you, Garrett. Looking sharp. I'm Claude."

"Glad to meet you too." Garrett wore a crisp blue button-down with slacks and no tie. It took him close to an hour to settle on his clothes.

"You ever been to Louisiana before?" Claude asked. Where Marie had a faint accent, the twins sounded as if they could've been national news anchors.

"I haven't."

"We'll make the best of it, but don't let this experience taint it for you. Great place." With well-groomed scruff, a dapper sweater, and a charming smile, Claude had all the makings of a French Casanova. Not what Garrett expected after Marie described him as a family man.

"We should get going," Julie said. "We're an hour away, and the clouds keep darkening."

"Sounds good," Garrett said. Clear skies loomed overhead, but he was eager to move. *Butts in seats, answers to follow.* He rolled Marie's behemoth of a checked bag and his own suitcase to the trunk. She followed with her carry-on and a tote bag so stuffed it must have broken airline regulations.

"That's all you brought?" Claude popped open the trunk, eyeing Garrett's luggage. "Marie, didn't you tell him to pack more?"

"He *always* packs light," she mocked, staring at Garrett to highlight the many times she'd tried to convince him to do otherwise.

"You have a washer and a dryer, right?" Garrett asked.

"Of course, but—" Claude whistled low. "We'll get you some clothes."

Waiting to sit down before asking questions started to pain Garrett. With his tongue jammed against his back teeth, he helped Claude hoist Marie's larger bag into the trunk. The two of them alternated loading the rest. After they finished, the four of them slid into the car, twins in the front. Marie reached over and met Garrett's hand on the middle seat. She gave a look that opened the floor for questioning.

But as Claude shifted into gear, he beat him to the punch. "What do you do in Boston?"

Marie's eyes apologized.

"I worked as a financial analyst for a few years out of college," Garrett said. "Now I'm getting my MBA at Harvard. Delving deeper into the management side of things."

"Harvard." Claude affected a snooty voice and rolled the 'r'.

"Claude," warned both sisters.

"He said the H word first, not me!"

"Nobody cares, Claude," Marie said. "Nobody cares."

Claude drum rolled the steering wheel. "Sorry, Garrett. I work with this guy from Harvard. He drops the name whenever he can, and I like to poke fun at him. Automatic response at this point. Harvard's a good school, obviously. Smart to get all your education out of the way before starting a family. A lot harder to find the time once you have a kid. If you have a kid." He glanced at Marie through the rearview mirror. She turned to face out the window.

Garrett wanted a family, but they'd never seriously discussed it. Too far in the future. At least, it was before proposing and jumping on a plane to meet Marie's entire family. She avoided children out in the open world, but did that mean she didn't want her own? He had the oh-so-generous time frame of a week to find out.

"What do you two do?" Garrett asked.

"I'm an analyst too," Claude said. "Nothing fancy. Hard to move up when duty calls at a moment's notice." He veered onto a two-lane highway. Flat grassy plains in various states of liveliness rolled alongside the road. Yellows, greens, and browns alternated in random arrays. Not a tree in sight.

"Yet he manages to afford extravagant vacations every year," Julie said, "and as far as I've seen, dresses this way every day." Her finger drew an invisible line from his head to his waist.

"My reward for staring at a computer screen all day. Wish I could say it was worth the work. Not sure if ghosts or spreadsheets give me worse nightmares." If the haunted house was one big gag, Marie had her whole family in on it.

"I get what you mean," Garrett chuckled. "The spreadsheet part at least. What about you, Julie?"

She raised her chin in the direction of the white clouds above. "I live at the house with Dad and Grandpa," she said, as if unconcerned whether anybody heard her. She was old enough that her grandfather might've needed assistance at home. Was she a caretaker?

"It doesn't bother you living in a," Garrett paused, feeling silly, "haunted house?"

"It does."

He was wondering what to make of that when Marie snapped out of her daze.

"What's it like at home?" she asked. "Any big changes?"

"The usual turnover," Julie said. "Spirits coming and going. Dad bought a new gas range. Decided it was worth the risk." She made ghosts sound like a picnic conversation.

"Not going out on an empty stomach."

"Not him."

"Why is buying a new oven risky?" Garrett asked.

Awkward silence. Julie's siblings glanced at her. Through practiced disregard or truly not noticing them, she didn't react for several moments. Simply looked up and out the windshield. As the silence tickled the back of Garrett's neck, she shook her head.

"Nobody?" she asked.

Marie tucked her ankle under her thigh. "You're the best at this. I can't remember all the specifics anyway."

"He doesn't need specifics." Julie sighed. "Fine. The house itself isn't haunted. It's where it's built that's the problem. The ground sneaks through worlds, bringing back whatever it finds. We keep everything as consistent as possible. Repairing furniture before we replace it. Reupholstering it before that. An oven, couch, or bed may not look the same, but it will feel, smell, and sound the same. The more sensory aspects we maintain, the safer we are."

"How so?" Garrett asked.

"Ghosts can alter how we perceive the world. Keeping furniture as a constant grounds us, allows us to recover more quickly once we spot the inconsistency. Once the Breach opens, and we're contending with mekari in addition to ghosts, we want the deck stacked in our favor as much as possible."

"Breach? Mekari?"

"Dammit, Marie. Did you tell him nothing?"

Marie blushed and shrank behind Julie's headrest. She mouthed, *Uh oh,* to Garrett before responding. "I told him the basics. Said it would be better to show than tell."

"You mean pass it off to your sister and dad."

"You know my memory is bad, and Garrett needs a strong foundation. I'll fill him in on details later, but I'd mess up laying the groundwork. You're like the brains between us. I'm the heart."

"She's right about that," Claude said.

With a curt wave, Julie cut them off. "I'll disregard the insinuation that I lack a heart. A Breach is the event we're gathering for. Those living at the house alert everybody else once we see the signs. There are preludes to ghosts and mekari—"

"Basically, demons," Claude clarified.

"No. Mekari. You didn't want to explain, so don't interrupt. Mekari are the yin to humanity's yang. They're as evil as humans are good, and vice versa. Whatever you think of humanity, most are good. Foolish and easily brainwashed, but good. They care about their people. They love them and will sacrifice for them. Mekari are the opposite. They seek entry into our world for selfish ends, to terrorize and consume. A single mekar is more dangerous than several spirits, but they're rare. Our world isn't as tightly linked with theirs as the spirit realm.

"Ghosts don't intend to hurt us. They wander over from wherever they died, stop halfway through passing over, and decide they want to walk this world again. They're balls of emotion, guided more by whims than logic. Their chance at freedom comes as the divide between our worlds weakens, what we call a Breach."

"A portal between worlds," Garrett concluded. It sounded like a twisted fairy tale. One meant to scare off or tease a potential suitor as a rite of passage.

"Exactly."

Marie and Claude stared at Julie, presumably expecting her to elaborate. She ignored them.

Garrett poked Marie's leg, shooting her a *what gives* gesture. She gave him an innocent shrug. Questions were piling up faster than answers. "Who opens the portal?"

"God. Satan. The Easter Bunny. We don't know. It's a natural phenomenon."

"Marie said everyone bound by blood or oath was better off dead than not returning. Why? What happens?"

Julie stiffened, stroking her eyebrow, obviously growing tired of the conversation. "Once the Breach begins in earnest, an electromagnetic field forms around the grounds."

"Like a force field?"

"Sure," she snapped. "That field is at its strongest when we're all gathered. Each person tied to the family through blood or oath that's missing weakens the field and widens the Breach. More spirits and mekari can then cross over, turning a leak into a flood and placing our lives and the world's well-being in jeopardy. Bottom line: anyone who puts us through that hell will wish for death once the Breach clears. Fortunately, nobody who's married into or been born into this family is that big of an ass." With a final stroke, her finger flicked away from her brow.

Claude grinned. "Don't fuck it up."

Behind the front seat, Garrett pointed to his ring finger and shrugged at Marie. She shook her head. She hadn't said anything about his proposal. He leaned back. "Marie also said romantic interests are a weak point. That ghosts, and I guess mekari, can use them against you? What about close friends?" Like the group he'd abandoned Saturday night plans with to take this trip.

Julie huffed. "At least she told you something. Close attachments outside of the family are undesirable, but not nearly as dangerous as an off-site lover. It's safest not to get attached to people. Some of us adhere to that better than others." She shot a warning glance at Claude, who ignored it or didn't notice. "We can teach you precautions to keep you reasonably safe."

Reasonably? Nothing about this typified reasonable. He tried to indulge Marie and her family while supporting his theory that this was a hazing ritual. He expected them to break down, laugh at him, and move on by now. These details went beyond jokes and campfire tales, but if ghosts existed, where was the proof? Every ghost story he'd investigated, Wikipedia either debunked or portrayed in a way that made drinking hot coffee sound more dangerous. The longer this Q&A lasted, the more Marie's invitation bore its oppressive weight against him. He'd barely passed her father's test, yet Julie indicated she appreciated more help. Was he walking into a cult? Marie had tried so hard to steer him away, he felt it even less likely than a haunted house. Cults also didn't tend to reveal their craziest tenets until snaring their victims.

This had to be a joke, but what else could he do besides continue to play along? "Is there some benefit to agnosticism?"

"Oh, I can answer," Marie said.

"Good," Julie said. "Claude and I need to focus on the road. The storm's close."

Not from Garrett's angle. The clouds were white as snow.

"You're asking because of Dad," Marie said. "It's hard to hear all of this, right? Agnostics handle it better from our experience. An open mind goes a long way."

Like every other answer, it invited more questions. How old was their home? Why had she said *a* Breach site? But Garrett focused on something else. "Then why was he on the fence about me?"

"You'll have to ask him. Everyone gets a different set of criteria. Could just be the youngest"— something caught in her throat; she squeezed her eyes and coughed it out—"youngest child syndrome." Uncertainty tapered the end of her suggestion. Marie unlatched her seat belt and scooted closer, clicking in the buckle of the middle seat. She nestled her head between Garrett's neck and shoulder, wrapping herself around his arm.

The family seemed spent on answers. Garrett chewed his lip. He trusted Marie, loved her, but the commitment this family required made marriage look like a first date. If there was any truth to Breaches and otherworldly portals, Garrett counted abandoning her as an act of cowardice. He studied the crown of Marie's head, and his heart fluttered. He was too committed to risk such a betrayal.

Lightning crackled, then exploded above. Garrett's chewing slipped into a deep bite. Blood flowed into his mouth. He stanched it with his left hand. Rain played the car's roof like a drum. Droplets smashed into the windshield. A vertical wall of shifting white currents replaced the clear skies. Anything past the next lane disappeared in the downpour.

"Let me drive," Julie said, calm and commanding.

"I got it." Claude waved her off, slowing down to parking lot speed.

"It'll rain the whole way home. There's no way you can see in this. Pull over and let big sis handle this."

"Big sis," mocked Claude. "Fine. Can you climb into the driver's seat?" He veered off the road, onto flat grasslands.

"In a skirt? Barely, if I hike it up, but it beats getting soaked." She whirled in her seat at Garrett. "Close your eyes." She noticed Marie somehow sleeping through the commotion. "Close your eyes," she repeated, quieter.

Garrett complied, covering his face with his hand for good measure.

The driver-side door clicked open. Nature's cacophony deafened all other sounds. Handfuls of water splashed onto Garrett. The door slammed shut. Leather creaked from the front. The driver seat rattled for a second, then the seat belt clicked. The passenger car door opened, amplifying the buzz of the rain, before the door closed and quieted the furious deluge.

"You can open up," Claude said. Garrett peeked out before opening his eyes fully.

Julie shifted the car into gear.

Claude took off his sweater, then his shirt, and tossed them onto the floor. He was toned like a runner. He opened the console, withdrew a folded collared shirt, and dangled it before Garrett. "More clothes. Always more clothes." Then he pulled on the shirt.

Within a minute, Julie was driving as fast as he had with clear skies. The rain poured harder than ever.

Garrett tensed. He'd rather take the wheel but fat chance of that happening. He tugged on his seat belt, double-checking it held taut. He tightened his grip around the bar below the door handle. Marie shifted to adapt, remaining asleep. *Does this family have superpowers too? Driving this fast seems like a death wish, yet nobody minds. And Marie . . .*

Loud noises often woke her with a start, but she slept soundly through this chaos. If Marie felt comfortable enough to pass out, the family trusted each other as he trusted her. The argument failed to convince him to completely let go, but he slacked his grip, returning some blood to his fingers. He found further comfort in the fact that they raced *toward* a supposedly haunted house. Julie wanted out of the storm so bad she risked speeding through solid waterfalls. How bad of a threat could the house present? A reasonable conclusion, assuming the Renaults were reasonable people. Of course, none of this sounded particularly sane.

The torrent intensified. Julie sped up, refusing to be cowed by the lack of visibility.

A big joke, he told himself. *One that's getting less funny by the minute.*

3. Orientation

Once Garrett's lip stopped bleeding, he settled into borderline comfort, mesmerized by the car's clock. Each minute that ticked by, he tore himself free to glance out the window. Torrents of rain continued their assault for the next half-hour, even as Julie pulled onto a paved driveway. They passed through an open gate, brick pillars to either side. Country fencing circled the perimeter of the visible yard, grass peeking out in spots through the deluge. A mansion emerged as they drove on. Interest in the burgeoning shape entranced him.

A jolt ripped through Garrett's insides. "What the hell!"

Marie woke and frantically patted her body, as if searching for a wound. Claude gasped, stiffening in his seat. Julie drove on, unaffected.

"What was that?" Garrett thought lightning had struck the car, but a second later the physical shock faded for one purely emotional.

"We're officially here," Claude said. "Remember that electromagnetic field? We call it the Ring. Stings worse the closer we get to Breaching. Lucky Julie here has lived here long enough to get used to it."

"Lucky," griped Julie.

Claude chuckled. "Either way. We're home."

The odds of the haunted house turning out to be a big practical joke sank, along with Garrett's stomach. What natural force produced such fleeting pain? He squeezed his fist and released. The shadow of the estate, obscured by unrelenting rain, demanded his present attention. "How many rooms are in there?"

"Thirty-five," Julie said.

"You'd be surprised how crowded it can feel," Marie said.

"Compared to the past twenty-four hours, that's a surprise I can handle," Garrett said. He didn't intend it as a joke, but Marie and Claude laughed. They rolled into a seven or eight-stall garage with immaculate white walls and ceiling. A jeep and an old truck sat near an elegant but worn door. Julie parked at the other end. She turned off the car, and the Renaults threw open their doors. Garrett joined them outside a moment later.

"Y'all can take it from here." Julie walked around the hood, handed Claude the keys, and approached the jeep and truck. "I need to check on something." She disappeared behind the vehicles.

"Do you need all this space?" Garrett asked. Only twelve people were slated to live here, including him.

"Better too much than not enough." Marie spun around in the garage. "I guess the others aren't here yet. Did Kelly and Tommy come in with you?"

"Nope," Claude said. "Picking them up Friday. Kelly doesn't want to stay any longer than she has to. She's pissed it's only been two years since the last Breach. Aunt Iris's crew lands the day before. I'll start unloading. Garrett, you want to help?"

Marie locked eyes with Garrett and shrugged. She was as happy carrying her luggage as letting him do it. His mom, however, cared greatly. If she learned any woman he dated walked through a door carrying anything besides her purse while Garrett had free hands, armpits, or teeth, she'd flay him alive. Or worse, lecture him.

"Go on," Garrett said. "I'm sure you and your dad are excited to see each other."

Marie beamed, gave a cursory wave goodbye, and jogged up to the same door Julie had passed through. As she entered, a hollow sensation carved out Garrett's insides. He watched long past the fading of her footsteps.

"Good news is you'll see her again," Claude said. "Bad news is it isn't in The Bahamas."

Garrett shook off his daze and joined Claude at the trunk.

"Also, about Marie. I don't like playing big brother when it comes to love, but there's something we should get out of the way. Especially since you still have to deal with my dad."

"What? Ghosts and demons aren't enough?"

"Ha. Good attitude." Claude opened the trunk and pulled out Marie's carry-on bag. "Those are the real enemies, but heartbreak's a bitch in this family. We can't expect people to sacrifice what's needed to marry in. I'm not saying I'll beat you up if you decide this life isn't for you. Not even sure I can take you." He smacked Garrett's bicep with a little too much familiarity. "Just . . . don't get her hopes up by proposing prematurely or something."

Garrett's brows twitched. "Sure."

Claude sized him up, seeming to accept the response. Grabbing as many suitcases as possible, he waited for Garrett to grab the rest so they could walk side by side. "I meant to ask you this in the car. Hope this isn't rude, but what's your"—he circled his luggage-filled hand around looking for the word—"ancestry?"

"Like, my race?"

"Yeah. No problem if that's too weird."

"Uh, it's fine." Green eyes and chestnut hair deviated from his otherwise predominantly Asian features. "Dad's German and English. Mom's Chinese. Emigrated as a child. Why?"

"A little curious, but mostly a haunted house thing. Speak any Mandarin?"

"A couple dozen words."

"Shame. China's a big country. We'd love a translator. Ghosts are as bad at staying put as they are with following directions to the afterlife. Anything we can do to communicate, to convince them to go"—Claude tapped the handle of Marie's rolling suitcase—"anywhere else, is a win."

The only communication Garrett had imagined involved a Ouija board. "I know Marie speaks some French and Spanish. Is learning a foreign language one of those safety precautions Julie mentioned?"

"It helps. I'm not saying this to scare you, but anything can go wrong. Every tool on your belt is another chance to come out of this unscathed. My wife's family is German, so I picked that up when we got serious. I talked to a soldier from World War 1 last time here. He tried to stab me with a bayonet. Fortunately, weapons don't follow them into the afterlife. We got things sorted out, and he went on his merry way. A hundred years in purgatory, but who's counting?"

Garrett stopped near the jeep, and Claude followed suit. "World War 1? Aren't these ghosts recently deceased?"

"Some take their sweet time finding their way to a Hellspot."

"Hellspot?"

Claude winced. "Oops. A little early for that. You'll get a primer during orientation. We'll fill you in on the rest throughout the week. Hauntings really aren't bad until a Breach." He nodded toward the door. "Come on, this stuff is heavy."

Garrett pressed on without a response, taking the lead. He didn't want Claude rushing him past a warning sign.

The garage led into a storage room. Marbled tiles lined floors plenty wide enough for their luggage. Upper cabinets with nickel handles rested above heavy-duty doors that resembled deep freezers, or perhaps morgue lockers. A decade-old refrigerator whirred from the far wall. Next to it ran a long counter a few feet high, with a wicker trash bin and a stocked wine fridge beneath. Claude nodded at the four-shelf unit and grinned.

From there, they entered a kitchen bigger than Garrett's studio apartment. Another refrigerator, the same model as in the storage room, nestled in its cove. A gas range fit for a high-end restaurant looked mismatched compared to the other older appliances. Dark granite countertops were barren outside of a bowl of oranges on a big island. The fruit tempted Garrett's empty stomach, but exploring the house satiated him in a way that food left him wanting.

Something's off. Everything looks so—he patted his slacks—*sterile.* Recalling that the Renaults kept old fixtures around for a reason didn't alleviate his unease.

They passed into the dining room. *A* dining room, at least, given the house's size. Wood floors, the real thing, not manufactured tiles. Worn, but with character. Twelve traditional chairs sat tucked under a long, polished table. French doors led out to the backyard. Embedded in the walls were multiple pairs of rectangular pillars with fluted molding. Ornate crown molding lined the perimeter of the ceiling. The solid wood hutch in the corner held hand towels and knitted trinkets on its two shelves. It met all expectations for an elegant dining room, save for the leather that framed two paintings of a sunrise and a sunset.

The sound of a cage rattling above Garrett snapped him to attention. He stopped mid-step, scoured the room. The enormity of the house had caused Garrett to forget why it was special. "Are any rooms more susceptible to," he hesitated, "hauntings?" He was starting to believe.

"Want to know where to avoid?" Claude laughed. "Don't worry. The AC makes that sound every day. It's on life support. For a real answer, no room's more or less haunted. Everywhere in and around this house, up to the Ring is fair game. But I'd limit my time in the kitchen. Flying knives make poor companions, even though they're locked up. Don't linger on staircases either. Ghosts have a hard time touching us directly. It'd take several to push you down the stairs, and ghosts aren't exactly team players. But . . . you never know."

"Thanks." After another scan of his surroundings, Garrett pushed open double doors into yet another large room, one he was pretty sure stretched to the front of the house. Marie casually stood from one of two oversized chairs. An older man—clearly her father—rose beside her.

Garrett wheeled his luggage to the nearest wall and approached the pair. Three sides of the room were painted a textured cream with slate streaks. Strips of stained wood accented the wall farthest from Garrett, its sole window covered by a thick Roman shade. Ribboned paneling of a darker wood ran the perimeter and grazed a hand-plastered trace ceiling.

Mr. Renault's handshake was delicate but firm.

"Good to meet you, Mr. Renault. I'm Garrett Mueller."

He held his grip for an extra moment as he appraised Garrett. "Not what I expected." The 'I' was pronounced like 'Ah'.

Garrett tensed for something worse than a haunting. Friends had warned him about minority life in the South when he started dating Marie. Her open-mindedness hadn't given him a reason to consider those warnings before now.

"I figured ya'd be built less like a jock and more like a scrawny artist."

Then again, his friends barely left the East Coast. A strange comment, though, coupled with Claude's earlier insinuations about his build. "I played baseball in college."

Mr. Renault nodded. He motioned past the chairs he and Marie had been sitting on, toward the wide sofa at the other end of a thick ornamental rug. The cream upholstery looked a tad fresher than that of the oversized chairs.

"Go and sit." Mr. Renault spoke with either a Southern or Cajun twang—Garrett couldn't tell the difference. "Did you play any pro?"

Garrett skirted a long leather ottoman and sat down. To his right, marble encased a dormant fireplace. Marie joined him, sat hip to hip. Felt too close for meeting her dad, but Mr. Renault acted unfazed. He sat in the same chair as earlier. Claude took up a spot near the edge of the couch, standing with his hands folded on top of his head.

"No," Garrett said. "Went straight to work. The small chance of making it big combined with a minor league salary convinced me I was better off in finance. With proper investments, I'll come out ahead even if I had gotten called up, which was low odds to begin with."

"You did a cost-benefit analysis on your career," Claude said, jovial as ever. "Damn."

"Fair analysis," Mr. Renault said. "However, somethin' to be said for passion."

Garrett flipped his palm face up, ceding the point. "That's why I'm getting my MBA, Mr. Renault."

"We'll be close. Call me Dad." Completely deadpanned.

He resisted looking at Claude for a reaction or turning to Marie for guidance. She said she hadn't mentioned the proposal to anyone. Unlikely it popped up in their fifteen minutes alone. Had he guessed or . . . ?

Marie leaned over and whispered, "Call him Dave."

Garrett mulled it over. Risking too-forward friendliness with his potential father-in-law paled in comparison to living in a haunted house. "Dad may take me a few days. What about . . . Dave?" His throat didn't dry out until he closed his mouth.

David Renault crossed his fingers, tapping his thumbs together with the rhythm of a metronome. He looked somewhere between an old forty-something and a young seventy-something. Healthy and robust, but tired. Dressed in a light sweater and high-waist dad jeans. Crew cut, sheet white hair. A trimmed beard covered wrinkles where it could. Small scars marred his hand and neck. "Children are such a delight."

Marie and Claude chuckled.

Garrett's toes curled in his shoes.

"You can get away with David," Mr. Renault said. Calling him David was one thing, but *thinking* it was something else. Garrett's parents would kill him for his audacity thus far.

"David it is." Garrett didn't relax until Mr. Renault cracked Marie's classic mischievous smile.

"Glad that's settled," Claude said. "Time for a drink. Guest chooses first."

Garrett drank alcohol maybe twice a week and wanted the entirety of his faculties working here. He scanned the room's inhabitants for cues, concerned about stepping on tradition.

Claude bailed him out. "Whiskey. Wine. Water. It's all fair game. There's plenty of time for booze later."

"Water's good, thanks."

Marie signaled one for her too. Mr. Renault waved off the request.

Claude jaunted toward the kitchen, leaving the doors open and luggage leaning against the frame.

Garrett examined the left side of the room, waiting for what came next. Exquisitely crafted end tables supported cheap-looking lamps and leather-framed family pictures. Beyond those, French doors led into a grand foyer. Above them were rolled-up shades that he'd never seen on interior doors.

"We should begin orientation," Mr. Renault said, drawing Garrett from rationalizing the conflicting design choices. "Ask your questions. Whatever they didn't tell ya in the car."

Marie's reassuring face indicated there was no wrong response, but Garrett's mind prodded him with reminders that he barely passed the test to sit here.

He played it safe, starting small. "How old is the house?" Marie crossed her legs and leaned against Garrett's arm, intently observing the conversation.

Mr. Renault showed no reaction at Marie's affection. "Focused on the natural. The foundation. Good." Would he comment similarly on a bad question? "Built in 1912. Added onto and renovated a few times in its first several decades. Groundskeepers keep it looking good without messin' up the feel of the place. Cuts down on accidents."

Groundskeepers? That had slipped Garrett's mind. He hadn't seen any around with the rain. He leaned forward. "Do they know about the hauntings?"

"A bit. They know the rumors. They see things, but we send 'em home before the Breach poses a danger." He paused, resuming after

Garrett nodded to demonstrate his familiarity with the term. "Yesterday was their last day 'til we call 'em back. Quite the busy bees getting everythin' up to snuff beforehand."

"It's like prepping for a party," Marie said. "The house always looks its best at the start."

Claude returned holding two glasses of water, with a third braced between his forearm and chest. He set two down on the ottoman, inside of a copper tray. He sipped at the third, melting into the chair beside his father.

Garrett reached for his water.

Inches from his grasp, the glass lifted itself, levitated for a split second, then nosedived at the floor. The rug cushioned the blow, absorbing the liquid and the impact.

The siblings jumped up. Marie hoisted up the copper tray. Claude took out a towel from inside the ottoman, blotting the spill. They reacted with a routine air, like cleaning up after an old pet cat.

Garrett retreated deeper into the couch cushions, holding his shaking hands out as if apologizing to the floor. "I didn't touch that." His voice cracked.

"We know," Marie said. "Like I said, the house goes downhill from here." With a singular motion, she set down the tray, swiped the remaining water glass, and handed it to him. He chugged half of the cool liquid before realizing it was in plastic, not glass. In fact, he hadn't seen glass anywhere in the house except for on windows and doors, all of which Roman shades protected. He realized even the kitchen's bowl of oranges was made of plastic, and the dull sheen on the room's lamps and family pictures suggested the same material. Like the dining room, leather framed the art in here too. Whatever potential projectiles decorated the room were picked to minimize damage. He'd never seen such precautions, not even in a horror movie.

Then, he remembered to breathe.

"It's really haunted." Garrett saw what he saw. Hard to dispute their claim now. In a way, the observation relieved him, releasing an underlying tension. The Renaults weren't an unaware family, freshly moved into a haunted house. *He* was, though. "How bad does it get?"

"Depends on who shows up to party." Claude methodically stamped his foot all over the towel. "You might stop shaving though. Razors near the neck? Not smart."

Garrett wanted a more direct answer. Assessing risk was the point of this week. He sipped his water. No—right now, impressing Mr. Renault took priority. "Why do you choose to live here in between," he hesitated, "Breaches?" Despite his near-conversion to believer status, it still sounded fantastical.

"My eldest daughter and I are like lighthouse keepers, watching for signs of danger. We signal to the rest of the family when we see 'em. We do it so others don't have to. The Breach shows up like a ship outta darkness. Unless we pay attention, we miss it."

"Does Marie's grandfather help? He lives here too, right?"

"Yes."

Guess we'll circle back to that one. "What's a Hellspot?"

Mr. Renault glanced between his children and puffed his cheeks. "It's where we are. A location tha' bridges the world of man, spirit, and mekar. The science is lacking. E'ery so often, the worlds merge together."

A, not the. "How many are there?"

"More than one, as you've supposed. Not currently relevant. Please forgive me. Some secrets must remain 'til your trial period's over. Until you're bound by oath."

What was this? A secret society of ghost hunters? Even if the Renaults were pros, did he want to tie his life to them? Garrett silently counted the seconds of his breath. He didn't have to make a decision yet. A week of listening and learning awaited—tasks he excelled at. Time enough to fill in the missing details.

"Is it possible for humans to use this bridge the other way around?" he asked. "Could we enter the ghost world? The demon one?"

Marie shifted uncomfortably.

"Now why would you want to?" Mr. Renault clasped his hands.

"I don't know." *I don't understand why ghosts or demon-what-you-call-its are coming here in the first place.*

"No's the answer. It'd be like trying to visit purgatory. Souls are too tethered to their living bodies to pass between."

"So, how do . . ." he stalled until recalling the name of those demons. He should remember that much. "How do mekari get in?"

"Breaches aren't entirely physical manifestations." As if that answered everything.

Garrett had clearly pushed Mr. Renault's instruction to the limit. Onto the next phase: opening himself up for questions. A chill reminiscent of a Boston winter cascaded down his spine.

"I'm the newest variable here. What do you want to know about me?"

"Nothin'. Everythin' I needed to learn Ah've figured out in the past twenty minutes. Marie told me about Harvard. Means you're smart but doesn't prove ya can think for yourself. Your questions and actions—they do. Ya keep glancing at the marble fireplace, the Brazilian teak floor, the reinforced shades I guarantee ya've never seen anywhere else. Ya probably don't even notice you're doing it. Means you're not rich, which at Harvard means you work hard. Ah'm not worried about you." Mr. Renault never touched the armrests, never leaned back all the way into his seat. Practically avoided any unnecessary contact. "You and Marie must be hungry. How about lunch?"

The house answered instead.

Double doors behind Mr. Renault slammed shut. Windows rattled in the aftershock. Garrett sank into the cushion, uncertain whether to fight or flee. Marie and Claude flinched but settled quickly. Mr. Renault dismissed the incident with a wave, his face calm. Garrett's heartbeat sped, but the reactions around him kept his adrenaline in check.

"Or a snack for now," Mr. Renault said. "The sunroom pantry's stocked. We can watch the rain, and you can fill me in on what Ah've missed from the outside world."

4. A Necessary Tour

A trap. That's what Garrett felt like he'd slipped into by sleeping in the same bed as Marie. He initially resisted when she led him into their spacious room. She reassured him that ghosts and mekari presented bigger worries than her purity or other nonsense that concerned other fathers. Nonetheless, the door kept drawing Garrett's gaze, buoyed by images of her dad barging in one moment, followed by spirits the next. He worked on his laptop until he relaxed enough to fall asleep, hours after Marie.

Garrett woke when Marie did, his laptop still in bed between them. She tsk-tsked him at that, then stealthily led him to the kitchen for breakfast. After a haunting-free meal, they returned to lounge in bed. He asked if he could help prepare for the Breach, and Marie told him he could later. Right now, she was bribing him to stay—the lazy Sunday way.

And they were lazy for a bit. They reminisced about when she got them lost hopping buses on their New York weekend getaway. Outside of the Manhattan fray, they indulged in a trip that felt entirely theirs. Garrett figured out the bus routes back to the hotel, but they opted to walk four hours and take one bus instead—once he checked the safety of the neighborhoods they would pass.

That memory flowed into Marie joking about the first time she played catch with him, until she got tired of throwing the baseball everywhere but at his glove. He countered with how badly he'd fared at his one class of improv theater, even when partnered with someone as talented as her.

From there, they fell into a long gaze. Propped on their sides, facing one another, they stacked their hands under the sheets. Her slender frame, covered by a rainbow tank top and polka dot underwear, enhanced her irresistible silliness. He wanted her, but time ticked down. Six days until the Breach. Six days to determine his future. He'd never last without proper rest.

"How do you sleep so easily in a haunted house?" Garrett asked, a slight headache stirring.

"I sleep easy and I wake easy. We all do. You'll get used to waking up and falling back asleep like it's nothing. We're also gonna start sleeping with water balloons."

Garrett tilted his forehead toward her, his eyebrows wiggling up and down.

She giggled. "Just the reaction I was looking for!" She lurched forward and kissed him. "Gare, we've got this haunted house business down. Like the water balloons. We use them for Dreamers."

"Dreamers?"

"Glad you asked. You never disappoint." She scooted closer so that her foot grazed his. "We break down ghosts into six types based on how they haunt. One's a Dreamer. They give you nightmares, sometimes bad ones that leave marks when you wake up. Water balloons—thin as a bubble—are our defense. People tend to thrash during nightmares, especially supernatural ones. If you hit the balloon or roll over it, it's splash! Then you wake up. I used to toss and turn as a kid until I kept waking up soaked every night. You already sleep pretty still, so you should adjust fast."

Dreamers? Six types of ghosts? He touched the tip of the iceberg of what he needed to know—both to survive and to decide whether to stay. "What about the other five? What about ghosts who throw things at you?"

"Deviants. Claude calls 'em the pop culture ghosts. If it's throwing lamps or tossing your water on the ground, they're your undead guy or gal."

"And how do you protect against *them?*" Considering the lack of projectile accoutrements in the sitting room and the obvious safety precautions from things like leather frames, he added, "while you sleep?"

She pointed up at the rails of the four-poster bed. He'd chalked the frame up to aesthetics, balancing out the high ceilings. "Claude's washing everyone's drapes. We'll hang them up tonight. Made out of the same stuff as the window shades. Super durable and *super* private. Think of it like one of our camping trips."

That explained the inset lighting on the bedposts and the room's lack of lamps—as much as anything explained anything else here. "But what if—"

"The ghosts move the curtains?"

"Yeah." He normally hated when people finished his sentences. With Marie it felt like blissful synchronization, a band playing in harmony.

She wiggled a victory dance. "They've got these bells. They're louder than when you snore. Not that you do that often," she hastened to add. "If you want, we can lock the drapes in place. They're like a wall that way."

Logical as these safety implementations were, he couldn't wrap his head around how little the haunted house concerned her. Was she putting on a show for him, or did ghosts really not worry her?

"I know that look!" She booped his nose. "Gare, you'll see it's all good. Until then, I'll keep you safe. I promise. Now, it's my turn to ask a question. What's the weirdest thing from yesterday?"

Breaking his mind free from his—and her— safety took effort. He focused on the dimples of her expectant smile. His world gradually shrank to the size of one woman. *What's the weirdest thing from yesterday?*

Where to begin? Expectations for the haunted house ran far in every direction. He had hoped for a casual laugh at his expense, followed by the reveal of an elaborate prank. That dream was dead. Her family welcomed him, grew friendlier with every interaction, yet there were oddities. Julie's driving. Not meeting the grandfather yet.

But what bothered him most was more subtle. Apprehension would've kept him from revealing it to any of his exes. With Marie, he opened up.

"Kind of strange how Claude and your dad both commented on my build. Julie checked me out before bed too. Scientifically, like a specimen."

"Are you worried they're gonna chop you up and put you in a stew?"

"That's not weird to you?"

"Relatively speaking, casual compliments don't measure high on the weird scale."

He racked his brain for a delicate response. It wasn't as if his clothes yesterday highlighted much of his frame.

Marie withdrew a hand from their stack and pressed her finger over his lips. "You're not wrong, Gare. But don't blame them. They *are* complimenting you. They see your potential: a better chance for all of us to make it out in one piece."

"That's great, but is that all I am to them? A tool? Is that what I am to you?" His heart beat faster, but he let the question linger.

She drew her arms in, folding them across her chest. As she curled her legs, her bare shins grazed his thigh. "I don't know. I don't think that way when we're together. You're just Gare. But somewhere in the back of my mind, I probably gave you a bigger chance because you're smart and athletic."

A wave of shame-induced nausea struck him. Garrett trusted her, knew she loved him. Was anything unfair about the Renaults assessing individuals for their survival merit? He stroked her thigh, ran his hand over the bump of her hip, crossed the ridges of her ribs, and rounded her shoulder en route to rubbing her arm. There was strength in her litheness. "I love you. It's fine. You promised me a tour today. Want to deliver?"

"I . . . Okay. Yeah. Let's do that." More confident and excited with every breath. "I love you too. You're great. Thanks for trying this out."

Both dressed casually, the awkward moment fading. They stepped out into a long hallway of closed doors. More leather-framed art decorated silver-gray walls. She pointed out empty and taken bedrooms, and bathrooms meant for each. About fifteen doors total on their side of the central stairs.

"This place is massive," Garrett said.

So many places for ghosts to strike from.

He suddenly regretted bringing up the tour. Wandering the house without a specific destination made him feel vulnerable. He focused on his bedrock—Marie. "Was your family ever big enough to fill it up?"

"Never," Marie said, gloom darkening her features. A chip in his rock already.

Garrett froze, half concerned for her, half for his own safety. He recovered before she did and embraced her, the hug returned without delay. She was herself again, and with his arm wrapped around her waist, his agoraphobic feelings waned.

But they still lurked.

He reminded himself of *why* the tour was important: knowledge. Knowledge kept him safe and calmed his mind. "What about the other ghost types?"

"Oh, right." The question brightened her mood. "You remember Julie talking about keeping stuff the same in the house? That's because of Shifters. They take your senses and twist them up or . . . well, take your senses. No seeing, no hearing, nothing. They can't take everything at once though. Stay grounded, and you'll recover fast."

They walked by the stairway. An antique clock stood near the top, placed so if it fell, it would land near the stairs instead of tumbling down them. He sped up so that it wouldn't fall on *him*. He took

Marie's advice to heart, touching the banister, then the smooth wall, as they funneled into the next hallway.

Marie grabbed his hand, and he jumped. Her eyes grew big, but she didn't giggle like normal after a jump scare. "People are good for grounding too."

He took a deep breath. Yesterday's realization that he might live in a real haunted house for a few months seemed to be settling in. His armpits started to perspire. "I need to know the other haunts."

She squeezed his hand. "Feeders feed on your emotions, but I don't get the name. They ramp up negative emotions—the ones that make people lose control. Anger, sadness, fear, loneliness, the whole shebang. Amplifiers fit better to me, but some old coot named these a way's back, and that's how it is."

"Which old man? Someone in your family?" He hazarded a guess, prying for details left unsaid from yesterday. "Or one from another Hellspot?"

Marie abruptly stopped, Garrett following suit once he felt resistance. She added her hand to their pair and waited for him to do the same. "I can't tell you. I'm sorry. Dad says I can't say much about Hellspots unless you commit. It opens a"—her voice dipped into a low octave—"whole bag of worms about the world no one's supposed to know but family." She returned to her normal pitch. "I promise it has nothing to do with your safety. I'll break the rule if it does."

The house's enormity weighed on Garrett. His knees sank, cutting the height disparity between him and Marie in half. No matter what he learned, a world's worth of clandestine details awaited.

When he didn't respond, she added, "You believe me, right?"

If that ceased to be true, he may as well bolt for the airport, but his trust held. Right now, that's what mattered. "I do."

She practically skipped into the sparsely decorated study. A desk had a few books stacked on it. Two chairs touched the room's back corners. Marie made a big show of yawning and closing the door, then led them next door, into the game room.

She challenged him to foosball by lining up on the red side and making a face. He accepted the invitation, taking his place opposite her, wishing he could reciprocate the carefree gesture. After they'd knocked the miniature soccer ball around for a few moments, she said, "The last two possess you. Claimers and Hiders. Hey, don't stop playing or I won't tell you more. Better! Claimers are quick, temporary possessions. They latch onto emotions, sort of like Feeders. If you're calm, they can't get you. So, make like Bobby McFerrin, and don't worry, be happy!"

"You know who sings that?" He chuckled.

"Oh my God, you laughed." She leapt across the table and would've fallen headfirst into his gut if he hadn't caught her. She kissed him and gave a quick tilt of her head back to her side of the foosball table. He eased her down. "And of course, I know who sings it. Spotify tells me I'm in the top 1% of listeners every year."

He laughed even harder at that, until the plethora of projectiles in the room sank in: board game boxes, ping pong paddles, and chairs. Innocuous entertainment or tools of supernatural war? Unable to shake the question, he asked to see more of the house. She complied, and they made for the foyer downstairs.

"Back to Hiders." Marie gave an extended sigh, then spoke quickly through her explanation. "They're semi-permanent. They slowly take over, edging your thoughts toward whatever the ghost fancies. Eventually, that settles into trying to copy how the host acts, so they can escape into the world undetected. But," she slowed her speech, "there's an easy solution called catching a lie. If someone calls the ghost out on an out-of-character behavior—like you turning down Ronny Chieng's stand-up—then ta-da! We got 'em, and the ghost gets kicked right on out. Eight months in, Gare, and it feels like we've known each other for half our lives. Hiders can't fool us."

Garrett gave a half-hearted smile, feigning the confidence she projected.

Marie finished her explanation as they reached the landing between the upstairs and down. The shade was rolled up on the house's largest window. The fenced backyard extended as far and wide as a baseball field. Trees dotted a field of manicured grass, all stretching upward to soak in the rain. And between Garrett and that yard was a pane of glass, waiting for a ghost to splinter it into a hundred daggers. He nudged her down the remaining stairs.

Six types of ghosts, all with powers akin to superheroes. Marie had tried to make them sound as if they posed no threat. Outside of the house, he might have felt flattered by the effort she put into convincing him. Here, the feeling of walls closing in made him feel powerless.

"What's to stop a single ghost from ruining your family?" Garrett death-gripped the banister. "I know you have your precautions, but how does a ghost constantly possessing or blinding people not end in—" He cut himself off from mentioning death. He couldn't handle that fear right now. "Catastrophe?"

"Well," she strung out the word, "remember Julie saying ghosts are balls of emotion? Side note: I'm glad she laid down the primer. No way I could've handled all that. Anyway," stringing out the word again. "They don't think, just act. There's no planning. Plus, hauntings are over fast, in minutes at most. They don't belong in our world, even during a Breach."

"Except Hiders." He stepped off the stairs into the grand open-air foyer.

"I wish you weren't such a good listener sometimes." She started to laugh, stopped at his straight face. "We've never not caught a Hider."

"How would you know?"

"Why would a Hider return to a Breach? If someone doesn't show up one year, we'll worry about it then."

Another antique clock tick-tocked between two of the foyer's myriad of closets. Canvased paintings, with leather frames, hung on the wall surrounding the front door. The wall directly across from Garrett separated a short hallway to the left and a wide arch to the right. Standing against it was a vintage black hutch similar to the one in the dining room. A stuffed dog and donkey, Marie's two favorite animals, sat on the top shelf. The hutch's other knickknacks had been cleared between yesterday and today. The lack of a chandelier made the room feel empty, with too much space. He had to admit one thing: the family put great care into ghostproofing the house. But despite that and Marie's explanations, he'd never feel at ease unless he could dive into the details on his own.

"Is there a book on any of this?" he asked.

Marie's pressed-together hands rose to her chin, and she excitedly clapped her fingers together. "You're gonna love our last stop."

She snatched his hand and led him with a new pep in her step. Marie waved off the door behind them, the one led into the sitting room, and brought them under the arch into the breakfast nook. Garrett barely had time to take in the round sofa or the dining bench before she abruptly stopped. "Actually, you saw all this yesterday. Onto the last stop! Then we can go back to bed." She bit her bottom lip seductively and turned them back.

Garrett grinned but tugged on her hand. He'd seen the sunroom off to the left, but he wanted to check out the other way.

"Isn't there a gym to the right? Can I see it?"

Marie hesitated with her back turned to him, then smacked her forehead. "Oh, yeah. You would want to see that. Sure."

A doorless entryway led into a gym with dark-paneled walls that looked as out of place as its hardwood floors. Inside were two stationary bikes and one weight bench, all atop a large mat. An armoire better fit for a bedroom stored an assortment of dumbbells. Though dated, none of the equipment looked touched.

"Does anybody use this place?" Garrett asked.

Marie's eyes glazed over at the sight of the bench, her mouth falling open. She grasped his hand as if it were a lifeboat.

He rubbed her shoulder. "Marie?"

"Nobody uses it."

What misery had she endured here? Protective instincts smashed those for survival. His worry mutated into spite. He wanted to strangle whoever hurt her—even if it didn't work that way with a ghost.

"You're welcome to," she said. "But lock up any dumbbells you're not using. Got to be safe, you know?" She rubbed his forearm and scanned the room, reviving her lively self. "Maybe I'll start biking. We can come down together." Her offer sounded forced, more than usual for any exercise that wasn't hiking.

"I'd like that."

She pulled him out of the room, and he couldn't help but think she put on a happy face for him. Imagined tragedies that might've befallen Marie assailed him in succession: a near-death strangling under the weight of a barbell, imprisonment in the room while being tormented by ghosts, watching a loved one die.

By the time he recovered, he was moving faster than Marie. They cut back to the foyer and into the hallway across from the stairs. Entryways to either side led to two generic offices. They looked identical, except the exterior-facing office had a window and a door, while the interior office had neither. A curious choice Garrett might've questioned had Marie not blazed past him to their destination: a library thrice the size of the dining room. Hopefully, it would provide the one thing that could hold his imagination at bay.

Answers.

5. Knowledge

Many trees gave their lives to build and furnish the colossal library. Rich walnut shelves surrounded Garrett and Marie as they entered. Books with laminated, colored sleeves spanned wall to wall, floor to ceiling. The colors looked out of place, like children's books in an ancient library. Frameless, plexiglass double doors, each pair the width of thirty encyclopedias, separated the books from the interior of the cavernous room. The shelving units were further divided into thirds from top to bottom, with a small gap between each. A thin rail, rounding at the room's corners, ran along the highest shelf. Connected to the rail, a nearby rolling ladder leaned against the shelves, locked in place by a chain linked through one of many hooks near the ceiling.

Marie was right about him loving their final stop. He stumbled into the room, overwhelmed by the grand representation of what he didn't know. Then came the soothing consideration that humanity may have actually solved otherworldly dangers, which calmed him more than any Renault assurance or explanation.

Two large tables, with rope cord designs etched into their aprons, stood on equally large rugs. Papers and books lay strewn about on top of each. Two smaller desks braced themselves against the room's longer walls. A few chairs rested under the tables, a few against the wall. The floor's dulled stains, scuffs, and scratches marked this as the most frequented room in the house—a far cry from the pristine gym.

Standing at the nearest table, Julie's finger lined the text of an encyclopedic tome. Ironically, she'd abandoned her librarian attire from yesterday for sweats and a t-shirt. "Enjoying your tour?" She didn't look up. "We should open up in the off-season and charge people."

"How *do* you pay for this place?" Garrett asked, curiosity overriding his earlier concern.

"Gist of it is rich folks pay us to keep their investments safe."

"Investments being the house?"

She flipped a few pages, bent down closer to the text. "Investments being planet Earth. Money runs the world, Harvard MBA. Loose ghosts and mekari incite fear. Fear is bad for business. Though our success has turned them stingy. Maintaining a mansion and researching rare phenomena aren't cheap. Luckily, the one thing Claude is serious about is money. He manages the family finances, keeps us going. Dad and I don't have the time, nor interest, for it."

"Who are these rich folks?" Tech giants? Old money? Foreign investments? The implications excited Garrett too much to care about the juvenile tinge to his voice. There were more Hellspots, presumably scattered around the world. Financial backing added another layer of legitimacy to all of this.

"Ask Dad," Julie said. "Not my place to tell."

Of course, he'd have to wait on that too.

Marie ambled from shelf to shelf, perusing the books, hands behind her back. She stopped in front of an opened-door shelf. Book-sized holes matched what lay near Julie. "Where is he?" She looked back. "And Claude?"

Julie straightened her legs and rubbed underneath her glasses— different ones from yesterday's, with both plastic lenses and frame. She scooted the tome toward the table's center. "I needed a break anyway," she sighed. "Dad's with Grandpa. Claude's in town picking up his wife's demands and clothes for Garrett."

"I really don't need—" Glares from both women shut him up. He'd have to accept some of their bizarre rules. "Are all of these books related to ghosts and mekari?"

"Most," Julie said, "but not all. There are also precognition, ESP, and curses."

"Oh my." He'd seen that famous 'Lions, Tigers, and Bears' clip from The Wizard of Oz more times than he cared to admit.

"Yes." Unimpressed as a scarecrow overseeing her literary crops.

"Be nice, Jules," Marie said. "This place needs brightening."

Julie tossed up her hands.

Thinking about it, Oz characters matched the family well. Only their idealized versions instead of the lacking ones. They'd even hinted at it in the car. Julie, the brains. Marie, the heart. Claude, the courage. Mr. Renault fit the enigmatic wizard role. That made him Dorothy. After the small amount he'd experienced, could he go back to his Kansas? Back to Boston as if none of this existed?

Marie continued. "These books are so big, even the novels. You should try a hobby that gets you out of here and lets you live a little."

"What?" Julie asked. "Like improv?"

"If you're interested—"

Julie's expression made it clear she wasn't.

"Okay, but we've lived more adult lives than most people twice our age. Try mixing something lighter into your life, Jules. It'll keep you young longer."

"I wear clothes like I'm retired." Julie plucked at her shirt. "And I'll be blind before fifty." She tapped the frame of her glasses. "Staying young is for people who don't live here full-time."

Marie stammered, arms swaying at her side.

Julie stopped her. "It's fine. I don't blame you for leaving."

Movement on the far wall put an end to their quarrel. A handful of books beat against the plexiglass. Every fifth book or so joined the uprising. Belligerent texts continued ramming each of the doors locking them in, convincing their neighbor to do the same, advancing toward the corner closest to Marie. She froze like a thief caught in the act.

Helplessness gouged a void in Garrett's gut. He'd finally felt calm touring the house and dropped his guard like a fool. His fingers writhed to act. He rose on the balls of his feet, prepped to follow either sister's lead.

"Billy," Julie snapped. "Stop it."

The chaos halted at the corner.

"Who's Billy?" Garrett coughed at the sudden parching of his throat.

With her forefinger held up, Julie crept toward the corner, half the length of the library away from Marie and Garrett.

Silence pervaded, but within his head, an explosive timer ticked down.

Julie's head whipped back. "Duck!" she shouted, as a book from the open shelves launched itself at her sister.

The binding struck Marie's forehead, sending her tumbling to the floor.

Garrett sprinted to her aid, skidding on the knees of his jeans. He would've run through a buzz saw before noticing it. Marie propped herself up and pressed two fingers to her forehead. He wrapped his arm around her back.

"Impetuous brat," Julie spat. "Claude'll be in for a treat in a few years."

Garrett had no idea what she was talking about, and right now he didn't care. "Are you okay?" he whispered to Marie. She touched the pink injury site, wincing but nodding all the same. He babbled at Julie's approach. "What happened? Is Marie safe? Did you know it? Him?"

"Hold on." Julie slammed the plexiglass doors shut, then squatted near Marie. She raised her forefinger near her younger sister's face. "Look at me. Open your eyes. Watch my finger tick side to side. Take your hand away from your face so I can see. Ugh, this light is terrible. Okay, good Marie. Keep watching, keep watching, keep watching. Alright. Looks fine. Tell me if you get any headaches in the next twenty-four hours."

"I'll be okay," Marie said. "Let me get up."

Garrett ached to help her, but both he and Julie stood and backed away, staying close enough to catch her if she fell. Marie took another moment, then rose without issue.

"Stop staring at me." Marie shooed her sister away.

Julie grunted and picked up the hardbound weapon from the floor. After sliding the crimson sleeve back over the faded cover, she set it down with the others on her table. "Back to your question. I See things related to the Hellspot. Or See through them, like the rain yesterday."

Garrett flinched, flipping his attention between the sisters. Julie could *See* the ghost? See *through* the rain?

Julie meandered back over. "It's a gift for staying around so long. And recompense for losing my eyesight. Nature's balancing act for living on a Hellspot. Anyway, Billy. He's an Aware spirit, and all those show up early, most commonly as Deviants. Which I can tell from your blank stare Marie also didn't explain."

"She covered the six haunt types. What's an Aware spirit?"

Julie's head reared back. She doled out an impressed expression for Marie, who danced a victory jig reminiscent of the one from bed this morning. "Awares are semi-civilized, usually encountered in the real world, so to speak. They're capable of limited communication. Instead of fulfilling unfinished business, they cause chaos, especially young ones like Billy. Bothersome and sometimes painful pranks notwithstanding, he's harmless. Most cross over on their own during a Breach once they've had their fill. We're always too wrapped up in everything else to notice." Then she pointed at Garrett. "I'm going to give you some homework. Marie won't read it, but you should."

Marie stuck out her tongue. Julie poked it. Marie wiped it across the back of her hand and closed her mouth, glaring.

Julie carried on as if nothing happened. "It's a more detailed account of the six haunts. There's something similar for mekari, but we won't see many of those. No Hellspot has documented more than two simultaneously, and there hasn't been more than one per Breach here since I was born. You'll need one of us to deal with them anyway." She walked toward and up the library's rolling ladder, entered the combination into the directional lock, and unhooked the ladder. She scooted it in front of a column of magenta-sleeved books, climbed up to relock the ladder, then descended halfway to the middle shelves.

"I guess this isn't online anywhere?" Garrett asked.

"Online?" she scoffed. "Trash written by amateur ghost hunters." She slid her hand underneath the middle set of shelves, fiddled with something there, then pulled on the door-length nickel handle with her other hand. "People like us write and update these books. Most have less than a hundred copies in circulation. A lot can go wrong with books, but they're more reliable than computers. Speaking of, I have edits to make." Her finger slid between the books until she plucked her target off the shelf. She came off the ladder pushed the book into Garrett's chest. "Read this. Put it back when you're done. The lock works the same way as the kitchen cabinets, your bedroom dresser, and any other drawer or container."

"There are locks on those?"

Julie stared dead-faced at Marie, who cleared her throat and made a popping sound with her lips. She answered Garrett without looking at him. "Up, in, up. Pull on the handle while pressing the last up. The ladder lock's similar. Up, right, up, repeat once. Put that book back when you're done. Ask me if you're interested in a particular topic. I'll fill in the details if others can't." She let that hang until Marie's blush deepened. She faced Garrett at last, only to raise her chin, looking up and beyond him. "Or I'll point you to the right book." She stepped out into the hallway before he formed a response. The door to the nearby office opened and closed.

Garrett turned to Marie, still blushing. "She's not worried about the ghosts hearing that?"

"Listening isn't exactly their strong suit, and balls of emotion don't translate well to fine motor skills."

Garrett shrugged acceptance and then opened the book, feeling the worn paper between his fingertips. He flipped to the title page. *A Beginner's Treatise on Disparate Hauntings.*

Julie's assignment filled his void of helplessness. What he lacked in experience, he'd make up for with knowledge. And athleticism, once he knew how to put it to use. Earlier criticisms of the Renaults appraising his usefulness no longer mattered. He *wanted* to contribute. Assuming, of course, that he stayed.

6. Free Rein

Garrett sipped his tepid coffee from the confines of the breakfast nook. The decor reminded him of an old diner. Cushioned bench seats formed a U and butted up against a solid wall. Plastic bottles of condiments stood at the table's end.

A chill wind tickled his neck.

He tightened his grip on the mug, forced himself to set it down rather than drop it. He searched for the culprit. The AC vent was too far to reach. A ghost then, a Shifter based on Marie's overview and his readings the past few days. Able to alter the sensory perception of an individual, or in some cases, anyone caught in a small area.

It's harmless.

His fingers, fidgeting with the coffee mug's handle, disagreed. He'd asked Marie for alone time after she and Julie finished breakfast. He needed to reduce his reliance on others. She granted his wish with hesitation. Her primary goal so far had been to convince him to stay. She acted as if *she* had proposed to *him*.

Garrett blinked hard, breathed harder. The chill wasn't any worse than the past few days' experiences. Random objects flew around like in the library. Spectral screams, breaths, and whispers broke silences and interrupted conversations. Heat and cold flip-flopped with erratic gusts of air. All were random, inconsistent, and most importantly, infrequent. No more than twice a day and over in a flash. Benign enough for Claude to joke about a light year. But Garrett had faced all those with Marie.

Now he sat alone in a room too large to watch for every potential threat.

The only other furniture was a royal blue lobby sofa, rounded with a cylindrical backrest in the middle. Natural light poured in through uncovered windows. Basking in the late morning sun tempted him as much as lowering the shades. He'd have to fool with the lock on the head rail to do so—using the same up, in, up pattern that Julie described in the library—and that required standing in front of unprotected glass longer than ideal. Compromising, he sat up to spy for anything strange, and merely straightened his jeans when he found nothing. If the Renaults were comfortable with it, he had to be as well.

He lowered his head toward his breakfast plate, placing his nose inches above the food. Hearty scents eased his mind, settling his stomach enough to resume eating. He stirred his sweet potato hash before taking a bite, letting the food linger in his mouth. Though now lukewarm, the flavors of the locally sourced eggs, sweet potatoes, sausage, and peppers rivaled fried food, without the greasy sickness. He split a biscuit in half and spooned honey on top. Soon the Renaults would be pulling meals from the freezer or cans, so they lived it up in the days preceding the Breach.

The buttery biscuit crumbled in his mouth, thick honey coating his tongue. He swallowed, but the stickiness remained, started to spread. Valentine's Day treats overwhelmed his taste buds. Truffles, lollipops, cotton candy, cheesecake, and peppermint assailed him with sickening sweetness. His mouth bloated to twice its usual size, as if forced into a marshmallow stuffing contest, preventing him from swallowing. A chocolate heart the width of his plate replaced his breakfast, cracked, then oozed blood. Garrett's hand crashed down, thrusting the plate off the table and spraying the booth opposite him with hash. Blood vanished, and he savored swallowing his saliva more than any bite of breakfast.

You're safe. No real danger before the Breach.

Garrett clenched his fist and slackened it to the rhythm of his bouncing leg. He turned in the direction of the front yard, where the

Renault sisters waited for Claude to arrive with the next batch of family members. Come tomorrow evening, he needed to decide whether to stay. Breach timing was too imprecise to guarantee his departure past tomorrow.

He straightened his hands and placed his palms on the table.

You're safe.

Staying meant officially binding Garrett by oath. Marie's father acted unconcerned by the implication: that someone little more than a stranger would marry his daughter. Worse, real dangers existed beyond errant sensory threats. Marie casually revealed yesterday that her mom and uncle had died here. Not just died, but were killed. Supernatural murders practically defined haunted houses and hadn't surprised Garrett. That they averaged only one death every other Breach was a small comfort. The way the Renaults acted in certain rooms, like Marie in the gym, told him they'd endured other traumas. Mr. Renault had barely left his father's room since Garrett's arrival.

The chill returned, gusting so strong it ruffled his shirt. He readjusted his collar and brushed his neck, but the cold remained. Slippery wet cold like a melting ice cube stroked his shoulder blade and slid out under his short sleeves. The ice melted, spread, and submerged his forearm in the glacial chill. An invisible finger, cold and thin as an icicle, worked its way from his elbow to his wrist.

Garrett jumped out of the booth. Wetness textured like a tongue lapped at his ear. He whirled around. Saw nothing out of the ordinary. Warmth returned to his arm as if it had never left.

Safe. Safe. Safe. He forced a stiff, confident posture. He approached the closest of the room's windows, risking it shattering in his face. Better to experience that now than after losing the freedom to escape.

Condensation formed on an eye-level windowpane. An unseen entity squiggled a heart into it. Instincts took hold; Garrett reared his fist back. He waited for a follow-up. Let his arm drop when none came. Close to a minute passed in a series of rapid, uneventful heartbeats. He racked his brain, cycling through the hauntings he'd crammed into memory. A Feeder? Shifter? Deviant? All fit. Did that mean multiple spirits, or did he simply not understand enough?

His feet itched to flee. He kept them planted. His first solitary meal unnerved him more than anything prior, but fear wouldn't control him. He was his master. He breathed until the thumping in his chest subsided. Then he walked measured steps back to the breakfast table. He scooped food from the bench onto his plate and returned it to the kitchen. After a harried depositing of his dishes and silverware into the dishwasher, he left to join the sisters.

As Garrett shut the house's front door, Marie spun around. Seeing her rejuvenated him. She excitedly clapped her hands and smiled wide. She and Julie were underneath the shade of a tree, just off the driveway. "That was fast. How was alone time?"

"A bit too lonely." The reference to breakfast snuffed out Garrett's rejuvenation. He jogged down the front stairs and along the walkway toward the sisters. *Calm down. If you can't handle the spirits without her, you don't belong here. You don't belong with her.*

He pecked Marie on the lips. "I thought you'd wait closer to the gate."

"And miss watching you get shocked again?" Julie asked. "Perish the thought." She monitored a phone she held near her chest.

"Do we really need to go through that again?" As much as Garrett loved Marie's company, the anticipation of another violent jolt served him far better in dismissing his recent haunting.

"What's the first rule of improv?" Marie asked.

"Always say yes?" Garrett tapped his pants. "How does that apply here?"

"You don't know until you try. Passing through the Ring might sting. You might also brush it off. Whatever 'appens, you're done, and you move on."

"But then I have to go back through . . ."

"Live in the moment!"

"I don't think—"

"More practically," Julie interrupted. "It's important to feel the difference in the Ring tightening up. It'll help you understand the progression of a Breach."

Pain seemed unlikely to help with anything. Julie ran the show here though, at least with their dad predisposed. He didn't want to risk ticking off his potential sister-in-law by declining. Maybe he could distract her, keep her talking long enough for the car to arrive. "What happened before your family lived here? When nobody guarded against the Breach? I don't imagine ghosts caused less trouble prior to the advent of civilization."

"Good question." She waved her phone at him before returning her attention to it. "Evidence suggests Native Americans migrated to these lands periodically. Notably, *not* seasonally. Meaning they came for a reason," Julie said this in a way that warded off asking for clarification. "But you're right. The world carried on. The commonly accepted theory is the increase in modern societal pressures leads to individuals opting not to pass on. Larger populations also mean more ghosts. The world can handle a few escapees. A critical mass, and that's that." She smacked the phone against her palm.

"How do you know? I get the world is better off without rampant ghosts and mekari Breaching the Ring." Finally getting comfortable with the terms. Marie looked more impressed than Julie. "But how do we know what's end-of-the-world bad?"

"Do you want to find out?" She shook her head, as if dealing with a child. "Let's go. They're almost here." She slid her phone into the seam of her pants.

So much for his distraction.

"We can hold hands." Marie grinned, beckoning him with a curl of her fingers until he reached out. She jabbed at the air with her other hand. "We'll punch through that Ring together and show it who's boss."

"Good luck with that," Julie said, already walking away. Garrett spotted the blade of grass her foot struck as she passed through the Ring. Her whole body stiffened. Infinitely more reaction than in the car. Spelled great things for him.

Marie patted Garrett's chest. "Try shallow breathing. Hurts less if there's less air. Oh, and keep your nose scrunched." He tried. "No, not like that. Like this." Her forehead and cheeks squeezed together so the slits of her eyes barely showed their whites. He imitated her as best as possible. "Last thing. Fist up. Pound the air near your face like this."

Garrett sighed, then mirrored her jabs, walking forward while feeling a fool.

Where was that blade of grass? He'd lost it focusing on Marie.

"Look at me," Marie said.

He did. And took another step. Lightning jolted his body. Fire seared through the fibers of his muscles. Bones and joints he didn't know existed popped and cracked. Worst of all, he moved through the Ring as if submerged in molasses. Torturous pain for five feet feeling like fifty. Once free, he leapt, dragging her forward, crunching her knuckles.

Marie pulled her hand free once Garrett relaxed and shook it out. "Was trying to take your mind off it. Oh well! You looked cute at least." She leaned in and whispered, "If it makes you feel better, I can sleep naked tonight."

It did. Too much. He stuffed his hands in his pocket until his bulge receded. The pain of passing through the Ring faded into a residual memory, leaving no long-term effects save for knowledge of the precise location to avoid. "Thanks, Marie."

She half-curtsied while walking.

"But let's make that a one-time thing. I'd rather not associate *that* with the Ring and develop some sort of Pavlovian response."

Her high-pitched hum didn't inspire much confidence.

Off in the distance, a speck appeared on the empty road. It slowly grew, taking the shape of the Mercedes sedan. Within a minute, it turned off the highway toward the house. Tires dragged loose gravel from the highway. The engine purred as it drove through the gate. Tinted windows prevented Garrett from seeing inside. The car drove past them, not stopping except for a sudden break at the Ring, then continued into the open garage. Julie chuckled and marched past Garrett without concern. He half-wished he'd stayed in the breakfast nook, accompanied by whichever of their uninvited guests.

"I don't know why I agreed to this," Garrett said. "I would have gladly taken your word that this would be a lot worse."

"You need to know that there's truly no escape," Julie said. "Once the Breach opens, that pain will feel like a mosquito bite in comparison. Your next time through is either tomorrow or four months from now. Make your pick." She didn't miss a beat in her return through the Ring. Was she human anymore? He pursed his lips and turned to Marie.

"Sorry, Gare," she said. "But we're here now. And the house is there." She pointed at the mansion. He took in the grand sight without the rain obscuring it. Limestone facade with green shingles and solar panels. Short balconies jutted out from two of the second-floor bedrooms. Inset pillars separated each column of windows. The giant garage connected to the right side of the house. Overall, a normal looking, albeit large, house he'd think nothing about. That is, if it weren't for the psychic moat that locked in the supernatural and an ominous grove just off the property.

"Fine," he said. "Let's get to it."

As they passed through that invisible asshole of a Ring, Marie leaned over and whispered, "Na-ked."

Growing up in a haunted house explains so much, Garrett thought, right before explosions of pain returned for an encore.

7. Desires

Trudging to the front door drained Garrett's willpower. The Ring's splatter shot of molten hot pinpricks amplified the pain of his previous passing. It enveloped him completely, stabbing wounds that reopened for the express purpose of deepening his suffering. Once he passed through hell's gate, he followed Marie up the steps of the house and stopped.

Pain faded, apathy taking its place. He wasn't tired. His limbs didn't ache. As before, there were no physical aftershocks. He just didn't have the drive to continue.

"I'll catch up," he said, too indolent to face Marie.

"You want me to stay?" she asked.

"It'll pass."

"You sure?" She bent down to look into his downcast eyes. "I know that wasn't fun."

The front windows rattled, as if the world's strongest man had slammed the door.

Adrenaline roused Garrett's listless limbs. Protective instincts pushed the Ring to the back of his mind. He threw open the front door, ready to act. Several adults and two kids stood in a circle in the foyer. All clearly unconcerned with the errant noise.

Marie came up behind him, whispered, "You can meet them later if you want to rest."

Garrett shook his head and approached the circle. Its members turned to greet him. The latest arrivals eliminated any remaining concerns of racism. Iris, Marie's aunt by marriage, had skin as dark as midnight. She played herself like a grandmother, walking stiffly and slightly hunching when standing. Yet her few wrinkles and streams of black hair among a sea of gray made it hard to believe her older than sixty. She wore a long skirt, black boots, and a necklace of navy spheres half the size of golf balls. She didn't offer Garrett a handshake or hug, but he didn't take it as a slight. From the moment the conversation began, she observed with keen eyes that belied her age.

Her son, Derrick, gave him a solid shake and a pat on the arm. "Nice shirt."

Garrett realized his seafoam collared top almost matched Derrick's. A brighter color than his usual attire. Still, he was thankful that if Claude had to buy him extra clothes, he chose something nice. "Great minds think alike."

Derrick tapped his temple. He shared many similarities with Claude. Long and lean with a disarming smile, wide cheekbones and forehead. His clear glasses frame was as sharp as the rest of his outfit. Easy to see the relationship after looking past their skin colors, though he was shades lighter than his mother. The conclusion hit Garrett almost immediately, but Derrick confirmed it nonetheless; his dad was Marie's deceased uncle. Derrick's wife, Nia, took the floor a moment later.

She resembled Marie, though the two dressed nothing alike. A smooth face enhanced by gold eye shadow and otherwise subtle makeup. Slender with slick, short hair. Tall heels and a knee-length, sleeveless dress made of solid auburn hugged her skin. Hoop earrings. She and their son, Grady—a young child with thick, curly hair—shared a similar complexion with Derrick. With a yawn, she offered Garrett her pleasantries and made her way upstairs with Grady in tow.

All the faceless names Garrett had researched on his plane trip started to fall into place.

Derrick pointed his thumb up the stairs and whispered, "If the ghosts don't kill me this year, she might. We were supposed to be in the Dominican in two weeks." He turned to Claude. "How's Kelly taking it?"

"In stride. We were also married five years before she saw a Breach. Not like him." He tapped Garrett with the back of his hand. "Starting off with a bang. Must really like our girl."

Garrett surprised himself by not flinching. The familial camaraderie had pushed the Ring deeper down. He smiled at Marie, deciding to stay silent on his intentions until he discussed it with her.

As was so very her, she had no such qualms. "Of course he does!" She squeezed Garrett's shoulders. "But he hasn't decided yet, so stay on your best behavior, because *I* really like this boy. Unfortunately, we didn't leave him with a lot of time to decide."

"If you expect an apology"—Julie pointed with her knife-edge hand—"for not giving you more warning." Her shaking head finished the statement.

Marie moved in and grasped her sister's hand between both of hers. "No, no, no. Jules, that's not what I meant."

Julie slipped Marie's grasp and mouthed, *Okay.*

"Whatever." Claude waved dismissively. "Twenty-four hours is plenty of time."

"I missed this." Derrick playfully shook his finger at his cousins, laughing. Like them, he barely had an accent. "I don't know if you intended to make me feel better about Nia, but I appreciate it all the same. We should hang out more outside of the house."

Marie wrapped her arms around Garrett's waist from behind and laid the side of her head between his shoulders.

Julie sighed, a heartfelt look on her face. "Would be easier if we weren't already enduring a multitude of lifetimes together here."

As if on cue, a child's shrill scream tore through the walls. Grady. Screaming until out of breath then restarting a split second later. Crying so loud, Garrett imagined the tears streaming down his face. He readied his legs for a dash up the stairs. The casual, if somber, reaction from the others halted him.

"Guess I better go check on them," Derrick said, his words dampened by his son's cries. "Good meeting you, Garrett. Let's talk when it's calmer."

By the time Derrick climbed halfway up the stairs, his wife's consoling coos overtook the cries, and the gathering returned to normal. Claude poked an annoyed Julie. Iris studied them. Marie pressed her ear against Garrett's spine. Within him, astonishment over everyone's lackadaisical response welled until he could no longer contain it.

"Why are children even allowed here?" Spoken aloud, it sparked another question so obvious he didn't know how he missed it. "And come to think of it, why no animals? Aren't they supposed to be good at spotting the supernatural?"

"Kids are the safest ones here." Marie rubbed his shoulder as she stepped to his side. "Losing them would devastate us . . ." She hung her head, seeming lost in terrible thought.

"But it would also piss us off," Claude said. "If ghosts and mekari take away too much, leave us with little to lose, they know they'll never make it out. They could bring the hordes of hell with them. We'd ruin ourselves to stop them out of spite. So, their best strategy isn't targeting the weakest link, but cutting off the head"—he brushed his neck and smirked—"so to speak."

Marie recovered. "Plus, the children aren't threats. Some are perceptive like you see in movies, but they're not good at processing it." She stared in the direction of Nia's motherly coos. "Atmosphere alone can set them off. Cats and dogs though, they know exactly what they're seeing."

"They're like alarm bells," Claude said. "But not knowledgeable enough to defend themselves or know when to run. That means they're the first to go. They'd help early on, but it's cruel to bring them here. Kids, on the other hand, distract us. If anything, their presence helps the spirits."

"Doesn't this all assume ghosts and mekari act rationally?" Garrett asked. "I thought spirits were guided by emotion."

"So far, so good." Claude's gaze, supported by his rigid neck and shoulders, locked onto Garrett. "Maybe they retain some of their humanity in the afterlife. All I can say is they've never directly caused a kid serious harm."

"More importantly," Julie said. "They're the next generation. Better to educate them now than throw them in the deep end once we're dead. I'll also remind you that everyone bound to this family by blood or oath must return. Not bringing them significantly increases the chances of their parents dying, or worse, the invading horde breaking free. It's a calculated risk."

A calculated risk? With kids? Irritation heated Garrett's body, but the Renault siblings appeared satisfied with their explanation. They were the experts. He crossed his arms, gripping his right triceps so tightly he pushed against bone. Marie countered by stroking his left, cooling his spirit. He trusted her enough to consider living in a haunted house for months, to consider putting off his career. This was no different. If they forbid pets based on safety, the calculated risk had to hold merit. Surely they cared more for their kids than adopted animals? As he relaxed his grip, he noticed Marie's trembling fingers.

"Are you okay?" Garrett asked.

She took a moment, then nodded. Her caress grew stronger yet softer. "We talk big, but I still worry about them. We're okay as long as we have each other. That's what I believe."

The way she imparted wisdom and confidence through a gentle act reminded him of everything he loved about her in a powerful instant. Filled him with a sudden desire, intensified by her scintillating insinuation whispered right before they passed through the Ring.

"If that's all, I have notes to finish up." Julie eyed Marie's continued caress. "I'll be in the library if I'm needed."

Iris humphed and sauntered up the stairs, her lack of speed not appearing due to age or injury.

To Garrett's satisfaction, the group was breaking up and only Claude remained. Hopefully, he wasn't sticking around. Desire for

Marie was lifting Garrett's spirit, and he craved alone time with her before the house crowded them further.

Claude jogged over toward Julie. "Need some help?"

"No," she said. "But I'll find something."

After the twins passed out of sight, Garrett's hand enveloped Marie's. Her personality mixed equal parts of her two siblings. Independent like Julie, sociable like Claude. Funny how she looked less like a sibling than Derrick though. Thinner, with cheek dimples absent from the rest of her family. He attributed the latter to her persistent smile.

He leaned in for a kiss.

She granted it. "Schwaz! Let's split to the kitchen. I could use a snack."

"Sure." He let her lead, admiring her backside as they moved through the house. Could they sneak into the bedroom? Probably too suspicious. They'd always stayed out during the day unless Garrett worked alone while she caught up with her siblings. He'd have to make it until tonight—a tall order. Marie didn't realize how a few silly words would wind him so. She glanced back as she opened the kitchen door, her dimples deepening a smile that insinuated she knew very well. He had to shift his mind elsewhere.

She opened the fridge and rifled through its contents. "I'm thinking a turkey roll-up. Mustard, cheese, and a strip of lettuce so you don't bug me about veggies later. You want one?"

Too early for a snack. Unless he hit the gym, which would be a great way to sway his mind from lusty desires. He walked behind her to inspect the shelves. A chill wind passed through him. Too cold and indirect to have come from the fridge. His attention trailed in the direction from which the gust left his body. He shook it off.

The house didn't lack for food. The shelves were packed. Two more fridges held just as much, with several deep freezers also split between the two storage rooms. Garrett drew closer for a better look. His hand grazed her bare thigh, his waist almost touching her backside. She pushed her butt back so that it did.

The chill returned, seeping into his skin, piercing his muscles. Ice spread from his heart, filling his veins. His chest numbed. Sensation in his fingertips and toes dulled. He craved to dive under a mountain of blankets in a desperate search for warmth. He knew what was happening and couldn't respond. Couldn't even feel his heartbeat.

Marie patted his frozen hand. "Are you okay?"

The girl asked, and then, he was. More than okay. Her sweet, sonorous voice tickled his ears. Overwhelmed him with newfound strength. Carnal desires erupted. Her body would be his. He sank his teeth into her neck, nibbling on her delectable flesh.

His prize giggled. "Not here. And definitely not while I'm eating."

He ignored her. Ran his hands over her small breasts, down her stomach, and fiddled with the button of her shorts. He smelled her skin. She was in heat, and he'd oblige her desires.

"Hey, I said stop." The girl tried to whirl around.

He held her in place, flicked off the button of her shorts. Started sliding them down with one hand.

The girl resisted, grabbed his wrist, trying to slow him.

He cackled. She was weak. He was strong.

"Garrett, this isn't you. Stop." She sounded worried, yet unafraid. Fool girl. He would hear her scream. Excitement, eagerness, and hunger overwhelmed him like feelings trying to escape his skin.

"Garrett," she said with fondness. How sweet this would be. With her shorts near her knees, he slipped his thumb into her panties. Salivated. Anticipation yearned to take her. His thumb stroked her hip. He started tugging. After the first yank, his hand resisted. Cramped. He tried to drive it down, but it opposed him. He hissed, growled. Felt infernal warmth coursing through him. Bit by bit, his limbs thawed, and he felt himself fading away.

Garrett's hands flew up. He shot back, struck the island counter square on his spine, and grunted. The pain sparked, then faded to a distant, dull ache in comparison to the guilt that strangled him. Marie righted her clothes.

"Marie, I'm so sorry," he said. "What happened? That wasn't me. I couldn't. Wouldn't. I don't even know why, why, why." In control of himself once again, he clasped his cheeks, saw his hands below, and hated them. Loathed them. Wanted them cut off. He dug them under the back neckline of his shirt.

Marie stood there in silence, holding her upper arm, her thumb circling just above the elbow.

He waited for what felt like an eternity. Waited for her to kick him out of the house, out of her life. He was too weak to cut it here. Not worthy of Marie's all-encompassing love. But when her hand fell from her arm, she didn't berate him. She stared deep into his eyes, seeming to search for something. If he was lucky, she'd find the earnest regret in his soul.

At last, she reached toward him. Stopped short of his face when he recoiled.

He wouldn't—couldn't—lose control again.

"It's not your fault. I put those thoughts in your head."

Garrett's jaw dropped. *Her* fault? In what manner? *He'd* lost control. Given into his basest instincts. Turned into another man. "It wasn't your fault at all. I did that. Not you. How can you look at me like nothing happened?"

"I know who you are. Knew it wasn't you almost immediately. I trust you." Flat, matter-of-fact speaking replaced the usual vibrancy in her voice. "Once it started, were you ever in control?"

"It doesn't matter." Garrett glanced away, keeping her face visible through his periphery.

"It matters here." She turned her palms up and gestured around the kitchen. Whirled toward the bulk of the house, then back to face him again. "Possession latches onto suppressed emotions. There are ways to protect yourself, but not for you. Not yet. I teased you, having fun like we normally do. More than normal because of how you looked after the Ring. I was selfish, worried you'd run off. I said a few words, touched you how you like, trying to keep your eyes on me. It was careless. We're too close to the Breach for me to do that until you adjust. But nothing 'appened, so let's both learn from it. For at least as long as you're here."

How could she entertain him staying? Consider taking even a fraction of the blame?

"Give into your emotions and let them out." She reached toward him again. This time he stayed still. As she touched his cheek, she jerked back. Then, she returned to lay a hesitant touch on his stubble. "This is what 'appens when they linger. That wasn't you. And I should've known better. I'm sorry."

He'd tried to rape her, and she felt guilty over it. Her! The only innocent involved, living or dead. Vigilance of strange sights, sounds, and sensations was to be his shield. Knowledge, his sword. All of that failed him in the moment of the house's first true test. Within him, two distinct emotions competed. Shame for his body's actions, for not controlling them better.

And anger.

He'd kill the damn ghosts if they weren't already dead. Years ago, at a baseball game, his bat had cracked during a swing. The tip hurtled at the opposing pitcher, who suffered a concussion and left the game. Though nobody blamed Garrett, he barely slept that night. But he'd sleep soundly after strangling whoever did this to her . . .

Your emotions are winning. He knew of only one way to quickly quell his hatred.

He looked up into Marie's eyes. Two oval orbs encompassed everything he wished for in the world. She wasn't over it—not yet. How could she be? Yet she already forgave him. His wants and needs no longer mattered. The only question was whether she was safer with him.

Or without him.

8. Reinforcements

Past relationships had taught Garrett that merely showing up late for a date merited penitence.

Not with Marie.

After his crime in the kitchen, she froze for one moment in the bedroom together, and then never looked at him differently again. Same smiles. Same touches. Same exuberance. Her love radiated through her forgiveness. He couldn't reciprocate. Last night, he edged away from her in bed, almost slept in a different room. Marie had vowed to follow him.

Why wasn't she concerned? He posed a danger to her—couldn't she see that? He could overpower her, force upon her the heinous whims of a vile spirit. Almost raping her was the worst of it, but his loss of control crafted a lingering fear within. For a short time in the kitchen, a stranger dictated his future.

Garrett grunted and clawed at his face. The sharp pain refocused his energies. He honed in on the book Julie had lent him. Sequestered in the study upstairs, he searched for what he really needed to know: how to fight back.

Possessions came in three forms. Mekari, which interacted with the physical world by stealing into people's willing bodies—who would will *that?*—or their dreams. Spirits did so as Claimers or Hiders. Marie had explained the gist of those, and this book clarified the details. Claimers differed from Feeders similar to how compulsions compared to anxiety. Intense desires, from love and lust to guilt to a maternal instinct to protect, opened one up to possession, granting the ghost a form with which to live out their twisted fantasies. Willpower aided in severing a Claimer's hold, and the book recommended ambiguous tips like staying calm and thinking who your body was hurting. But it read like anyone who ever said 'relax', generating the opposite effect.

Hiders snuck into bodies, mirroring a parasite. The longer their possession lasted, the more energy they leached from the body, leaving less for the human. The best defense was to trick the ghost, to make it think in a manner it believed was genuine, while in fact acting in complete disregard for their host's personality. Ultimately though, someone else had to catch the Hider in a lie to cast them out.

Each word had him gripping every page in a hunger to learn more. He craved to understand the principles behind these threats, treating the supernatural like a corporate problem to analyze in a spreadsheet and assess. He wouldn't—couldn't—let possession corrupt him again.

He returned to Julie for more reading, fretting she'd discover his crime in the kitchen with a glance. She pointed him in the right direction without question. Nobody else knew of his transgression. Guilt assailed him so fiercely, he didn't mention a missing page in an early chapter of the book. Apprehension over revealing something stifled him, convincing him to quietly return to the study.

Between bouts of research, he contemplated the breakfast nook ghost. A chill had passed through him there too. Was the Claimer stalking him? He clicked his tongue, then pinched the next page to read more.

A knock at the door interrupted him.

"Come in," he said, half-suspecting a passing spirit and surprised at his calmness. Maybe it was exhaustion.

Marie entered and blew him a kiss. She wore a sweater and a pair of jeans, both new to him. Despite the extra covering, she tempted him more than yesterday—her compassion heating him up and flushing his face. He looked away.

"Hey, don't do that." She snapped her fingers. "Eyes on me, Gare."

"What?" He plucked at his cheek, staring at a stain in the wood the size of a cigar burn. Footsteps creaked on the boards. Marie's shins and shoes blotted out the sight. Her soft hand cupped his chin and tilted his head up.

"Kelly's here."

"Kelly's here?" Garrett's eyebrows tightened. "How do you act like nothing happened yesterday?"

"First"—she pressed her forefinger to her lips—"shhh. Second, short memory." Another smile he didn't deserve.

"Even then, you're—"

"Shhh. You know what, let me help you out." She skipped over to the door, closed it, and returned to his side. "Still, shhh."

He lowered his voice. "I can't guarantee yesterday won't repeat itself." Books were supposed to feed him knowledge to face the house's threats. Instead, learning shined a light on his ignorance, leaving him with a depressing conclusion: he should give up the woman he loved and trusted to spare her. He had more to consider than himself. "You're in danger with me here."

"I love that you're worried about what I can handle. So, so much." She smirked. "Come on. I grew up in a haunted house. Don't throw yourself on the sword to save me. Use that sword to slice through ghosts. Metaphorically, of course. Swords are as useless as guns here."

He *would* sacrifice himself to save her. His contemplation the past day made that clear. But she was right. She had grown up here. He hadn't, but neither had Kelly or Nia. Speaking to them might teach him how to adapt. With Kelly waiting downstairs, he needed to jump on the opportunity. Nia had barely left her room since arriving.

"What's going through that head of yours?" Marie asked. "You're not bottling anything up, are you?"

"Trying not to." Easier said than done. He didn't live on whims like her.

"What do you want to do right now?"

Find forgiveness as easily as you found it for me. Kiss you without worrying about losing control. Those weren't options, not at the moment. "Go downstairs. Meet Kelly."

"Alright, then." She sandwiched one of his hands between both of hers, then nodded at the stack they created.

He added his free hand. *Stronger together than apart.* They'd crafted that saying a month into dating, after an unexplained bang startled them while they watched a movie at his place. This house twisted their mantra into a liability.

She pulled him to his feet, and they left the study for the stairs. Garrett focused on placing one foot in front of the other.

A group consisting of Claude's immediate family and Derrick congregated at the foot of the foyer stairs in a semicircle. Iris sat a few feet outside of it, in a chair pulled from a nearby office room. She knitted with a bag of balled yarn at her feet, watching the group of her juniors.

The image Garrett had conjured for Claude's wife flew so far off the mark it didn't hit the dartboard. In place of a slender French woman with a cigarette glued to her mouth, she looked positively ordinary. Not unattractive, just someone who could get lost in a crowd. About Marie's height. Blonde hair past her shoulders. Freckles. Curves barely noticeable from oversized clothes. Her t-shirt and jeans contrasted against Claude's designer clothes.

The child at her side, Tommy, was even younger than Grady. There must have been a few years between Claude and Derrick's kids. His features made specific resemblances to either parent hard to place. A ghost across his shirt said, *Boo.* A bit too on the nose for Garrett.

Marie gave them hugs. Garrett shook Kelly's hand and waved to Tommy.

Energetic steps pounded down the stairs behind them. Garrett jumped away, hands raised to fight. Marie sidestepped toward him, applied gentle pressure to his forearm. The last step halted three from the bottom. Nothing looked out of place, yet he felt watched. *Knew* he was.

Derrick shifted to occupy the abandoned space. "It's nothing."

Iris snorted and shook her head. Kept knitting.

"If y'all could leave the ghosts upstairs like we did, that would be great." Claude smirked, then pointed at Garrett. "Glad you could join us though. Thought you might stay tucked away the whole day."

As if that were an option. He was leaving the house or marrying Marie tonight. What time did that leave to sort out complex emotions barely a day old?

"Yeah, figured we'd catch up yesterday," Derrick said. "Couldn't find you the whole evening. Got spooked by something? Maybe by this follower of yours?" He pointed his thumb over his shoulder, where Garrett imagined the formless specter standing. Experienced or not, how did they act so calmly in the presence of the supernatural?

"Something like that." Garrett willed himself to turn to the group, lowering his arms. "Not proud to admit how I acted."

"Don't be ashamed of anything here. We've all lived it."

I doubt that.

"Really. No shame." Marie stared at him, reading his thoughts.

Garrett turned away. He caught Iris staring too. He felt—or imagined—her judgment, and shifted back toward the group.

"We offered to sit in the sunroom." Derrick gestured toward his mother. "She said we were too young to sit around all day. I grabbed her a seat so she could join in."

"Don't put words in my mouth." Iris paused mid-stitch. Leaned forward an inch. "You need to stay strong. Sitting makes you weak. In fact, do some jumping jacks while you're up. Good for blood flow." She spoke with a Southern drawl, different than Mr. Renault's accent.

He blinked, taken back. "Then why're you sitting?"

"Because I'm smart. Don't need stren'th." She refocused on knitting as if having erased all doubt.

Derrick tossed his hands in the air, looked at Garrett. "Anyway, I can't blame you. Grady must've woken up five times last night. Not sure when we'll move him into his own room."

Two other isolated individuals posed a greater concern to Garrett. "What about your dad and grandfather?"

Claude gave a helpless shrug. "Dad's been cooped up more than usual before a Breach. As for Grandpa, Dad's better at explaining, but Derrick will do his best."

"Me?" Derrick shot back. "He's your dad."

"I'm older. I'm delegating the best person for the job. Or we could grab Julie?"

"I'm not interrupting her."

"Then it's settled."

Derrick sighed. "Fine."

Garrett's stomach clenched. *Where is this going?*

Kelly rolled her eyes and reached down to help Tommy stand. She held his hands like a puppeteer as the boy danced on the floor.

"I was going to talk to you about it yesterday," Derrick said. "Figured Julie was too busy, and Claude and Marie too optimistic to give an accurate take. But again, I couldn't find you. So, here's the deal. Grandpa can speak with mekari. Have full conversations with them. Uncle Dave must be busy with that."

Kelly hoisted a squealing kid in the air, then slapped Claude on the arm with her free hand. "You didn't tell him about this until *now*? That's not something you leave out 'til the last minute." Wrong about her again—Garrett had taken her for the quiet type.

Claude scratched behind his ear. "Like Derrick said, we were hoping for good news to pair with the bad."

The bad? Was the time Mr. Renault spent with his father atypical for a Breach?

"I'm sorry, Garrett," Kelly said. Marie swayed in place, not meeting her furious stare. "Go on, Derrick."

"Sure." Derrick tapped his thumb against his forefinger. Calmly, methodically. "First, did they fill you in about mekari at all?"

"Of cours—" Claude started.

Kelly silenced him with a swipe of her finger.

Garrett's neck stiffened. He barely understood what they were discussing. Everything felt like such a well-oiled machine until now. "Demons," he said, "but less Satan and more dualism of man. I know the basics. I take it mekari have their own language?"

"Languages," Derrick said. "Like humans. Grandpa speaks them all and hears what we pick up as silence. He learned them over the years, but his English. His French." He swiped his hand across his chest. "All gone. Can't relearn it either. Once he realized what was happening to him, he and Uncle Dave created a new language that draws from both worlds. Luckily, that one's stuck around. No other way to communicate with him."

"Great gifts at big prices." Claude mocked the cadence of a used car salesman.

"Right," Garrett said. "Julie mentioned something similar about her sight. Your dad seems fine though."

"Not at all," Marie said, dropping into a somber tone. "He's got it worst of all. Feels spirits but can't feel the touch of anything . . . or anyone else." She leaned into Garrett, her hip tagging his dangling fingers.

He panicked, lifted his arm, and slid it high around her shoulder. He hung off her like a platonic friend.

She frowned. "His hugs aren't what they used to be. They still feel good, because it's Dad, but yeah, not like how it was before."

"Remember these sacrifices." Iris wagged a knitting needle at the group.

"We will, Mom." Derrick stole a glance back at the stairs. Concern for the spirit, at last? Or something to do with these family powers? Would the house eventually twist Garrett in the same way? "Anyway, the two of them have a system that involves a big diagram and lots of pointing. Gets us a semblance of useful knowledge from what sounds like ramblings. The problem with more ramblings . . ."

Marie looked up, an apology twinkling in her eyes. " . . . is that it means more mekari."

The scene slowed. Garrett pulled his arm away from Marie, massaged the back of his neck. A Breach with bonus demons. Great. Just what he—

A pop near the front door sped everything back up. Window shades shuttered down. Sailed back up.

Tommy stared in wonder. Kelly jogged over and placed herself between him and the erratic shades, keeping a hand on him.

"Y'all didn't lock all these yet?" Derrick moseyed to the nearest window as if approaching a docile pup to correct him after accidentally barking.

Laughter of a young woman emanated from the door, trailing off toward the library halls.

Everyone followed the sound with their eyes, Claude with his feet. "I'm going to check on Julie." He waited for Kelly's approval before moving.

Derrick pulled the shades down and engaged the lock.

"Is the same thing with your dad and grandpa keeping Julie stuck in the library?" Garrett asked. "More mekari? More spirits?"

"She's there a lot normally," Marie said, "but probably. She usually wraps up the recon stage days before a Breach."

Garrett had assumed Julie and David's dedication was normal. If their workload concerned seasoned veterans—it should horrify him. It didn't. Because unlike the Renaults, he had an out. Even if a major reason to leave was to protect Marie from himself.

Marie touched him. Garrett raised a staying hand. The space blurred where the foyer turned into library halls. He verged on an epiphany.

The last Breach was two years ago, the one before that eight. Four times as long. How long was the one before that one? He focused so hard on preparing for the now, he didn't think to research the past. As if he had the time. Project updates for his professors had already sunk to the bare minimum.

Focus.

Is there a connection between haunting frequency and Breach timing? The more recent the Breach, the greater the danger sort of thing? The Renaults should know. They're prepared in every other way. If so, why didn't Marie tell me until, well, never?

Garrett shifted away from her. His hands formed a reverse steeple, thumbs bouncing off one another near his waist. "How bad will this Breach get?"

"We don't know," Marie said. "Julie suspected the rash of ghosts might be an aberration. They're more benign than usual." Garrett's eyes opened wide at that. Marie's nose twitched. "We were hoping it'd taper off. The last Breach wasn't that bad."

"Seriously?" Kelly's nose twitched. She obviously strained not to raise her voice. "Caring for a baby while dealing with the last one gave me nightmares for a month. You're telling me it'll be worse this year?"

"We don't know." Marie shuffled her feet. "The hauntings this week have been worse than the past Breaches, but Julie's recon always rises to the occasion. And mekari can even be good. If we just wait and see how it turns out . . ."

"I don't care," Garrett said. *Stay calm.* Everyone watched him while he regulated his breathing.

She nibbled on her lips.

He thought to let it go. A small repayment for his crimes. But these weren't insignificant details.

"You didn't lie," was the best he could muster. He thought he could trust her with his life, his future. "But you hid things. Why?"

She inched toward him, froze when he stiffened. "I'm sorry. I would've told you before tonight, I promise. I hoped it would turn around. Breaches are scary, but we usually keep everyone safe." She wrapped her arms around her torso. "We have our precautions, so ghosts have to cooperate to be dangerous."

"More ghosts means more cooperation, though." Inadvertently, if not on purpose. He didn't ask because he knew it as a fact from Julie's latest book recommendation.

A growl, then an angry yell burst from the library. "Get the fuck out!"

Julie.

Footsteps pounded the floor toward them. Garrett braced himself for a bull rush of invisible force. He delayed the briefest moment before shielding Marie. That short window twisted his anger and hurt by adding a dose of guilt.

Claude slowed his sprint to a jog as he rounded the corner. A sheepish grin partially relieved the room of its tension. With Garrett's adrenaline fading, a light headache replaced the surge of energy. He'd been grinding his teeth in anticipation of an angry spirit.

"Good news is the ghost didn't follow," Claude said. "Bad news is sis can't take a joke."

"That's not exactly news," Derrick said. Then to Garrett. "Why don't we talk in the sunroom? I'll explain everything that I figured we'd get to yesterday."

Marie's omission, her betrayal of uncertain proportions, left him wary of Renault blood relatives. He preferred to speak with Kelly, but she knew little more than him. Derrick seemed to take everything in stride. Maybe he'd coax the truth from him. He needed distance from Marie either way. He still loved her, but it might've been as she said when he proposed. That this whole idea of marriage was preposterous.

Kelly pointed casually at Marie. "Can you watch Tommy for a bit?" Then whirled on her husband, pointing the same finger at him with full extension. "Claude also has explaining to do."

Marie stuttered, "Sure." Treading toward the child, she glanced between him and the pairing of Garrett with her cousin.

Kelly reassured Tommy she'd be back soon and handed him off to Marie. The boy went on playing as if nothing had changed. Claude took advantage of his wife's diverted attention. He winked at Garrett and Derrick, oblivious to the air in the room. He returned to all seriousness as his wife marched over and dragged him upstairs.

Derrick raised a questioning brow. Not at Claude though.

Garrett realized he hadn't answered. "Lead on."

"Wait." Iris stood up, not fast, but sprier than expected. At this point, expectations felt meaningless. "Take my chair back. I'm locking myself in the sitting room so I don't have to hear y'all's nonsense."

"The kitchen's through there," Derrick said. "What if we get hungry?"

"Don't."

"Actually." Marie flapped her nephew's hand around. "Can we join you?"

Iris grunted and shuffled past, casting a whiff of subtle earth, as if she'd been gardening. Was that smell real or a ghost's work? She gripped the handle to the house's only interior glass doors. "Come if you're coming." Marie picked up Tommy awkwardly and hustled over, setting him down as soon as they passed the threshold. Iris shut the doors to coincide with her parting words, leaving no room for argument. "Renault brains are better than this."

9. Second Chance

Plexiglass windows wrapped around a sunroom that better exemplified beachfront property than heart of Louisiana. A sturdy coffee table lay in the center, surrounded by a cushioned couch, matching chairs, and end tables, all made of wicker. Plastic plants with large leaves decorated the corners of the room. Big square tiles covered the floor. Beyond the windows, the backyard offered plenty of space for a pool—if it wasn't such an obvious safety hazard.

Garrett sat on a cushion of blue and white palm trees. Dusk was settling on the outside world. "Do we even have enough time to talk about this?"

In the chair beside him, Derrick made a show of inspecting the outside world. He sipped on a glass of wine. "Plenty of time."

Garrett's own glass sat empty on the narrow table beside him. He instead held a ceramic mug full of tea in his lap. The longer they sat, the more he swayed back and forth in miniature motions, as if jostled by shallow waves. His nervousness reminded him of the time he gave his first presentation to a corporate Board of Directors. He filled the silence by pursuing a curiosity. "Why aren't the rest of the house's windows made of plexiglass? Seems safer."

Derrick tilted his head, admitting the point. "For one, glass looks nicer. Not a great justification, but when you're here for several months, balancing psyche comes into play. Two, broken windows aren't common, and our window shades are reinforced to withstand serious abuse. It'd take multiple simultaneous hauntings for the glass to pose a real danger. Three, and this is the big reason, sometimes we want to break out. Uncle Dave had to one year. Threw a chair straight through the window to escape a rare combo of ghostly unity—a Claimer taking my dad, and a Deviant flinging pens, books, and broken-off chairs legs at him. Without the window, a locked door would've spelled his end, especially if a Shifter shut down the hearing of any potential rescuers nearby. You're looking at me funny. Did nobody explain the different ghosts?"

"It's not that. The shades are locked. How useful is an escape route when you have to fiddle with that first?"

"Those locks'll be second nature before long. You know how the library and next-door supply room don't have doors?"

"Yeah. Same as the gym and an office downstairs. I meant to ask Marie about them."

"That's because there aren't any windows, and they don't connect anywhere else. Every room has a backup exit or an easy way out. We considered using thinner doors, but ghosts would break those as easily as glass. Wooden stakes aren't much better than glass shards."

"You make it sound like everything in the house can be a weapon." Garrett's free palm moved to rest against the warm mug.

Derrick plucked at the armrest. "It can. That's why we take these precautions. We can't fully ghostproof a house, but we can reduce our risk while maximizing our options. Serious injuries only occur in rare moments where ghosts unintentionally string together their haunts. Further, the last two to die, my dad twenty-two years ago, and Aunt Sophie six years later were"—his lips writhed as he searched for the word—"troubled. I don't want to say they lost the will to live, but it was sort of like that. You need to be in the right headspace here. We all see therapists. If you suffer from something like unmanaged depression, I'd recommend booting it over to the airport now."

He didn't, but that revealed another detail Marie had kept secret. At least this one he could chalk up to her forgetful nature. But which was it? Could he truly trust her? His need to know likely surpassed anyone else in the world contemplating marriage.

Derrick turned his attention to the backyard, seeming to take Garrett's silence as a cue for wanting to think.

Garrett focused on the earthy-yellow liquid between his palms. The warmth and vanilla scent comforted him, soothing a voice that screamed, *Get out!* The house wasn't safe. Renaults *had* died here. But everyone walked around without a care in the world. Either acting ran in the family, or they had honed supernatural guardianship to a fine point.

Night consumed day as Garrett's mind ping-ponged between potential truths.

"Okay." Derrick shifted in his seat. "I said we've got plenty of time, but I didn't count on tangents like that. In case we have a few more, let's get started. You deserve space to think over what I tell you here." He tapped the bowl of his wine glass. "This'll sound like a strange starting point, so stick with me."

Strange. The word had lost its meaning.

"Have you ever experienced racism?"

Garrett blinked. "Sure."

"What's the stupidest thing people say to you? Not a particularly heinous incident. Something you've heard multiple times."

The answer came in a flash. He hesitated because he knew others had it worse. Knew friends with true horror stories. Imagined the bullshit Derrick might have endured. But bullshit was bullshit, and after the past day, he was sick of any and all of it. "That I'm lucky to be Asian. Lucky because my smart brain makes working easy." He tapped the side of his skull. "That it must be nice to like studying. That I love working hard, so it makes succeeding easy. It's asinine. Yeah, I'm smarter than some others. Dumber too. I work my ass off because I give a damn, not because working is fun.

"The person doesn't even think it's racist because hey, it's a compliment. They don't think they're chalking up every hurdle I've overcome to genetic luck." He grunted. "Sorry to unload. House is getting to me, I guess."

"Nothing to apologize for."

Garrett sipped his tea, then started idly flicking his mug. "I've never really been threatened at least. Uncomfortable stares sure, but rare. Friends warned me to watch out if I ever went south."

"There are bad folks here," Derrick said, "but we hardly have a monopoly. It's not like people of color only suffer where it's warm. I've got to watch my language around certain people, you know? Some that supposedly protect us. People walk faster when they see me if I'm wearing anything besides a suit. Despite that, and you might laugh at this one, what bothers me most is the assumption I play basketball. Not just from white people. I've jogged by courts with my headphones in and been harassed to join a game. I hate basketball. There's no sport where scoring is less satisfying. It's all up and down the court. Over and over. The most repetitive game on the planet."

Garrett nodded, trying to relate. Playing third base, multiple innings might pass without a ball hit in his direction. He'd never considered it boring though. The batter drew his full focus. He didn't care much about other sports, but he imagined they all shared this element. Attention to the present allowed little time for boredom. He would've thought Derrick interested in something competitive based on his lean build, but his vitriol for one game cast the idea in doubt. He supposed that was the point of this: the foolishness of making assumptions based on appearance.

"I see that." Derrick pinched his glasses frames for effect. "The *he's built for sports* look." Heck of a read. He waved off Garrett's attempt to defend himself. "I'm not calling you out. It's natural." He shrugged, flipping his free palm face up. "This is all genetics, staying handy around the house, and chasing a child." He took a sip of his drink. "And wine."

Derrick lowered the stem and leaned on the armrest closest to Garrett. "The point is: appearances can be deceiving. They tell us false facts that are poor substitutes for real experience. People see our skin color and think they know us. The ones who hate us make a cruel and unfair world. That puts the onus of survival on us, even though they're in the wrong. Hiding details about ghosts and mekari looks bad." He frowned. "It is bad, but not as much as it seems. I don't want you to make a wrong assumption here because it's easy to do, and you know how often it can be wrong.

"This house is all kinds of fucked. What you've learned so far is a drop in the bucket. Julie's library is a testament to the incomprehensible adversity of living in this house. I worry about death every time I walk in here. I worry about my wife and my kid, even when I don't show it. I worry that one day, ghosts will start working together and put us in a real bind. I worry over mekari doing something we can't counter because no Overseer has ever lived to report on it.

"I could go on, but point is: there's a lot to worry about. What saves me is family, whether they're bound by blood or oath. Bet you're sick of hearing that." He flashed a grin, then returned to his somber tone. "I'm able to compartmentalize these fears because of the people here. In the outside world, people make stupid assumptions because of how I look. People pit themselves against each other for even stupider reasons. Here though, we're all on the same side. We've got each other's back. It's a total war zone, and I feel safer here than anywhere else in the world."

The back of Garrett's neck tingled. He felt power in those words. A sense of belonging, like a coach pumping him up for a game. Greater, because this went well beyond prepping for a game.

He didn't have to live there though. The Renaults' dedication to one another had nothing to do with his relationship to Marie. He wanted to buy into logic that enticed him to stay, but logic didn't change that she withheld vital information. "I see what you mean. I do. I just can't help but think: what else is she hiding?"

"There's the problem. You're asking the wrong question. We all hide things. Marie more than others, but not for nefarious reasons. She looks beyond the bad to spy the brightest futures, then paints that scene for the rest of us. Julie would never admit it, but Marie's optimism helps her to keep her cool in the worst situations. Without it, she and Uncle Dave wouldn't have the energy to tackle all the threats this house throws at us." He tilted his head. "I'm not saying this to convince you of anything, just giving you the defense she won't supply for herself. The real question is: do you believe she would have told you before y'all got to the wedding ceremony?"

An answer came immediately. Uncertainty pushed it down. Garrett drank his tea, propped it between his legs, and watched the ripples fade. He had to dive deep to discover that he believed in Marie. Forgiveness for his crime in the kitchen came so easily to her. She hadn't done any irreversible harm. He had. For any relationship to work, he had to reciprocate. And this wasn't any relationship. It was one he jeopardized his future for, because he deemed the sacrifice worth it. Derrick was right—holding her optimism against her made him little better than those who attributed his successes to his heritage.

Garrett sighed, folded his hands on top of his head, and leaned back. The sun descended into the horizon. Backyard shadows turned into patches of darkness. Trees dotted the fields of grass, looming like monsters. Except, the monsters weren't outside. They were here, in the house, preparing to escape over the dead bodies of everyone inside. Marie lay in danger, even graver than he first suspected. Leaving her now felt cruel. If only he could think on it for another day.

But he couldn't.

He had to decide whether or not to marry Marie. Here, now, in this room. Relying on his gut for an answer was out of the question. So many details went unnoticed. One might cost his life, and there wasn't time to *think*. Either he joined her tonight in blessed union or flew out on a plane to likely never see her again.

He pulled his hair taut. His analytical brain made a habit of overthinking problems, worsened by stressful situations like living in a haunted house. The past week had been full of back-and-forths. He needed to simplify the equation, and how better to do that than focus on his dilemma's most crucial element: Marie.

She trusted him, even when a spirit stole his body for its heinous assault. She trusted him, knowing that the wrong spouse in this house could end her family. She trusted him, with secrets only a handful of people in the world knew. And she hadn't truly done anything to extinguish the trust he felt a week ago.

What else was there to go on but his mother's sage advice? Find someone he trusted, who trusted him. He'd already done the hard part.

"Thanks, Derrick. There's something I need to do." Garrett pushed down on the chair's armrest and started to rise. Stiffened at Derrick tutting and wagging his forefinger.

"This is a happy moment." Derrick swirled the remainder of his wine in the bowl of his glass. "They'll soon be few and far between. I want to savor it a bit longer." Droplets of wine descended from the glass's rim, forming their iconic legs. He drained the rest while creeping movement entered Garrett's periphery.

Black tendrils spread over a pane of plexiglass. Slowly, but faster than the sun cast a shadow. As a coil touched the pane's edge, the entire form shrank and lost its fringes, leaving the shadow of a human head and shoulders. The darkness broke at its mouth, grinned, and vanished, leaving no trace on the clear window. Garrett felt pride that his heart skipped only a beat. Pride that he didn't squeeze his tea mug, but merely firmed his grip.

The rim at Derrick's lips gave the impression he missed the shadow, until he lowered his glass and stared at the spot. "That reminds me. Not all mekari are bad."

"Marie said that. Julie too. She also said most *were* bad." Garrett pointed at the window. "That wasn't one, was it?"

"Oh, no. Mekari can't do that. The smile just made me hopeful we'll find some otherworldly allies this year."

"Do you"—Garrett drummed his mug—"believe that?"

Derrick surveyed the room, inhaled a deep breath, then shook his head. "No, I guess not. It's better not to trust them in any case. Before meeting Nia, I felt this corruption inside of me, calling me to wicked acts. Resistance grew harder, and as it did, a mekar visited my dreams, offering relief for a future price. Seems like the architect of the virus selling the cure, right? Thankfully, we never made it to negotiations. Meeting Nia was my salvation."

"And the corruption went away?"

Derrick snapped his fingers. "Like that."

"What kind of temptations?"

"No offense, but that's well in the past. I don't care to revisit it more than I've said. Just keep in mind that though mekari may not be true devils, they make deals like them."

"And you feel safer here than anywhere else in the world?"

"Unity. It's what keeps us together." Derrick admired the room's walls and ceiling with the reverence of a pilgrim visiting a holy site. He seemed to see through the plaster and wood, to the house's inhabitants. His genuine admiration for his family contrasted the plethora of Garrett's classmates who used theirs to climb the corporate ladder. "So, still planning to propose?"

"I didn't ever say I was going to."

Derrick laughed. "The only other sane option is to ride out to the airport. Really, the only sane option. But love is love, and Marie is Marie. You're lucky to have her, in spite of our family baggage. Make sure you do it right. You don't get a second chance."

Irony almost caused Garrett to reciprocate the laughter. Derrick was wrong about a second chance, but wisdom incarnate imbued his other words. Dusk fell faster now, urging him along. But he sat still, cemented himself to the chair until he mustered a smile. Even if it wouldn't be his first proposal, Marie deserved his best effort. He pictured her standing in street clothes, a giant grin plastered on her face, rocking back and forth with her hands behind her back. Her swaying grew bigger and bolder with each cycle until she tipped too far and fell, landing square on her rear. Her grin stretched even wider.

Garrett snorted, once twice, then broke out in laughter.

"You okay?" Derrick's eyebrows were already raised. "Not losing it, are you?"

"No," Garrett said, still smiling. "Not losing anything at all."

10. Blessed Union

The wedding turned out even more low-key than the marriage proposal.

Either of them.

Everyone except the grandfather met in the backyard, where mowed grass stretched to the perimeter of the country fence line. Trees dotted the flat landscape until they clumped into a grove outside the fence. Humidity restrained itself more than at any point during Garrett's stay, and both bugs and ghosts alike were content to leave them alone.

The family gathered near the limestone walls of the house. Drinks on a cast iron table on the patio provided the sole sign of the event. Nobody sat, and aside from Julie using the excuse to wear heels, only Garrett and Marie dressed formally. He went for the full suit, but she forced him to drop the tie and jacket. She surprised him with a pastel blue, floor-length dress. For a brief moment, he forgot his worries, mesmerized by her beauty and rare attire.

Her collarbones lay nestled between short, narrow straps. A hint of cleavage peeked from the top. Her slender arms swung freely in the sleeveless dress. The fabric clung to her body like a second skin. She still wore her sneakers and lifted the hem of her dress before the ceremony to show them to the crowd. Chuckles ignited the air. Garrett joined them, but the joy of it eluded him. He wanted to marry her as much as he feared what followed.

The ceremony lasted no more than ten minutes. Mr. Renault officiated. He wore the same sweater and jeans as the day they met. He smelled cleaner than his appearance suggested, and his voice showed no sign of the tired look in his eyes. He opened with a prayer, then led the couple through an exchange of vows foreign to Garrett. In place of expected topics like love, communication, and honesty were steadfastness, unity, and strength. It sounded closer to an army pledge than a wedding vow.

Mr. Renault slid two identical golden bands onto their ring fingers and announced them bound by oath. He congratulated the couple with a distant smile, then left to return to his father's room. The only one who seemed disappointed by his short attendance was Garrett. Afterward, everyone mingled with a moratorium on talks of hauntings or mekari. Nobody except Claude drank more than a couple of glasses. He still walked as straight as anyone.

Garrett and Marie exchanged hugs with everyone then walked a short distance from the crowd. They held hands and half-full glasses: champagne for her, wine for him. Imbibing worried him more than usual, but he didn't want to spurn celebratory drinks meant in their honor. When they halted, Marie showered him with affection. Leaning on him, kissing his cheek, wrapping her arms around him from the side. She exuded adoration, moonlight enhancing her dimples. He nursed his drink with her by his side, smothering his desire to indulge his feelings. What if he lost control again?

Marie jabbed his arm. "If you don't stop worrying, you're gonna die. And now, if you die, I die."

He frowned. He didn't intend for either of them to die. That was the point of staying distant, keeping his emotions in check. How would he ever balance this? "Is that how it works?"

"No. It's not magic." She raised her shoulders like Garrett was an idiot. "I spent my life thinking this day would never arrive. Me, married? With all my baggage? When we started dating, I never believed or expected you'd give up so much for me. I was happy to enjoy the ride while it lasted. But then you proposed, not once but twice, and married me in a rush to beat the Breach. You represent my impossible—I can't handle you losing yourself. Whatever it is you need to move on, I grant it." She exaggerated the sign of the cross between her head and shoulders. "You are absolved of your sins and transgressions. Now, I demand you enjoy the fact that we're *married*." She cupped his chin and drew his lips to hers.

Her words convinced him into reciprocating her kiss. What was the point of marrying the woman he loved if he didn't enjoy it? Diligence enough to play baseball at Harvard was diligence enough to keep his body off limits to undead thieves. He'd find a healthy middle ground between love and lust to defend against losing control. That balance necessitated not bottling up his desires. He pulled her toward him, his hand finding equal measures of bare skin and lace on her back.

Clapping started up from the crowd. One of the kids howled. Claude yelled, "Go get 'em." No clue if that was for him or Marie. Garrett cracked a smile all the same.

Feeling in a better place, he poked fun at something she'd said. "So, you wouldn't have died before if I'd died? Only now that we're married?"

"Who's to say? The past is the past, remember?" She wagged a playful finger at him. "I don't want to imagine it. I've got my Gare back, and that's all I care about. No dying for either of us." She motioned toward her family. "No dying for any of us."

"Agreed." Garrett stretched around her back, caressing the back of her arm. "Oh, I found your stash of friendship bracelets when I was hunting for the engagement ring. Why'd you bring so many?"

Marie blushed. "We're so cut off in a Breach. I like having some things from around the world."

Garrett kissed the crown of her head. "I get it."

Hard to believe he had chosen to live in a haunted house for several months. Hard to believe spirits haunted the place at all—to the point where he'd cracked his first joke about it. This wasn't some ramshackle house. The backside of the mansion invited even more photography than the front. The patio ran half the width of the house, covered by a roll-up cloth awning. A hip-height wall enclosed all but two exits. A lonely tool shed filled the space around the corner. Windows gave him inside views of the sunroom, dining room, and breakfast nook. It all seemed so quaint and normal, as quaint as possible for a thirty-five-room behemoth.

Marie turned, catching a strand of her hair in his burgeoning beard. She stroked her bob cut back into place. "I was so wrapped up telling my family about the wedding, I forgot to ask: how'd the call go with your parents?"

After he had proposed in the solitude of their room, Marie jumped to spread the news and gather her family. He let her go with a parade of kisses, then called his parents. "I kept it simple. Said I proposed, you said yes, and that I was staying with your family for a few months. My dad immediately realized it would delay my graduation and tried to convince me to stay over the summer instead. I countered with the opportunity to learn the family business here. My mom was the one who eventually settled him down. Speaking of, I need to text them a pic of your engagement ring. Without the other jewelry."

The golden ring given by Mr. Renault didn't match the platinum band in front of it, nor the diamond on top. She didn't mind the mismatch, but it was already needling at him. He assumed replacing their wedding bands was out of the question, given the almost ritualistic nature of the ceremony.

"Better get to it then," Marie said. They set their drinks onto the grass. She slipped off the wedding ring and handed it to Garrett, who put it in his pocket. "Who knows how much longer we've got cell service."

Ideally, long enough to hear back from his professors. He was committed to his decision but hoped for a positive response to his semester withdrawal. Their support factored into whether the school offered a tuition refund, and thus one less worry. He took her hand in his and pulled his phone from his pocket, angling the ring for different pictures, talking as he did so.

"Mom and Dad were a little disappointed not to have met you first, but their chief concern by the end of the call was that I'd miss Christmas. It wore off as we talked. They eventually said they trusted me." He had almost laughed at that. Trust, trust, and more trust. The word was inescapable this week. "We'll have to make sure we play off our big wedding with straight faces. Your family too." He inclined his head toward the crowd. "Truth is one hole I can't dig myself out of."

"We're good with secrets." Marie winked.

"I guess you are." He chuckled, scratching his jawline with his shoulder. Itchy stubble didn't suit him. "I also gave them the address in case they needed it."

Marie raised her eyebrow. Nobody knew of this house except for the people living in Ajaccio, and some tax assessors he supposed.

He massaged in between her knuckles. "I had to tell them in case, you know, something happens to me. It's a risk, but I can't leave them completely in the dark. I said that I'd be out of touch for a few months." That took convincing, stretching the truth with an elaborate excuse detailing Renault traditions—when you were with the family, you were *with* the family—to see if a person meshed with them before marrying in. He didn't earn his parents' buy-in until promising something similar from him and Marie. "They're not the types to show up unannounced."

She glanced at the second story. "It's okay with me, but keep that from my dad. I trust you."

That word again. Garrett smirked and sent the best three pictures to his parents. Then he stepped back, pointed the lens at Marie, captured her from the waist up. "You're wearing something different for the big wedding, right?"

She hung her hand on her hip, elbow bent wide. "Would it be a problem if I didn't?"

He hadn't considered the dress might be special.

"I'm kidding. Of course, I'm picking out something new. Why?"

Garrett exhaled budding tension. "Thought my parents should also get a picture of you. Didn't want them later wondering why I sent pictures of your wedding dress well in advance of the wedding."

"In that case." She posed like a goof, arms in a flourish, mouth open. Garrett snapped the photo, then pursed his lips with his *act serious* face. She blew a raspberry, clasped her hand at her waist, and smiled. The first pose captured her spirit better, but he sent the second. He flipped to his email after. Still only word from one professor, a lukewarm response.

"Everything okay?" she asked.

"Nothing new from school, but it'll be fine." He slid the phone back into his pocket and pulled out her wedding ring. "Ready to go back to being married?"

She tilted her head, jutting her chin. She clearly suspected his feigned confidence but happily donned the gold band. Together they stacked their hands and stared at one another. Determination to come out of these next few months filled him with a newfound strength. He didn't control his future any less than before. There were simply more obstacles in the way, but he'd overcome them like others in the past. He pressed his forehead to hers, savoring this moment of bliss. Savoring the smell of grass like from the sport he'd played for so long. Savoring a joy and love in the air that cast away the horrors of what these grounds entailed.

A deep roar pierced their serenity. Glass shattered from a second-floor window on the other side of the patio. Rasped cries descended from above. Something had fallen halfway to the ground by the time the newlyweds turned. Arms and legs flailed against gravity. A body crashed to the earth, landing with a thud.

11. Breach

Marie picked up her dress and raced to where the body had fallen, kicking over her champagne flute. Her siblings and cousin sprinted twenty steps ahead of her. Kelly and Nia picked up their children and darted for the house.

Adrenaline shot through Garrett, pressing him into an alert state. He approached the scene cautiously. No glass or other projectiles levitated for a follow-up attack. He searched for signs of whether the fall was self-induced or from a push. Other than the shattered window, the house offered no clues.

Cries of "Grandpa!" rang out, followed by the clamor of arguing. The four grandchildren circled the prone body, with Derrick and Julie kneeling on opposite sides.

Where was Iris? Had she already fled inside?

Claude yanked his sweater off and tossed it to Julie, who presumably placed it under their grandpa's head. Garrett couldn't tell for sure; from this angle, he saw only the man's waist and bare feet. He found himself walking to maintain that concealment. He realized he wasn't just watching for danger. He feared what lay on the ground. A man who spoke to mekari, living holed up in his bedroom. What would he look like? What would he say?

Did he survive?

No sooner had the mothers disappeared into the dining room than did Mr. Renault take their place. He flew from the mouth of the French doors as if escaping a fire, dashing to the cramped circle.

"Is he alive?" he cried out. "Did he say anything?" The circle parted.

He crouched down, biting his thumbnail.

"Breathing, barely," Julie said. "Can't speak. The glass cut him up, but nothing looks broken or out of place."

"It will soon."

Her eyes widened. "Dad, no."

Marie's hands flew up to her mouth, muffling a gasp. Claude shifted uncomfortably and Derrick lifted his grandfather's shirt in search of something.

"Don't bother looking yet." Mr. Renault reached for his father's hand, then pulled back as if sensing a trap. He settled for a light squeeze of his thigh and stood up. "It's there. We'll find it after. Leave him the peace we can for now. And keep your ears on."

Derrick pulled the man's top straight, then he and Julie backed up a couple feet.

What was this? Curiosity pushed Garrett the last few steps to join Marie and inspect the scene. His fingertips grazed the back of her arm; she didn't give him any notice. Grandfather Renault appeared asleep, his head turned up and his eyes closed. Claude's sweater supported his head. The family kept their distance. Shards of glass created a minefield, likely digging into the knees of those kneeling on the ground. Blood flowed from Mr. Renault's forearms to his wrists, staining the grass and his pants in equal measure. Garrett looked above. The window had shattered from the center. Did that imply a push?

"What happened?" Julie voiced the question that Garrett wanted to ask but felt he had no right.

"Grandpa was ranting." Mr. Renault sighed. A barely discernible sorrow tinged his voice. "Like he was mad I left 'im. Or mad he missed the wedding. Normally, he gives me time to translate by repeating what he hears from a mekar. Not the case tonight. Whichever mekarian language he shouted got angrier the longer I stayed. He wasn't having a thing to do with our chart translations, so I tried calming him. Made things worse.

"I left the room. Poured myself a drink in the kitchen and waited some minutes, knowing I couldn't leave him alone. When I returned, something had taken hold of 'im. I thought it was a spirit at first. I watched 'im walk the bedroom as if young again, inspecting the walls like he'd never seen 'em.

"Then he turned, suddenly aware of me, and charged. I held back. Didn't wanna hurt him. Tha' was a mistake. The longer we fought, the clearer I saw a mekar possessed him. Our tussle pushed me near the window. I managed to twist around before he threw me out, but the momentum carried him forward. I tried to grab him as he fell, but . . ." he waved to the near-corpse. "Ah'll sift through old tapes to see if I can make sense out of what he said. And to see how a mekar got inside 'im."

Garrett clamped the joint of his forefinger between his teeth and wrapped his other arm around his ribs. Mr. Renault's bloody forearms supported his account. But if he tried to grab his father, he should have been seen out the window, at least for a moment. And who had roared before the fall? Uneasiness festered in Garrett as he reexamined Mr. Renault's wounds. Wouldn't he be a prime target to possess? And if this man, who had grown up in the house, could be possessed to push his father to his death, Garrett stood no chance. Worse, if possession drove Mr. Renault to fabricate his tale, it meant the entity still lurked inside.

Everyone else had turned back to their grandfather. Why did he doubt Mr. Renault's story? Nobody else seemed to. Probably because a Hider wouldn't attack outright, and a Claimer wouldn't last.

Everyone's on the same side here. You're just scared.

Eerie seconds of silence passed until Marie shook her head. "Whatever 'appened, he's still alive. We have to help him."

"Should we carry him back to his room?" Claude asked.

"Not 'til he speaks," Mr. Renault said, steadfast authority replacing his sorrow.

"If he has a concussion," Marie said, "he could die for nothing. We've got to at least—"

"You know that's not how this works." Julie studied the body as she would a book.

Marie shifted in place, her hands searching for a comfortable place to perch without success. She bumped Garrett and only then seemed to realize his presence. She let herself fall into him. Everyone besides her appeared calm. She spoke true though. If her grandpa hit his head, broke his ribs, or incurred one of a dozen other injuries, he could die if they did nothing. He needed medical care.

The closest hospital was fifty miles away, the closest doctor at least twenty. *If he's not okay and has to stay overnight, he'll miss the Breach.* A worse fate than one individual death, from what he understood. Was his family already writing him off? Garrett imagined himself laying on the ground, verging on death while the Renaults treated him like a science project. He clutched Marie, the reason for his illogical sacrifice.

Footsteps approached from the right, plodding onto patio tiles. Iris in her matronly skirt cast a grave look at the gathering. She stopped at the edge of the patio, spinning a chair toward them, and sat in it with a stiff posture. Metal scraping on stone coincided with the grandfather's returning consciousness.

He blinked a few times, each one drawing his nose deeper into a sneer. He perused those gathered until his sights fell on his son. The calm before the storm passed in an instant.

Grandpa Renault growled, lifted his head, and fell back down. Tried to rise again and again, faster and faster, as if attempting to carry the momentum to the rest of his body. Growls as deep as an idling car engine sputtered, finally ceased with a huff. Nothing but his mouth moved. Nothing but hatred poured from the pupils of his eyes. He spat a language that sounded like a mix of German, Russian, and something inhuman.

Marie rocked in Garrett's arms. The tirade continued from the ground. Julie and Derrick leaned back, still kneeling, hands on their thighs ready to act. Spit flew from their grandpa's mouth like a broken sprinkler system. Claude and Mr. Renault chewed their lips, looking more like father and son than ever.

Their grandpa channeled his anger into furies of gibberish. His eyes darted around. His cheeks twitched as he ranted. He funneled the purest vitriol one could muster into his face and voice. His movement left no doubt that a fractured spine left him paralyzed below the neck. The foreign language carried on and on. Each sentence sounded different than the last: an angry rant overflowing with unmistakable loathing.

Grandpa Renault no longer spoke human languages, but this went well beyond that. He no longer spoke for himself at all. Garrett tore himself away from the supine man's convulsions to inspect Marie. While her family prepared to handle whatever situation arose, she expressed nothing but the purest concern. Pride buoyed him against an uncertainty that tried to topple him. *This is my wife,* he thought, giving her a quick kiss. She nestled her backside into all his remaining crevices.

A guttural groan blasted from their grandfather. He spoke a final line directed at Mr. Renault and then ceased all movement. Nobody reacted until blood pooled from the back of his head, painting a deep crimson onto blades of healthy grass. Each person uniquely mourned the loss: turning away, breathing deeply, or fidgeting in various manners. Tears dropped from Marie onto Garrett's arm. Iris alone displayed no signs of grief. She narrowed her eyes when she noticed his stare, then returned to inspecting the scene with a blank expression.

"Julie." Mr. Renault coughed. "You comfortable looking for it?"

"Now?"

"We should bury him as soon as possible. If you don't wanna look, I will, but time's an issue."

Julie frowned, gravely inspecting the corpse of her grandfather. After a moment, her shoulders slumped. "I'll do it. Get everything prepared."

Absent nods made their way around the circle. One by one, everyone besides Julie dispersed. Iris's nod signaled a certain finality. She stood up to approach the tallest of the trees in the yard. Marie led Garrett to join her, none of them speaking as they advanced. The other males snuck around the corner of the house, toward the tool shed.

Halfway to the tree, he heard clothing moved around. He did his best to resist looking at the corpse, but the sounds demanded he look. The grandfather's shirt was rolled up to his chest. His pants hung below his hips. Julie investigated his bare skin with her plastic glasses up in her hair.

"What's Julie looking for?" Garrett asked.

"A mekar's." Marie sniffed. "Branding."

"A branding? What do you mean?"

Marie sniffled, but Iris beat her to the answer. "Keep Marie from falling to pieces, and I'll explain." She paused, considering Garrett with those piercing eyes. In response, he inched closer to Marie, who took a calming breath after a moment. Only then did Iris continue. "Mekari leave a small, unique marking to show a claim to their second skin."

"Their second skin?" Garrett's head ached.

Iris snorted. "Ghosts sneak inside bodies. Mekari take control. Claimers and Hiders are imitators playing a role, judging how others perceive them so they ain't get caught. Mekari, though, they see inside us. See our needs, our wants, our likes, our hates. They're natural deceivers with all the tools needed to impersonate us."

But for a mekar to take hold of a human body . . .

"Can't a mekar only possess someone if invited?" Garrett asked. Marie tensed at that, and he matched her for it.

"Far as I know," Iris said.

And the only person who knew for sure could say no more. But other details didn't add up. "So, if the goal is to sneak out from the Breach, why would a mekar inside Grandpa attack Mr. Renault?"

Iris gave him a disapproving look. Garrett didn't have time to ponder why.

The shed door slammed shut, startling him and Marie. The Renault men started toward them, each carrying a shovel.

How many bodies were buried in this yard?

"Don't know why he attacked," Iris said. "Could've been trying to escape before the Breach."

"How is any of this possible?" Garrett asked. "I thought mekari couldn't even cross into our world until after the rift opened? And that the Breach wasn't until tomorrow at the earliest."

"Seems we were wrong." Mr. Renault walked past them and planted his shovel's blade in the grass.

"Like a shitty Christmas." Claude came around Iris, holding the shaft of his shovel.

Derrick circled the other way, handle in one hand, his thumb tapping the metal socket in the other. Facial tics betrayed his anxiety at the task before him.

Garrett's stomach sank. He knew the possibility of an early Breach. That's why her family pushed him into deciding tonight, but he assumed they acted with caution. He had factored in another day before bearing the full weight of a haunted house. Another day to learn of this place without stressing over someone dying. Another day to . . .

Garrett let go of Marie's hand and dug into his pocket for his phone.

"What is it?" she asked.

He flipped through his text messages. "The pictures I sent my parents. The first batch went through. The second didn't. My signal's dead." He grimaced. "Gone."

"What time was that?" Mr. Renault asked. Claude and Derrick pulled out their phones, frowned at the displays.

"9:03." Too, too early. He counted on answering messages until bed. What if he missed something from his parents? Would they try to come, despite his assurances to Marie? And he'd have no idea whether Harvard would offer that tuition refund.

"Thanks," Mr. Renault said. "Might be useful later."

"Better get to work." Iris pointed past Garrett, toward the corpse.

He didn't look. "Julie's found the mark." Derrick started digging before his mom finished. Mr. Renault and Claude both stretched their necks in a circle, then joined him.

Garrett tightened the grip on his phone, glancing between it and Mr. Renault. "Do you need another set of hands?"

"It's your wedding night." Marie's father didn't look up, speaking between feats of earthly excavations. "Don't make it worse by diggin' a grave. We'll take care of everything after we give Grandpa his rites."

What would they even do with alone time at this point? "I'll try rebooting my phone," Garrett said. "Just in case."

Nobody had to tell him it wouldn't work. Not only did he have to survive a haunted house, he had to do so wondering about the outside world. And as his first husbandly duties, had to console his wife over the loss of her grandfather. Hopefully, the second wedding went better, assuming they survived. It couldn't be much worse.

12. Processing

Poking and prodding into Garrett's ribs startled him awake. Like needles jabbing for organs through his soft flesh.

The Breach!

He pushed himself back, threw the sheets and comforter at his aggressor. His back struck a stiff drape. Bells jingled, and he shot back to where he'd woken. He whirled around, recognized the material as the same he'd fallen asleep near, and scanned the confines of the enclosed bed for the original instigator. The overhead light was on, along with the one from the opposite-side bedpost. Marie, laying on her side with his bedding tossed over her mid-section, gave him a quizzical look. They were alone.

She leaned toward him, propping her head up in her palm. Her eyes were swollen and red from hours of crying, but she wore a smile that disregarded yesterday's horrors. "Glad I took the water balloons off the bed. I tried waking you up the nice way." She eyed his boxers. "But all you did was snuggle into the covers."

"So you started poking me?"

"It worked, didn't it?"

"Can you at least cut your nails next time?"

She examined her nails, aghast. "Sorry about that!" She yanked open the drape on her side, put on a pair of shorts from the floor, and left the room. She returned a minute later, carefully opening his drape and waving clippers in the air. "I'm such a dutiful wife, aren't I?"

Garrett sat up, scratching his scalp. "I'm not answering that."

"Because you're such a smart husband!" She hopped over and kissed him, then used her hip to scoot him toward the foot of the bed. She plopped down near his pillow, clipping her nails on his nightstand. Couldn't she use a magazine like a normal person? He swallowed. There were more pressing topics.

"Are you okay?" he asked. "Last night was hard." *For everyone.* "You can't be done grieving."

"Wrong. All done." She switched hands, pausing at her ring finger to admire her new jewelry. "Don't get me wrong, I'm still sad. Today though, happiness is my priority. We're *married,* and I won't let this house ruin that."

She tossed the clippers on the table and whirled on him, bending her knee and propping it on his thigh. She poked him in the rib again, softer this time, grinning as she twirled the culpable forefinger. "We're gonna celebrate all day to make up for yesterday." She glanced away, taking a deep breath. "Grandpa would've wanted that."

He cupped her knee, his thumb stroking just above. "It's okay to grieve. We'll be married for a while." Pending their survival. Opening the Breach with a death had cracked his confidence, but he couldn't let her notice.

"That's right, so we're not starting it off by moping around."

"That's not—"

"Enough worrying about me. How'd you sleep?"

He'd have to return to the problem later. "Better than expected." For the few hours he wasn't consoling Marie.

The funeral had lasted about an hour, with each family member recounting a fond memory. Their grandfather sounded a lot like Garrett's, almost stereotypical once they stripped away the supernatural. Always interested in his grandchildren and their children. Happy to help during hardships.

Afterward, everyone separated to grieve in their own way. Garrett cradled Marie while she cried. He fell asleep minutes after she did and slept soundly.

Too soundly.

"Where are the ghosts?" he asked.

"Do you want ghosts?"

"No, but isn't that what happens after a Breach?"

"I guess they got lost." *Got lost? Will she ever take this seriously?* Before he could figure out how to voice his thoughts without upsetting her, she added, "Did you have any dreams?"

Garrett rubbed his forehead. A scene set near the funeral tree lurked in his mind, too foggy to recall. "I can't remember. What about you?"

"Nope. One minute I'm cuddling with you, the next I'm up, ready to go. The future awaits." She invited him with a wink, though to what he didn't know. Grogginess from his sudden waking dulled his mind. The mattress beckoned his return, and he yawned in response.

Marie's deepening frown yanked him back.

He slapped his cheeks. "Some future. Four months in a haunted house."

"And more than that for many decades after." She leaned over, her hair sweeping his shoulder. "Are you regretting marrying me?"

"Of course not." He caressed her knee again. Her eyes fluttered. In his foggy dream, a stranger had lifted his hands, touching him with leathery and calloused palms. "I just want to stay realistic. This place is dangerous. There's no guarantee we'll both survive." *Not to mention doing this again, however many years from now.* "We're not supposed to bottle up our feelings, right? Optimism is your M.O., but I don't see how you've already recovered from last night. I haven't begun processing it, and I never met him."

"That's the thing. I told you that I'm still sad. I also told you I choose happiness. That's easy when I'm with you. I'm not pushing down my emotions. They're still there. It's just that with you, joy is stronger."

"Joy." He pursed his lips, staring into her hazel eyes, her brows lifting as she waited for him to continue. "I love you." He snorted a chuckle. "Partly, because you can feel joy in a time like this. But me? I don't feel it. When I look at you, I'm concerned, determined, and protective." He shook his head, having missed a feeling so new that recognizing it proved difficult. As he did, warmth spread through him. "And complete. I am who I am, and who I want to be, with you. But there's no room for joy today."

She pulled her hands back to her hips and smirked. "I can think of a very good reason why."

"What's that?" He couldn't hazard a guess. The half of his brain actually awake spent most of its processing power recalling his dream.

"We haven't consummated our marriage."

Oh. "Technically, we got that out of the way a while ago." *What am I saying?*

She wiggled her finger. "No, no, no. Everything resets after the wedding." She unbuttoned her shorts, her underwear peeking out.

Electric excitement swiped away more distressing emotions. He reached for her, stopping as he brushed her side, his face inches from hers. Suddenly, the dream fog lifted, and memory of its events returned, all but a key element. "That dream is coming back. I was laying on the ground, half alive. Your grandfather helped me up. He said something to me in English." The elder Renault's mouth moved silently. "Can't remember what though."

"Gare." Her playful demeanor faltered.

"I thought it might be important."

"It might be. That won't change in a minute. I need this moment to be about us, okay?" She smiled as her shorts hit the ground.

He indulged in the sight of her legs and her fair skin above her shorts line. Her dimples sold him the rest of the way. He stripped his undershirt, almost threw it onto nail clippings before grimacing. She giggled as he dropped his top to the floor. "A minute, huh? It's our wedding night-morning-day. Ten minutes guaranteed."

He leaned forward. She dipped back, wrapping her arms around his shoulders. He ran his hand up to her waist. Soft and smooth up the side of her thigh. Blood rushed to his groin and froze him in place. His hand stiffened against her hip. His crimes in the kitchen lingered. "You want this, right?"

"That's why my shorts are on the floor." Realization dawned on her face. She squeezed his shoulders. "Gare, that moment is long gone. I don't think about it. It wasn't your fault."

He looked down, where his hand rested on the band of her underwear.

"I'm a willing and able participant." With a kiss, she dispelled his guilt, hopefully forever.

His shoulders lowered, their tensions eased. They fell into one another, tugged and yanked off the rest of their clothes. He pressed his knee to the mattress and then, in a blurred flash, remembered what Marie's dream-grandfather told him: *Forgive the past.* It didn't ruin the moment, simply stalled it. He had a feeling the message didn't relate to *his* past.

"I told you," Marie said. "Willing and able."

"It's not that."

"What then?"

Should he tell her? He wanted to press every inch of his body against hers, touch every curve and every crease. He paused as his mind replayed the sound of glass shattering. *Dammit, Garrett, choose joy. You can figure out what it means later—in ten minutes, hours, or days. What's happening now isn't going to wait.* He focused on the resplendent sight before him. "I was thinking how much trouble I had getting out of bed. If I get back in, I'm not sure when I'll be able to get out again."

"That's okay with me." Marie jerked him toward her, and on top of her he fell. She was a whirlpool of optimism, pulling him in with no chance of resistance, directing his attention fully where it belonged.

13. Theories

The strangest thing happened in the two weeks following Grandpa Renault's death: nothing.

Garrett geared himself for a whirlwind of chaos. He expected flying pans, demonic snarls, chills stabbing his skin. In their place, a gentle calm prevailed. Other than the AC's morning rattle, the house's serene nature made for a relaxing, almost enjoyable, stay. Each morning, he jumped a little less at the metal yawn. But his apprehension hadn't faded. It shifted elsewhere, sank deep within. Frightened him in a more subdued manner.

Marie kept it at bay. With her, he could focus on the present.

The two were leaving their bedroom for the stairs, en route to a brainstorming session led by Julie. Garrett's head ached from Marie's latest bomb.

"So let me get this straight," he said. "There are eleven other Hellspots. Families who run them, like yours. Ours." He grunted. "They're called Overseers. Benefactors for Hellspots are mostly old money but include billionaires like Jing Liu and Margaret Applebaum? But these benefactors don't know the locations of these Hellspots outside of one in Rome. They pay what's basically an insurance company to limit disasters like mass shootings—which are actually curtailed versus how bad it could be. That company then pays the Overseers. And nobody else outside of families like yours. Ours." He cleared his throat. He'd get used to it eventually. "Nobody else knows? Not even the President?"

"Not even the President." Marie grinned with what looked like subtle pride on anyone else. On her, it whispered amusement. "Okay, that's not entirely true. About thirty years ago, the benefactors decided the Overseers needed an audit. They assembled a team of so-called professionals and ousted the Overseers for the next Breach. Everyone died and disaster spread across the Italian countryside. That made for a big cover-up, but they leave us alone now, other than reports Julie sends via that intermediary organization."

"Wow." Garrett stopped for a moment while he absorbed Marie's tale. "Is there any way to communicate with other Hellspots during a Breach?"

Marie's lips curled in. "Nope. We're on our own." She and Garrett turned their backs to the window as they hurried by the middle landing. Shades remained lowered everywhere except here. The few rays of sunshine beaming in seemed dimmer than natural. Once they cleared a safe distance, she perked up, offsetting the afternoon twilight. "But that's okay with me. Our family's bigger and better than the others. Most Overseers keep their families small."

"Why?" Logic dictated that bigger families provided more stability, more help.

"Exposure to Hellspots usually leads to fertility problems. We're special it seems. Don't worry though. I haven't stopped birth control. I'm not sure what would happen to a child conceived during a Breach."

"But eventually?"

"We have time." Her smile encouraged him, but he didn't prod.

For now, he reveled in simply being with her, an eternal spring of optimism that relaxed the tensions of suspicious inactivity. He swept her up at the base of the stairs. She slung her legs horizontally and giggled. He carried her the rest of the way to the sitting room.

"Glad someone's having fun." Julie was reclining in one of the two stuffed, oversized chairs. Iris sat next to her. Across the rug, Nia perched on the couch, makeup and attire better suited for clubbing than a haunted house.

"Lots of fun," Marie said. She whistled her descent as Garrett whisked her feet back to the wooden floor. "Aw. Party's over."

Iris and Nia's stares followed them to the end of the couch. Garrett fidgeted with his wedding band as they sat. Marie wore hers too, but like the other wives, now kept her pointy engagement ring safety tucked away.

"We can party later," Julie said. "We need to get back to business." They were on the third day of a rotating discussion group, theorizing reasons for the spirits' lull in activity. While one group discussed, others searched for physical clues.

"Nobody's experienced anything lowkey unusual?" Julie asked. The trio on the couch shook their heads. Iris continued knitting. "Creaks from a floorboard you mistook for an aging house? Voices in your head that sound familiar, but a little off?"

"You tryin' to scare us?" Nia asked. "Can't we enjoy this while it lasts?" Garrett and her had barely interacted since her arrival. Her accent differed from the rest, more pronounced than the Renault children, less regionalized than Iris and Mr. Renault.

"Sure, if we want to die because we didn't heed the warning signs. Our only goal is survival. Enjoyment isn't important."

Nia folded her arms and receded into the cushions. "Not suggestin' we throw a party." She scoffed at her couchmates. Garrett's cheeks warmed. "But quiet isn't the big bad you makin' it out to be."

"You're right. It's worse."

Marie and Garrett shared a look. Their life had improved since the Breach. Schoolwork no longer competed for his time, and ghosts left them alone. He studied other books, listened for noises, and spent the rest of his time with his wife—his *wife*! She reassured him they did nothing wrong acting like the newlyweds they were. Reading his thoughts, she ran a subtle fingernail up and down the side of his rear. He patted her knee to stop. She didn't. He let himself enjoy her playful touch but focused on the others, tempering—no, controlling—his desires.

"Maybe so," Nia said, "but some of us have children we're tryin' to keep calm. Grady's sleeping through the night. I won't ruin that by stressing about nothin'." Nia parted a stray wisp of hair. "You expect ghosts to just drop clues in your lap?"

Marie stopped toying with Garrett and covered his hand on her knee. "What if there's a lot less of them than usual?"

"I'm confident that's not the case," Julie countered. "Pre-Breach activity has always correlated with Breach hauntings. I cataloged fourteen distinct ghosts with suppositions on another six. We had seven last year. Then, there's the mekar who possessed Grandpa. Dad's still deciphering his last words." She bit her lip. "His decision to tell us nothing until finishing his translation spells more bad than good. The ghosts are here. They're just inactive."

Garrett's throat clenched. Marie instilled an easy complacency, but Julie's warnings choked him with reality. The others may have grown up here or lived here for extended periods, but the older sister's permanent residency gave her theories greater weight.

"The way you gather intel," he said, "could ghosts turn that around on us? Spy on us?" It seemed feasible, even if his research confirmed that spirits acted with animal-like instinct rather than careful scheming.

Iris nodded, approving either of his idea or a particular stitch.

"To what end?" Julie asked.

"Find our weaknesses?" Garrett suggested. "The Breach lasts for months. What's a couple weeks of planning the best way out? Especially once they're all assembled."

"Way to give 'em ideas," Nia said.

Garrett's attention swung from Nia to Julie. He didn't think it worked that way, but there were several thousand books in that library, and he'd read four.

"You're both right," Julie said. "You're both wrong. Assuming a spirit was listening in on us, they'd first have to know English. Not uncommon, especially for spirits who showed pre-Breach. However, there's no indication they can process anything besides a direct request. Secondly, they wouldn't know what to do with the information.

They're individuals with a fixation on the present and escaping out into the world. Third, they're *individuals*. They don't work together, except by accident."

"They also don't keep quiet like this," Iris said, not looking up.

"No, they don't." Julie tilted her head to the side. "Garrett, as much as your idea runs against the ghosts' normal behavior, it's a good launching pad."

Quiet contemplation lulled over the room, the occasional click of Iris's knitting needles providing the only sound for several moments.

Marie snapped her fingers. "What Gare said, plus what Dad finds. That's got to be it."

"Sounds good." Nia leaned forward, halfway to standing. "We can stop these focus groups 'til David tells us what he's learned."

Julie gestured for Nia to stay seated and addressed Marie. "You want to expand on that?"

"I don't know exactly. Hold on." Marie stood up, drumming her thigh as she paced the room. "Grandpa must've been trying to send us a message. A mekar interfered. The message has something to do with what Gare said." Julie tried to interrupt. Marie wagged her finger. "Nuh-uh. I've got this. The ghosts who want out know something we don't. Maybe the Ring will be weaker at a certain point, weak enough to slip through. Or the mekari are taking the first crack and scaring ghosts off from acting."

"Assuming any of that is true, there's nothing we can do about it."

"Sounds normal to me. We can't attack the ghosts, and a little extra insight helps us prep for whatever they throw at us."

A sound like a machine gun rattled above. Garrett flinched.

Damn AC. The thought lingered until bulky footsteps plodded from the foyer.

Motion took the form of Claude shuffling into the room. He carried a stack of five books, their sleeves creating a rainbow of color. "Hello, hello," he said. "I've got some good news and some bad."

"Out with it." Julie crossed her arms.

"Friendly atmosphere." Claude whistled. "Good news is I found some missing books. They were buried all over the backyard. Not sure how they got past the plexiglass—I'm guessing someone left them out for a Deviant, or a Hider got sloppy. Depriving us of boredom isn't very devious though, and these books are drier than an encyclopedia. So, I'm thinking Hider. Any spirits in the room want to come clean?"

Garrett sat up straight. The only surefire approach to finding a Hider mandated listening to one's words and watching their actions. Catching a lie required constant vigilance. In the lull of the past two weeks, this served as a good reminder of the dangers that loomed. Others scanned the room, but none displayed the unease he felt.

"Worth a shot." Claude shrugged. Maybe it was a joke. "Either way, the ghosts are active." He hoisted up the first book from the stack. "At least this one has pictures. I think it's pronounced *Methlaser's Pictarium?*"

"Mathlazar," Julie corrected. "A kook who thought we could assess a ghost's threat level by the volume of their footfalls. What's the bad news?"

"With a name like Mathlazar, he never stood a chance. Classic case of bad parenting."

"It's. His. Last. Name," Julie retorted. "What's the bad news?"

"Bad news is the same as the good news. I just like that saying."

Only Marie cracked a smile, but she let it fade in the gravity of the room.

"You can't stop joking, can you?" Julie buried her face in her hands, rubbing the sides of her skull. "Even during a Breach potentially more serious than any other. Why can't you—"

"Say the other books." Iris cut her off.

Julie glared at Iris. When it became clear that her aunt would pay her no mind, Julie rolled her eyes and nestled her chin in her palm. She blinked at Claude. "Well?"

"O-kay." Claude treaded toward the ottoman as if approaching a viper pit. He set down the first book and announced, "*Mathlazar's*

Pictarium." Then flipped to the next cover, reading each title and setting it down on the cushion. "*A Grand Symposium on Spirits. Deciphering Silence. Crossworlds. Gateway to a Doorway.*"

Who might be the Hider? Garrett rubbed his jeans until he broke off his train of thought. He shouldn't dwell on it if others didn't. *Ignore the Hider. How can you help?*

Julie crossed her arms tightly around her chest, dragging her forefinger down her shirt sleeve. "What are the authors' names?"

Marie plopped back into her seat. Neither the titles nor authors clearly meant anything to her. The four books Garrett had read nearly matched her lifetime total.

"I'm still up, huh?" Claude exaggerated snapping his fingers and bent down. He picked up each book in turn, read off its author's name, then returned it to the ottoman. "Please tell me I'm done with these. Dirty earth mixed with library musk is not a pleasant aroma."

Garrett reached for the tangerine-sleeved book. *Crossworlds.* Rotten fungus scents urged him to retreat. He stopped flipping through it halfway in. "There's a page missing. Is that normal?" He swallowed hard to keep from retching as he placed the book back.

A gasp spurted out from Julie before she settled into stoic silence.

"You okay?" Marie asked.

As suddenly as Julie had gasped, she broke into a dry chuckle. "Good work, Garrett."

"You mean the missing page?" he asked.

"No." She waved her dismissal. "That's been torn out for years. Your spying suggestion. It didn't register because I'd imagined the spirits took charge. They didn't. Ghosts don't have the capacity for forward-thinking, but mekari do. While these books mean nothing to a spirit, a knowledgeable mekar would identify these as five individuals who survived a mekarian possession. And a sloppy Hider supports this conclusion. It makes no sense to risk exposure on such a meaningless act for a spirit. A mekar—or worse, mekari—are running the show. It's the only logical explanation." Julie shot off her seat, starting for the foyer. "I need to talk to Dad."

Repressed worries over a Hider punched Garrett in the gut as Julie's conjecture gave them new life. "What's the significance of a mekar ordering a spirit?"

Claude snorted. "The ghosts are unionizing." He fell into an uncharacteristic gloom following his quip.

Marie slipped her hand into Garrett's.

He gripped her tighter than he intended. "Why not burn the books? Or tear them apart?"

"Ghosts aren't fond of fire," Claude said. "And I guess destroying them is too obvious? Who knows."

"So, we do need to be careful of what we say."

Julie had taken her first step into the foyer. She coughed and turned her head. Alarm painted her face. "We need to be more careful of *everything*." She stopped short of breaking into a run as she fled the room.

Her flight, and the way everyone stiffened in near-perfect synchronization, alerted him to a threat much greater than a single Hider. Marie, Claude, and the whole family's optimism about surviving a Breach stemmed from a simple constant: ghosts acted independently and at random, indulging a whim before vanishing as their efforts severed their connection to the real world.

And it seemed that constant no longer held true.

14. Blitzkrieg

Table saws buzzed all around Garrett, chasing him through the wide expanse of a workshop. Dust puffed up in a cloud, poisoning his lungs and obscuring his vision. He veered left and skidded to a halt two steps in. His shoes streaked across the floor. A row of autonomous nail guns were shooting into waist-high planks. He darted right. Ducked underneath the table with a sander pressing down on it and sprinted toward the open door. He was picking up speed when his shins collided with an invisible obstruction that toppled him over. His head struck something pillow soft. He bounced off and landed elbow-first onto a spongy surface.

Garrett opened his eyes to a tiled floor beneath him. What he *felt* was a cushion kissing his cheek. A familiar touch grazed his back. He flinched, and the touch vanished.

Jagged-cut boards lay within arm's reach. Chainsaws droned and sliced wood behind him, then squished, as if cutting flesh. The faint cries of a woman joined the chaos. Instincts begged him to flee. He pushed himself up. His hands passed through the floor, his wrists flickering in and out of sight as they submerged below. He was sinking. How was he sinking?

The pressure on his back returned, firmed up. Tender warmth radiated from it in a circular pattern, penetrating his sweat-damp shirt. It reminded him that the tiled floor should be rigid and cold, not cozy like the touch on his spine. He eased into the phantom hand this time, accepting the comfort it offered.

Sandpaper scraped against a solid surface several feet above, scratching toward him at the speed of a falling feather. He resisted the temptation to look. He needed to focus. Why were his senses fighting one another? He pulled his right arm from the sinking floor and patted the air around him. A plushy texture stopped him. He felt around the invisible obstacle, absorbing the touch of stuffed fabric.

The deadly workshop was a lie. He lay prone on the circular lobby sofa in the breakfast nook. He squeezed his eyes shut, then released. The sounds of saws and sandpaper disappeared, leaving only a desperate cry from behind.

Marie was sitting next to him, breathing as heavily as him.

Groaning, Garrett pushed himself up, practically falling into her. She caught him, then folded her arms into an embrace. He clutched her back, not considering the potential trap until firmly in her grasp. Her heart beat fiercely against his chest, his own keeping pace, and the worry subsided.

He wished Julie's theory had been wrong. The honeymoon the house had so graciously granted them shattered two nights ago. Or was it three? Shifters stole their senses and transformed their reality, working with uncommon unity to conceal the sun and cast them into darkness. The house's antique clocks sped ahead and fell back to new times at each perusal. Unseen spirits hungered to inhabit their bodies, their cold wisps of air slithering on their skin.

And a likely Hider still lurked among them.

"How are we going to survive?" Garrett asked. Neither moved to release the other.

"It can get a little bumpy. No big deal. We'll make it. We always win."

At what cost? We're already down one. At least with her grandfather, there were signs. Incidents like Garrett's living nightmare came without warning. He'd been in the dining room, eating lunch with Marie. She left for the bathroom. He was chewing his sandwich, not tasting it, merely sustaining himself. He leaned back in his seat, closing his eyes for a brief respite. He sat like that for a forgotten time, until saws jolted him into awareness.

Marie had rescued him, as she did daily. He nestled his face into the crook of her neck. Tears escaped the corners of his eyes as he settled into some semblance of safety.

Steady footsteps echoed from the library hallway. He pulled away, shifted his body between Marie and the arched entryway. The noise sounded casual, but he tensed all the same.

Claude shuffled into the breakfast nook. Days ago, he would've peeked around the corner for a cheap scare. "Guess everything's okay."

"I wouldn't go that far." Garrett wiped the wetness from his cheeks.

"What did you see?" Marie hugged him from behind.

"A workshop, like in a classroom. Except filled with way more saws, sanders, and nail guns than necessary. It was massive. An auditorium's worth of tables. I didn't think I'd make it." He pictured Marie crying over his gravesite, forcing him to sniff back a fresh set of tears.

"Haunted obstacle courses are no joke," Claude said. "Have you ever seen that Japanese game show? You might give them a call after the Breach."

Marie propped her head on Garrett's shoulder. "Now's not a good time for a joke."

Agreed.

A door slammed against a wall upstairs, reverberating down the hall.

"You're not her," a man shouted. "You can't be her. You try to make it work. I try to make it work, but it can't ever work."

Derrick, yelling with a mix of panic and anger.

Claude bounded back under the arch and up the stairs on his long runner's legs. Marie shot up after him, Garrett following without thought. He didn't want to let go of her—not ever. They darted up the steps. He gulped air in duets of sputtered breaths, once for fear, once for exhaustion. The trio skirted around the middle landing, shielding their faces from the uncovered window.

Derrick's wife responded, her voice firm. "It's Nia. I'm not going to hurt you. You're safe."

"It's not about safety. It's about truth, and I can't avoid it in this house."

"What're you talkin' about?" she snapped.

"The truth. You can't be my wife. It doesn't fit the pattern."

"Oh no? Who do you think I am?"

In the upstairs hall, Derrick stood facing an open bedroom. Claude paused two doors away and held out his arm, stopping Garrett and Marie.

Derrick shook his head, mouth agape. "A replacement," he said at last, before toppling over sideways.

Claude sprinted forward. He caught his cousin as his shoulder slammed onto the rug beneath. If Derrick hadn't swapped out his glasses for contacts when the Breach opened, they would have flown right off.

Nia joined them a moment later, slinking out of her room. She wore plain yoga pants and a white tank top that conformed to a frame as slender as Marie's. She stared at Claude like a detective interrogating a suspect. "You know what he was talkin' about?"

"No clue." He patted Derrick on the cheek. "Wake up, buddy. The bad ghost is all gone now."

"Scoot," Nia said.

Claude's lips twitched, but he complied. He craned his neck over her shoulder as she took his place. Marie fidgeted by Garrett's side.

Kneeling beside her husband, Nia felt for a pulse, nodded, then touched his cheek. "Honey, you need to wake up." Softer than she'd spoken to Claude, but with that same underlying expectation of obedience. "We got to figure out what you saw. I need an explanation for the nonsense that came outta your mouth. If you sleep all afternoon it'll be gone by evening. I know how this damned house works. Wake up."

Her thumb stroked under his eyes. After moments of motionlessness, she pecked him on the lips. He continued to slumber, if that appropriately described his state. "Think about Grady. You don't want to give him a scare. He's probably gettin' tired of playin' with little Tommy. And if he's not, I bet he's givin' Kelly a helluva an afternoon running around that deathtrap of a backyard. So." Her strokes turned to soft taps, her words timed to the beat. "It's time. For you. To wake up."

The heaviness of her sigh highlighted the despondency in the air.

"Can I try?" Marie asked.

Garrett nearly tightened his grip on her into a vise. A surge of willpower steadied his hand.

"Be my guest." Nia's slapped her thigh.

Marie was patient while Garrett relinquished her hand. He stepped after her, drew as close to the group as felt reasonable. Then he inched closer.

She squatted opposite Nia. "Hey, Derk. It's Marie. Garrett's here too. You like him, remember? That's four people watching you sleep. You've gotta hate that." After an uncomfortable giggle, her head sank. She chewed her lips and stared.

Was this the work of a Dreamer? Usually, the victim tossed and turned. This stillness differed from any symptoms Garrett had read about.

Marie whistled a foreign, uplifting tune. A long deep note, followed by warm rising and falling tones. "The bad times are over. You're free to come out now."

Still nothing.

Marie pressed her palm against his forehead and whistled again.

Derrick's eyes fluttered open. "Marie?"

She pulled back.

He turned his head, massaging his temple. "Nia? What am I doing here?" He started to sit. Both women nudged him down. He put his weight on the side that didn't strike the ground. "Whatever happened, I could use an ice pack. My shoulder is killing me."

"I'm on it." Claude hopped up, dashed by Garrett toward the stairs.

"You don't remember anythin' you said?" Nia asked. "Do you remember what happened right before you lost control?"

"Right before." Derrick closed his eyes, his head moving as if in silent conversation with himself. He cleared his throat as he stared back at his wife. "The blatant lie about when you met my family. You—or the ghost, I guess—mentioned Marie offering to babysit your sister. After I caught the lie and you'd woken up, I asked if you'd found a way to trick the Hider. You smiled that way that makes me say yes to anything and then . . . I don't remember anything between then and waking up to you two. Can I get up yet?"

"I 'spose," Nia said. Both she and Marie hovered near Derrick as he sat up. He scooted himself to the wall.

"You buried the books in the backyard?" Garrett asked. "You were the Hider?"

"I did, and I was," Nia said. "Don't worry. I'll even the score." She pointed like there was a scoreboard hanging up on the wall.

How? he wanted to ask. But that thought, and any would-be relief over one less possession, conflicted with his other question: why was Marie babysitting Nia's sister an obvious lie? Had she avoided kids for that long?

Derrick's chuckle interrupted Garrett's thoughts. Propped against the wall, he rubbed the small of Nia's back. She stiffened at first, then mellowed as her gaze shifted to Marie.

Garrett's wife—his loving, amazing *wife*— took on a bashful demeanor. The last time she'd reacted like that, an idiot former teammate was hounding her at a party for dating him. He almost told Nia to back off, even though she wasn't doing anything.

"What is it?" Marie raised her eyebrows.

"What'd you whistle to him?" Nia asked.

"A tune we used as kids." Marie glanced at Derrick, who cracked a faint smile. "When the coast was clear."

"Clear from what?"

"Ghosts. Parents. Claude and Jules. Not necessarily in that order." She stifled a laugh. "When you're only a couple years apart living in a haunted house, you stick together. Whether that's getting into or out of trouble."

Their ages took Garrett aback. He had pinned Derrick closer to the twins' age. He must have married Nia practically out of high school. Garrett had taken marriage advice from someone younger than him.

"How've I never heard it?" Nia asked.

Marie wrinkled her forehead. "There hasn't been a need for it, I guess. The last two Breaches were relatively calm, and the one before those, the ghosts seemed to have other priorities." She glanced away with a sadness that burned away Garrett's curiosities. He wanted to hug her—her mom had died in that Breach—but it felt wrong to interrupt.

"Can you teach me it?" Nia asked.

"The"—Marie leaned forward—"whistling?" She grabbed Nia's hand and smiled. "Of course."

Nia inspected the sudden touch, murmured, "Hmm."

"I mean Derrick also knows it."

Nia gave Marie a gentle caress, then pulled out of her grip. "No, I want to learn it from you."

"Sure. I'd love spending more time together."

Thudding stairsteps cut the moment short. Marie stood up. Derrick tried, but Nia's knee pushed him back down. Garrett crept for a view of the landing. A swallow caught in his throat. Julie's brunette scalp rounded past the landing, and his tensed limbs relaxed—mostly. Where was Claude?

She held an ice pack in one hand and a plastic glass of water in the other. She strode toward Derrick so stiffly the strands of her ponytail barely budged. She gave him the aid package, then leaned against the wall, her sweater-covered arms behind her back. "I know you were expecting Claude. He's recently indisposed. Nothing to worry about, but it's clear that the Breach is fully underway."

"What do you mean, nothin' to worry about?" Nia asked.

"I mean exactly that." After an awkward moment, Julie huffed. "Iris was having a scuffle with her knitting needles. Claude yelled for help and told me to come upstairs with ice and water. I'm surprised you didn't hear him. One more note to jot down."

Marie grazed Nia's wrist, whose nose twitched in response. The evolution into a thin smile gave Garrett the impression that anyone else trying to comfort her would've invited a verbal lashing.

"I need to check on Grady." Nia kissed Derrick and patted his chest. "If I come back to you unsupervised or not in bed, you'll wish that ghost had got you."

He chuckled with a slight incline of his head.

"The kids are fine," Julie said. "I saw Kelly through the landing window on the way up, no worse for wear."

Nia was already marching toward the stairs, ignoring the reassurance.

"Probably a good idea to check all the same," Julie trailed off, then muttered something under her breath, followed by a snort from Derrick.

"Can you two watch him?" Julie asked. "I was in the middle of something."

"Sure," Garrett said, same time as Marie. *As long as I'm with her.* "Also, on the frequency of these haunts. Will they all be as bad as today?"

"We're in uncharted territory. I'm confident our theory on mekari working with the spirits was dead on. How they're planning to take advantage of it, we have to wait and see. We're used to riffraff offshoots, not an organized effort." She huffed. "I've got to go." And like Nia, seemed unlikely to care about any follow-up he might offer.

Garrett stepped behind Marie and Derrick. His mind drifted as the two cousins bantered. *An army,* he thought. His dad made a hobby out of studying historical warfare. Not that he needed help to define this tactic. The Germans popularized it nearly a century ago.

Blitzkrieg.

This wasn't a batch of hauntings. It was a coordinated strike, and despite the Renaults' preparations, they were no more ready to repel the initial assault than the French.

15. Research

Garrett sucked in air with a prolonged yawn. His ears popped, and his brain cleared his thoughts without consent. Half a day poring over texts in the library had pushed his focus to its limits, especially now that he couldn't pretend strange creaks and thumps came from a house screaming its age.

"What's the matter?" Julie asked across the large walnut table. She tapped the top of the chair she had been sitting in until half an hour ago. Garrett had just risen from his. "Miss Marie?"

He grunted in feigned amusement. This morning, he'd suggested to Marie they work out in the gym. She agreed but changed her mind as they approached through the breakfast nook. Her furtive glance instilled new worries: the bike toppling over and pinning him or the bench giving out while he lifted weights. She made no attempt to dissuade *his* exercising, but the anxiety she embedded had percolated within. He managed three sets before retreating. Unsure of where Marie went, he headed to where he knew another person was—the library.

"Or is it trouble in paradise?" Julie asked.

Then again, he had suggested working out to escape an argument. He asked Marie why Nia's mention of her babysitting made for an obvious lie. His brief attempt to pry turned her sour. He backpedaled, apologized, and defaulted to his prime stress relief: working out. Was it possible she left the gym not due to anxiety, but because she remained upset at him?

"We're fine," Garrett said.

Chuckling came to Julie as easily as a fish breathing air, but she gave a convincing attempt. "Sure."

Garrett returned to reading. He tilted his head, confused. Letters blurred together, one word ending where another began. He rubbed his eyes. Fatigue begged him to rest. Fear demanded he occupy his thoughts.

Back to the book, a hundred tiny Rorschach tests splattered the text. He flipped a page, then another, and a dozen more. None of it made sense. Was there something in this book a spirit didn't want him to see? Turning on his heels, he marched to the shelf, dug his hand underneath the plexiglass to find and open the lock, then snatched a teal-sleeved book.

Julie interrupted him. "You can't read either."

He opened it anyway. Chinese Hanzi would have made more sense. He sucked in rapid, short breaths, almost hyperventilating. He forced a deep inhale, closed the book, and grabbed another from the shelf. A black river flowed from one page to the next. He took another book, reading the indecipherable squiggles of a toddler.

It's worse than gibberish.

Gibberish normally kept to a pattern. These books were all over the place. And if he couldn't read, what use was he? He felt pride in providing this family—his family —some modicum of value. He stood on the brink of finally contributing, and in an instant, a spirit had stripped that from him.

Julie walked to the shelf Garrett had left open for ghosts to procure literary weapons. "Put the books back before you do something stupid with them. This will pass. Spirits can't haunt indefinitely, remember?" She locked the doors and leaned against them.

He wanted to pull out his hair. How could someone so devoted to reading stay so calm? Garrett stormed back to the table, slammed the books down. Julie's face flashed as the texts slid like an avalanche across the table. What did he care? Grady read better than him now.

"And how do we know there aren't enough Shifters to keep this stint running?" He fought to keep his voice level. "We're reading how to shut down a Breach of a historic magnitude. Seems like keeping us illiterate is a smart strategy for coming out on top." Memories flashed of him, controlled by another, tearing at Marie's clothes in the kitchen. "How can we win when they can control and subvert us at a whim?"

"It's not us, specifically. It's the text or the room itself. I'd wager nobody in this house could read these right now."

His gut didn't buy it. Perception was relative.

"In any case, panicking doesn't help," Julie said.

"I'm not—"

"Well, you're not thinking straight."

"In what way am I not—"

"You're acting like a child. Think! What vital piece of this situation is not being *seen*?"

Words of the open book below writhed like serpents. *What's not being seen? What is there to see?* He scanned the room, shrugging as he tried to humor her. Was she just trying to get his mind off this? He didn't want to argue with his new sister-in-law, especially not now, but certain actions necessitated certain responses, and—

In the corner of the room closest to him, a shelf of crimson-sleeved books drew his attention. The library ghost had hurled one of those at Marie before the Breach, and Julie witnessed it all in crystal clear detail.

"You," he said. How had he forgotten? "You can't See what's doing this, can you?"

"There's that Harvard education paying off."

Confusion sank into gloom. One less weapon in their struggle. He thumbed the pages of his original book. "You may be surprised to learn that doesn't make me feel better."

"I don't care how you feel." Julie made her way toward Garrett. "I care that you make yourself useful. I have a strong suspicion as to why I can't See, but I want *you* to think about it. You're an outsider, or were until recently. Your opinion isn't tainted by decades of history and hundreds of books." She yanked the book from his grasp, slid it out of arm's reach. "Class is over. I should check on Dad. He must be nearly done translating." If she intended to allay his fears by smothering them with conjecture, then . . .

Garrett chewed his knuckle. If she intended that, then it worked. He pondered an answer to her query. He found none, but a curiosity grew in its wake. He pocketed his hands.

"Wait."

Julie stopped midstride. She crossed her arms, tilted her head.

Technology offered the means to check on her father without leaving the library. "Why don't you use walkie-talkies?"

"Good." She extended her hand, palm facing up. "You're feeling better, right? Less panicked?"

"I guess. What does that have to do with—"

"Let that be a lesson. Don't bury your fear. It only makes things worse. Distract it with something else. Claude uses humor, Marie has her optimism, and so on. But we"—her finger flitted between them—"think. To answer your question, spirits interfere with radio wave transmissions. When frequencies do pass through, the responses can be intercepted and impersonated. That's not to say they never work. You can find walkie-talkies in either storage room if you want to learn more on your own. There's even a book over there"—she waved her arm in the direction of the yellow and white-sleeved books—"theorizing the mechanics of interference and interceptions." Her sly expression seemed to say, *once you can read again.*

No, he couldn't let that get to him. Julie was right—seeking solutions calmed him better than dwelling on problems. "What about using walkie-talkies to communicate with the spirits? Take a diplomatic approach?"

Julie laughed with a dismissive shake of her head. "No. I'm sure Claude has told you his story about the World War 1 vet." She waited for Garrett to nod. "Most ghosts are drawn to a Breach like feral animals. Claude's particular ghost was Aware. It spoke to him first, a willingness we see maybe once a Breach. And Claude happens to speak German. Suffice to say—"

"It's a rare event," finished Garrett.

"You're firing on all cylinders. Now, get out of here and give your brain a chance to decompress. I'll happily answer more questions— *later.*" She turned and strode toward the exit, raising the back of her hand and wiggling her fingers goodbye. She stutter-stepped before passing over the threshold with a glance at the top shelf. A tangerine-sleeved book leaned against another, filling the space of a missing book in between. Were the spirits raiding the library again?

Garrett briefly considered finding a walkie-talkie before moving on to more current concerns. His arms and legs itched, pleading with him to finish his abandoned workout. Solitude exacerbated his apprehension, smothering the consideration. *I'll work out another day. Soon,* he promised.

A single book slammed against the plexiglass behind him. Wherever his next destination, he had overstayed his welcome here. He fled the room between a march and jog, focused on the shelf from where the book shifted.

The room stayed quiet.

With a violent shake of his head, he turned back to the foyer and startled. He almost bowled over Derrick, whose son held his hand beside him.

"Surprised to see me?" Derrick asked, then leaned in for a whisper. "I know what you're thinking. Can't believe Nia's letting me wander alone with our child after the other day, right?"

Given Garrett's other concerns, it hadn't crossed his mind.

"What you talking about?" Grady asked, juvenile in pronunciation but easier to understand than most his age. His carefree air gave no hint of the house's horrors. It had barely bothered the children since the Breach.

"I was telling Uncle Garrett your mom is sleepy and needs her rest. Nobody is to bother her, including you, got it?"

"I know! Mom already told me."

"Nia's alone?" Garrett asked at last. She proved herself braver than him.

"Grady shooed away all the ghosts so she could sleep safe and sound," Derrick said. His son beamed with the effort of a job well done.

If the ghosts were truly avoiding the kids for some reason, it might clear the spirits from the library. His mouth dried at the idea of returning, but the prospect of learning what the ghosts were obscuring gave him a backbone.

Garrett cleared his throat. "Something happened in the library."

"I figured by the way Julie ran out," Derrick said.

Nervous laughter trickled out of Garrett's mouth. "I'm a bit hung up on it. Would you mind taking a look at a book in there?" He gestured at Grady. "If you think it's safe."

"Sure. Lead on." Derrick led Grady into the room.

Potentially exposing a child to a ghost twisted Garrett's gut, but Derrick knew the risks better than him. Both about the house and his son. He hadn't even asked for specifics regarding the haunting. Garrett turned around, sensitive to the pairs of footsteps following him.

"Dad," Grady said. "Aunt Julie said this room is bad for kids. I don't want to get in trouble."

"She's right. But, if you're holding your Dad's hand, it's okay."

"Really? Cool! Can you hold my hand for a hundred hours? It's so big."

Derrick chuckled. "Another day."

Garrett walked to the book he had been reading. He flipped it open to a random page. The text showed some semblance of structure, but the words spiraled in an indecipherable cursive font similar to Arabic. "Can you read this for me?" And walked away to give him space.

Standing over the table, Derrick hesitated. He rubbed his eyes, blinked in rapid succession, then nodded. "Scientifically speaking, the presence of a spirit is difficult to discern."

Garrett crept closer.

"Molecules in the air shift in their supposed presence, in a manner similar to clouds in a thunderstorm. Positively charged ions float to the top, negative ions to the bottom. Unlike a cloud—" He scratched his beard. "What am I reading?"

Garrett hunched over the table. The text had returned to small-font English. He leafed deeper into the book. Same situation. Julie was right. He had only needed to wait. Or were the spirits messing with him, letting the environment seem normal until they stripped it all away again?

"You okay?"

Garrett snapped to. He flipped through the other books on the table. "A few minutes ago, these words were all gibberish. Julie and I were reading for hours, then everything turned into abstract art."

Derrick touched his arm, eyeballed his kid.

Garrett softened his voice. "I can't believe it all went back to normal the instant you touched one. It was as if . . ."

Don't make new problems. Distract your fears.

"We all need a sanity check sometimes," Derrick said. "Glad I could help."

A knock rapped near the entryway. Garrett whirled around, fists ready to fly into action.

"How cute." Julie rested on the cased opening. "Grady, what did I tell you about coming into the library?"

The child's eyes widened.

"It's okay," Derrick said. "Aunt Julie forgot that it's okay for you to be in here, as long as you're holding my hand. Isn't that right?"

"Apparently." Julie grunted with an expression that guaranteed a smattering of choice words later. "There are more important issues.

Dad's done with his translations. Or as done as he can figure out. We need to find the others. Garrett, take the bottom floor. Derrick, the top. I'll take outside. We start in twenty minutes."

"Are we meeting him in Grandpa's bedroom?" Derrick asked. "Won't that be cramped?"

"Yes. Now, get moving." She snapped her fingers several times.

Instincts told Garrett to flee, as if he could run to anywhere meaningful.

"Sure," Derrick said, "but we need to work out who's watching the kids. Adult talk is pretty boring anyway, isn't it?" He squeezed his son's hand.

"Yeah." Grady's fist shot into the air. "I want to play outside!"

The skin underneath Julie's eye twitched. "Do what you need, as long as you're there in twenty minutes. Time's getting pricier by the second." She retreated into the hall, not waiting for a response.

"Mind if we stick together until we find someone?" Garrett asked.

"And risk Julie's wrath?" Derrick's grin turned sour in the face of Garrett's grave expression. For a moment, he showed signs of a burgeoning weariness that Garrett had believed only he suffered from, right before recomposing his confident facade. "Sure. Nia and I have a side project going, so let me grab a book while I'm here, then we'll be off."

Julie had proved herself right yet again.

Garrett missed Marie. He missed her very much.

16. Translations

Stale air, like that of a forgotten crypt, lingered in Mr. Renault's bedroom—formerly his father's. Garrett shuffled into the room, wrinkling his nose as he took his place near his wife. He stiffened at the unshaded window, the glass replaced since the grandfather's fall. He tore his attention away only when nobody else paid it any mind.

Despite the stench, the room looked tidy, if dusty, except for the desk. A spiral notebook with perfect handwriting rested at its center. Scattered around, several loose-leaf papers brimmed with scribbling eerily reminiscent of his library incident moments ago. Water rings and food stains marred the rare open spaces.

The room was a self-imposed prison.

In this prison, the group waited for Iris's arrival in silence. The rest of the attendees, all the adults except Claude and Nia, crowded the room. Cramped space required everyone to stand, save Mr. Renault. The alternative was climbing onto the bed where Grandpa Renault had slept until four weeks ago. Marie's grave expression summed up everyone's opinion on that notion.

Slicking her blonde hair behind her ear, Kelly broke the room's passive introspection. "Is gathering most of us in the same room a smart idea?" She directed the question at Mr. Renault.

With his head buried in his hand, squeezing his temples, he gave no indication of having heard her.

Julie, who stood beside him, grew tall. "Dad hasn't experienced any incidents in this room since the Breach. This year, it's safer than anywhere else in the house."

"Why?" Kelly's gaze lingered on the naked window, at last justifying Garrett's concern.

"Nothing concrete." Julie gestured toward her unaware father. "Once we get started, our collective brain power is meant to solve that. And more pressing matters."

The answer seemed so obvious. Garrett paused nonetheless. He had to be missing something for nobody else to have said anything. He chewed on the inside of his cheek. This wasn't the time for juvenile shyness. "We think the mekari are in control, right?"

"So?" Julie asked.

"This room contains vital information. Scaring us has its advantages." Recollections of possession, loss of literacy, and fleeing from buzz saws flashed one after the other. He coughed, buying time to steel his voice. "But so does knowing what we know, to use it against us. Gathering intelligence is a high priority in a war."

"You think of this as a war?"

"That's what it feels like." *A war with the supernatural. How is that not terrifying to these people?* Around the room, impressed faces showed fearless interest in the exchange. Marie smiled at him. When he and she had met up before coming here, he baffled her by asking if she was mad at him. He'd already apologized for prying, so why would she be upset? Her affirmation strengthened him. Without her by his side, he might not have kept his voice steady.

Julie tapped her lips, then mimicked her family's approving expressions. "It's an apt analogy. However, if there were ghosts lurking, Dad would Feel them."

"You," Garrett hesitated. Again, it was so obvious. Except, he supposed, when the rules all changed. "You couldn't See them in the library."

Derrick brushed the side of his nose. "You didn't tell us that."

"It's barely been half an hour since it happened," Julie snapped, glaring at Garrett. "I'm working out the reason." She had told him she had a theory but wanted him to figure it out. Was she lying?

Kelly's face flushed, highlighting her freckles. "Why does this family insist on hiding things?"

"I'm not hiding anything. And I don't think it has any bearing on Dad's ability."

"It's okay, Jules." Marie clasped her hands and slightly bowed, looking saintlike. "You're doing a great job."

"I don't need—"

The door cracked open. Derrick jumped sideways, alert. Iris swung it open the rest of the way, sauntered past her son and Kelly. She propped herself up at the head of the bed. Her back touched the wall as she sat up straight, facing Mr. Renault.

"Glad you could join us, Iris." Julie huffed. Her aunt flipped her wrist. Julie had already turned away. "We're all here then. Regardless of conjecture, we can't not know what Dad has to say. Let's get to it."

Mr. Renault yawned as if waking from a long, desperately needed nap. "Thanks for coming quickly. Knowing what I know now, I wish Ah'd pushed myself harder. I apologize for the translation speed and passing out last night. If i's any consolation, this journal makes a bad pillow." He spoke without mirth, patting the spiral behind him. "Julie's kept me in the loop about what's happening outside. The spirits' behavior largely aligns with the last words spoken by my dad's body."

Garrett's shoulders crept toward his ears. They lowered ever so slightly as Marie stroked his arm.

After another yawn, Mr. Renault leaned forward, assessing the room's occupants. "At least four mekari interacted with Grandpa on his final day, some diplomatically. Some forcefully."

Marie's stroking tightened into a clench.

The significance of this revelation flipped on like a switch for Garrett—rarely did Breaches involve more than one mekar, and no records existed with more than two.

"They spoke in two distinct languages," he continued, "one split into three dialects. It's possible there are more, but i's already more varied than Ah've ever seen."

"Get on with it," Iris said. "Read us your journal."

"'Course." Mr. Renault swiped the notebook, flipped it open on his lap. "First, you'll need context. These accounts are chronological, starting with Grandpa's one-sided rants. He alternates speaking *to* two different mekari, each using different dialects of a shared language. Ah'll refer to 'em as Alpha and Beta. Pauses in their conversation are the mekar in question responding. Ah'll note the seconds tha' elapse during interludes.

"Then, sometime between my leaving for water and returning, at least two new mekari overtook his consciousness. After that, he speaks *as* these others, who I denote as Charlie and Delta. Translations aren't exact, and I filled gaps logically. Unfortunately, I missed the first thirty seconds or so. Didn't start recording on my phone 'til I realized Dad wasn't waiting for me to translate."

"Excuses ain't relevant to context." Iris lashed out with the same venom as the night Grandpa Renault died. Her and Mr. Renault's bad blood was another mystery that took its place in line.

"You're right. Ah'll begin. Remember, these words are my dad speaking his piece with the first pair. Pauses mean the mekar's talking back." Mr. Renault cleared his throat, reading the journal in a monotone.

"*Alpha*: . . . lay here, and let you take my family. We've lived here for over a damn century. A century. Your kind comes and goes, and we always win. Fly off to another Hellspot. Ah'll make damn sure you never pass through the Ring here." With a deeper voice, "*Ten seconds pass.*" He flexed his hand before starting again. "So tha's your reason? You'll bank it all on mekarian witchcraft? Even if you killed every one of us, we'd find a way to prevent your passing. Yet ya insist on this plan."

"*Five seconds of silence. This is when I left the room, my phone still recording on the dresser.*" Mr. Renault's head hung a little lower, as likely from fatigue as regret.

"*Alpha*: Of course, I want my family safe. Ah'm not a mekar. Humans care about their descendants, but Ah'm not so foolish as to appeal to your decency. Spirits can turn on you as easily as help you. They were once human after all. Your daring plan stands a better chance of setting you back decades than accomplishing anythin'. *Two seconds.*

"*Beta*: Lithyipur, reason with her. *Twenty seconds.*" He paused longer for the longer gaps. "Preposterous. You're all insane. Lithyipur, you know this is a fool's errand. If ya don't work with me, it'll make things worse for both of us.

"*Alpha:* And Tiliminia, i's not a matter of compassion but of logic. A sociopath could see the reason in my arguments. Why can't you? *Eight seconds.* Ya've said tha' for days. I don't know why you're telling me. *Three seconds.* To prepare me? For what? *Twenty-three seconds.* You think Ah'm more useful with you in my body? Be my guest. I barely rise from this bed as is. Ah'd love to watch you suffer, trapped in my hell.

"*Beta:* No, Ah'm not afraid. Ah've lived longer than expected. I only want to know what role ya played in all of this . . . *Grandpa cries out in pain.*" Mr. Renault cleared his throat. "*Eighteen seconds.* Then prove it. If not to me, then to—"

"*Alpha:* He won't be alone. He'll have us. *Four seconds.*

"*Beta:* I do. Not every mekar is evil. *Eight seconds.*

"*Alpha:* Your goal isn't cohabitation. It's parasitic. If ya wanted peace, ya woulda had peace. You try to slip in beside innocent spirits. *Another painful cry. Ten seconds.* Yes, they're innocent! Selfish and greedy, but ignorant. Few in this world understand death as well as we do. I can't blame those who wish to return to the world of the living when they don't understand the danger. You may take advantage of 'em, but once they realize . . . *More pain, followed by heavy breathing for the next forty seconds.*"

Marie shifted closer to Garrett. For the first time, he noticed how uniformly this tale absorbed the room. Even Iris dropped the fierce loathing from her stare. The strangeness of this reading for veteran Overseers heightened his already alert state.

"*Beta:* I'm aware. It's ultimately my fault they're like that, but how else could they protect our Hellspot?

"*Alpha:* Silence. I said silence.

"*Beta:* They're strong though. They'll overcome. *Five . . . seconds. Then, a prolonged groan.*"

The delay seemed unintentional, as if choosing to skip over something at the last minute. Was Garrett reading too much into it? Too on edge?

"*Alpha:* Ah've warned you. This isn't —"

Mr. Renault's head lifted. "After this, Alpha and Beta disappear. They're replaced by Charlie, using a different language entirely, and Delta, with a dialect of the previous language. Remember, Grandpa is now speaking *as* these two, rather than *to* these two." He pinched his nose bridge, squeezing his eyes tight until he composed himself. "Grandpa is wandering the room in silence when I return. There's no further dialogue until our altercation begins. Half of it is unintelligible over our fight, so I've left out those parts."

"*Charlie:* Let me go. Freedom awaits.

"*Delta:* Useless. Useless. This is useless. I want to go back.

"*Charlie:* Ah'll kill every last one of ya, then Ah'll feast. You're living on borrowed time, old man. My allies are coming in full force, and your pathetic family can't hope to stop us.

"*Delta:* I want to go back. Useless body. Useless. *Variations on this statement follow. Then Grandpa falls*"—Mr. Renault steadied himself with a breath—"*from the window. I grab my phone and race downstairs. The recording resumes forty-four seconds later, but Grandpa's silent for another minute and thirty-three seconds after.*

"*Charlie:* What're you all waiting for? This man killed your grandfather. He killed you all. Yet ya look at me with doubt and uncertainty. Fools, all of ya. We're converging while you wait idly. *Lengthy snarling.* You idiots can't understand me, can you? Your language is so primitive, so dull. Ah'm gonna rot in this corpse. I can't believe I let Tiliminia convince me. Heinous bitch.

"*Delta:* Why do you get to be in control? You wouldn't have taken this body if—

"*Charlie:* Because Ah'm better than you. It's insufferable enough tha' you're privy to my thoughts. I won't let you speak them aloud. Perhaps one of these fools will grasp a shred of my words. Do not bury this body. I want Tiliminia dead. The bringer of the one who doesn't belong, the one who mocks your bindings of blood and oath, should nail me up standing in this yard. In return, Ah'll make sure tha' bitch pays. All of you are already doomed. What do ya have to lose? *Deep, croaking breath. This* body's wretched son, what do ya feel as you watch your father die? Is patricide a fair price to destroy two mekari?"

Rubbing his fingers through his beard, Mr. Renault stared at the journal. "My father dies immediately after."

Six human statues kept their vigil in silence. A squeal, childish and joyful, sailed from down the hall. Nobody moved. Had only Garrett heard that? Insinuations of patricide pushed the phantom sound from his mind but remained too unclear to consider the implications. With pained deliberation, Mr. Renault closed the journal.

"That's a lot to unpack." Derrick patted the side of his crisply pressed jeans. "I don't know about y'all, but I'm having a hard time moving past the mekar's recommendation. Any clue about the bringer of the one who doesn't belong?"

Everyone shrugged or stared blank-faced.

"That's what I thought. Regardless, Grandpa's long since buried. Exhuming him is bad enough. Propping him up like a scarecrow is vile. I can't imagine what it'd do to Grady and Tommy."

"We can't do that to him." Marie's focus flitted around the room, like a rabbit searching for a hound. "We can't."

Julie rolled her shoulders a couple times and leaned against the wall. "That, plus it's foolish to trust a mekar. On the other hand, why lie?

Mekari are individualistic. They don't care about preserving their species. It's possible Charlie used their dying breath to deceive us, but they seemed certain we were doomed anyway. Finding a way to avenge their death at the harm of their kin is plausible. As terrible as the suggestion sounds, we must consider it. Our survival is paramount."

Garrett twisted his wedding band. "I'm inclined to believe the mekar, to a degree."

Betrayal flashed across Marie's face. "Gare, no."

Garrett hadn't realized how bloodshot her eyes were. He gave her a reassuring smile and turned back to the room. "I bet the act would get Charlie his revenge on Tilm . . . Tiliman?"

"Tiliminia," corrected Julie.

"Tiliminia. Thanks. I believe the mekar, but evil laces truths with deceit. Helping a mekar get their revenge doesn't mean it helps us. I think this is a *two wrongs don't make a right* situation, rather than *the enemy of my enemy is my friend.*"

Marie exhaled in relief. Garrett caressed her back, her warmth radiating through her shirt.

"Right," Derrick said. "Plus, that thing wanted us to nail Grandpa up immediately, with no burial. That ship has sailed." A train of nods circled the room, save from Mr. Renault.

"I almost thought you all were considering it." Kelly raised her hand into a stop sign. "I'm sorry, but I'd burn his corpse before I let you nail him up."

"Would ya now?" Iris asked.

"Yeah." Annoyance flashed across her face. "Tommy doesn't need to see that."

"No, he doesn't." Iris ignored Kelly's quizzical assessment.

What's the deal with Iris? It's like she resents being here. Maybe she did.

"There is one good thing," Marie said. The room's mood immediately lightened, as if her simply stating it—regardless of the ensuing rationale—made it so. "Beta from the first duo—Lithyipur, I think. He sounded like he and Grandpa were working together in some capacity."

Derrick clapped his hands together. "He did. We could try communicating with him."

"Is that possible?" Garrett asked, worried he knew what it would take.

"Definitely. Though it's not up to us. We can call for him, but if Lithyipur doesn't want to talk, we can't force him."

"It's also dangerous," Julie said.

"Are we talking like a . . . Ouija board?" Garrett hoped for an alternative to the obvious. "A seance?"

"Nope." Marie's cheeks creased in the way that normally preceded a giggling fit, but she adopted her family's serious composure. "Those are for spirits. They also don't work well. Fine motor skills deteriorate in the between-life state. Unless Dad or Julie can pick something up with their extra senses, we have to offer a vessel."

"Assuming Julie's problem isn't more permanent," Derrick said. "And Uncle Dave doesn't start up with similar problems."

Julie backhanded the air near her chest. "It happened once."

"That we know of."

"Move. On."

Garrett did just that, confirming what he knew all along. His chest tightened, leaving room only for shallow breaths. "So, to speak with a mekar, we have to let them inside one of us?"

"Yep," Derrick said. "At least to get a direct response."

"A willing possession," sighed Kelly. "Thank God Claude is cute. He owes me that for this family. No offense. Saving the world is great, but I'd rather be on the sidelines."

"None taken. Pretty sure Nia feels the same."

Claimers and Hiders caused enough mayhem. What would a mekar do? A sour taste crept up from Garrett's stomach. He wanted to argue, but he knew next to nothing compared to anyone in this room.

"It's an option," Julie said. "But a dangerous one, as I said. Grandpa wasn't worried about a mekar controlling his body because of his frailty. He must have let them in, hoping to take them out of the equation, maybe hoping to trap Tiliminia herself."

"Or to give us a chance to listen to the mekari directly," Marie said, "like we're discussing now."

"Probably both, knowing Grandpa. He knew the recorder was running and could've banked on Dad translating like he did. Either way, with a mekar inside his frail body, he put up a solid fight with Dad. Offering a healthy vessel isn't just a risk to the individual, but to everyone."

"Then it'll be me," Iris said. "If it comes to it." She made a shooing motion. "Continue."

Who would sacrifice themselves for those they resented? Garrett had read Iris wrong but couldn't hazard another guess as to the reason for her sporadic vitriol.

"The big, obvious news," Julie said, "is confirmation the mekari and ghosts are working together. Either the spirits were deceived or Grandpa misjudged their integrity. Regardless, this is a major operation on a scale unseen. To Garrett's earlier point about spirits potentially spying on us, it's a risk we must take. We don't know if the spirits can report back to mekari. As Dad demonstrated, human and mekarian languages are incompatible. Spirits would have to use symbology or images to translate what they've heard. That's not a big deal when the two sides are planning who or where to haunt, but it's significantly harder to communicate concepts and ideas like we're discussing now. Most importantly, we can't afford to risk not communicating." She pushed herself off the wall. "There's a lot to digest. I'll photocopy Dad's notes so we can review them at our leisure. Let's adjourn and discuss later."

"Why the rush?" Derrick asked. "Yesterday I was a raving lunatic. This morning I saw a frying pan bang itself on the stove. I'm loving this quiet place."

"What? You want to camp here?"

"If it keeps the ghosts away, I'd sleep standing."

"Me too." Kelly rubbed the back of her neck.

Marie's hip nudged Garrett. When he investigated, she was staring innocently at Julie. Was she reassuring him or suggesting something carnal? Wistful desires of returning to when spirits and mekari let them enjoy their newlywed status led to imagining family life with Marie. The two of them with their little kids, all safe and sound, away from this house. He admonished himself for slipping into a fantasy with real threats all around, until that same fantasy jolted him with the memory of a particular line from the translation.

"Actually," Garrett said. "One other thing sticks out."

"Yes!" Derrick clapped and rubbed his hands together. "I knew you'd find a reason to keep us here." Marie and Kelly chuckled.

"When Grandpa Renault was talking to the less bad mekar. *Limsomething?*" He couldn't remember the names like the rest of the family, but he moved on before Julie's inevitable correction. "He took blame for something. Seemed related to your ability to protect the Hellspot? What did he mean?" Though interested in the answer, he mainly intended to unearth the lines he suspected Mr. Renault of skipping over. He didn't want to risk that section not making it into the photocopied notes.

A shrug jumped from Derrick to Kelly and made it all around the room. Only Iris showed genuine interest in his question, peering in the direction of Mr. Renault's slumped head. Snores grunted in response. No one noticed Mr. Renault had fallen asleep.

"We should let him rest," Julie said. She tugged at the journal. Mr. Renault's grip held tight. "I'll get the notes later."

Garrett tensed. Had he imagined the missing lines?

"Are they safe?" Kelly asked.

"In this room, sure. If I'm wrong, Dad spent so much time translating he's probably memorized it all anyway. He needs any sleep he can get. We all do."

If he's actually asleep at all, Garrett thought, but it was clear nobody—save perhaps Iris—shared his doubts.

17. Children

By the time Garrett and Marie walked under the foyer arch and into the breakfast nook, Derrick and Nia were already sitting. On one side of the cushioned U-shaped booth, the couple faced the sunroom hallway, sharing an open book on the table. Garrett's shin brushed the royal blue circular sofa on the way over. After the plush material had woken him from a Shifter-induced hallucination a few days ago, he'd developed a habit of making contact with it whenever he passed by.

Garrett slid onto the open bench facing the gym hallway. He took a baby carrot out of his bag and bit it in half. The Renaults still cooked the occasional large meal, but most food lately came in easy-to-prep and fast-to-eat snack form.

Nia closed the book they were reading and drummed her fingers on its crimson-sleeved cover. Another brown-sleeved tome lay shut in front of Derrick. Scant afternoon light entered the room from the two lowered shades bracketing the sides of the booth.

Marie stayed standing at the head of the table. "Do y'all mind if we swap? That corner slot"—she gestured with her uneaten apple toward Nia—"has been my Breach seat since I was ten or eleven. With what Dad told us a couple days ago, I'd like to keep to traditions."

"Sure." Derrick popped right out of his seat. Nia shrugged like she didn't see the point. She scooted out anyway, grabbing her book and a zipped soft cooler.

Garrett certainly didn't mind the swap. His compulsive touching of the sofa mirrored Marie's reason for wanting her seat. Staying grounded kept them safer. The pairs swapped seats, Nia set her belongings on the bench between her and Derrick, and Marie bit into her fuji apple.

"Glad the four of us finally got together." Derrick placed his book on top of Nia's, clearing the table. "Took a while to convince Nia to leave Grady with my mom for more than an hour."

Nia tilted her head down and crossed her arms. She spoke fast, her Louisiana accent thickening. "We're in a 'aunted 'ouse. No, worse than that. A place called a *'ell*spot. I don't care what y'all say 'bout kids safety here. Nobody knows my baby like I do, and I don't mean this as disrespect"—she raised her hands in placating manner—"but I don't think y'all two would die for 'im."

Garrett's ears flushed at the likely accurate read. Prospects of death lingered, casting a paralyzing gloom over the table. Eager to move on, he floundered for a follow-up question. "What made you change your mind?" He crunched another carrot, keeping that ominous silence at bay.

Derrick's forefinger tapped his lips as he recalled a memory. "That was all Grady. He wanted to play pillow fort with his Nana and didn't want Mom messing up their fun."

"As if I'm not fun," Nia said.

"You sure are. When you're not in mom mode."

Nia took her husband by the chin and lightly squeezed his cheeks. "Haunted. House."

Derrick took her hand and kissed her knuckles, like a routine they'd practiced countless times.

"Well," Garrett said, "if you get more comfortable with the idea, we'd be happy to watch Grady for you too. I'm sure you're right that our protective instincts don't match yours, but we'd watch him like hawks."

"Not the best analogy," Nia said. "Hawks are predators. But you should learn from Derrick's mistakes and ask your wife. She's squirmin' good."

Marie ate more of her apple, her eyes seeming to search for an escape as she chewed. She didn't find one by the time she swallowed. "I'm just uncomfortable watching kids."

"You watched Tommy earlier, though," Garrett said, holding himself back from prying more.

"That was before the Breach. And only for a few minutes before I left him with Iris. I didn't want to be responsible for him."

Was that how she felt about all kids at all times? Including potential kids of her own?

"Hey, Marie," Derrick said. "You don't have to watch Grady if you don't want, but we trust you with him, right, Nia?"

"As much as anyone else here," she said.

Derrick smiled and made an amused puff from his nose.

"Thanks," Marie said. "Maybe? We'll see. You never know."

Derrick rescued her from her train of non-committals. "We also brought gifts." He transferred the soft cooler from the bench to the table. "Four of Nia's fresh baked cookies, as of this morning. So good, they're worth her pressing her butt against the oven for fifty straight minutes to make sure no Deviant messed them up. They're mostly for bribing Grady, but we figured he wouldn't miss a few."

Marie had her apple half-raised to her mouth when Derrick mentioned cookies. With an apologetic look at Garrett, she set her apple on the table, and pilfered a treat from the cooler.

He smirked. Three months into dating, he'd started trying to impart how she'd feel better eating nutritious food first, but nothing could stop her sweet tooth. At the end of the day, he couldn't change her eating habits any more than he could control ghosts.

To her credit, she nibbled the cookie instead of devouring it. Her eye roll and relaxed shoulders spoke to how good it tasted.

Nia clapped her hands and chuckled. "I knew you couldn't resist. Best batch I've made since Grady's school fundraiser."

"These cookies are insane. You've been holding out on me!"

"Had to warm up to ya first. Brown butter is the secret." Nia picked out her dessert and took a quarter bite.

The jovial air ignited a warmth already stirred by Derrick's invite to hang out. Garrett liked him before this, and Nia now showcased a more pleasant side of herself. Thinking nothing of it when he eyed the books stacked between them, he asked, "What were you two reading when we came in?"

The couple shared a look that signified a subject too private for discussion.

Crap. But after a few facial expressions Garrett couldn't read, Derrick calmly answered.

"It's a long story that starts with me trying to convince Nia to move back home on a more permanent basis."

Nia cleared her throat.

"Okay, not *home* home," Derrick said. "Back to Louisiana. Somewhere within driving distance. We don't all get together enough, and this lets us see y'all whenever you or Claude come back. Plus, Uncle Dave and Mom are getting older. We might shoot for somewhere like Baton Rouge. Kind of in the middle of them."

Marie's nibbling turned into scarfing the rest of her cookie. She peeked into the cooler, presumably for a bonus treat. "Schwaz, that was good. I can't speak for Gare, but I'd come back just for these cookies. Gare, you've got to try yours." Content to wait, Garrett pursed his lips and pulled his hands closer in. Marie blew raspberries at him. "So, you really might move back?"

Nia unwound further after Marie's compliments. "We'll see what the books say. But before I bring Grady or another kid to this house more than necessary, I'll be damned sure it won't mess 'em up. Something's wrong with the vibe of this place. Don't know. Mother's intuition or sixth sense, I guess."

"Do you have something like Seeing or Feeling?" Garrett ate the last of his carrots and shoved the bag in his pocket.

"Oh, no." Her head reared back, as if dodging the possibility. "And I better not wake up not smelling or hearing one day, else Derrick's paying for the nicest spa week of my life every month in perpetuity."

"Fair," Derrick said.

"So, yeah. These books." Nia's knuckles rapped the top book of the stack. "One's on—"

Without warning, Marie and Derrick yelled, "Hide!"

Both slid underneath the table, crouching catty-corner from one another. Marie's knee bumped Garrett's shin, and she curled into an even tighter ball.

"What are you doing?" Garrett asked.

They both started shivering.

"Shifters," Nia said.

"Don't listen," Marie said.

"They'll go away," Derrick said.

Of course.

"Follow my lead." Nia moved so quickly, apprehension didn't have time to touch Garrett. She leaned over, extended her arm towards Derrick. She placed her hand on his shoulder, then leaned over her side incrementally, as if expecting a strike from below. None came, and she rested her head against Derrick's former seat. "Wake up, Derrick. Wake up."

Garrett mirrored her, step for step, in addressing Marie.

Nia's hand slid down to Derrick's. After a purposeful pause, she brought his palm to within an inch of her face. She never let go. When Garrett followed suit, Marie resisted, about as long as Nia's pause. When she relented, he moved her hand next to him. They stayed like that for several seconds, Nia and Garrett whispering encouraging words to wake. Then, Nia whistled a familiar tune, the one Marie had used to wake Derrick.

The pair underneath the table recovered in quick succession, confusion lining their faces as they scanned their surroundings.

Nia and Garrett sat up to give them space. She raised her eyebrow, to him suggesting he should learn that tune too. He already planned to the next time he was alone with Marie.

Marie and Derrick grabbed the table's edge and dragged themselves back to sitting.

"Sorry about that," she said.

"Same," he added.

"It's fine," Nia said. "'least you didn't bump the cookies."

"Speaking of." Derrick took a calming inhale and released, then reached inside the cooler, coming back with a cookie. "I think I deserve this."

The silent interlude that was inevitable for every conversation—though it originated from a source that was anything but natural—came at a terrible time for Garrett's anxiety. He reminded himself of his best defense: knowledge. "You think that haunt was over your books?"

"Who knows?" Nia said. "That's for Julie and David to decide. I just know I'm not lettin' one of those damned spirits cut *me* off." She defiantly scoured the room before continuing. "One book's on curses. The other's about tainted air, tainted water, tainted whatever we're takin' in while that Ring out there traps us like zoo beasts."

"Found anything interesting so far?"

"Interesting? Sure. There's a sort of blood ritual one can offer up to a mekar. Curses people to make 'em see somethin' sort of like ghosts. But it's as likely to curse the ritualist too. Dumb and dumber, but interesting, yeah. Useful? Different story. There's a possibility Hellspots are why Overseers can't have all the kids they want. Gets into the bloodstream and makes it harder every generation."

"Except us!" Marie decreed.

Nia's nose flared and her jaw clenched.

Derrick ran his hand back and forth on the table's smooth surface. "We've been trying for a year, actually. So, the jury's still out."

Marie's fingers covered her mouth, then slid down to her chin. "I'm so sorry. I had no idea."

"Mhmm." After a moment, Nia sighed. "That's just you bein' you. Side note—how're you so happy all the time and your sister's a grumpy maestro? When Derrick told her what we were thinkin' and asked for help, she gave us a country-mile-long list of books and told us to get started."

"Jules always has a lot on her plate. Especially with Dad focused on Grandpa's translations. It's a little easier for me, you know? Plus, I have Gare now. Best Breach ever. Well, minus mekari and ghosts working together."

"That's one perspective."

Derrick caught the crumbs of his last bite and threw those back too. Marie scooted closer to Garrett and held his hand under the table.

Garrett gave Marie a loving squeeze. "Tell me to shut up if this is too personal." Nia's stern face implied a shorter leash than she allotted Marie. His hands felt a bit clammy, worse than when dealing with the Shifters. He carefully chose his words. "There's one thing about kids I don't get. I want to read about it, but I'm still catching up on the need-to-know stuff. I understand if this is something you or others don't want to do, but why don't Overseers adopt instead? It would solve the reproductive dilemma, and that seems like an oath to me."

Nia apparently approved of his tact, turning to Derrick for an answer.

"A one-sided oath," Derrick said. "But not sure if that's the problem. What we know is the last two families who tried adopting died out their next Breach. Maybe it's a coincidence, but nobody wants to be the third family that makes it a pattern."

"What happened?"

"Well"—Derrick shot him an expectant look, then answered after no response came—"they died. We don't know. Overseers record most things, but not so much when in survival mode. Most figure a four and five-member family all dying in a single Breach says enough."

"On a happier note," Marie said. "Garrett still has a cookie to eat. What are you waiting for?"

Garrett processed Derrick's answer before responding to Marie. Then, he took the last cookie and chewed on it. Her reaction hadn't been for show—the dense, crumbly sweetness tasted divine. "Good things come to those who wait."

He couldn't help but hope that statement held true with Marie and starting a family of their own, however silly the concern was compared to the one that loomed ever-present: their survival.

18. Happiness?

The silence outside reminded Garrett of prey hiding from a predator, who in turn waited for his prey to err. Every outdoor creature must have felt the Breach coming because no bird had sung nor cricket chirped in a month. Trimmed grass fed the eerie undercurrent, like the most basic elements of nature absconded taking root here. Though Garrett knew Claude had recently taken a manual mower to the backyard—to keep it *familiar*—trying to apply logic only deepened his fear.

Fear that evil had befallen his wife.

"Marie?" he called out, hoping she'd hear him where he couldn't see her.

Predatory silence answered, daring him to venture into its maw. He held onto the cold door handle leading back into the sunroom. Instinctual drive pushed him to return inside, for all the good it would do. What if a Deviant pulled his shoelaces as he walked down the stairs? What if a Claimer made him hurt another, as it already had once? And he seemed long overdue for a Dreamer to corrupt his sleep.

The house wasn't any safer, but he could find people there. People meant help, as the family fought together to keep their sanity and their lives. Outside provided no safety nets. If he walked to the edge of the backyard, would they hear him if he screamed?

Stop it. You're looking for Marie, not a hiding spot.

He released the handle, one finger at a time. He made contact with the patio furniture as he walked out onto the grass. Marie had woken up earlier and earlier the past few days, but today was the first morning she was missing when he stirred from sleep. Nobody had seen her since last night. He'd tried reading to wait for her before jumping to conclusions. When a picture, one of a young Marie next to a younger child, fell out of the book, he took it as a sign and pocketed it as if a protective talisman.

Half the house asked if he wanted help finding her, but every offer carried the air of a favor to him, rather than a fear for Marie's safety, like this was a normal occurrence. He'd wanted to accept their help anyway. He declined because of how diligently each worked on their task. Julie and Mr. Renault, researching. Claude taking a break from jokes to tidy the house and scour it for hazards. Derrick, Nia, and Kelly watching the kids while brainstorming new theories. Even Iris, who mainly knitted, made rounds between rooms with available seats, overseeing everything.

Garrett yawned as he approached the fence line. Sleeping and waking throughout the nights had started to take its toll, but he had to be able to handle a simple task like finding his wife.

Even if it meant trudging through an outdoors as quiet as a devil's hush.

I'll feel better when I find her.

"Marie," he yelled. "Marie?" Trees blocked large swathes of vision opposite the fence, but he remained on the mowed side. What if a predator—supernatural or otherwise—*was* waiting for him? Where better to hide than among a row of trees? And beyond those trees, the Ring's vicious barrier defined a searing-yet-invisible line to the depth of his search.

The hair on his neck and arms stood on ends.

Had a Claimer taken hold of her, brought her here for a Deviant to deliver a killing blow? The Shifters who had struck Derrick and Marie simultaneously all but proved the theory that spirits now worked together. The Renaults' safety precautions were all predicated on ghosts acting individually as they had in Breaches before. Serious injuries only occurred when they inadvertently teamed up—an act set to occur with ever more frequency.

And here he was, out on his own, without a single piece of protection.

"Marie!" It came out as a frightened plea. His heart beat rapidly, and his stomach clenched tight enough to shatter a stone. He turned back to the house, seeming impossibly far away. He swam in an ocean of sharks hungry for blood. He would die—

Garrett made fists, brought them to his chest, and closed his eyes. He shakily breathed in every ounce of air his lungs would hold and released it to a countdown from ten. Derrick had said the last two to die during a Breach—well, before his grandfather—were his father and aunt, both troubled individuals. Garrett would survive only if he stayed sane.

He crept on, past another few rows of trees, about fifteen yards before the fence hit a corner and ran perpendicular. He stepped once more, and the silence broke.

He heard *something*. He heard . . . crying.

Garrett took another step.

In a small clearing, Marie stood before a tree whose branches stretched around as if frozen in the act of offering a hug. She wore the same ripstop shorts and long-sleeved shirt as the day he first proposed. The grass under her feet looked particularly trampled, with a pile of friendship bracelets in the clearing.

Garrett stepped onto and over the fence, moving carefully but making an intentional racket. "Marie?"

She didn't turn.

Was a ghost luring him into a trap? *They're balls of emotion. They don't think.* But mekar do. *She's not possessed by a mekar. She wouldn't let that happen.*

He ambled up behind her, timing a timid tap on her shoulder with his voice. "Marie?"

She screamed, turned, and backed straight into the tree, bumping her head on a thick branch. "Oh God, Gare. You scared me."

Garrett had jumped back a step too. "*You* scared *me*. What are you doing out here?"

Marie wiped both sides of her face in turn, then beamed. "Never mind. Finish this sentence with the first thing you think of that's not paper: the dog ate my . . ."

"I don't know." Confusion sheared away at Garrett's distress. "Cat?"

Marie whistled low with furrowed brows. "Too gruesome. Anything not an animal."

"Okay. How about hat?"

She giggled. "What a leap, all the way from cat! Okay, I can do that." She closed her eyes and inhaled like she was . . . getting in character for an improv show.

But why?

Marie planted her hand on her hip, bent over, and wagged her finger. "Fido, that was my mom's hat. Why would you do that?" She swung her arm across the ground in a 90-degree arc. "You can't bark your way out of this one." A pause, presumably for imagined barks. "Talk, talk, talk. That's all you do. I want action. I want you to prove to me this won't 'appen again." Pause. "Hey, now. Those puppy eyes aren't fair. If I let you get away with this, then . . ." She clamped her other hand to her hip and looked up, lost in momentary thought. With a jolt that yanked her head back to neutral, she locked onto Garrett and rushed him.

He only had time to shield his chest and think, *This is wrong*.

When she reached him, she took his hands and curled her fingers around his.

"I'll make you a tip-top breakfast. Black pudding, eggs, bacon, beans, and toast. Black tea, nice and strong. *Extra* strong. We'll end on a scrumptious blueberry scone. With a full belly and warm touch, you'll hold me in your arms, and we'll sleep. Sleep so well. Sleep forever, embraced as we pass from this world to the next, the poison in the tea coursing through our body, leaving only a scant moment to share one sweet, final kiss. Come, my love. Our forever awaits." By one hand, she tried to pull him toward the fence.

Garrett's mouth had dried with every word she uttered, but he managed the strength to hold firm in place. If a Claimer didn't have her earlier, it did now. "Marie, stop."

"No, no, no." She bounded back at him, she ran her hand up his arm and under his sleeve. "Can't you see the beauty? With a final act, we'll declare our immortal love to the world. A love so beautiful, so pure, no creature earthly or otherwise can strip us of it."

"I want to be with you here. With your family." He felt foolish arguing with a spirit, but that was how she handled his possession, and what he'd read corroborated it as the best approach. "Let's wait here until the stars come out."

"I don't want to wait. I want it now." The innocent sweetness of her voice slipped to that of a demanding crone. She smiled as if realizing her error and turned from talk to action. She kissed him. He pulled back and she bit his lip.

With a wince, he came back to her.

She stroked his hair and ran kisses down from his lips to his bearded cheek to his neck. One hand slipped under his shirt and started down his pants. Garrett took her wrist, harder than he meant, and she moaned.

"Want to play dirty?" Not-Marie asked. "I can do that." Her lips had moved aside his shirt where his neck joined his shoulder. Her teeth clamped onto him, muscle, flesh, and all.

Garrett groaned but stayed still until her jaw released him. He ran his hands along her cheeks and under her ears, holding her a safe distance away. She stared in wonder at him, and he pecked her on the lips. "Wake up, Marie."

"We are awake, my love." Not-Marie rummaged through his hair with both hands now, then curled her fingers, pulling his hair taut. "I'll allow one final sin from your body to mine, and then we begin our lives in eternit—" She lost her grip on his hair, followed by her form. Marie crumpled toward the ground. Garrett caught her around the waistline and propped her back up on his shoulder.

He felt the dampness of her tears before he heard them.

Marie's whole body shook with the force of her sobs.

Garrett pressed his lips to the crown of her head. Still holding almost half her weight with an arm around her waist, he started rubbing her back. "It's okay."

She sobbed, slowed to a cry, and started sobbing again. He held her and waited. Then, like a valve had turned off, she stopped, pulling away from his shoulder. Red shaded her fair skin, a combination of tears, face-to-shoulder pressure, and blushing embarrassment.

Marie propped her hands on Garrett's hips. "Does being around me make you happier?"

"Of course it does." He massaged her forearms up to her elbows. "I love you."

"That's not what I mean. Does my staying upbeat matter *here*? Does it keep you calmer? Keep your mind from wondering what we're facing?"

"I wouldn't make it here without you. What are you getting at?"

"I just—" She sniffed. "I needed to hear that. To make it all worth it."

"To make what worth it?"

"Always acting happy."

"You don't always have to be happy."

She backed away, shaking her head like she was dealing with an idiot. "What else do I have to offer? Julie's smart. Derrick's hard-working. Claude's funny. Dad is wise. What else am I good at besides being happy?" She verged on hysterics but recomposed herself with a staying hand at her side. Her speech still bordered on frantic. "I can feel when people are hurting or scared. Not in a supernatural way. I guess I pick up on little tells. I know their sadness, fear, and grief. When I force myself to stay cheery, I think it lightens their load, but it's so draining, always pushing down my own sadness and fear. If it makes life easier for others to do what they do, then it's worth it. But maybe I'm not helping. Maybe I've been deluding myself into thinking I make a difference."

Garrett closed the gap she'd created and brought her hand to his lips for a kiss. "You do so much for this family that it's hard to quantify. Your upbeat mood matters." He recalled what Derrick had told him prior to his second marriage proposal. "I don't think she'd say it, but I bet Julie couldn't handle everything she does without your optimism. That doesn't mean she needs to see it all the time."

"Thanks, Gare, but you're wrong. If I'm helping, and I'd really, really like to think I am, then she does. I brought you into the worst Breach our family's ever dealt with, and I should've just said no to your proposal and left it at that, but you were so sweet, so charming, so understanding. I love you, and I was selfish. I've been so selfish, taking and taking from this family. All I can do is help the best way I know how. I'll be smarter. I won't come back to this spot until after the Breach, and I promise not to lose myself again."

"I knew what I was getting into." Even if that wasn't exactly true, she needed to hear it. "There's no reason to blame yourself." In an attempt to pull Marie from a deep well of guilt Garrett never knew she harbored, he playfully blew the side of her head, ruffling her short hair. Her lips ticked up, and he hoped to summon more genuine—not forced—happiness. He pulled out the photo in his pocket and offered it to her. "This fell out from a book I was reading. I guess it's you and a childhood friend?"

Marie made it halfway to accepting and stopped, frozen in the act. Her mouth hung open, like he'd said he wanted a divorce. When she spoke, her voice quavered. "A book? There shouldn't be photos of him anywhere here."

"Photos of who? Why not?"

"My," she stuck on the word, each ensuing blink bringing her closer to finishing her thought. As she took the picture from Garrett, she answered his first question. "My brother."

"Claude? That can't—"

"My younger brother." She stared at the photo, kept still between her forefinger and thumb. "He . . ."

Another death. One Marie hid the truth about. What else explained a family member's absence? At least one more had died in recent Breaches beyond Marie's mom and uncle. Joining that list was a child—one who should've been safe according to the Renaults' assurances. Garrett's stomach clenched. How many more—

No, he was overthinking again, filling the silence while she put words to this tragedy. There was an explanation for why she kept this from him.

Marie shook her head, then turned and knelt before the pile of friendship bracelets. A few inches over, she dug a shallow grave in the soft dirt and buried the photo.

Garrett grimaced at his festering doubt in his wife. There was more to the story, if he just waited. Marie had earned his trust ten times over. The house and her recent possession had put him on edge.

At last, she rewarded his patience. "He died a few months before a Breach. Sixteen years ago, when I was ten. It was an accident, and—" Her breathing hitched, and she whimpered. "We don't keep photos of him in the house. The emotion opens us up to possession. Me, especially, like just now. I don't know how that photo ended up in your book, especially after all these years. We were so careful."

There it was. His explanation. After all, how does one bring up a brother who died as a child? She could have easily lied about him when Garrett asked. The possibility of a death not caused by the supernatural had never even crossed his mind. He squatted behind her and caressed the top of her arm.

Marie didn't react at first, maybe didn't react to him at all when she resumed speaking. Tears were more audible in her voice than in the droplets that trickled down her cheeks. "This place is my memorial to him. We and my mom used to make friendship bracelets together. Now I buy them from all over and bring them here, for him. To give him pieces of the world he'll never visit. I know it's stupid and unsafe to visit, especially in a Breach. I'm usually better at controlling myself in our special place, but when you snuck up on me, I got hit by a rush of emotions, and then . . ." She rubbed her face, her hands muffling her words. "I can't talk about it anymore. I'm sorry. I'll be better. Happier than ever."

"It's okay," Garrett said. "It's not your fault." When her cries only intensified, he pressed his chest against her back, hugging her from behind. "I'm sorry about your brother. You don't always have to be happy around me though. Husbands are meant to help with those kinds of things."

She laid her head on his forearm. Flutters of her eyelashes beat against his skin. A leaf sailed down from a tree limb above and landed in her hair. The act of Garrett picking it from her hair seemed to prompt her to speak.

"I don't want to associate you with sadness. There's already so much of that here. Thinking about you makes me smile, and I don't want to taint that with sorrowful memories."

"What if you let it out in small doses?"

Marie slowly spun in his embrace, bringing her flushed face inches from his, a weak smile gracing her lips. "Okay, I can do that."

"Good. But if you ever need more—"

She shut him up with a kiss. Lips locked, they pressed together, not seeking anything more than to imprint this capsule of a memory. Their eyes closed as Garrett forgot the Breach, even the world outside of them, existed. Their chests loaded and unloaded with the several breaths that passed, until Marie finally pulled away.

"I love you, Gare. I'm ready to go back inside. And thanks to you, I won't have to force my happiness for quite a while."

As Not-Marie had tried with Garrett, the real Marie tugged him toward the fence line. This time he followed, reassuring himself that the feeling she still concealed something vital was either another case of overthinking or related to tragic details he simply didn't need to know.

19. Portents

Garrett blinked awake. Darkness enshrined the bedroom. In place of faint morning sunlight, night continued its reign. He felt rested and aware, as though he'd slept into the next evening. Marie's head shifted on the crook of his shoulder. Surely, they hadn't slept that long. Spirits wouldn't allow such an extended recovery. He considered peeking into the hall, but hollow silence warded him away. He closed his eyes. Sightless darkness radiated panic in every limb, causing his arms and legs to seize.

He abandoned sleep so fiercely he thrust himself from bed. He sprung up into the air, levitating above Marie. Without a destination in mind, he passed through the bedroom walls. His journey took him to the foyer, his head inches from the vaulted ceiling.

Standing in a circle were eleven individuals: the inhabitants of the house, Garrett included. Half of them—Mr. Renault, Iris, and their children—faced inward, arguing and discussing too quietly to discern anything said. The others—the spouses and children—faced away from the group in frozen stasis. He willed his body closer. The house expanded, keeping the conversation at the same muffled distance. Before long, he floated thirty feet above the ground, the same distance separating him from the ceiling.

Metal rattled above, imitating the AC's morning ritual. As the clattering subsided, silence lifted the heads of the inner circle. They locked onto Garrett. Then, the actors of the scene burst into a choreographed routine, like a flash mob.

Marie wailed in pain. She stretched her arms out, hands tense in a strangling motion and shaking violently. Derrick tapped his chin, examining her from head to toe. Julie flicked a lighter, igniting rolled-up paper. Claude showered the crowd with stacks of cash. Mr. Renault and Iris beelined for one another, the start of a bizarre dance routine. They strutted toward the circle's center, sidestepping before coming into contact, and continued to the circle's edge where the other started. Like their children, their impromptu actions played out in repeat. Those turned away from the circle, Garrett's doppelganger included, remained as statues, unconcerned with the bizarre actions occurring an arm's length away.

Spirits and mekari, he cursed. He was clearly dreaming, but the vivid perception felt as real as the waking world. Yet unlike his mad dash through the imagined workshop of horrors, he felt no fear. Felt nothing at all. Numbness permeated his skin. Safety and danger lost all meaning.

He tried again to move closer, to search for clues that could explain the scene. The room expanded as before. Only this time, another force fought back. Garrett convulsed, and the entirety of the house quaked like a snow globe. His body sped through the mansion, blitzing through in a rapid slideshow of a million pictures. He halted his travels at the tree under which Grandpa Renault rested.

"You have to get out," a croaky, incorporeal voice panicked. "These aren't your dreams."

"What's happening?" Garrett asked, in control beyond reason.

"She's showing you a version of the truth, worse than a lie. Find a way out before you lose yourself. I can only help so much."

"Who are you?"

"Maurice Renault."

Stars peppered the sky. Moonlight generously shared the gift of illumination with the backyard. Earth's greatest celestial satellite had last loomed this large on his wedding day. "Marie's grandfather." Garrett had never heard his first name.

"Yes." Exhaustion replaced the panic in his voice. "If you remember nothing else, remember this: forgive their past."

"You said that to me before, didn't you? In another dream. Are you a spirit now?"

"I'm trapped . . ." He continued speaking, too quiet to hear.

Whichever direction Garrett leaned, the words eluded him. Faint static buzzed until his companion faded. Now, only the quiet night accompanied him. Cold logic calculated the conversation's meaning. It must relate to the scene displayed in the foyer. Was he to forgive the Renaults for past misdeeds? Or was this a trick by those who trapped him here? Trapped, like Maurice Renault. Unless Maurice was actually a Dreamer impersonating him, currying favor with obvious warnings.

If this wasn't Garrett's dream, he should flee, regardless of who summoned him here. But how? Earlier attempts to move in the foyer met resistance. He walked toward the sunroom, each step bounding him forward the distance of a full leap. When he pulled the handle, a mirror image of the backyard greeted him. He stepped one foot through, scanned for any major differences, then backpedaled.

Chanting came from behind him. Shadowy figures hung their heads around Maurice's burial plot. Garrett strode back to the site. Hooded robes concealed eight adults with their heads tilted down. Two lifted their gaze.

"Not what I expected," Mr. Renault said, his cheeks bearing four distinct tattoos: a dollar sign, a book, a heart, and the Greek male symbol, all with a crack through them.

"Heartbreak's a bitch in this family," Claude said with a sly smile.

How dare Mr. Renault judge him? His daughter's love should have been all the acceptance needed. And Claude! Garrett had trusted him. This was a sign—a *warning*. Claude and his father intended to split Garrett from his wife.

His arms flew up over his head, his fury ignited. The sky cracked, cleaving the Little Dipper in two. His mouth twisted to yell. The words caught in his throat. Throaty exhales failed to shove them out.

Claude and Mr. Renault bowed their heads and returned to chanting. How dare they ignore him when he had so much to say? Garrett grabbed Mr. Renault's arm, pulled with all his might against a force as sturdy as a house. His father-in-law gave no reaction, except to focus on the grave plot. Grady and Tommy slept soundly at its center, six feet above their great-grandfather.

Garrett reeled back. Breath escaped him. *Have they always been there?*

"This is ridiculous," he barked. Nobody paid him any mind. None of this was real. He traversed a sick dream controlled by a damned spirit, it in turn the puppet of a vile mekar. Worse, the dream was sucking him in. Making him believe its lies. His rage boiled, the heat of a sun fueling his fury. His body readjusted to temperatures that would disintegrate him in the waking world.

Stars turned to ash, plummeting from the sky.

"That's my escape." He channeled his anger into each word. "None of this is real. You can't control me." Violent gestures rent the sky into fragments, tearing the heavens apart. "I won't succumb to your games. Mekar, spirit, whatever you are. Leave me alone. Leave us alone." Volcanic magma welled within, sputtering from his mouth onto the hooded figures, blanketing them in lava. Tree roots sliced through the earth, splitting the ground into dozens of tiny islands, each floating above a black void. "Or my fury will make this display seem timid."

His dream ignited like a canvas set ablaze. Black emptiness surrounded him. Heat radiated from his body, blurring the surrounding air. A white flash blinded him. As his sight and the void returned, heat expelled was now absorbed. His skin broiled from his shoulders to his thighs. Flames smothered his body, burning him alive until scorched from existence. Garrett screamed, silent in the void despite his efforts. Silent, all the way until he woke supine in bed, dimness shrouding the room.

His screams pierced his own ears. He scampered to standing, frantically patting his body. He was naked. Beads of sweat rolled down his chest. Singed skin replaced where his boxers and shirt began and ended. Fingernail-width rings of hot pain wrapped themselves around his biceps and thighs. He clamped his hand to his neck, his skin raw and warm.

The mattress underneath rocked. Bedpost light dispersed the gloom. Sweat and a burst water balloon soaked his half of the bed. A gentle caress rubbed his side. He recoiled from the innocent touch.

"I'm here," the voice whispered. "You're safe."

Catching his breath, neck still shielded, Garrett's eyes trailed up from the sheets. A familiar pair of legs led upward to Marie's face, inches from his own. Her worried lines matched the fear in his bones. From that fear sprung tears, a trickle loosened by painful manifestations of his fiery dream.

A dream he remembered as faint sensations rather than definitive instances.

Garrett wrapped himself around Marie. Squeezed her tight. Loosened his hold as she stiffened, then buried his face in her shoulder. His lips unintentionally brushed against her collarbone, their familiarity a welcome reprieve.

"What 'appened?" she whispered.

"A nightmare. I—"

Great thumps beat against the hallway floors, approaching their room. Thick canopy drapes hung taut around the bed, protecting them.

Am I awake? Is this real?

A knock rapped at the door. "You okay?" Derrick—or something impersonating him— asked.

"We're okay," Marie said.

Was he okay? Of course. He trusted Marie. Knew this was her. In the same way the Renaults' familiar furniture rooted them in reality, intimate knowledge of his wife grounded him.

Floorboards creaked away from them. Muffled conversation slowly dissipated from the hallway. Others had come to check on him. Danger had chased him, but he found sanctuary.

Garrett heaved all the relief his lungs could muster. He pulled back to see Marie's face but dared not let her go. Her gaze wandered to the blisters marring his arm. Her eyes widened, darting over the rest of his body. She lingered on his thigh, biting her lip, then rested her hand on his forearm.

"Do they hurt?" she asked.

He nodded, wiping away remnant tears. "It's fading quickly though. It was iron hot when I woke. Now, it's like a bad sunburn." He glanced at the arm she held. "I wish the marks faded as fast. I don't know what caused it. I can't remember the actual nightmare, but to mark me up like this . . ." He didn't need to finish. Marie's expression showed she understood the significance. According to the books he'd read, it usually took multiple Dreamers to manifest physical effects from a dream. Another sign of the spirits working together. "Why didn't the water balloon wake me?"

"You must've stayed still. Any rustling would've woken me up. We can ask Jules about it in the morning. All that matters is you're safe now. Want me to stay up with you? One good thing about growing up in this house is learning how to survive on limited sleep." She massaged him from his forearm to his wrist, then sandwiched his hand between both of hers.

He completed their hand stack. "I'll be okay. You should sleep, but can we change the sheets?" A realization hung at the edge of his mind. He might identify it if he acted quickly.

"While we're at it, should we get you some clothes? Not that I mind the sight." Her hesitant smile showcased her concern, and he loved her all the more for it. He kissed her, and his tension softened.

"Clothes sound great." Faint sensations of Garrett's dream faded too, leaving him scant time. He delved deep within its fleeting moments, grasped at the shards remaining and found something of greater substance than expected. "By the way, was your grandfather's name Maurice?"

"Yes. Didn't you already know that? Why?"

If he'd heard it before, he didn't know where. Attached to the name, he felt certain of two truths, though he couldn't say why. The sensation of their veracity seared itself into his confidence as fiercely as the red rings on his limbs.

One, he needed to find forgiveness for something. Past or future, that part was easy. Garrett's near-rape of his wife still weighed on him, her absolution saving him from himself. He owed it to her to find forgiveness for whoever wished it, especially with the pressure he now knew she placed on herself to act in kind.

Two, he shouldn't trust Mr. Renault or Claude. That presented more difficulty. He didn't know either of them well enough to spot peculiarities, to determine if they acted out of turn. And he couldn't reveal his mistrust to those closest to them. At best, they'd wave it away as phantasmal delusions. Maybe they were—a mekar or Dreamer might have tainted Garrett's dreams—but his suspicions arose from a confidence deeper within.

If Mr. Renault and Claude betrayed their family, he would stand ready.

20. Watchman

Afternoon twilight ruled the skies. Though light merely trickled in through the Ring, warmth entered in droves, accompanied by boggy humidity. That heat never crossed into the house, where a chill permeated the air. Garrett had found passable comfort in a thick sweater and jeans, along with sitting in the sunroom that sucked in the sun's narrow rays. As a bonus to the passable temperature, the room put him in position to keep watch on his brother-in-law, to study him for signs that justified the mistrust born from last night's dream.

Keeping watch. Was that what the Breach had come to? Better than discussing his dead brother-in-law, he supposed. If the family determined it best to hide the memory of Marie's younger brother, Garrett didn't want to risk bringing it up unless necessary.

Claude made a sizzling sound from the coastal-chic sofa. "Bet you're glad for those extra shirts now. You think this is their latest strategy? Burn up our clothes and freeze us out?"

Kelly slapped his arm. "You're an idiot. Ghosts set him on fire, and you're making jokes?" Despite admonishing him, she snuggled right back into him, sparing a quick study of the room.

An empty chair separated Garrett from the couple. After he and Marie properly woke this morning, she had deposited him here so she might spend time with her father. Spurred by his dream, Garrett stumbled to dissuade her, but no practical reason found its way to his lips. Buying pity with his wounds had popped into his head—a dirty option given the red rings' pain had healed. He dismissed the idea, forcing himself to entrust her safety to herself.

Garrett picked at the wicker armrest. He needed to pretend all was well. "Thanks, Kelly. Though it doesn't sound much worse than your kitchen Deviant."

"The real sharp stuff's moved off-site before a Breach. It wasn't so bad." A downtrodden expression belied her claim.

"Speak for yourself." Claude rolled his left sleeve up to his elbow. A long scratch marred his forearm. "Those pop culture ghosts throw like pros, and a speeding butter knife still hurts."

"Then you shouldn't have left one out."

"Was keeping the ghosts honest." With his other hand, he raised a plastic champagne flute full of mimosa. "Worth it though." He took a sip, resting the flute's base against his crossed leg. A bottle of orange juice and sleeved champagne rested on coasters on the coffee table.

"How are you so chill?" Garrett asked.

Claude chuckled. "Is that a pun?"

Garrett rubbed his nose for circulation. "Not on purpose. We're living through a Breach for the ages. It doesn't seem to bother you."

"Not much does," Kelly said. "Raising a three-year-old and dealing with ghosts are a lot alike, mortal threats aside. Neither phase him."

"Why let it?" Claude asked. "We'll deal with whatever comes. We always do." He drank with confidence, his other arm settling behind his wife.

"You sound like Marie," Garrett said.

"She *is* my sister." A charming grin. "Plus, I need to double-check all the shades' locks today. That boring job is a lot easier with a touch of alcohol."

Déjà vu struck Garrett.

"You okay?"

"Yeah, sorry. Just thinking. We still have two months minimum before the Ring lets us out. That's a long time."

"The rules have all changed," Claude said. "Could be whatever deal the mekari worked out with the spirits seals the Breach faster."

"What does Julie think?" He could trust her opinion. Objectivity guided her better than anyone else. Garrett leaned forward, elbows on his knees, listening for a hint that a spirit controlled Claude's actions and words.

"Nothing without proof. When she announces a new theory, you know it's legit." Claude tapped the champagne flute. "You sure you don't want a mimosa? Either of you?"

Kelly plucked Claude's drink, gave it a sip before returning it. "Yours taste better."

He pecked her on the cheek with another chuckle.

The idea of imbibing any of that toxin revolted Garrett. "I'm good." The couple showed no hint of the inescapable dread suddenly plaguing him. Sweat percolated under his arms. He coughed in a fit, giving pretense to check his midsection for physical malady. What was he doing here? His dreams were lies, his feelings of mistrust a misdirection. "We have no way to tell when this will end?"

"Nope," Claude said. "Sit back and enjoy the ride. Think of it as a roller coaster where the restraints come a little loose."

"That's not reassuring." Garrett massaged his forearm to keep himself from acting out.

"He's not good with metaphors." Kelly rubbed her husband's leg. Claude shook his head with a smirk. Both acted innocent of any knowledge of a future grand betrayal.

Garrett should relax and enjoy their company. Instead, he crossed his arms, shielding his chest. He couldn't stop fidgeting. "Can't we do something more productive?"

"Are you okay?" Claude tilted his head. Genuine-seeming concern creased lines on his face.

Kelly started to rise. Garrett leaned back, and she dropped to perching on the couch.

Hurriedly, she asked, "Did you see something?"

"No. I don't know. I think it's a moment of," he slowed his spastic speech, "feeling overwhelmed." Pressure never affected him like this.

Uneasiness and uncertainty blanketed a lull over the trio. Garrett gulped, rubbed his throat. Blood vessels pounded his skull. *If there's nothing to talk about, think!* He stared at the windowpane where a shadow once smiled at him. Had that been a warning? Now, it was too late to leave and death awaited.

The sunroom door flung open. The metal knob slammed into the tiled wall. A Deviant had entered to begin the final assault. Garrett wheeled around, pushing himself and his chair back against the wall.

Julie stormed in, balancing a laptop on her forearm. "Claude, what the fuck is this?"

Half a breath fled from Garrett. Not a spirit, but an incensed Julie stirred the stew of fear all the same. Bubbles of dread popped in his stomach, poisoning him with nausea.

"It's a computer," Claude said. "You really spend too much time in the library."

Garrett scooted toward the wall. *What's happening?*

"Do not start." Julie blew past Garrett as if he wasn't there. She slid her laptop onto the table. Would've clipped the champagne bottle had Kelly not snatched it. She thrust her finger at the screen. "Are you stealing from us?"

Was this the betrayal Garrett's dream portended? He wrinkled his nose and moved to the edge of his seat. If this suggested even a minor threat to Marie from her father, his legs were ready to bolt.

21. Fracture

Palm on his thigh, Claude leaned forward, examining the screen.

The accusation had rendered Kelly feeble. Her thumbnail dug into the neck of the champagne bottle, splitting the gold aluminum wrapping.

"What are you looking at?" Julie's face flushed. "You're stealing from us. Do you deny it or not?"

Claude leaned back and brushed a stray brown hair from his forehead. "I thought you wanted me to look at what you found. Why bother with the laptop otherwise?"

"So that you know what I've seen."

"Well, I don't know, because I haven't finished—"

"Answer. The fucking. Question. Are you stealing from us?"

With a sigh and a stolen glance at his shell-shocked wife, Claude nodded. Garrett may as well have been a ghost in the room. One of many. *One of many . . .*

"Why?" Julie flailed. "Are you too impotent to provide for your family? Is the job you brag about a facade? You've siphoned two million dollars that I *know of.* What idiot thinks they can get away with that? Can you comprehend how serious this is? That money pays for groundskeepers, food, maintenance, last-minute plane tickets, esoteric research, and everything we need to survive. You risk it all because what? You want to fucking look pretty? Your idiocy is unreal."

Julie's restless limbs writhed chaotically. Her normally cool and collected manner gave way to an uncharacteristic fiery state. Everyone in the house would hear bits of this argument. Kelly froze in her corner of the sofa.

Terror akin to waiting for the executioner's axe pelted Garrett. He struggled to control his breathing, to keep his hands steady. Buzz saws had threatened his life more than this family altercation, yet that moment felt like a holiday by comparison. Why did this room have him so on edge?

The spring of Claude's eternal carefree confidence dried out. He shrank before his sister's wrath, meekly offering his rebuttal. "I wanted a reward for our sacrifices. I come back here to help when I can." He wavered in his seat, hesitant to continue. "More than some others."

Julie slapped Claude so fast, the motion didn't register until after the sound. Her fist balled at her side. She moved fast—unnaturally fast.

Then it all made sense.

"Julie, hold on." Garrett's voice cracked. He still butted up against the wall.

She drilled her forefinger at him. "Don't think that because you're fucking my sister, I'll listen to a damn word out of your mouth."

"It's a Feeder." His unceasing dread. Her explosion of anger. Both explained by a spirit that amplified emotions, bolstering natural feelings into unnatural responses.

Her forehead wrinkled. She massaged the creases. She squeezed her eyes so tight her brows concealed her lids.

Claude touched his sister's forearm.

She swatted his hand away. "Feeder or no, you duped us."

Kelly thawed from her frozen state. Betrayal had a different look on her. "I have half a mind to slap Claude myself, but if Garrett's right, shouldn't we talk about this later? Without the spirit twisting the conversation?" Both her and Claude locked onto Julie.

Julie's rhythmic breathing mellowed the scene. She fell into a trance-like state. When she snapped out of it, the crazed fury had vanished, but a harshness remained. "I'm fine now. You're catching on quick, Garrett."

He flipped up his palms, rejecting the praise. "It was festering doubt in me before you came in. Despair," he corrected, not wanting to draw attention to his mistrust, however justified.

"In any case, this is about you, Claude." Julie clutched her hips, arms akimbo. An occasional facial twitch threatened to incinerate her icy coolness again, but she maintained her composure. "If you need a vacation or a new suit, we can cover that. Two million dollars, though. Where does it go? We trusted you to invest the funds, not embezzle them. Especially while our benefactors grow complacent and pull funding."

Claude scratched his beard. He started to turn toward his wife and stopped. "That's the thing. I did invest. Repeatedly. The craziest things would happen to sure bets."

Julie scoffed. "Unbelievable. You gambled it away."

"No," Claude said. "I mean, maybe. I swear those investments looked safe, at least until they fell apart. It's like something kept me from seeing the red flags. And," he struggled to expand, scratching behind his ear. "It's not as if I'm the only one with a compulsion."

Garrett tapped his wrist. Certain subtleties of this conversation were flying over his head.

"Kids"—Julie briefly donned a pained mask—"can't help it. Besides, you don't trade stocks from inside the house." Her fingers flittered near her brother's face. "There's no excuse. You're an adult. Act like one."

Are they talking about their younger brother? Had he been self-destructive? That would further explain Marie's reluctance to discuss him. Garrett realized she never even told him his name.

"I know," Claude said. "I'm just saying. Maybe there's more to it?"

"I can't deal with this. Take responsibility. I've got enough on my plate without absolving your theft. I came to find if there was a good explanation."

"There could be."

"There's not."

Claude raised a relaxed fist to his lips. He didn't seem to have noticed that Kelly had picked up his mimosa, her empty drink, and fled the room with the bottle of champagne. She left the door wide open.

Garrett moved to follow her out. Whether or not Claude's excuse related to his younger brother, this reveal had confirmed his dream's suspicions. He needed to check on Marie.

"I was sifting through Dad's translation," Julie said. "I'm pretty sure all the mekari who would normally haunt the other Hellspots are here, focusing entirely on us."

Garrett halted midstride, turned around. Part of him thought to call out to Kelly, but an overwhelming urge to know *now* kept him from interrupting.

Julie paced near the plexiglass windows. Outdoor twilight darkened her fair skin. Her incisors seemed to glisten as she curled her top lip.

She looks like a vampire. He pinched himself. *Don't let the feeder feed.*

"We're dealing with an unprecedented assault," she said. "At least four mekari spoke with Grandpa before the Breach. Hellspot Overseers haven't identified more than two in a single event in the past century. Spirits number more than I've ever Seen, yet they prod us in controlled bursts. We know mekari are directing them, and that takes more leadership than the two who didn't die in Grandpa's body. These facts, combined with reading between the lines in Dad's translation, leaves me confident. We're taking the heavy brunt of the world's Breaches this year."

"I don't get it." Garrett clenched the back of a chair. His tongue was sticky-dry. "Why does that mean all the mekari came here? Why not a bigger invasion at other Hellspots too?" The thought didn't offer much comfort but more than having a target on their back.

Julie walked her fingers along the plexiglass's metal dividers. "The Mekarian world is difficult to navigate. Moving from one location to the next isn't as simple as riding an airplane. Plus, the Breach is as sudden for them as it is for us. They would have had to have been in place, ready to go."

"But why not do this before? Surely, a couple dozen mekari have always offered better escape odds than relying on one or two. Why change this year? Why target us?"

"I don't know. We and other Overseers assumed some force prevented mekari from gathering en masse, or they were too independent to work together. All I know is they chose us." Her eyes lingered on Claude before she shook it off. The Feeder continued testing her too.

Garrett's thoughts wandered to the translated text. Had she made a copy or was she using the original? If the latter, he wanted to see it for himself—to discover if Mr. Renault had indeed skipped a passage. Those missing words could hint at the betrayal that awaited. He opened his mouth, but Claude beat him to speaking.

"How did you come across those numbers?" He gestured at the laptop.

"Does it matter?" Julie snapped.

Claude calmly shifted out of his sister's reach. "I can't imagine you were exploring accounting records to fight mekari. And we don't have the Internet. I'm surprised you even had the data downloaded. So, how did you come across them?"

Julie crossed her arms, tapping her biceps. The motion slowed until halting entirely. "After reading through the translation, I wanted evidence to support what I just laid out. I was comparing historic damage reports between Hellspots, looking for anomalies." Warmth in her voice plummeted into an icy frost. "Either way, it led me to your theft. And of course I have the records available. Anything related to this house is pulled on a regular basis. I don't leave paper trails unattended."

"Well." Claude held his arm in front of his torso, using it to direct his speech. "I'm not saying this is definitive, or even likely, but . . ." His arms settled into a protective shield. "It's possible you're compromised.

What if something's inside of you? Giving hints that would push us apart?"

"What if something is inside of *you* trying to trick me?"

"That's possible, but—"

"You already admitted to stealing from us. Outside of this house, where there's no chance of a spirit or a mekar corrupting you. It was your responsibility—not just to manage our money but to keep it safe. To not steal it."

Worry for Marie tugged again at Garrett. He couldn't leave these two alone though, not like this.

"I mean you're right," Claude said. "You're always right. Except think of the possibilities if you're wrong. We shouldn't be fighting. You can ream me for this later all you want, but let's survive first. What do you say, sis?"

"We'll survive fine. The Breach is under control."

"I don't doubt it, but it's better odds if we work together."

"Not if you stab me in the back."

"I'm telling you. Every one of those stocks was a safe bet. You normally get my reasoning, even when I don't say it as eloquently as you."

"Safe. Bet. Do you see the problem?" Julie looked ready to drag Garrett into this. Then she stormed out of the room, leaving with a final, "This is pointless. My time's better spent on something productive."

With her went access to her father's translations. Garrett considered following but didn't have the stones to ask her for anything in her current mood.

Claude, rubbing his arms for warmth, turned to him with a sad smile. "Good news is a Hider isn't always immediately threatening. If it's me or her or whoever, we can adjust appropriately. Hopefully, the host can drive out the little devil before it becomes a big issue. Bad news is I've pissed off half the women in the house. One of whom I normally sleep with. An empty bed makes for a lonely Breach. I don't know how Julie and Dad do it."

Garrett offered a prolonged shrug, buying time for a measured response. A man who stole from his family would've disgusted him in a normal setting. Here, he didn't know what to think. He knew only that he cared more for his wife's safety than Claude's conjectures or feelings. "Then you better apologize," he said. "Sorry, I need to go."

Claude thanked him, spouting off something else.

Garrett tuned out the words as he marched from the room, visualizing his route to Mr. Renault's room. He seared his destination into his mind in case a Shifter tried to alter his reality. He quelled the urge to run and instead counted uniform steps, picturing his route along the way. Closing his eyes here and there, he constantly reaffirmed his location. A ghost could drive him mad, and he'd still find his way to her. An army of mekari would have to intercept him to prevent his reaching her. Even then, he'd put up a hell of a fight.

22. Break

"I missed you." That was Garrett's best excuse for interrupting Marie's father-daughter time. He embraced her in her father's stale-smelling room, then politely waved to Mr. Renault behind her back.

He responded with an equally polite nod.

"That's so sweet." Marie backed out from their hug, eyeing the door he'd just walked through. "How about we play outside when I'm done here? Won't be too long." She wrinkled her nose. "I could use some air."

"Sure." The message was clear. Marie wanted time with her dad. Who knew how many more Breaches they would share? More importantly, she was safe. And protecting her all the time made for an impossible task—if she even needed protecting. "I'll be," he paused. Where was he going? He knew only that he wanted company. "Around," he finished.

Marie's dimpled smile followed him as he backed out of the room.

Fortune, in a manner, answered as Garrett closed the door.

Derrick jogged barefoot toward him. Leather-framed canvases flung themselves at him. He dodged each but the last with the grace of a dancer. It struck his arm, bouncing off as he slowed to a stop. He brushed off the impact. "Thank God, I found you. I need a favor."

Garrett's hands trembled near his chest, his heart racing to do more. Two landscape paintings beyond Derrick mocked him with their stillness. "What? We need to get out of here."

"Oh, the art? It's fine. That's why they're in leather." Derrick rotated his arm to show where he'd been struck. An inch-long red mark was the only evidence of the attack. "Plus, it makes for good cardio."

The joke was lost on Garrett. "Uh . . . okay." He massaged the back of his neck, trying to instill a modicum of Derrick's calm. "What's the favor?"

"It's Nia." Derrick's confidence faltered. "The house is getting to her. A Feeder maybe? I don't know. I've never seen her so sullen, and we've been together since high school. I wish we had a psychiatrist in the family, but I'm trying to make do. Two kids in tow is all the sudden getting to her. Kelly's sleeping, Dad and Marie are busy, and Julie's the only other person I could find, but she's a ball of fire right now. I was hoping you could watch 'em?"

The enormity of the responsibility—and Nia's chiding the other day about handing off her kids—weighed Garrett down like an anchor. He choked on his response, ambient cold air worsening the burn in his throat. "Are you sure?"

"Yeah. Nia and I agreed a fresh pair of eyes was safer than a worn-out supermom. It's more likely the kids hurt each other than anything supernatural." Derrick blew air into his hands and furiously rubbed his forearms. "Ghosts seemed tied up with the hallway weather anyhow. If you want a family and Marie ever gets over—" He bit his lip, cutting himself off. "Ever also wants kids, then this is good practice. It's a dive off the deep end given the setting, but I trust you." He signaled down the hall, toward his room. "What do you say?"

"What were you going to say about Marie?"

Derrick sucked his teeth. "Shoot. As you might imagine, this house can be traumatic for a kid. Even with everybody watching you, things can go wrong. She'll tell you when she's ready, but don't prod her. Now, not to make this about me but what do you say about babysitting?"

With the way Marie acted around the gym, Garrett once again considered it the source of an unspoken trauma. Maybe it had to do with her brother though, and the little memorial she kept for him? Either way, she'd tell him when the time came. For now, he owed it to her to help the Renaults in any way possible. Garrett stepped to

Derrick's side, eyes glued to the two hanging paintings. "I'm in. Got any tips how to handle two kids?"

Derrick gave a relief-uttering sigh as he led the way. "Yep. Don't play favorites. If they act up, tell them you're calling me or Nia." He picked up the closest fallen canvas. "Nia won't feel comfortable if the first thing she sees is a graveyard of deadly art." He remounted the frame, steadied it until level, then moved on. "Do you have your phone?"

Garrett patted his pockets. "Nope. Left it in the room today. Isn't super useful anymore."

"Until now. We can grab it on the way. The kids don't have a clue the phones don't work. Pretending to call us is the fastest way to settle them. I wouldn't actually dial of course, unless you want to speak with a ghost. It's no walkie-talkie interruption, but a specter's voice is hard to get out of your head." He hung up another painting.

"Speaking from experience?"

"Oh, yeah. Normal kids come up with silly dares like saying Bloody Mary to a mirror. We dared each other to speak to the dead. Walkie-talkies are best for that."

Garrett passed the paintings he'd been watching and folded his arm across the back of his head. Just in case. "Best how?" he sputtered.

Derrick chuckled. "Good question. Safest, I guess. Spectral threats of slitting your throat chills the bone, but they're only threats. We'd eventually fall asleep after a dozen reminders that it's only talk. Still, Claude and Julie had fun messing with me and Marie. We occasionally got 'em back."

They approached where the hall split around the stairs. Thankfully, all the window shades were lowered. Derrick walked by at first, then cut back toward the front of the house. A painting was twenty feet from its usual place. He grimaced as he picked it up. "Darn. Got a tear in it. Marie loves this one."

Garrett joined him, forcing his hands down to his sides. In between the leather frame swirled an abstract mix of reds, yellows, oranges, and blacks. He had passed by it a hundred times but never inspected it. The image formed quickly and clearly. "Two people holding each other. Is the second one looking away?"

Derrick grunted with amusement. "Only you and Marie see people. To me, it's a sun rising out of a black hole. No idea how you get a couple out of it."

"Surprised Marie's never said ..." Garrett's voice trailed as he spotted a lone figure through the landing window below. Styled hair with a head that nearly reached the tree limb above. "Is that Claude?"

"Huh. He wasn't there a moment ago. Probably paying homage to Grandpa. They were close."

Suspicion wormed its way into Garrett given, but he'd seen weirder things on this walk alone.

"Can't imagine it's that cathartic with the permanent day dusk," Derrick said, "but at least it's warm out there." He carried the painting back to its home, showcased by sun-bleached silver-gray walls around a darker rectangle.

Garrett followed, distancing himself from the covered windows as much as possible. *It's a game of odds,* he thought, justifying his caution. *Shattered glass can cut through the shades as easily as slide under them.* Though thick material reinforced the fabrics more than anything in a retail store. *Nothing wrong with extra safety.* He massaged his palms, alternating sides with every knead. *Just don't show the kids you're scared.*

"One other thing." Derrick snatched the penultimate painting and deftly hung it. "Don't fall asleep watching the kids."

"Why's that?" Garrett's hands made another rigid clasp.

"I guarantee they'll find something to draw on you with."

Garrett countered with a grin he almost felt.

"You'll be okay." Derrick picked up the final painting and brought it halfway up.

Glass shattered. A rapid succession of high-pitched breaks followed, echoing down the hall. The leather frame slipped from his grasp, struck the floor with a soft thud.

Garrett turned about, instinctively inspecting the windows he'd fearfully passed. Their immaculate condition and a memory falling into place spun him back again. He placed the sound—two doors down. The room where Nia was watching Grady and Tommy.

Derrick bounded into a sprint before a woman's scream split the air; the cry died as quickly as it came. He threw open the door to his room, dashed in and out of sight.

"Mom?" Grady quavered. "Mommy?"

"Nia!" Derrick's steps boomed through the upstairs halls.

Garrett hesitated. He should have been running too, but his feet felt like lead.

"Nia, no!" Derrick cried. "Stay with me."

Dread stalled Garrett. What horrific scene awaited him? Was he walking into a trap?

That doesn't matter. Not in a house where every member depended on one another. This could have as easily been Marie. He pushed on, entering through the open doorway.

Nia lay on the ground, smiling through a grimace. Blood drowned her blouse and drenched a dagger-sized sliver of glass on the floor. Smaller shards speckled the ground. Derrick, muttering, had jammed his shirt against his wife's neck. Lime green cotton turned crimson like a paper towel cleaning up a bottle of wine. Pebbles of glass stuck to his bare arches, oozing blood. Grady clutched his mother's ankle, lips shuddering. Tommy, bracing against the wall, stared into his lap.

Mouth agape, Garrett stood motionless, waiting. For what? For the divine to whisper guidance? By the time he considered cauterization and its impracticability, Nia's smile drooped.

Her face lolled away from her husband. Her eyes stared at the ceiling.

Derrick stroked her arm. Tears ran rivulets down his cheeks and onto the hardwood floor, diluting her blood like rain on a pond. The children's high-pitched wails merged with his deep lament into a somber chorus. He whistled a familiar tune, breaking it into half a dozen segments to recover from his hitched breathing. "The bad times are over, Nia." A sniffle. "You're free to come out now."

Garrett recalled the song—Marie and Derrick's code for the coast was clear. The same tune Marie had taught him the other day.

A literal lifetime ago.

23. Intermediary

Garrett was a useless spectator, rubbernecking at the scene of a tragedy. However much he panned his inaction, he couldn't will himself to move. Marie brushed by him, beelining for her grieving cousin.

Derrick swayed over the lifeless body of his wife. Crying in silent communion with her, he held her hand between both of his, unconcerned and unaware of his wounds. Blood trickled down the undersides of his feet, joining the pool on the floor.

Marie came to a halt behind him. "God, Nia, no!" She recoiled, raising her arm to block the scene. Slowly, she let her arm fall. Her head jerked away only for her gaze to wander back. Tears now fell as freely from her as from her cousin. She locked onto the lifeless body and brought a shaking hand to her lips. "Derk, I . . .I'm so sorry."

Mr. Renault hustled in behind his daughter. He absorbed the scene like a detective rather than a family member.

Because he doesn't care. This is his betrayal in the making. Garrett cursed himself anew once Mr. Renault acted. The family patriarch coaxed the despondent boys into taking his hand and following him from the room. If this was betrayal, what described Garrett's idleness?

Marie hesitantly reached for Derrick, her hand falling at last on his shoulder. He ignored it, as he did the blood on the floor and his son's sobbing.

Until with a sudden twist of his torso, he snapped, "Get away. I can't have you here."

She reeled back but stood her ground.

"Get out!" Veins bulged from Derrick's forehead and neck.

Grady's wails magnified from the hallway.

Defensive hands raised, Marie backpedaled. "I'm sorry." She turned away, her eyes meeting Garrett's. She staggered out of the room and mouthed, *Watch him,* before joining her father and the boys.

Derrick's face softened. Harsh lines softened into sad droops. Had lingering spirits latched onto his fragile state?

Stop suspecting everyone and find a way to help. Garrett's vantage point near the room's bed let him watch Derrick while peeking into the hall. Mr. Renault crouched before Tommy and Grady. The children sat against the wall, knees pulled toward their chests. Marie popped into and out of sight as she alternated comforting the children with pacing away from them. It was the most affection he'd seen her show them, which stirred the desire for kids at yet another inopportune time.

Be useful!

Garrett straightened his back, focusing on the murder scene. The window shade gusted with the wind, its edges frayed all around but especially at head height. If not for Nia's blood-soaked blouse and the drenched shirt around her neck, one could have mistaken her for sleeping. At rest, her domineering demeanor faded, and she resembled his wife more than ever. *If this was Marie . . .* He covered the left side of his face, leaving only Derrick in view and cutting off the thought.

"Is there anything I can do?" He sounded panicked. He realized they were his first words since the window broke.

"Bandages," Derrick choked. His face was a wet mess. "I'm—I'm bleeding a bit." He flaked off shards stuck to his feet and cleared a safe space around himself, then leaned on his hands over his wife's body. His arms shook, verging on collapse.

Watch him. His foot did need dressing though. "What about pillow-cases?"

"Don't want to leave me alone?" Derrick murmured, low, pitiable. "I'm not leaving Grady like that but fair enough. Hand me the pillowcases. My cuts aren't deep, and everything in this room"—he scanned around briefly but flicked back to Nia as if a timer dinged for her checkup—"I don't want to see again."

Garrett undressed the pillows. Wetting one of the pillowcases would help clean the injury, but that meant leaving the room. "Marie, can you get—"

"Leave her." The harshness in his voice faded quickly. "Out of it." His abrupt ferocity juxtaposed the sweetness with which he caressed his wife. He stroked her cheek with the back of his hand. Gave her a kiss on the forehead.

Asking Mr. Renault for assistance was an option until he started consoling the children. His choices spent, Garrett resigned to keeping the makeshift bandages dry. He tossed the last pillowcase onto the comforter.

Where is everyone else? They'd had more than enough time to arrive. If the shattered glass happened too fast to notice, the grief-stricken sobs and wails screamed for attention. He swept up the bundle of makeshift bandages and crept toward Derrick, staying at arm's reach. Sporadic vitriol aimed at Marie, a cousin he loved dearly, gave Garrett cause for concern.

Glass shards taunted him from the floor. They could rise in an instant, several as long as steak knives, and end his life as they had Nia's. Her corpse cautioned him away.

He rooted himself to the ground.

You have to help.

Perspiration building under his arms, he pressed on. As long as he didn't see her hair or her motionless face, he could keep it together. He focused on a glass-free grain of wood that blood had yet to reach.

"Here you go." Garrett extended a pillowcase from his pile.

"Thanks," Derrick sighed, turning just enough to extend a hand.

Garrett's trembling hand fumbled giving him a linen, then two more until Derrick pulled back. "Anything else I can do?" Sickening acid crept into the back of his throat.

"No." Derrick sniffed a few times. He didn't move his feet to stanch their bleeding. He brought his hand to Nia's face.

Garrett's intentionally obfuscated view made it hard to discern the act beyond its gentleness. He rushed back to his post beside the nightstand and deposited the spare coverings onto the bed.

Coward, he admonished. *You watched her die, but you can't look at her now?* If he couldn't face death here, he was letting down Marie. He risked it, and spied what Derrick was doing with the linens—wiping the blood from his wife's face. Cleaning her off. With the final pillowcase, he shrouded her face. Sobs burst forth anew.

Out in the hall, Grady's shuddering cries joined in lament. "Mommy," he whimpered. "Was. Crying." A pair of tearful gasps. "Then she. Went to. The Window." Sob, gasp. "To look. Outside." He bordered on hyperventilating. "It. Attacked. Her."

"Did she say anything before she looked out the window?" Mr. Renault asked.

The boy managed to regulate his speech. In place of sobbing stops, he doled out his words in shaky sentences. "She said she wasn't going to let anything bad happen to us."

"Do you know—" A moment passed. Mr. Renault glanced left. "What's that?"

Whispers passed, too quiet to catch in the hall, but Garrett recognized Marie's voice.

"Sorry, Grady. Do you know what your mom meant by that?"

"No," Grady said with a deep inhale. "She was acting funny. I didn't want to upset her."

"In what way . . ." Mr. Renault's voice trailed off. When he spoke again, he spoke deeper, his attention focused above the seated children. "It's okay. You can go. Try and find the others."

"Thanks. I'm," stumbled Marie. "I'm sorry I couldn't do more."

"Ya did well. We'll talk later."

Footsteps moved in the direction of the back staircase. What had

Marie whispered to her dad? Garrett's heart wrenched, useless in his ability to comfort her.

Grady returned to bawling with the attention off him. Tommy tried to match his flow of tears.

Mr. Renault brought the boys in for a quick hug and squeezed them tight. Then he let go, keeping his hands on their shoulders. "Now, Grady, in what way was your mom acting funny? Take your time. You're very brave."

After recovering with a series of sniffs and cries, he answered. "She said to stay away from the birds. But there weren't any birds, Peepaw. And she made us wear jackets and hats. It wasn't even cold."

Not cold? But . . . Garrett realized the room was as warm as the outdoors. Nearby hallway air had turned more temperate too. His sweat wasn't purely from fear.

"Auntie Ni said pro-tek," Tommy piped in.

"Yeah. Protection," Grady agreed.

"From what?"

Uncertainty struck Grady's voice. "Don't know. Can I see Daddy?"

"Sure. Stay right here. Ah'll get him. It's okay to be sad, but I don't want you to worry. Everyone is gonna keep you safe like Nia wanted. You're both very brave boys." Mr. Renault waited for an unseen confirmation, then stretched his legs as he stood, an unreadable expression gleaming down below. He shuffled into the bedroom, focused on his nephew.

A moment of contemplation passed. He hushed his voice into a whisper. "Has he done anything strange? Anything indicative of a Claimer or Hider?" He added with a grimace, "Or a mekar?"

"He was snippy with Marie, but he's acting like someone who just lost his wife." Garrett spoke with robotic candor, else he risked raising his voice and disturbing Derrick's private memorial. Where was an uncle's concern for his nephew?

You weren't better moments ago.

Mr. Renault nodded. "You probably wanna check on Marie, but can ya watch the kids for a minute? Not sure if . . ." He gestured from Derrick to Grady and back, indicating it may not be safe. "We'll also need to figure out what 'appened to the others."

Watch him. Surely, Marie meant for him to protect Derrick from himself, not his uncle. And he couldn't deny someone needed to assess Derrick's mental state.

"Sure," Garrett said. His father-in-law's gaze trapped him for agonizing seconds, then he walked over to his nephew. The two spoke in hushed whispers.

Garrett's insides wrapped themselves in knots. Someone had to take charge. Only, why did it have to be the person he trusted the least? He balled his fists, then released.

Constant suspicion threatened to drive him mad. Vigilance was an effective enough tool. If proof of Mr. Renault's misdeeds ever materialized like it had for Claude, Garrett could act then. Besides, Derrick's uncle could easily manufacture alone time with his nephew.

Grady and Tommy made watching them easy as they crawled into view.

Garrett blocked the entryway with his body. He doubted they could see the grizzly aftermath from their place on the floor but better to be safe. "Did Aunt Marie give you two good hugs?"

That was the best he had?

Grady rubbed his swollen eyes. "I guess."

"You know we'll all keep you safe, right? Like your mom wanted." He felt silly questioning Mr. Renault's motives while repeating his lines.

"Okay," Tommy said, whose head drooped when he noticed his cousin doing the same.

"What's wrong, Grady?" Garrett asked.

He poked at the floor. "If everyone keeps us safe, who keeps everyone safe?" He looked up with genuine concern yet shrunk away as if scared of the answer.

The innocent selflessness pained Garrett. "We'll find a way."

Grady nodded, returning to poking the floor and sniffling in equal measure. Spending time in this house at its worst imparted a strength upon these children few others knew, a strength that highlighted Garrett's weakness.

Who *would* protect the adults? He suddenly itched to flee the room. Would have bolted if not for his responsibilities. He almost jumped when Mr. Renault tapped his shoulder.

"He's doing okay, given the circumstances. Plan's to keep the kids watched in Grandpa's room since it's stayed safe since the Breach. We'll split up, look for everyone. Derrick said ya saw Claude outside?"

"Yeah."

"Good. One less to worry about. Once we account for everyone else," he said, lowering his voice into a whisper. Garrett had to lean in to hear. "We'll bury Nia. When it's time, would ya help me cover her and bring her downstairs? Ya don't have to answer now."

Garrett's neck tensed. "I'll help how I can." How could he say no?

Mr. Renault clasped his shoulder. Looked beyond him. Something lay hidden and unsaid in his perusal of the hall. Whatever it was, the smile on his lips spat in the face of the room's grim mood.

24. Reprieve

Everyone crowded around Nia's gravesite, a bulging mound of dirt that Garrett helped dig an hour ago. His attention clung to the shapen earth while others shared their favorite memories of her. Round and round they went, closing out her funeral ceremony. They stood under a tree fifty paces from where Maurice's family buried him barely a month prior. The speaking circle reached its final member, and Derrick stepped forward.

"The day we met, I was a mess. Had been for several years. I kept it to myself, but you saw through me. I was sitting alone for lunch when you came by. You said you wouldn't stop chatting 'til I said something back. We didn't take long to hit it off after that. We skipped our afternoon classes and did, well, nothing. There's not much for high schoolers to do in a town like Ajaccio. Good company was its saving grace, so keeping to myself just tore me up worse every day. I didn't realize how badly until one time we'd spent so long together, I missed the bus. You were so cool, you even had a car. You dropped me off at home, and I'm pretty sure Mom yelled at me for an hour. Probably made me skip dinner. I can't remember. I was on cloud nine.

"But my most cherished memory of you comes a few hours later. You weren't even there for it, and I never told you." He rocked back and forth, struggling to continue. "I slept more soundly that night than any since my father died. Back before a permanent sense of wrong started to fester in my teenage years. My mom, my cousins, and Uncle Dave were my cornerstones as a kid, but this *thing* twisted inside of me until I was afraid to be around them. Marie and I used to play all the time, and then one day." His balled fist rapped his thigh. "One day, I couldn't see her anymore without imagining the horrors that might come to pass.

"When you came along and I slept that night, I shed so much of that apprehension I'd grown accustomed to over the years. I woke with a carefree sensation I'd nearly forgotten. You gave me my family back. You gave me a family." Lips quivered into the uptick of a smile in Grady's direction. "You gave me my life back. I wish I could give you yours."

Derrick wiped his eyes, his head hanging for several moments more. Then, he turned and lumbered away. His downtrodden trek brought him toward the dining room, the house consuming him as he entered.

Iris laid her Southern drawl on thick. "I'll take care of 'im." She held her grandson's hand as she had throughout the service. "Grady, say g'night."

"Goodnight." The boy's somber tone barely rose above the quiet night air.

Everyone responded in kind, their combined voices a dreary monotone. Iris left as Derrick had, following his path with Grady in tow.

Derrick's sorrowful brooding spread to Garrett like a virus. He replayed the moments before he carried Nia's lifeless body downstairs. Mr. Renault had shocked him by meeting him with a fresh body bag. They'd probably used one for Maurice too, but Garrett had been inside for the burial. Knowing those were on hand twisted fear's knife edge into his side, fear he'd pacified with despondency. From then until now, he acted as little more than muscle to lift and dig, or a shoulder to support Marie.

Kelly rescued him from his dark spiral. "I can't believe I slept through it all," she said. "Two doors down. I could've helped if I'd woken up."

Others lifted their heads in unison. He hadn't been the only one lost in thought.

"No," Mr. Renault stated. "Ya couldn't have." His harsh tone, devoid of support, strengthened his words. He spoke in objective facts. Rendering aid was an impossibility.

Kelly didn't see it that way. "Even if that's true, what if next time I can get there, but I sleep through it again?"

"We were all kept from her." Julie, arms crossed, shrugged. "Iris acted wisest, staying seated and safe. I almost sprained my ankle trying to leap over a puddle that wasn't there. We can't control what the house does to us, only how we respond. A Shifter probably seized your hearing. You can only act on what you know."

"I guess." Relief softened Kelly's face. "Thanks." She stroked Tommy's hair with one hand. Slipped the other into her husband's palm.

Claude didn't react. His face was as flat as his body was frozen. He merged gloomy and penitent into a single package, maintaining the same disposition as when Garrett and Mr. Renault had found him. He was standing under his grandpa's tree when they arrived with Nia's shrouded body. When his dad asked what he was doing, he said, 'just thinking'. They left it at that. As Garrett's mind thawed, he now wondered whether a Claimer drove Claude outside. Whether a Claimer drove him still. But to what end?

Would Garrett ever stop seeing betrayal?

"We should get going," Kelly said. "It's late, and it's been a long day."

Julie's nose twitched. "Indeed." Only this morning, she had confronted her brother about his embezzlement. They'd never reconcile if the house assaulted them at this pace.

If they even survived that long.

Garrett's body stiffened.

"Maybe tomorrow will be better." Marie's usual pep sounded particularly forced.

"Maybe." Kelly scanned the crowd, seeming to buy time for any lingering words. When none came, she turned her family toward the sunroom. The trio walked away, Claude showing some life as he opened the door inside.

After a quiet transition, Marie said, "I'm gonna shower, and I could use some alone time. Do you mind waiting twenty minutes to come up?" Red, puffy eyelids hinted at how she'd spend her solitude. She deserved a big, bold hug, but Garrett was running on fumes.

"Is that safe?" he managed.

"As safe as anywhere here. I'm a big girl."

"Right. I'll see you in a bit."

"Thanks." Marie pecked his lips, then hugged Julie and her dad, who squeezed her with the embrace she deserved. She sniffled, then darted away fast enough that she beat the door closing behind her brother.

What was Garrett to do for twenty minutes? His focus slid to Mr. Renault.

He kept us from breaking today. He could have broken us further. Had Garrett's dream misled him?

"With the effort spent by the spirits and mekari today," Mr. Renault said, "tonight should be relatively calm. We should indulge in the reprieve." He glanced at Nia's resting place. "As best we can."

A break from overanalyzing every little movement sounded divine. He needed distance from family members that he kept mistrusting. "Do you mind if I take a look around the storage area next to the sunroom?"

"You're a Renault now. No need to ask permission. It's your house too."

"Thanks." Garrett wasn't seeking anything in particular. The room just happened to be one of two places that spirits had yet to bother him. He gave a faint wave to Mr. Renault and Julie, and received an equally faint response from each in return.

He intentionally plodded over to the sunroom, worried he'd catch up to Claude and Kelly and find them arguing if he moved too fast.

Once inside with no one in sight, he rushed to his destination. Plexiglass panes and the hallway's single painting passed by in a blur.

The storage room was twice the size of his bedroom. Three narrow rows of wire shelves stretched to the ceiling, each full or nearly so. Clear containers—locked like almost everything in the house—held goods ranging from food to first aid to forgotten heirlooms. Underneath each shelving unit, the floor dipped into a shallow drain. One refrigerator stood at the back next to a row of squatty freezers, all practically touching. The room was temperate, nothing like the chill preceding Nia's murder.

Was the weather shift another way to incite unease?

He massaged his temples and approached the fridge, inspecting its contents. He snapped the seal on a bottle of water and downed half of it. Cold revitalized him, spurring him forward as if he drank a pot of coffee. He rummaged through the shelves, box after box, stopping to handle a plush doll he imagined Marie toted around when she was Grady's age. Why had she and her siblings grown up here, and Grady and Tommy lived offsite? He dropped the plushie where he found it and locked the container. After fifteen minutes, he chanced a final search. Amid heaps of discarded electronics, he found a pair of blue walkie-talkies.

He tapped one of the bulky plastic antennas against his chin. Warnings regarding their use seemed relatively innocuous. Worst case, a ghastly voice responded, and he'd dump the radios back into storage. Maybe he'd stumble on an Aware spirit. Any help was welcome, even from the other side. He might have tried them out here, but he didn't want Marie fretting over his tardiness, especially tonight.

He left the room with his goods, keeping them hidden behind crossed arms until he opened his bedroom door.

Marie sat cross-legged atop the comforter, wearing her loosest pajama pants and tightest tank top, a weird and yet entirely her outfit. She lifted her head. Cheeks more flushed and eyes more irritated than he'd hoped, but she giggled when she spotted what he held.

"What are you doing with those?" she asked.

"Honestly, I have no idea. Searching for answers, I guess."

"You always have to be doing something, don't you?" With a tilt of her head and a wiggle of her eyebrows, she invited him to sit beside her.

"Guilty as charged." Which summoned an image of his father-in-law, and the baseless suspicions surrounding his potentially devilish deeds. Was the problem with Garrett, rather than Mr. Renault? A Hider slowly taking over? But Claude's embezzlement proved his dreams true, didn't it? Perhaps Mr. Renault's betrayal lay in the past too.

More giggling pulled him from his rumination. "Wakey wakey, Gare."

Grinning, he shook the walkie-talkies beside his head and then deposited them on the dresser before joining her.

"Claude and Julie used to make me and Derrick talk to spirits on those. We'd spend hours surfing channels until we found one scary enough to make us scream."

"He mentioned that."

"Yeah . . ." she drifted into silence. Their hands inched toward one another, forming a stack of knuckles, fingers, and lifelines. "I feel bad for him. But you don't need to hear my sappy stories."

"I want to. Tell me. I'm here for you, remember?"

She smiled, then eased into regaling him with tales of their youth. Her redness faded as they spoke deep into the night.

25. Breakfast

Within a scant few bites of breakfast, chaos descended on the quartet seated at the dining room table.

It started with a steady thump on the tabletop. Double doors leading to the sitting room glided open, then slammed shut. Julie swiveled her head, eyes tracking an unseen actor to the kitchen. A violent force thrust open the door, rattling the frame and briefly revealing tiled floors. Across from Julie, Mr. Renault rubbed his arms as if caught in a snowstorm. Marie's hand went rigid, her plastic fork holding hash browns over a paper plate.

Garrett's attempt to cook had spun into a wretched affair. Fatigue made it difficult to care.

These were the sounds of normalcy, of everyday life in the week since Nia's funeral. Between watching for signs of betrayal from Mr. Renault and the ongoing bustle of haunted activities, occurrences that didn't directly threaten his or Marie's safety melded into background noise like the tweets of a bird—a sound he sorely missed.

"Guess the ghosts are hungry too." Garrett failed to lighten the mood.

Marie forced a faint smile. Julie and her father continued as if they hadn't heard, she studying the kitchen door and he shivering with diminishing tremors.

Bags weighed down the foursome's eyes, drooping ever further with each incident. Garrett would have put aside his mistrust of Claude for one of his jokes. Not that Julie would've agreed to breakfast had her brother joined.

The spectral earthquake subsided, leaving only a faint patter on the backyard French Doors. A shrill scratch on a random windowpane occasionally joined in.

Mr. Renault gave a final shiver and nestled into his seat. "Nice to feel a friendly touch." After his first bite of eggs, his head bobbed appreciatively. "Ya use soy sauce?"

A friendly touch?

The transition threw Garrett off guard. "Uh, yeah. My mom cooked them that way, and the green onions were on their way out." He pointed between the three doors. "Do you know who was just here?"

"It's good. Ah'm getting chili powder too. Can't wait to cook for real again."

"Right. Chili powder. What about the—" Garrett stopped at Mr. Renault's raised finger, waiting for him to swallow his food. He ate more than the other three combined.

"It's tha' couple who introduced themselves the day we met. I think they'll try to make a home of the estate. It won't work of course, but it's comforting tha' some ghosts strive for settling here rather than trying to tear us apart."

"Does that mean you can Feel again?" The implication hinted at the first bit of good news in ages. Tempering his excitement, Garrett spun his coffee in a wheat straw mug. He'd never heard of the material before, but it didn't melt and more importantly, didn't break. "And Julie, did you See them?"

She looked out from the corners of her eyes, gave the slightest of nods. Her brownish eggs remained as perfectly plated as when Garrett set them before her.

"Isn't that good?"

"It is," Mr. Renault said.

The ominous silence left Garrett yearning for the familiarity of the spirit couple trouncing through the room. He clamped onto his mug.

Marie placed her fork across the top of her plate and rubbed the base of her neck. "What's going on?"

Julie snorted once, then again, devolving into a cackle as she leaned forward. She intertwined her fingers on the table's edge. Garrett pulled back. "Dad's apathetic for the same reason as me. He Felt something when Nia died."

Mr. Renault stopped chewing and narrowed his eyes.

Marie raised her hand to her face, warding off tears as she struggled to keep her head held high. Bouncing back from Nia's death proved more difficult for her than from her grandfather's. Garrett placed his hand on her knee. Her hand fell on top of his.

"The spirits that stopped you from reaching Nia," Mr. Renault said. "You Saw them."

She answered him with a look.

He interpreted it as only a father could. "Why didn't ya say so earlier?"

"Why didn't you?"

"Derrick and Grady take precedence. We didn't have time to indulge in theories."

"But now we do."

Mr. Renault tapped the walnut table.

Julie nudged him along. "Spit it out, Dad."

He cleared his throat, locking onto his eldest daughter. "In the hallway, multiple spirits brushed by me. Some heading into Derrick and Nia's room. Some heading away. But inside the room itself"—he shook his head—"nothin'."

Julie crossed her arms, her eyes wandering the room. Then she gave a knowing huff. "As if protected."

"Yes, but from what cause?"

Julie's raised an eyebrow. "Really? You don't have any ideas?"

Spirits stalled his response. The table shifted beneath and drove itself into the wall. Friction singed Garrett's forearm. Marie yelped.

Plates moved with the table. His collided with his arm, flipping food into the air, peppering the tabletop with his wasted efforts. The table leg at the end yanked two empty chairs toward him. The closest lifted up, struck him square on the thigh, and launched him at Marie. He caught himself between the back of her chair and the table's edge.

Plastic cups and paper mugs crashed down, spraying water and coffee over the surface. A muddy pool dripped onto the hardwood below. Four plastic forks levitated and shot off to the room's corners, falling harmlessly to the floor.

Julie scrambled to standing. She put her hand out for a cursory check on everyone. Marie gave a tepid thumbs up.

Garrett winced, then did likewise. His fatigue vanished, his fight-or-flight response activating at last.

Mr. Renault sneered in the direction of the dented wall. "Be right back." He stormed off, disappearing into the kitchen. The door slammed shut behind him as a noise rattled behind Julie.

The massive corner hutch—wider than the room's double door frame—shifted and quaked, preparing to topple. Julie sprung over, and Garrett jumped up to help. The middle of his thigh seized, the earlier collision deadening his muscles. He hopped the rest of the way, arriving just quickly enough to steady the furniture.

Ethereal forces writhed to free themselves from their combined grasp. Hand towels slid off the shelves. Harmless knickknacks bounced off the defending pair. Marie joined the effort, pushing against what surface area remained.

From the kitchen, metal clanged against metal and thudded against wood.

"It's me. Jus' me," Mr. Renault asserted. "Let me out." After a final bang, the kitchen's barrage ceased. The door clicked open, and he emerged with a determined look.

The hutch rocked once more, then abandoned its violent rumblings. Nonetheless, the trio held firm until Mr. Renault plopped a handful of damp towels onto the table.

Julie eased off her post. "What did you do?"

"Nothin'." Mr. Renault wiped the table and piled the remnants of breakfast together.

"Then why did you go into the kitchen?"

"Wanted to check if I could Feel the couple in there."

"And?"

His answer: a single, solitary nod.

"Ah." As if that adequately explained his behavior, Julie grabbed the two towels left on the hutch's shelves. She joined her father cleaning the table while Garrett and Marie shared a look.

He pursed his lips. She shrugged and followed her sister.

What did Feeling ghosts in another room matter for the haunting in this one? A voice in Garrett's head decried betrayal, but that didn't make sense either. Julie accepted the explanation for a logical reason. Anything else, she'd throw a fit over.

"What am I missing?" Garrett asked.

Marie collapsed into a chair at the table's end and started scooting food onto a plate.

Julie dried up the wet streaks left by her father. "The obvious, apparently. Maybe helping instead of holding onto that hutch will shake something loose."

Obvious? Hardly. Garrett pushed himself off the furniture. Phantom needles pricked his thigh, but remnant adrenaline dulled the pain. He willed himself forward, inspecting the damage. Chairs out of place, a table-edged dent in the wall, plasticware and food chunks on the floor. He followed Marie's lead, picking up a plate off the ground and filling it with trash at the speed of a recovering hip surgery patient. Why was Julie making him work for an answer he clearly didn't have?

Marie piped up. "Mekari are working together to block your abilities."

"Finally," Julie said.

Lack of sleep was hitting Garrett hard. He couldn't explain Marie's leap of logic. He chewed his lip and resigned himself to listening.

"Why not just tell us?" Marie asked.

"What use are you if you can't think on your own?"

"Julie," Mr. Renault and Marie said in unison, their tones mismatched. Him, admonishing. Her, despondent.

Marie set her plate on the table.

"I can't be the only one thinking of solutions." Julie tossed the rag away. "That's how we die. Everyone needs to pull their weight or—" She huffed, presumably under the brunt of the room's collective scrutiny. "Fine. I thought my Sight returning on the day Nia died was an aberration. A temporary lapse from our enemies. Given how many ghosts I've seen recently, it's clear that's not the case. But my Sight is useless. All I see are relatively benign spirits like these quakers and shakers. I'd wager Dad's Feeling is the same."

He gestured for her to continue.

"I'm overloaded with noise. Between spirits, the constant riffraff, and bothersome nightmares, I can only assume our enemies want to wear us out until we can't fight back." Her face also seemed to suggest, *If the Breach lasts as long as normal, it might work.*

Garrett abandoned his floor cleanup a couple of eggs short. He hurried to Marie's side, ignoring his leg's wailing. He rubbed her shoulder, briefly sparking life before her crestfallen mask returned. "How do you get mekari blocking your abilities out of that?"

Julie's lips sputtered. She massaged her forehead with the base of her wrist. "I thought you knew by now. You've had since that day in the library to figure it out. Do you know how many times an Overseer has lost an ability like ours?" She motioned at her dad.

"Never?" Garrett answered. No books he'd read mentioned it.

"Never. And do you remember how long it's been since a Hellspot has dealt with more than two mekari?"

That side note on the day she discovered Claude's treachery crawled back to him. "A hundred years."

"Over a hundred years." Julie crept toward him until only a chair separated them. "You were there the moment Nia passed. You saw the aftermath of the carefully choreographed assault. You heard the children's baffled account. You've experienced dozens of hauntings this Breach, and I know damn well none of them compared to the horrors Nia faced in her final moments. So, how many spirits do you think it took to orchestrate Nia's murder?"

"I don't know." He stifled a yawn, exhausted.

Julie slammed her hands on the table. "Am I boring you?"

"No, I'm—"

"Jules, we're all tired," Marie said. "The ghosts are wearing us out. You said it yourself. I haven't thought of half of what you've said. I took a stab at your theory and hit it because of dumb luck. After twenty-six years, I didn't know what to guess, but I had a lot I ruled out. There's no way Gare could've figured it out, and you would know that. Is it possible a Feeder is trying—"

"A Feeder? Wouldn't that be convenient? Let's blame the ghosts for everyone slacking off! Derrick and Nia were onto something, and now he's—" Angry facial twitches replaced whatever she might have said.

"It's also only a theory," Mr. Renault said. "There're other possibilities."

"Other possibilities?" she spat. "Yeah, sure. Winning the lottery is possible. God is possible. I'm wrong but dammit, nothing else makes sense. There must've been a couple dozen spirits in Nia's room. She didn't have a chance. She was too fucking smart to decide she needed a look-see out her bedroom window with every other warning sign the kids reported. Up until then, spirits have struck us with potshots, yet I couldn't See anything. If mekari are leading the majority of haunts, each one must only be able to direct a small number of spirits. With how many struck at Nia, they must've needed several in her room at once. That would've left the rest of the house clear of mekari, which is how Dad Felt and I Saw ghosts damn near everywhere else."

Mekari are blocking their abilities? Jolted by at last understanding, Garrett's fatigue eased up. "If all of that is true, what can we do about it?"

"I don't know every damn answer. Marie's over here throwing out guesses, her husband acts like he skipped college instead of attending Harvard, yet you two are the only ones trying. Even Dad's only good for the occasional quip now. Use your collective brainpower and come up with your own theory. Then, we'll talk." She flicked her wrist and marched toward the sitting room. "Y'all are nearly done with clean up. You can deal with it without me—for once." She exited the room with a slamming of doors that rivaled the ghosts.

One benefit to perpetual tiredness was an inability to feel the impact of Julie's chiding. Instead, his brain replayed key quotes from her tirade, focusing on one: Nia never had a chance. So why wouldn't the ghosts just repeat that strategy until they'd taken them all?

Warmth spread over Garrett's hand. He startled, almost twisted away until he recognized Marie's touch. With her chin level, she batted her eyelashes, asking without words that they finish cleaning up and leave. Her sister's words had done more harm to her than him.

"You two go." Mr. Renault had read the same message as Garrett. "Ah'll finish up."

"You'll be okay alone, right?" Marie asked.

"I will, precisely because Ah'm not alone. Tha' couple's back to keep me comfy. Little chilly, but warmer than Feeling nothin' at all."

Marie stood up, kissed her father on the cheek for all the good it did, then joined Garrett. He limped alongside her toward their bedroom without sharing a word. The silence suited Garrett, allowing him to indulge in his thoughts. Injury aside, he felt revitalized, though not for an ideal reason. Suspicion had wormed its way into him again. This time, the target was Julie.

Maybe Claude was right: that a Hider had snuck into her, using her to cast derision in an attempt to split the family apart. Her mannerisms *had* seemed strange, almost forced. Like she acted with an ulterior motive. She provided enough information to cause concern, yet failed to acknowledge the clear bright side—she could See and Mr. Renault could Feel again. That revelation likely meant the attack on Nia took a lot out of the mekari, the spirits, or both. Why lash out at her family for not reading her mind when there was a silver lining?

Her outburst, coupled with missing pages Garrett had found for two books, gave him a destination as soon as Marie was ready: the library, to investigate if Julie was hiding something.

26. Investigation

Marie slumped her head into her palm, her elbow propped up on a small desk near the library's inset bookshelves. Navy-colored spines filled the space behind her. She turned the page of the book below her like a rebellious student obliging her teacher. Three more tomes with differently colored covers sat stacked nearby. "Can we go yet?"

"You promised." Garrett pouted, standing at the room's center near one of its large tables. Truthfully, half an afternoon in the library was longer than he had expected her to last. After hours of consolation following Julie's outburst, Marie had perked back up to her usual self. To reward his patience and comfort him over his ruined breakfast, she offered him a deal. They'd go wherever he wanted, do whatever he wanted, as long as it was just them.

She probably hadn't expected him to pick reading in the library.

"It's a nice day," she said. "Let's go outside."

"It's the same as the others." He skimmed the last and first sentences of several successive pages. Nothing was missing or torn out. Searching for nonsequential pages instead of reading would've saved time, but he worried they'd miss something leafing through. Plus, some books didn't number pages, rendering the strategy moot.

"It's warmer though. Great for sunbathing without getting burned. Supernatural cloud covering has its perks."

"Guess so."

"You like it when I wear a bikini, don't you?"

Garrett chuckled, glancing up to visualize the outfit. He savored the image for a moment, then dismissed it. "There's no pool. What are you going to do? Have me hose you down?"

"If you want, but there's a blow-up kiddie pool in storage. Big enough for two adults to lay down comfortably and share a couple beverages."

"What kind of beverages?"

Marie's mischievous grin clarified her intent. Even if he stuck to virgin sodas, the shift in setting made a tempting offer.

"What if we stop after we find one more book?"

"With a missing page?"

He nodded. He had four now, three he'd found and one from Marie. They seemed related enough to suggest at least one more existed. A fifth book might clear up exactly what they held in common.

"Why don't you ask Julie?" She wagged a pinched page side to side. "She must have every book memorized."

Which was precisely why he didn't. Julie's knowledge of the library meant she knew what the missing pages referenced. If she was innocent then all he lost was time, a resource he counted more as an enemy than a friend here. But if the crime was more sinister and he played his hand early, she could render the mystery permanently unsolvable.

He couldn't admit any of this to Julie's adoring sister. Not without evidence.

"That sounds like cheating." He hoped he sounded convincing.

Creases formed between Marie's eyes and nose, drawing her upper lip along with them. Her scrunched-up face almost incited a nervous laughter. He held strong long enough for her to sigh. "Fine. One more book."

"One more *with a missing page.*"

"You. Are. The. Worst." But she smiled as she returned to reading.

Once again, the sounds of pages turning and hardbacks plopping onto tables occupied the room. He read as fast as his tired mind allowed. It wasn't just Marie impacting his timer. Julie had been speaking with Kelly when Garrett came downstairs, and their conversation was running well past their usual length. Ghosts and mekari also granted an atypical reprieve.

They were on borrowed time.

With each chapter, his focus diminished despite the invisible clock whipping his back. He chewed his lips, Nia's fate conquering his thoughts, a fate that could have befallen any of them.

His breathing grew labored, his stomach distended with a heaping of anxiety. Words below blurred into a blob of unfocused ink. He stared at the pages and saw nothing but the scene replaying in his mind: entering Nia's room, seeing her lying on the floor, Derrick's blood-soaked shirt pressed against her neck.

He cleared his throat, rubbed his eyes.

Marie looked up with a concerned face.

"Sorry." He redirected his attention to the pristine sheets of paper between his fingers.

Seven books later, he found his next clue. A fifth missing page which cemented the topic in question. All of them dealt with the tie between mekari and ESP that manifested in long-term Hellspot dwellers. The next question: if Julie was responsible for the missing pages, then why? What topic merited enough worth to desecrate her sacred books?

"Did you find something?" The rise in Marie's tone belied her hope.

He considered lying, buying more time to find the link. He had promised though, and a short break might spark something. "I did. Let's put the others back, and we can indulge in those adult beverages of yours."

"The work never ends." She shook a fist at the ceiling in a mock display of anger. Then she slid out of her seat and started shelving books with twice the energy she spent reading them.

He chuckled and matched her pace, all the while mulling over the books' links to each other. There was still the risk of Julie walking in on them or a spirit stealing his evidence. The sooner he figured out why those pages were torn out, the better. As they left the room, Garrett used one hand to brace the books against his hip and held Marie with the other.

Halfway through the hallway, they slowed as footsteps descended from the stairs into the foyer. They peeked around the corner. At the sight of the source, tension eased in their grips.

Derrick turned halfway toward the sitting room before he noticed them. If he had slept at all the past several nights, it didn't help. He looked a decade older.

"Hey," he said, listless.

Marie slipped from Garrett darted right at Derrick, her arms open wide. Her cousin pursed his lips as she wrapped herself around him. He stiffened, mildly patted her on the shoulder. Said something with three syllables, maybe an, *I'm sorry*, then backed away.

Derrick pointed a thumb at his original destination. "Good to see y'all. Just getting something for my mom. Not really in a talking mood."

"Of course," Marie said, dejected.

"We get it," Garrett added.

Derrick continued on, head slumped and shoulders hunched.

When he moved out of sight, Garrett came up behind his wife and rubbed the small of her back. "He'll be okay in time."

"Yeah." Her tone suggested she didn't believe him.

Garrett did though. He couldn't guess how long he'd take to recover if a similar tragedy befell Marie, but he'd need more than a week. Derrick confining himself to his room likely exacerbated his pain. Who knew what additional horrors the spirits inflicted on him? But that was up to him, and the fact he moved at all counted for something. Marie's bleeding heart didn't need to take on unnecessary responsibilities.

"Come on," Garrett said. "Up to the room and out to the pool." He directed her forward with his fingertips. She obliged with the meekest of walks, like a prisoner condemned to death.

"He was like this before," she whispered. "Avoiding me when we were teens. Like I was diseased. He never did it as a kid. I'm worried he'll be like this forever without Nia. I'm worried about what he sees when he looks at me."

"What do you think he sees?"

"I don't know, but she made it better."

Garrett embraced Marie, giving her his best public snuggle.

In the back of his mind, an idle feeling resonated: she did know what he saw in her and couldn't bring herself to admit it. To herself though? Or to Garrett?

He hung onto this new suspicion until the weight of tears burdened his cheeks. To lose trust in Marie was to lose himself. By the end, he was embracing her for his comfort as much as her own.

27. Epiphany

True dusk came at its usual time, relieving the day's orange haze with a blanket of navy blue. Underneath the darkened skies, Marie shifted in the blowup pool, lapping water against Garrett's chest. Tucked away near the side of the house, he yearned to indulge in the quiet reprieve as she had. Her sleek bikini made a convincing argument to lower his guard, and she swung her legs onto his lap for good measure.

He stroked her hairless leg—the wonders of Nair replacing shaving during the Breach—and briefly succumbed to the distraction. In and out of clothes, whatever she wore or didn't, she never ceased to mesmerize him. He started to assess his own shape, softening without his normal workout routine. That's when he noticed the rings from his incendiary nightmare had faded sometime between Nia's funeral and today.

He pulled away from Marie and reached out of the pool for his tumbler of melted ice and coconut-flavored sparkling water. "You're not worried about something attacking us? Pushing our heads underwater and drowning us? It's been too quiet outside."

"Gare, I've got you. I may act like I'm on a beach, but I'm always listening. Relax, and let your wife take care of you, like you took care of her when she needed it." She slurped at her second piña colada. "I was thinking when we make it out of here, we take a camping trip somewhere fun like the Rocky Mountains."

"I'd like that." Instead of giving reasons to say no—like getting back into school—Garrett tried to absorb Marie's positivity, talking about camping like their survival was a foregone conclusion. He massaged her two toes resting against his ribs. Her fair skin glimmered under the approaching moonlight. He leaned back and let his bent legs relax. His shin brushed Marie's hip as he stretched from rim to rim.

Trust issues of Marie's family aside, they seemed right about one thing. Ghosts and mekari needed time to recharge after their attack. What else explained this respite? He closed his eyes, taking solace in that logic. Rippling water serenaded him, stripping the Renaults and all else from his thoughts.

Blackness exploded into vivid imagery. Maurice's and Nia's final moments. Buzzsaws chasing him. Ruined breakfasts and other meals. Dreams incinerating his clothes. Altercations between siblings.

His knees jutted upward, piercing the pool's surface. Marie gently pressed against his shin. Her calming, soft touch erased the horrifying images, and he sank again. Sank toward oblivion, drifting in the water until an insatiable need pulled him back. He slitted his eyelids, spying Marie and grounding himself in reality. In balancing vigilance and relaxation, genuine peace found him at last.

An epiphany quickly followed.

Water slopped as he sat up bolt upright. Tangerine-sleeved books burned in his mind. "I think that does it for me."

"Aw. There's still some daylight."

"I know. Sorry."

"That's okay. You lasted longer than I thought. We should do this again."

"I'd like that." What would it cost them though? Marie didn't seem to consider that.

"And maybe next time, I'll get you to try one of these." She raised her tropical beverage. "It's really good." And downed the last bit as if to prove it.

"You know me. Probably none until after the Breach. I don't like celebrating until after a win." He set his water in the grass and pushed himself up. One foot after the other, he stepped out of the pool. He grabbed a towel from the chair they had brought from the porch.

Marie jumped out after him and rushed over for a great big hug in her dripping two-piece.

His towel was soaked, and he not any drier. "Thanks for that."

"That's what you get. Bet you wish you had a nice dry towel." She snatched the other one and pranced out of his reach. She shimmied the towel across her backside.

He grinned and made do, drying himself off at half her speed.

Would her playful attitude remain after he accused her sister of lying? Would Julie admit to what she'd done to the missing book from the top shelf—occupied by a hole she glanced at whenever she left the room? He didn't know, but he had to make sure he had his facts straight before confronting her.

"I love you," Garrett said.

"I love you too." Marie scrubbed her face. "Going back to the library?"

"I am."

"Want some company?"

"As long as it's you. Don't suppose you can guarantee privacy from otherworldly guests?" *Or from your family.*

"If I could do that"—she shook her head, her tone falling from jovial to grave—"we'd be a lot better off." Out of the water and into the night, even Marie couldn't deny their gloomy reality. Garrett drifted over to wrap his arm around her. She slid hers across his lower back, and both straightened with renewed confidence. Huddled together, they contented themselves in each other's company as they walked through the sunroom and up to their bedroom.

After showering, and a gentle kiss that might have turned into something more if not for Garrett's determination, they returned to the library. He carried the five books with their missing pages, hoping to find one more that confirmed his theory. Hoping to also find privacy.

Disappointment answered instead.

Julie wandered between shelves, her fingertips dancing between book covers. She slid a navy-sleeved book from the shelf and pretended not to notice them. After closing and locking the plexiglass doors, she returned to her large table with her prize.

"Hello." She opened her book to an early page.

"Hey, Jules." Marie leaned against the nearest shelf. "What're you up to?"

"Research, as always. What are *you* up to?"

"Garrett's . . ." She raised her brow at him, silently asking to discuss the missing pages. He glowered. "Onto something big."

"Oh?" Julie looked up.

"I think so," he said. "Hoping to find it tonight."

"What is *it?*"

A pit in his stomach sprouted vines and seized his torso, splintering his sides with stitches. Julie's imposing presence stifled his confidence. "I don't quite know yet. It's like a jigsaw puzzle missing too many pieces to see the bigger picture."

"And what? You thought Marie would help you find it? She's already itching to leave."

"Moral support!" Marie retorted. After a moment, she added, "Are you angry? What's wrong?"

"Nothing."

"We can come back another time."

"No, this is as good of a time as any." Julie huffed, staring off to the side until she continued. "I wanted to apologize for how I acted after breakfast. Marie, you were right about the Feeder. I was seething when I left the room. I made it worse by storming off. Another Feeder latched on as the other faded, and the cycle started all again. Took the whole afternoon and wearing Kelly's patience thin before I settled down. I should have apologized sooner, but I'm so busy . . ." She seemed to consider saying more. Marie approached her in those silent moments. As she stepped within arm's reach, Julie ended, "I'm sorry."

Marie hugged her sister. "That's okay, Jules. I knew that wasn't you. Whatever you need, I'm here to help. We both are."

"Thanks. For now, just"—Julie directed her sister back to her table with Garrett—"be quiet in here."

Marie bit her lip, assessing her sister with concerned eyes. She gave a defeated shrug and plopped onto her same seat from earlier this afternoon.

Apology or not, Garrett needed to explore his theory to its end. He focused on a particular shelf, the one which way up high held the empty space Julie gave too much attention. Tangerine-sleeved books took up nearly two full shelves below and beside the spot. All of them dealt with the same general topic: direct interactions between mekari and humans, the only topic the books with the missing pages had in common. Garrett sought a specific link between developed ESP, such as Julie's Seeing, and mekari. He jumped as a book two feet away pounded the plexiglass barrier, then slammed itself back into place.

Julie grumbled. "Really?"

"That wasn't me," Garrett said.

She didn't answer.

Garrett moved toward the book to examine the title. *Transference: Sibling Shared Senses.* Not quite his target, but interesting enough. He pressed up, in, up on the door's underside lock, then pulled the handle. He tilted the book toward him, held it in place for a moment before taking it.

Help from the other side? he wondered. That might've explained their calm poolcation.

He locked the door and pulled up a seat opposite Marie, offering her a goofy smile to compensate for his boring research.

No sooner had he opened the cover than another book beat against its prison from the far corner. It rammed itself back into place. Was he meant to take that book too? Garrett slapped his cheek, trying to focus. He skimmed the pages, fingers flipping through them as fast as his summarizing eyes allowed. At the onset of the second chapter, a book on an emptier shelf thrashed against its neighbors for several seconds before abating. The Renault sisters' heads tilted up, then fell back to neutral. He resumed reading about siblings whose talents worked in tandem.

Later chapters detailed one sibling's talents ceasing as the other's activated. Following that were talents first strengthened by a sibling's presence, then weakened by it. Each topic veered him further from his goal. Hope in finding a clue about the missing pages waned, as did his confidence in having found a ghostly ally.

Just a prank to keep me busy. But he pressed on. Almost ripped out a page himself as the storm of books surged. Several rattled the shelves, rumbling to strike their prison doors in unison like a well-timed battering ram.

Garrett's breath hitched. He scanned the room to reassure himself no books had broken free. *I'm close. That's why they want me to leave. If it's not this book, it's the next. Or the next.*

"Billy," Julie said, "is that you?"

Her library ghost. If he was indeed responsible, he gave no affirmation. The torrent of chaos continued.

"Can you See?" Marie asked.

Julie shook her head methodically.

"Should we go?" Marie asked. Loud enough for her sister to hear, but her touch signaled she meant the question for him.

Garrett reassured her with the feigned confidence of a caress, avoiding her eyes that might convince him to leave. Then he withdrew and read on. Shelves creaked from the efforts of their inhabitants. He skimmed the text faster, bypassing any page that failed to mention mekari.

An entire shelf of books shifted in unison, near the same corner as before.

Julie slammed her hand on the table, its density deadening the blow. "Stop it!"

Marie crunched Garrett's fingers.

Inconsequential topics blurred by. Unusual sibling relationships— forcefully dominant, woefully submissive, and everything in between. Volatile behavior with one's family that never showed elsewhere. Talents empowered by flaws detailed in prior chapters.

The library's now familiar sound played like a symphony with erratic intermissions. Gameday-like anxiety invigorated him, spurred him on. He fell in with the song, turned two pages to every supernatural book slam. When the tune stopped, he slowed.

Julie grumbled, flipping pages as she joined the chaotic chorus.

Marie placed her other hand on top of Garrett's, the simple act inviting him to do the same.

He couldn't. He was so close, driven by reckless faith. The first domino which fell in this barrage wasn't an accident. It was targeted. His persistence yielded another miss: chapters on the manifestation of talents due to sibling rivalries. He flipped several dozen more pages, potential success eroding to the tune of angry books. His limbs yearned to fling themselves about. Where was the answer?

Nearing defeat, one flip of a page revitalized him.

"That's it," he said. The next page was torn out. The chapter covered internal strengths and defects: primarily related to cardiovascular health, gastrointestinal regularity, and fertility. Like the other missing pages, the surrounding text prominently mentioned mekari. This time, the text specifically mentioned another book's name.

Or would have if not for the torn page. The sentence which started, *Relationships between these phenomena and mekari are under peer review at the time of this writing, but can be read about in more detail—*, flowed into an unrelated sentence. He opened the five other books to their marked pages. He couldn't say for sure, but two seemed to reference a book as well. He knew the answer: the tangerine-sleeved text missing from way above his head.

"What is it?" Marie asked.

"I'm sorry," Garrett said. In a relaxed setting, this would be a trying endeavor. Set to the backdrop of dancing books and Julie's recent apology, a piece of him cried out to try another time.

"About?"

"The pages. And Julie." What if he was wrong? With so much on the line, rewards merited the risk.

Partial realization dawned on Marie, and she gasped. "Later."

Acting later was not what Julie would have done. Not what she did when she confronted Claude. He shook his head, committing to the gamble.

"Julie, I need to ask you something."

"Please do," she said. "It's not like I can concentrate anyway."

"Why is there a page missing from each of these six books?"

Resistance pulled on him as he rose. He gave one gentle tug, and Marie's grasp slipped.

Julie waited expectantly while he gathered his evidence. He brought them to her, risked placing himself within reach of her. He removed the covers and read the names of three titles before she stopped him.

"I'm capable of reading, thank you." She pushed the texts away. "What do they mean?"

His lips and limbs froze up. This was him, inserting himself into his new family's affairs. This was him, attacking the brain of their resistance. This *was* him, wasn't it?

"The missing pages all reference a particular book." He spoke slowly to ward off a frightful stutter.

"How do you know? They're *missing*."

"Because it explains the empty shelf space up there." Garrett pointed to the spot.

Julie crossed her arms, didn't follow his finger. "So, explain it."

He opened the first book to a bookmarked page and scooted it to the neutral area between them. "Each book covers the same topics in the pages surrounding the one that's missing. They theorize or detail the link between mekari and humans in regards to extrasensory abilities. Like your Seeing." He opened and pushed the second book forward, eliciting no acknowledgment from Julie but drawing Marie toward them. "Which deviates from the idea that these abilities are strictly tied to the Hellspot. Mekari also play a role."

Marie stopped at the tableside opposite Julie. She leaned over, clutching the edge.

Garrett added a third book to the row. Julie had yet to touch them. Was she even listening? "These clearly point to a book for more information on the same topic."

"Theories," Julie said. "Just theories, but let's say they're true. What makes you think the missing pages all reference the same book?"

"Similar subject matter. It's not definitive, but what else would be worth tearing out six random pages from six random books? A reference to a seventh," he said, "missing like the books Claude found buried in the backyard."

"So what? You're suggesting I tore out these pages? Buried those books?"

He hadn't considered that last one yet. "I think you know what—" He broke off to search the room.

"What now?" Julie snapped.

"The spirits. They stopped."

"Yes, ever since you brought me your monumental discovery." Biting sarcasm oozed out. "You're late to the party, but at least that's a legitimate observation." She was hiding something—no surprise. The question was what?

Garrett tapped the three remaining closed covers.

"Julie," Marie said. Despite her quiet voice, her interruption commanded their attention. "We've never been good at hiding things from each other. Tell us what you know. If you did something you regret, nobody'll blame you. We know how rough this house is, but we're all on the same side, right?"

"How nice of you," Julie started, taking a moment. An apathetic coldness blanketed her, as if her sister's blind faith in her had solely fueled the warmth of her humanity. "How nice of you to absolve me. Will you forgive Claude too? Did you know he's been pilfering the house funds?"

"What?" Marie reeled back, her palms barely touching the table now. "He wouldn't."

"Ask your husband. He was there when Claude admitted it."

After a deep inhale with his eyes closed, Garrett admitted the accusation with an inclined head. He could lie, say it slipped his mind with everything that happened, but how would that help? "Sorry for not telling you. I didn't feel it was my place."

"Okay, Gare," she said. "Apology accepted." Her sad forgiveness struck worse than an angry diatribe.

"That's it?" Julie spat. "Why aren't you angrier? We're supposed to look out for one another."

"Then tell us what you know!"

"I don't know anything that'll help. You say you know me, but you didn't have a clue what your own brother and husband were hiding. What does that say?" She backhanded the air. Marie paled under the verbal assault. "He doesn't know what he's talking about, and neither do you. It's a waste of my time. You're both wasting my time and getting in my way."

Marie slunk from the table, cradling her stomach. "I," she said, "think I need a break. I'll be in our room, Gare." Shoulders hunched, she trudged out like an admonished puppy.

Garrett's tongue worked the inside of his mouth, prepping to lash out, the faint whisper of logic his only restraint. He needed Julie. They all did, even as her secrets splintered them further apart. He didn't buy her defense for a second though. Sure, her responses manicured a convincing facade, but an unplaceable detail called her consistency into question. It was as if a Hider was inside of her. Could he catch her in a lie if so?

Marie's steps faded into the hallway, and the echoes diverted his thoughts. Intending to follow her out, Garrett reached for the three books in front of Julie.

She seized his wrist. "I have words for you."

"I have some for you too." Garrett wrenched free of her grasp and pulled the books in. "I'll keep them to myself though. You've made it clear we're a nuisance, and I have more important matters to attend to." He stacked the books and carried them off. He made it a few steps before Julie whispered in a tone he never expected: one of regret, more earnest than her earlier apology.

"I burned it."

"What?" He turned back.

"The missing book."

"Why?" He set the books down.

"I don't know." She clasped her hands atop the table. Deference replaced defiance.

"What was it?"

"I don't know."

"You just admitted," his near-yelling quieted by Julie pressing her forefinger to her lips. "Admitted to burning a book. How could you not know anything?"

"I could know. If I think hard enough, I'll remember. That's the problem. You coming at me like this, trying to spark an idea I've long since buried, risks everything." Julie loosely balled her fist, running her thumb back and forth across her knuckles. "When you got into specifics earlier, I had to tune you out. If I theorize why a thing is the way it is too long, I get this insatiable compulsion. I rip out pages and burn books like I want to eradicate truth itself. I've done it before, and not just with these books. There are a dozen others."

Her thumb ceased moving, and she balled her fist tight. "I can't stop it. I can't help it. All I can do is stop myself from pursuing anything beyond general knowledge and topics I know are safe. So, I don't know because that knowledge would make me push this family closer to the brink than I already have."

Garrett soaked in her admission before responding. "How long has this been going on?"

"Years."

Which ruled out possession, unless Hiders or mekari had evolved. Or unless she was lying, he supposed. "Have you told anyone else?"

"Haven't needed to. I found ways to push Derrick and Dad down paths I couldn't walk. I did the same with you. Did you think I kept glancing up at that shelf accidentally?" She waved in the direction of the tangerine-sleeved shelves, but kept her sights trained on Garrett. "I sure didn't do it for my health. My insides knotted with every glance, fearing what I'd remember, fearing what I'd destroy. But it's the most I could do without these"—her brows furrowed as she struggled to say her next word—"cravings taking control. "

"You wanted me to expose you?"

Julie only blinked.

"Then why treat Marie that way? Why lie to her? You have no idea how much she does for this family."

"I have every idea. I also trust she's strong enough to handle what's thrown at her if it helps the family. And I didn't lie to her. I told her I didn't know anything that'll help. If I lied to anyone, it was to you." Julie smirked, but it didn't last.

"Whatever. What's the point of this confession?"

"That's the question I want to answer. But not in front of Marie. You remember my dad's translation of Grandpa's possessed last words?"

He nodded while fidgeting with the sleeve of the stack's bottom book.

"I'm not well-versed in any mekarian language, but I've heard it enough to understand the cadence. I've listened to the raw tape of Dad's recording a few times now. The timing of the events, the pauses, and the words themselves don't add up."

"How do you mean?"

"Something is missing from what he told us."

That pause in his translation. Garrett hadn't imagined it. "Why would he do that?"

"He probably has his reasons, like me."

"Why not tell Marie the truth?"

"Because if she suspects something, he'll know. She sees the best in us all. Normally, that's a positive. In this case, an inability to accept that Dad might've committed a grievous act would complicate the matter." Julie raised her brows, presumably waiting for Garrett to realize the truth of this. To realize that Marie couldn't act the same with such a burden. He nodded his understanding. "We can't have that until we know more. If he has a spirit, or worse, a mekar, inside of him, then we can't tip him off prematurely.

"First, we might make this misinformation work to our advantage. Second, Dad is cryptic to begin with. To catch a lie, we need to be certain, or the Hider will bunker down." She gestured at Garrett. "You've read about Hiders' truths and lies, yes?"

An ironic twist. "Yeah, I know about catching a lie. But how do I know there isn't a Hider or mekar inside of you?"

She chuckled. "I've considered that. Hiders care about one thing— not getting caught. They limit what they say, not put forth truths that complicate the process. And I very much doubt a mekar would try to limit the book burnings."

"There are worse things than burning books."

For a brief moment, Julie's face scrunched up like a child before crying. Then, she pinched her nose bridge near the corners of her eyes and groaned. When her eyes opened, she stared at Garrett, practically spewing flames. "I thought you would get this. Knowledge is our greatest tool. I'm taking all the cannonballs in our little fort and replacing them with feathers. The only worse act is killing everyone, and unless a Shifter has me hallucinating, you're still alive. Compulsion or no, I won't forgive myself for what I did, and I won't forget what I'm capable of. I can't fix this without risking making it worse, but you can. So, what will it be?"

He squeezed the stack's bottom book, his fingertips digging into the edges of the pages. Reassuring as it was to find an ally against Mr. Renault's behavior, Julie's actions gave Garrett's suspicion cause to linger. She claimed uncontrollable compulsions forced her actions, yet she berated Claude a week ago for a more benign crime. She could have also found a simpler way to speak with Garrett than harshly rebuking her sister. "If this translation is the key, why haven't you burned it too?"

Her fiery stare persisted. "I can't tell you because I don't know how the compulsions work, and I'm pretty damned sure if I tried to learn, I'd desecrate an entire shelf of books. My guess is that I only have a copy, and Dad would never part with the original. Or that the source is a tape and not a book. But even then, to be safe, I don't speculate too hard on any one theory. Now, time is at a premium, so I'll ask again: what will it be?" Her harsh enunciation made it clear she had tired of repeating herself.

But one niggling quandary persisted. "I'll help, for Marie's sake if nothing else. But why admit to the book burning and reveal all this to me? Why not just direct me as you said you've done with Derrick and your dad?"

She folded her arms, digging her thumb into her forearm and looking above and beyond Garrett. He knew, straight at the shelf that once housed whatever book she burned. "Secrets eat us alive. I was tired of having my flesh gnawed on."

Secrets. He had the feeling this wasn't the end of them.

28. Excavation

Seated on the bed, legs bouncing, Garrett mulled over whether to wait for Marie or seek her out. When he'd returned to their bedroom, she was gone with no signs of her destination. Opposing his budding fear was the logic of silence. No cries for help, no shouts of alarm. Bedtime came hours ago for most of the house, especially for the children. If they managed to sleep with those grizzly memories in their skulls, he didn't want to wake them by clamoring for Marie. Maybe she'd left to pay respects to her brother again.

He stroked a patch of the plush comforter between his thumb and forefinger, surrendering to its soothing indulgences. He drifted into the void of his subconscious, drifted deep until he slammed into a jagged bar of anxiety. Shifters had blocked Kelly from hearing the attack on Nia. Why not do the same with Marie? And why would she commune with her brother under the cover of darkness? He leapt off the bed, damning the consequences. Her safety trumped her family's tranquility.

As Garrett reached for the door handle, the dresser crackled and stopped him in place. Crackled again. Not the dresser, but the walkie-talkie on top of it. He crept over, pressed the transmitter button. "Hello?" Waited. "Hello?"

No answer. He backpedaled, hand outstretched behind him until he struck the door handle.

Static emanated again, this time covering a faint sound. He raced over to the dresser and grabbed the handheld device. "What do you want?"

Undulating tuning screeched, then sank into a deep bass. He waited for a voice, flipped through nearby channels when none came.

Returned to the original when his exploration didn't pay off. The reverberation continued. He tapped the device and considered walking the halls with it in hand.

Words spoke at last. Unintelligible, but with a clear cadence. Three beats, repeated continuously with a screech in between. He held the walkie-talkie to his ear to sift out the voice. The screech shrieked again. He winced and inched the device away. Static soon faded, rewarding his patience.

A nondescript male spoke as if reading a script. "Suicide. Disown. How." Garrett's heart skipped a beat. No, that wasn't right. Another couple of listens clarified the message. "Outside. Disown. Now." He hovered the walkie-talkie near his ear. Steadied himself to focus on the message. After another series of repeats, he heard it loud and clear.

"Outside. Alone. Now."

He listened once more to confirm.

"Outside. Alone. Now."

Marie. Garrett clipped the walkie-talkie to his back pocket and threw open the door. He sprinted through the hall, his sneakers a drum roll down the stairs. The middle landing's outside window flashed by in a blur. It took until he reached the bottom of the stairs to process he'd seen nothing but darkness out there. As he took his first step into the foyer, he tumbled a few feet down *onto* the foyer.

The steps had moved. A Shifter tried to keep him from Marie.

He'd avoided breaking anything and didn't care about bruises. He jumped up and raced under the breakfast nook arch. Blood throbbing in his ears deafened the radio behind him. He cut hard around the room's round couch and turned into the short hallway. His brain raced to catch his feet. The draw of his racket likely countered orders to come alone. The thought lasted until he hit the sunroom, where his all concerns melded back into one: Marie.

His senses scouted for her in their own way, every ounce of energy devoted to finding her. His eyes scanned beyond the plexiglass windows, then across the entire yard as he stepped into the ominous night. Ears listened for the sweet whisper of her voice. Nostrils sucked in air, hoping for a whiff of her subtle fragrance amid the musky humidity. Bare skin trudged through dense air in search of her touch.

Garrett flipped off the walkie-talkie. He crept forward, acclimating himself to the vast stretch of darkness. Patio lighting sourced his vision. The moon had fled far away. Intentionally timed or specifically manifested, no doubt. These mekari planned tactical strikes like Napoleon Bonaparte. Even the stars absconded the sky, hidden by invisible clouds or yet another inexplicable force.

A deep thump struck the earth as he stepped off the patio stone-work. His legs itched to work, and his concern for Marie demanded it, but his mind cautioned against a reckless advance. He settled on a steady pace.

A dozen steps coincided with a disorienting silence. He wandered blindly into a dreamlike void. He chanced looking down to ensure he still walked on solid ground. Another thump made him jump. His head whipped back up.

Dim motion captured a long stick-like object, attached to a human form, swaying to the side. The stick reached the end of its arc, made a scraping sound, then recentered before the mysterious figure. The object split the earth, and Garrett placed the sound: the shoveling of the dirt.

Nausea comparable to the most vile food poisoning stumbled his step. Marie's lifeless body filled the empty space at the stranger's feet. "What did you do?" he barked.

Thump.

Garrett staggered forward, caught between dashing to her rescue and fleeing from the reality of his greatest horror.

Thump.

When he neared, the corpse of Marie disappeared. He'd only imag-ined it. There was no body at all. Only a mound of dirt. He breathed a quiet sigh, inched deeper into the darkness. Stopped the length of a shovel away from the figure. A thick tree limb hung overhead, twigs nearly brushing against his or her head. Garrett recognized the location and the figure in simultaneous clarity. Maurice Renault lay buried here, and his grandson was digging him up.

Thump.

"Claude, stop."

The shoveling paused, the edge jammed into the ground. He glanced up, then returned to his task.

Garrett skirted a hole several inches deep. He grabbed the shovel's shaft. Claude twisted away, pulling him forward. "What are you doing?"

With a better grip on his shovel, Claude pushed back. "Fixing things."

Garrett stumbled, yanking his shoulder as he tried to hold onto the shovel and failed. He halted his fall with an outstretched arm and landed in a crouched position. "Fixing what?" It made no sense, but Claude hadn't been his usual self since Julie confronted him. Sinking depression might have opened the door for possession. Garrett kept his distance, settling on finding a way to bring him back.

"Our situation." Another thump. "You heard Dad's translation of Grandpa's final words. The mekar said to raise his corpse. That's what I'm doing." He twisted, swinging the shovel with him. Dirt tumbled from its metal blade.

"It's a mekar. They lie."

"If I don't stop, will you fight me?"

"I . . . what? Why?" Garrett stood up, examining the hole. He had time before resorting to anything drastic. By then, reinforcements would arrive.

He froze.

The others should've arrived by now with the ruckus he'd caused. The voice on the walkie-talkie said to come alone. Where was this leading?

"You'd win, I think." Claude brought the shovel near his chest, turning it horizontal. "Even with this. I'd be afraid to use it because what would be the point?"

Garrett's face wrenched in confusion.

"Nia's death is my fault." He rotated the shovel's shaft, over and over. His words poured out like a madman. "Everything Julie accused me of was true. Worse in fact. She missed a smaller account. Like an ass, I betrayed everyone who gives a damn about me. Kelly and I fought after that. She needed some alone time. I did too. I dropped Tommy off with Nia, then came out to have a conversation with Grandpa." He snickered. "A one-way conversation. It didn't help any, but it killed Nia. She was sharp as a tack. Spirits fled her for easy targets like me. With two kids though, two kids she'd already done more than her fair share to watch, it was too much." He heaved a snarling cry. "She died protecting them. I know she did. If I hadn't been trying to treat this Breach as a family vacation, hadn't stolen from them all, she'd still live.

"It helped me see one thing though. We're doomed if we don't do something desperate. I don't trust the mekar, but they're not all bad. Even if this one is, I trust its desire for revenge. When he spoke, he was speaking to me."

"What do you mean?"

"The bringer of the one who doesn't belong, the one who mocks your bindings of blood and oath. I'm glad I wasn't in the room for that. Not sure I could've stopped myself from reacting. When I read the translation . . ." Claude tilted his chin up, facing the second story near where Kelly and Tommy slept. He winced and averted his gaze as if glimpsing the sun. "I'm shooting blanks. Kelly and I agreed to adopt instead. I couldn't risk letting Grady take on the responsibility of the next generation by himself."

"What about those families who adopted—"

Claude planted his shovel in the grass. "The ones who died? Didn't know you knew. Yeah, I thought it was hogwash. A coincidence. I played it careful anyway. Those families adopted older kids, and I've never treated Tommy as anyone other than a blood son. That's why we kept it a secret—that, and I didn't want to disappoint Dad. We lied about Kelly's pregnancy to my family while we worked on adopting Tommy. Made up excuses to keep everyone away from his supposed birth. That's part of where that stolen money went. Healthy newborns are impossible to find without greasing someone's wheels."

A single one of those admissions would have thrown Garrett into a stupor. Hearing them all at once sounded so incredulous his mind refused to process any of it. "Why are you telling me this?"

"We're a month in, and things are already falling apart. I'm throwing everything I've got at you. I can't help anymore but through this." He paused, maybe smiling, maybe frowning. "Please don't tell anyone. Things are bad enough as is with Kelly."

Garrett clutched his beard hairs, pulling the skin near his jawline taut. "If you truly believe that, why stop digging?"

Shadows moved in a way that defined a faint shrug. "Trying to explain my side of it. I don't know what brought you outside, but I guess I'm hoping you go back. Like I told you the day we met, I can't take you. Even if I could, I wouldn't want to hurt you. That defeats the whole purpose of redemption. So, if any of this makes any sense, please go. I won't tell anyone if things go wrong here. Though they can't get much worse." He started flicking the wooden shaft like a ticking time bomb. "That said, if you do try to stop me, I'll resist. You'll have to drag me away and lock me in a room because I have to do something."

Garrett's hand slid from his face. *Claude isn't possessed. He's guilt-ridden. Why did that voice send me here? It must've wanted me to intervene.* Did that mean the fabled good mekar *was* on his side? He gazed back at the house, beacons of rectangular glass catching light between Roman shades and windows. His attention settled on the room he shared with Marie.

Unless this was all a distraction.

"Garrett?" The time bomb slowed but pressed on.

He stepped back, fists clenched. He wanted to run back inside, crying out for Marie.

"You leaving?"

If this was a distraction, it was a good one. He couldn't leave Claude to his task; trusting a mekar would doom them sooner or later. And regardless of Garrett's perception, a Hider could still be pulling the strings. He had to fix this, but how? Fighting took too long. Besides, Garrett didn't want to hurt Claude either.

"Say something."

Garrett turned, considering one other option: reassuring Claude he wasn't the only one guilty of betraying the family. Julie probably wanted her secret revealed to Claude even less than to Marie, but how else could he resolve the situation quickly and peacefully?

"Okay," Garrett said, trying not to rush through this. He committed to taking his first shot without revealing Julie's secret. "I know you feel responsible. You're not. You made mistakes, but one grand sweeping action won't absolve you of that. Putting your faith in a mekar won't either. It'll only put more guilt on your plate."

"I appreciate it, but I've already had this conversation with myself. I'm the only one without the excuse of a Breach to hurt this family."

Garrett grunted. *So be it.* "Julie burned a book between this Breach and the last. She tore out all the pages mentioning it from other books. And she's burned other books before. All not during a Breach."

The flicking of the shaft ceased. "What? Which books?"

"I don't know, but the most recent was about a link between mekari and human ESP."

"Julie did that?"

"Yes."

"That doesn't make any . . ." Before finishing the thought, Claude chucked the shovel away. It thwacked the base of the nearby tree and clanged to the ground. "I still think we should do this, but I'll wait until there's a consensus. Going solo is what got me into this mess."

The shift in his demeanor happened so rapidly, Garrett once again questioned whether a Hider was at work. This time, openly. "Were you possessed?" Garrett asked. "Are you possessed?"

Gloom concealed Claude's listless body language. "I honestly don't know."

That frankness comforted Garrett more than Julie's redirection when he'd asked her the same thing. "We need to go. I'm worried about Marie." He sidestepped to make room for Claude to join him but kept his distance. He still worried the capitulation was an act.

Claude walked as if sped up by an airport walkway. "Why?"

Once Claude entered his peripheral, Garrett broke into a jog, Claude joining him. "Gut feeling." Too long to explain the walkie-talkie.

"Is that why you came outside?"

"Not exactly. Come on."

It stopped the conversation as intended. Sneakers brushed through the yard, the pair splitting the grass underneath them. Right before they stepped onto the stone steps of the porch, the sunroom door opened.

Light poured out from the room, coalescing with the patio's glow from above. Out of the doorway emerged two figures. Garrett and Claude stepped back, then inched forward as their sight adjusted. Marie and Mr. Renault stopped their advance halfway across the porch. What was she doing out here? She should've been in danger somewhere. It was the only thing that made sense.

"Better get your gut checked," Claude whispered.

Marie approached without concern, her father following as a shield for her backside. Her casual stroll stunned Garrett, her voice sounding like an echo. "What are y'all doing out here?"

Maybe the voice from the walkie-talkie expected his encounter with Claude to go down differently. Maybe it went exactly as desired, stopping the desecration of Maurice Renault's resting place. Did the voice belong to a mekar? A spirit? Maurice himself?

Claude coughed. "Yeah, I should cover this one. I was—"

"Hold on. Gare, you don't look great." Marie grazed his knuckles. He hadn't realized she'd stepped so close. "Do you need to lie down?"

He must have looked catatonic. He lifted his head and closed his mouth. His wife's hazel eyes mended his remaining shock. Marie was fine.

She. Was. Fine.

What did the rest matter? Every facial muscle joined together in a smile. Tears of relief trembled to free themselves. "I'm great."

He pulled her in for an embrace, breaking only to kiss her cheek, then drew her in tighter. She hugged him back, not questioning with her words or her body, only pressing her hands against his back like the caressing stroke of an angel.

Mr. Renault interrupted. "Why's there dirt on your hands?"

Garrett and Marie separated, their embrace morphing into held hands. She glanced at his hands first, then followed her father's raised brow.

Mr. Renault was staring at his son.

Claude scratched his beard. It had grown disheveled since the morning he and his wife drank mimosas. "Right. Like I was saying. We're up against it a lot tougher than usual. I was feeling lost after Nia." He sniffed. "You know. I was helpless, hopeless, just . . . less." He sounded torn between joking and melancholic justifications. "I was thinking of a way to turn that around, and I had an idea. I knew it was risky, foolish even, but I wasn't thinking just how foolish until Garrett showed up and talked me out of it. It's what that mekar said through Grandpa, about propping him up in the yard. That's the reason my hands are dirty." Missing from his admission was his adopted son.

Mr. Renault's reaction didn't allow much time for it. "You were gonna string up your grandpa's *corpse*?"

One door from the dining room shuttered open. Garrett spun around, wrenching free from Marie's grip.

"It's okay," she said, obviously shaken by Claude's admission, but far from the fury of her father. "It's Julie. We split up searching the house when we heard the commotion, planning to meet outside if we didn't find anything within. We thought it wasn't likely with the dark." She gazed in the direction of her grandpa's burial site.

"Everything fine?" Julie shouted, still holding the door open, light enveloping her as a shadow. After an impatient silence, she yelled again. "Hello?"

Marie shook off her daze. "Everything's fine," she shouted back, satisfying Julie enough for her to head back inside, the door swinging shut behind her.

Mr. Renault grunted, stormed toward the house the instant after.

"Where are you going?" Marie asked.

"To figure something out." Hand on the door handle, with a glance that lingered on Claude, he yanked it open and returned inside.

As Garrett gestured for Claude to take the lead, a strange sensation struck him. He, as a guest of only several weeks, directed one who grew up here. Why had the walkie-talkie chosen to speak with him? Surely more than happenstance of picking up the device. Marie slid her hand back into Garrett's. Her look seemed to ask, *What will we do with him?*

I don't know, he thought. *But we've got a lot more than that to figure out.*

29. Unleashed

Two days passed in a murky haze, everyone caught up in their own affairs or those of the young ones they cared for. The walkie-talkie stayed quiet. Garrett saw glimpses of the family but spent most of his time consoling Marie, who brooded in their room. She'd forgiven Claude, but her cousin's continued avoidance of her tormented her worse than any spirit.

Try as he might to cheer her up, this morning she forced the issue. She left Garrett with a kiss and a new attitude, determined to force Derrick to speak with her. His constant dodging failed to dissuade her. Her cousin was hurting, and she knew others shunned him as he did her. Kelly and Julie admitted to her that they both partially blamed Derrick for Nia's death, overworking her with watching the children. Who else would support him besides his mom—a mom busy babysitting Grady? Derrick needed Marie, Marie needed to feel helpful, and that was the end of it.

Garrett didn't voice his disagreement. Derrick deserved better, and that shining beacon of hope in her eyes sealed the deal. It did leave a problem, which was how to spend his afternoon. A problem he resolved by checking on Claude. Spying on him, truthfully. His attempt to string up his grandfather's corpse burned fresh in Garrett's mind.

Why am I always on Claude duty whenever she's elsewhere?

Convincing his brother-in-law to join him in the game room was a breeze. His plan pulled double duty by placing him near Marie. The room shared a wall with the one where Derrick had stayed since Nia's death. In case of danger, Garrett stood ready to act under the guise of playing foosball.

Claude spun the handle nearest Garrett's goal. The plastic ball shot forward, bounced off the carved goalkeeper, and flew into the middle of the wooden field. Frantic spins from both players fought to drive the ball toward their opponent's side of the field. "Thanks for playing. Helps take my mind off everyone hating me."

"They don't hate you," Garrett said. "Hate is dangerous. Opens you up."

"Good news is you're right. Bad news is the situation's worse. They're apathetic. Thanks for the great pep talk. I understand what Marie sees in you now."

Garrett chuckled. Claude had been making jokes the whole morning. Almost enough to satiate the need to watch him.

Garrett spun his midfielders' handle so hard his hand slipped off. The ball darted through half a dozen miniature men and straight into the goal. Made him down something like twenty to fifty, but he was catching on quick. He preferred pool and pinball, but dense balls and glass sheets made for unnecessary hazards. Foosball, ping pong, and board game plastics offered safer alternatives.

Claude grabbed the ball and slid it down the chute back onto the field. Frantic spinning resumed. "Speaking of Marie, where is she? I didn't think you'd let her out of your sight with everything going on."

"She wanted some alone time with Derrick. She feels bad for him, but he's been avoiding her. Any idea what's up with him?"

"He was like that for a couple of years before meeting Nia. Marie and he were inseparable until something clicked in him." Claude stopped the game, hands up in surrender. "Look behind you."

From the long, rectangular shelf where a dozen board games sat, a copy of Monopoly levitated to eye level. The box tipped over, its top sliding off and dropping to the ground with a hollow thud. Plastic hotels and paper money spilled on the floor from the angled box. Garrett walked to Claude, placing the foosball table as a shield between him and the game pieces. The box's contents tumbled to the floor, then rose again into the air. One by one, they shot at Garrett and Claude.

They dodged the first several strikes, then crouched halfway, their eyes skimming above the table's lip. Copies of Risk and Scrabble emptied themselves onto the floor. Plastic army men and wooden letters joined the torrent. Gaming contents whizzed by, landing on their side of the room.

The direct assault morphed into a pincer attack.

The defenders propped their backs against table legs, covering their faces with their arms. The offensive intensified, pieces flying like machine gun fire at them and the foosball table. Handfuls struck Garrett in the leg. He winced, more startled than from any real pain. Then, like a tornado passing by a devastated neighborhood, everything ceased.

Claude stood up, surveying the room. "This'll be a bitch to clean up."

Garrett's pulse quickened, but not from fear—more like pre-game jitters. He joined Claude, chuckling as much from the comment as his lack of concern. "Yes, it will. Why aren't these locked away like everything else?"

"My bright idea. We replaced anything metal in the boxes, so it's all cheap plastic and paper. I figured those can't hurt much. The idea was to provide Aware Deviants another means of communicating, maybe help out."

"Any luck?"

"Nope, but hope springs eternal." Claude tapped the rim of the foosball table, then strolled toward the pair of empty game boxes on the floor. "Better get to it." He scooted Monopoly's bottom lid along the floor with his shoe, bending down periodically to place pieces in the box. Garrett followed behind him, mirroring his cleanup with Risk. Luckily, plastic soldiers were easy to separate from miniature houses and block letters.

"How'd this haunt compare to your past couple days?" Claude asked. "Better or worse?"

"Better, I guess." Marie's declining mood absorbed Garrett so completely, he didn't consider until now the relatively benign nature of the recent hauntings. Furniture rumbled for a few minutes one morning. That same evening, every sound came to him muffled. At one point he thought he'd entered a meat freezer in place of a bathroom. Annoying, but little more than interruptions. If he ignored the two tragedies thus far, he could even pretend he was growing accustomed to life here.

"Me too. Believe it or not, not a single haunt came my way." He stacked up piles of Monopoly money, jumbling up the denominations, then set them in the box. "It's like the spirit world wanted to torture me with my thoughts. Well, too bad for them. I spent all my alone time thinking up jokes for Tommy when Kelly lets me see him."

"She won't let you see your son?"

"Not without her supervision. But it's not like that." Claude snickered. "I mean it kind of is. She's pissed like hell, but she's right to be cautious. We don't know that there isn't something supernaturally wrong with me."

"How do you feel?"

"Like a million bucks." Claude pinched a red player pawn between his fingers. "Trampled by an armored vehicle."

"That good, huh?"

"Could be worse. I don't feel possessed. On a separate note, stop separating your pieces by color. You'll just get annoyed when everything gets dumped out again."

Garrett hung a blue cannon over the box, ready to place it with its matching army. He did it anyway, but all the rest he grabbed by the fistfuls and dumped them in.

"Better."

They continued cleaning while Garrett peppered in suspicion-alleviating questions in between Claude's silly jokes. Garrett actually enjoyed the moment. He relished his time with Marie, but he couldn't turn off his protective instincts around her. Bit by bit of casual conversation with Claude, he eased into relaxation. Eased into it so well, his mind cleared of all distractions. Calm thoughts left him with an image he spent half his energy pushing away—Nia's corpse. Pangs of guilt struck him at the memory. Why should he enjoy a pleasant moment when she never would again?

He was a monster. A disgusting, selfish monster, thinking of nothing but his own needs. He patted his thighs. Was that really what he thought of himself or was a spirit tainting his confidence?

"You done helping? Don't leave me stranded on cleanup isle."

Garrett finished with Risk, then moved onto picking up Scrabble. He stared at the contents in his hand, several tiles engraved with various letters.

"Get it? Because it's like a store aisle, but also an island isle where it's just us. Come on, man. What's up?"

Garrett didn't get to answer. A high-pitched scream caused them to drop their Scrabble letters and dash for the exit.

A desperate, "No!" from next door cried out as they entered the hallway.

Garrett pressed against the door to barge in and twisted the doorknob to Derrick's room, finding it locked. He reared back, rushed the door with his shoulder. It pinched against his chest. The door held, and another scream made an inaudible plea.

He stepped back, readying himself for a longer lead-up run.

"Move," Claude said.

Garrett sneered, ready to fight. *If he's going to try—*

"I've kicked in more doors than you."

Garrett moved over, gesturing frantically at the door.

Female cries of, "You can't," revolted Garrett. Sickened him. He shouldn't have left Marie. Derrick wasn't enough to protect her.

Claude lifted his foot and drove it just below the doorknob. Splinters flew, and the door swung in. His momentum carried him into the room, Garrett on his back heel.

Derrick had trapped Marie underneath him on the unkempt bed, a wolfish grin on his face. He was bare from the waist down. Marie's shorts hung around her waist. He gripped her underwear's waistband while lifting her shirt above her chest. She grasped his wrists, futilely resisting.

Claude flew toward Derrick, fought to wrestle him off. Savage determination kept Derrick in place. He continued trying to strip Marie. Garrett grabbed him underneath his ribs. Together, the pair wrangled him snarling off the bed and onto the ground. With his back on the floor, Garrett hooked his arms around Derrick's writhing body. Claude clamped his legs down, avoiding errant fists flying in his direction.

"She's mine. Mine. Mine!" Derrick twisted to break free. "I've waited my life for this. Who are you to take it away?" Saliva sprayed in the air, raining down on Garrett's arms.

"Check on Marie," Garrett shouted.

Claude's head bounced off the mattress as he dodged another strike. "You can't hold him."

"I'm fine," Marie said. Weak and barely audible over the chaos.

Derrick responded with a haunting chuckle.

"Can you turn him over?" Claude asked. "Face him to the ground?"

Garrett didn't think, just listened. He shifted to the side. Claude pulled when he pushed, and the two spun Derrick around until his cheek kissed the floor. Garrett sat on his mid-back, knees pinning arms, hands pinning wrists. Derrick bucked, nearly throwing him until Claude corralled his lower limbs.

"How long?" Garrett asked.

"Until whatever's in him gets the hell out," Claude said.

Garrett knew it was foolish, knew it a mistake, but he glanced back to check on his wife. She had redressed herself, and lay unaware of his gaze, her thumbnail pressed in between her teeth. Fury and sorrow split his organs. He pressed harder on Derrick, even as the resistance dwindled. His emotions rose like a volcano up through his mouth, and he screamed, "Why?" even as his own shameful tears welled up.

He wasn't any better. He'd let the ghost take hold of him weeks ago.

Banging from down the hall wrenched Garrett from his dark thoughts. He scooted down Derrick's spine, preparing to envelop him to free up Claude to face this new threat.

"Just what we need," Claude muttered.

"I've got him," Garrett said.

Banging morphed into faint footsteps that stopped at the door.

"Dad?" Claude asked.

Mr. Renault entered, shirtless but in jeans. He sneered at the entanglement on the floor, then moved to the bed. He comforted his daughter as any good father would. Garrett squinted, uncontrollably and unintentionally. Despite Claude's sins, and Mr. Renault's seeming innocence, he trusted the former more. But this wasn't the time for jealousy or suspicion.

The last bit of fight faded from Derrick's body. Garrett eased up, ready to pounce back down in case of a feint. Seconds passed with only Marie's heart-wrenching sniffs and shuddering sighs to pass the time.

Wild energy returned to the man below, and Garrett trapped him against the wood floor.

"Let me up!" Derrick squirmed for freedom, mere human strength resisting. Desperation replaced anger from moments ago. "I can't be here. I have to get away from her. Please let me up. Please!" His pleas blared loudest in the bleak song of the room's melody.

Garrett focused on Claude for an answer.

"It's him," Claude said. "We're . . . good." He stood up, backed against the far wall from the door.

Garrett rose moments later, keeping himself directly in the line between Derrick and Marie.

As soon as Derrick was free, he scrambled up and pulled back on his pants, his head turned so far from Marie he almost snapped his neck.

He sped away with enough energy to sprint a dozen laps around the property, but several steps down the hall the clamor ceased, and the sobbing began. Louder than either his snarling screams or desperate pleas. Sobs so deep he heaved for breaths in between.

"Marie." Claude's hand ran back and forth across his neck. "Marie, what can I do?"

Garrett blew past him, coming to his wife's side opposite her father. He tried to place his hands in hers. She recoiled and planted her hands in her lap. He responded in kind and apologized.

She kept crying, almost silently. A sprinkle compared to the torrent Derrick wailed out in the halls. Staring down at bed, moving only to wipe tears, she seemed oblivious to the world.

Mr. Renault inclined his head toward Claude and mouthed, *Watch Derrick.*

Claude hesitated, lips writhing as he assessed his sister. Then he nodded and left the room. He closed the splintered door behind him, quieting a fraction of Derrick's pitiful crying that suggested he was the victim and not the aggressor.

Moments passed. The noise from the halls progressively quieted, until a new speaker made their voice heard. Garrett couldn't make them out, didn't try. He ignored anything beyond Marie, ignored her father entirely. Whether Mr. Renault was guilty of anything, she needed both of them now.

He fell into a trance, to be broken only by Marie.

That break came when she extended her hand toward him, palm up. She beckoned him when he didn't respond. When Garrett took her hand, she loosed a calming shudder. Then, although nobody asked her what happened, she answered, her voice distant. "I wouldn't let him leave until he opened up to me. He tried sneaking around me to leave the room, but I stood in the way. He didn't want to touch me."

Her face writhed in sorrow, and she took a moment to recompose herself. "We were finally getting somewhere. He told me more about the day he met Nia. About some of their iconic dates. I knew they loved each other, but the way he talked about her was something different." Now she locked onto Garrett. "I love you, but they weren't like you and me."

"I love you too," Garrett said.

"I know. But this was different. We're good alone, but we're—"

"Stronger together than apart." He stalled his inclination to add a second hand to hers.

"It's okay."

He sandwiched her hand between both of his. She completed the stack, the softness of her palm a tranquilizer for his rising tension. He loosened a jaw he didn't know he'd clenched.

"Now, let me finish." She sniffled. "Nia was Derrick's salvation. He loves us. The Renaults, I mean. He loves us, but he needed an escape. With her, that was possible." She blinked out droplets of tears.

A strong, weathered hand moved from Garrett's periphery to Marie's face, holding a cloth of some sort. He almost jutted his hand out from Marie's to stop the threat, interpreting it as an attempted suffocation. He stopped after realizing the 'threat' was Marie's dad proffering a pillowcase.

"Thanks." She took the makeshift tissue and blew her nose. After a few rounds, she wiped her eyes with the other hand. With a long sigh, she began again. "Losing her lost him that escape. He's trapped now. He told me how tough it was being near me. I reminded him too much of her. He kept coming back to that same excuse, apologizing repeatedly while opening up to me. But as we talked, something came over him. I ignored it at first. Until." Her gaze fell. Garrett yearned to kiss her hand but didn't know what would cross her comfort line in the wake of her assault.

"I'm putting a stop to this," Mr. Renault said. "Nothing like this'll 'appen to you again."

She didn't respond.

"Is there anything I can do?" Garrett asked.

Whimpers and whispers out in the hall filled the gap between her answer.

After a while, she broke from her comatose state. She stared at Garrett. "Keep me company outside. We can pitch tents and do some light camping in the backyard. What I really need is a change of clothes and to get out of this house. Even if we can't go very far." She lifted her shoulder to brush her eyes.

"Absolutely."

She withdrew her hands and started to sit upright. Garrett straightened the pillow behind her before her back returned to it. "Also, drop the coddling."

Garrett's cheeks flushed as he pulled his arms back. "I'll do my best." As she came to a fully seated position, he raised his eyebrows, the immediacy of the dangers finally passing.

"What is it?" Marie asked.

"Who locked the door?"

"Nobody. That's why you can't blame him."

He nodded, resisting the urge to pick her up and carry her out as she made her way off the bed. Forgiveness came so easily to her. He admired her for it. It amplified his love. But even for her, the act wasn't so simple. It wasn't lost on him that she never used Derrick's name in defending him.

30. Relationships

Inside a yellow tent big enough to fit a queen mattress, Garrett and Marie sat atop their sleeping bags. He repeated the list she had just given him. "A turkey sandwich with provolone, lettuce, and mustard. Bottled water. Graham crackers, chocolate, and marshmallows."

"You got it," she said.

"About the s'mores—I know ghosts hate fires, but isn't it unwise to start one?"

"I agree. Good thing uncooked s'mores still taste great." She forced a smile.

He snorted with amusement. "And what if someone wants to see you?"

His question conjured a mental snapshot of yesterday's attack, souring his brief happy moment. Marie didn't answer immediately, and a loathsome seed sprouted in Garrett's gut. When a Claimer had briefly possessed him, it latched onto a sensation of lust so wild, it took on a life of its own. Barely enough of him had remained to retake the reins, but he'd recovered on his own. Derrick, however, required two grown men to subdue him. When forced off of his cousin, he struggled with supernatural strength to return. How much lust lived in his heart to surrender so totally to it?

"Tell them"—Marie fiddled with the drawstring of her pajama pants—"I'm not ready." She glanced down, as if ashamed.

Derrick, you bastard. "It's okay. Nobody will blame you."

Marie read his mind, as she so often did. "Nobody should blame anyone but the ghosts and mekari for anything."

"Right." Garrett realized he'd clenched his jaw and furrowed his brows. Marie's lips turned up in a reserved smile. She stared at him with a sweet softness until he composed his face. Regardless of the accuracy of Marie's statement, his relaxing made her happier, and his fierce anger on this Claimer-infested property threatened her more than it helped. "I'll be right back."

"Take your time. I don't mind sitting quietly with nature, and this tent is made of the stuff they use for stab proof vests. I'll be safe."

They leaned in toward one another for a peck on the lips, then Garrett grabbed his backpack and unzipped the tent.

Despite Marie's request, he walked toward the sunroom-adjacent supply room with haste. Thinking clearer thanks to her, and alone for the first time since Derrick's assault, he admitted another more palatable explanation for yesterday's atrocity. Marie's talk of Nia had stirred a batch of fervent emotions. Love, grief, sorrow, and anger led to unpredictable behavior in the real world. On a Hellspot, catastrophic consequences followed. A Feeder might have agitated his volatile mix of emotions. Shaken them until they exploded in his violent outburst.

From Garrett's loathsome seed sprouted a lightheaded dizziness and acid that gurgled up to his chest. How was he supposed to protect Marie? Whether natural forces or the supernatural drove Derrick, Marie was in danger around her cousin. He might talk to Derrick and clear up the situation.

He might also punch him in the face.

This isn't helping.

He focused on Marie's list. Once at his destination, he filled his backpack half-up with water and enough s'mores ingredients to make both of them sick. From there, he beelined it to the kitchen to make their sandwiches. He passed through adjoining rooms in quick succession, thankful for the quiet stroll. His lucky streak veered toward ending as he entered the sitting room. Iris was knitting in the closest oversized chair. Grady snoozed in a sleeping bag at her feet.

Garrett offered a faint wave as he passed by, exhaling as she ignored him. He left open the double doors leading to the dining room as he hurried through.

The kitchen's eerie quiet reassured Garrett as much as walking under a ladder. With frequent looks over his shoulder, he gathered what he needed for sandwiches and set them on the edge of the island. He kept the knife in hand as he assembled the ingredients, whether or not actively using it. Ghosts might invade his mind or assault him with nearby objects, but they'd have a hell of a time ripping something from his grip. He sealed the sandwiches in a pair of plastic bags and loaded them in his backpack. Only then did he relinquish the knife, placing it directly into the dishwasher. Until the moment he left the room, he expected at least a ghastly rattling. Perhaps the mekar in charge rightly assessed the quiet was more unsettling.

He tried to slip into the backyard from the dining room exit. A firm voice stopped him inches from the outdoors. From Marie.

"Garrett," Iris said with her country drawl.

She didn't look up. Didn't turn. Just kept knitting.

His palm danced inches from the handle. "Did you say something?" he asked, hoping he imagined it.

"Said your name." After a pause that begged Garrett to respond, Iris added, "We needa talk."

His head bobbed from side to side. "Marie's waiting on me. Don't want our sandwiches to get warm and all that. How about this evening?"

"Now's good."

"What about Grady? He's sleeping, right?"

Acrylic needles clacked against the table beside Iris. She stood up, hands on hips, with a predatory stare he imagined similarly glued to mekari faces. "Like an angel. Now, get in here. I'm tired, I'm old, and I ain't arguing."

With a longing glance outside, he gave in to her demands. She sat back down as he started toward her. He scoffed, then frowned at his thoughtless display.

If Iris cared, she didn't show it in her voice. Why should she? The past couple weeks barely seemed to have affected her. "Before you sit, close the doors. Both of 'em."

"Sure." A devious plot of slamming the doors to wake Grady and escape the situation entered and fled his mind. Weakness gripped his limbs, a punishment for the thought. If anyone deserved peaceful rest, it was Grady and Tommy. He did as instructed, then sat on the couch, planning to call it after ten minutes. He checked his phone to start the timer.

Iris clasped her hands, her stiff posture imposing. She pointed her sneaker at her grandson. "He got this idea from you and Marie. Wanted to go camping with the grownups. I told him no. You know why?"

Garrett slipped his backpack off onto the cushion beside him. "No."

"Stupid idea. We all sleep upstairs for a reason. No one's gonna hear you if something happens outside. Y'all on your own out there. Better inside, with family."

He didn't agree, especially lately.

"But family's a funny thing, ain't it? It means different things to different people. Some people call close friends family. Some call family their enemies. Here, we're bound by blood and oath."

"Been a while since I've heard that," he joked.

Her rigid face hid her emotions like a wall. "I know you wanna get back to your lovey-dovey. I've seen that doe-like stare. You and Derrick're a lot alike."

Bullshit. He might have thought that once, but not anymore. Garrett's fist tightened. He slid it under his armpit, hopefully before Iris saw.

She grunted. "I'll make this quick if you promise not to talk 'til the end."

"Sure." What other choice did he have besides pissing her off?

"Something's wrong with my son. I've known it for a while. Felt it for a while. Moms have this intuition 'bout their children. We can see the car crash coming. We just don't know when, where, or how. What happened wasn't his fault. Make all the dumb faces you like. Don't change the truth."

Garrett forced his sneer down. He curled his lips around his teeth to keep his nose planted. She was right about one thing: something *was* wrong with Derrick.

"I tried to hold my baby boy yesterday. He told me I wasn't safe with him. Said he's gonna stay in his room 'til the Breach clears, broken door and all. He knows what he did was wrong. Don't have to forgive him, but you should. Your wife did." She shook her head, judgmental and knowing. "Men. Always failing to learn from the women in their life. She don't even know the whole story."

Where was this going? Confusion sheared away at his vitriol.

"And she's not gonna learn. This is just you and me." Her finger flitted back and forth between them while she glanced at the slumbering child at her feet. "You're a fool, but a special fool. You don't trust Marie's dad." She laughed. "Thought they'd teach you to hide your emotions better at Harvard."

Garrett's uncurled his lips, aching from his teeth digging in. Was it that obvious how he felt about Mr. Renault?

"Don't worry. Secret's safe with me." She grinned. "I recognize the mistrust 'cause that's how I feel every damn time I'm in a room with him. Something's going on, and I'm tired of trying to figure it out. Sick of forcing myself into his presence."

Snapped out of his stupor, Garrett wiped the surprise off his face. He wanted to respond. Marie's solitary waiting stopped him. *Shut up and listen. This'll end faster.* But time passed so slowly that he almost spoke anyway.

Then Iris shot him a sneer of her own. "We slept together. Derrick's not his nephew. He's his son."

Garrett's brain short-circuited. Once his mind rebooted, he leaned in. "You? And Marie's dad?" he sputtered. He wanted to ask every major question. What? When? Why? "How do you know? Did you and your husband," he paused, "not," then faltered at the imposing figure of this slight woman.

Iris's apathetic expression never cracked. "Simon. My husband. Wasn't fertile. We didn't get him officially checked, but I knew. Like a mother's intuition, wives have a sixth sense 'bout their husbands. I'd made my peace with it. He never did. I wanted a child, but he *needed* a child. Felt some nonsense shame over David having two kids at that point to carry on the family line while he'd contributed none. Dumb competition between male twins."

"Mr. Renau—"

"David. Half the house is Mr. Renault."

"David and Simon were twins?" He didn't know why that mattered. It just struck him as odd that it hadn't come up before. He'd seen old pictures of the elder Renaults together. Clearly brothers, but nowhere near the resemblance as the residence's current fraternal twins.

"It's what I said, and you're not supposed to talk." She gazed in Marie's direction, clearly punishing Garrett with a prolonged delay. When she turned back, he was fidgeting with a couch cushion. "We tried and tried. Used to come back here more, before the Breach that got him. His frustration got worse and worse, and he pushed me away. Right into his brother's arms. I was young and stupid. Broke it off quick, but not quick enough. Got my baby boy out of it though, so I don't regret it."

She picked up her knitting needles, attached to what looked like a tiny half-finished shirt. "Simon died when Derrick was Grady's age. Never suspected his son wasn't his. Nor did Sophie, David's wife. Joy for a new generation of Overseers blinds us to the truth as much as not wanting to believe it. Just like I didn't want to believe anything bad 'bout David for years." She petted the yarn, seeming to draw comfort from it. "You can talk now."

His eyes darted back and forth between the two other living souls in the room. Would this knowledge have given Derrick the strength to stop himself? Would it have changed Marie's reaction to yesterday's horror? Less hypothetically, it didn't explain why she'd told him. "What does this have to do with—" He cleared his throat. Mr. Renault's first name still felt improper to say. "What does this have to do with David's secret?"

"Intuition. Mother's, wife's, lover's. All the same. He's hiding something, and I know it's got to do with Derrick. With all his kids' sins."

All? Garrett leaned back, crossed his arms in suspicion. What sin could Marie have committed? Trusting and forgiving too much?

"It's not their fault," Iris said. As if that should satisfy him. "My Derrick's a good boy. He's not to blame. Children are never to blame. You remember that."

Blame for what? Did she mean Claude and Julie? Or that younger brother whose name he still didn't know? If someone could handle him bringing it up, it was Iris. With everything else he'd discovered, the topic held merit. "Do you mean the younger brother? The one who died?"

He caught her off guard with that.

She recovered quickly, breaking her stoic stare to study Grady. "Tragic death."

"What happened?"

"Tragic death," she repeated. She frowned as she stared up at the ceiling. Above, her son had barricaded himself in his room after attacking his cousin.

Not his cousin. His sister.

Garrett realized he believed Iris's claim, and despite their infrequent interactions, probably trusted her more than anyone in the house after Marie. He wished she'd come clean on the younger brother too, but he needed to get back to Marie. He grabbed the hook strap of his backpack. "Why tell me about Derrick? Even if you can't go to the kids, there's Kelly. She's been here longer than me. There was also—" He bit his lip. He'd almost said, *Nia.*

Iris pointed at him. "You need to understand how hard it is to be a mom, young man. Here, of all places." Grady stirred at her feet. "I should charge you tuition for that lesson. I told you 'cause I thought you should know. Now, scram. I know you want to."

Garrett slipped out his phone to check the time. Over twenty minutes passed in conversation. He slung his backpack across his shoulders, clutching the straps in anger for not finding a way out earlier. He jumped off the couch in pursuit of his wife. His grip slackened in his first step forward. One question remained.

"Can I tell anyone about this?" he asked.

Slowly, the answer became clear as her brows furrowed into a scowl. "If you speak a word o' this to anyone, I'll cut your throat. Slice you five ways to Sunday. I'll rend your flesh like it's a piece of cloth and savor tearing you like threads of fabric." She licked her lips.

A Claimer had taken her. He would've fled the room and let the possession run its course, but there lay Grady, sleeping through it all. Garrett stepped forward, out of her immediate reach but close enough to protect her grandson. Muscles in his fingers and around his knees flexed autonomously.

Iris slipped her knitting needles off the yarn. "Maybe we start with a sweet little stabbing. We can watch your blood drain, ooze off your skin, and paint the floors that holy crimson color. And then with a dash of my thumb, savor a taste. A family's sticky sweetness is a treat." She stood up, her foot striking Grady's knee. She glanced down, then collapsed in her seat.

"Is it time to get up?" Grady mumbled.

"No." Iris's voice shook. She placed her needles under her thigh. "No, honey. Go back." She cleared her throat. "Go back to sleep."

"Okay. Night, night." Grady rolled over, never opening his eyes.

"Sorry," Iris whispered. "What's happening with my son. And what *that man* has done." She grimaced, holding out her hand to ask for a moment. *That man* could have only been Mr. Renault or his brother. With the torment she threatened Garrett with, her anger indicated a hatred she had let simmer but never let boil until speaking it aloud. Or maybe it was as simple as a mom defending her child.

"Do what you need with the secret," Iris said at last. "Just help my son. I put my faith in you." She hunched over, focused entirely on Grady, ignoring any potential answer from Garrett.

He had no desire to give one after the response to his last question. He stood there for a moment, ensuring Grady's safety. Then a single thought slammed him off his heels.

Marie.

Garrett bolted from the room, opening one door after the next with barely a break in his stride. Dusky, humid backyard air greeted him. Inside the tent, a couple dozen yards from the house, Marie's familiar shadow sat up within.

He breathed relief. She was safe for now. But as he inhaled, he felt the weight of all the house's secrets piling atop his shoulders.

31. Leaking Out

Secrets eat us alive. I was tired of having my flesh gnawed on.

Julie's words weighed on Garrett. Their relevance gained traction as the next days passed in the accursed, evil house. Haunted was too gentle a term. The Hellspot didn't simply test survival. It tested the bonds of trust. Tested what to tell Marie. Tested whether he should voice his mistrust of her father, now well-founded based on his latest discovery. Tested whether to reveal her cousin was in fact another brother.

His chief focus—the extent of Mr. Renault's misdeeds—was within his grasp. Marie chased it unknowingly by his side. Though the couple continued camping outside, Marie had returned to her normal self, at least on the surface. The pair strolled in the upper hallways to where Mr. Renault slept and worked most of his days, the room originally assigned to his now-deceased father.

Fires ignited within Garrett's chest. His ribs creaked to contain his trove of secrets. Marie acted calmly to learning of Claude's embezzlement. Why shouldn't he trust her with the truth about Derrick's relationship, Julie's book burning, and Mr. Renault's missing translation? Was he protecting Marie or himself?

I will come clean, he promised himself. *Once I have tangible proof about her dad.* The rest risked too many distractions.

But mere steps from their destination, Garrett about-faced and walked the other way.

"I thought you needed to ask my dad something?" Marie caught up with a jog.

"I do." *Just not with you around.* "But I think he's close to something. I know how hard it is to get my concentration back after an interruption, so it can wait. Not like we have any shortage of problems to tackle."

"Okay." The tinge of sadness in her voice hinted she knew Garrett was hiding something. The same sadness as yesterday when he told her, *Nothing's wrong*, on his return to their tent.

He reached for her hand, stopped just short, silently asking whether she wanted his touch. She did, and the guilt swallowed Garrett like an eclipse. He had to tell her something. Fast, before he openly accused Marie's dad. "The walkie-talkie in our room," he blurted out, "it's how I found out about Claude."

"Oh." They split wide around a cracked floorboard, stretching the reach of their hand holding before they returned to walking side by side. "Why didn't you tell me earlier?"

"It told me not to tell anyone. I got it in my head that it wouldn't help again if I did. It's been silent since that night regardless. Think it was a one-time thing."

"Why tell me now?"

"I guess there's always a time and—"

A door opened ahead of them, stalling his pathetic confession. Underneath the frame, Kelly poked out, holding Tommy in her arms. "Sorry to interrupt. I need some time with an adult." Her blonde hair was frazzled.

Worried creases on Marie's face gave way to a smile. "Happy to help."

"I could use a break, but I can't let him out of my sight." She pressed her head to her son's. Tommy clapped once, then started poking her shoulder. Relentlessly. "No matter how frustrating he is." She either didn't mind the poking or felt as defeated as she looked.

"At least he's safe with you."

"I don't know about that. Sleep's been tough. Or I sleep all at once and miss"—she leaned out into the hall, glancing at Nia's old room—"important events."

"Safer than with me at least," Marie said.

"I'm sure you'd do great. You're patient enough for Claude. Tommy's a lot easier."

"Maybe when they're older." She looked to Garrett for rescue.

"Might be genetics," he joked.

"What do you mean?" Kelly asked.

"Yeah, what do you mean?" Marie pouted.

He was thinking about Mr. Renault when he'd said that, stuck on Iris's suggestion that a previous act had twisted his kids. They might have taken his statement as implying any number of insults. But it did open another door.

"Your dad has been distant since I arrived. I don't know if he's always like that. It feels like he's worried around you—beyond a father's normal, loving concern. Like, I don't know, he's ashamed of something?" *Smooth, Garrett.*

"He's busy." Marie slipped out from Garrett's grasp to stuff her hand in her pocket. "He's helping how he can. All of us are doing what we can." She might not have revealed anything in the open ears of the hallway, but even in her face, Garrett saw nothing but an earnest reply.

"Sorry. I was making a joke and made it worse trying to justify it." He rubbed the corners of his eyes. "I'm not sleeping much either."

"Not easy in this house," Kelly said. "And the dreams aren't much better."

"Dreams?" Garrett asked. "From a Dreamer?"

"Nothing," she yawned. "Excuse me. Nothing like that. I always have weird dreams here. I doubt I'm important enough for the spirits to bother."

"You're important." Marie rubbed Kelly's free arm.

"Thanks." Kelly readjusted her son's weight. "Well, Tommy's getting heavy. Like I said, nice to see some adults. We should talk in the hall more often. Or preferably somewhere else once Tommy feels safe leaving the room for more than a few minutes."

"Glad we could help."

Garrett's forced smile vanished as the door closed. The pair walked the remaining steps to their room, facing straight ahead. As they stopped in front of their room, he broke the silence. "Sorry about that. That was weird. And sorry about not telling you about the walkie-talkie."

"We've got a lot going on." Marie's head drooped toward the floor and her shoulders sank. Garrett reached for her, hoping to rescue her from whatever dark thoughts ailed her. He paused as her head started bobbing as if listening to club music. She looked up with her dimples in full effect. "I love you. That's what matters."

"I love you too." He thought back to Marie's breakdown at her personal memorial to her brother. "You sure you're okay? You can always tell me."

"All we need is love. Now that that's settled, I need to run to the bathroom. Be right back."

"Sure." He never quite knew what to expect from her. He loved her for it, but a competing uneasiness lingered.

As Marie scurried away, Garrett entered their room, leaving the door open. Today's plan had centered on talking with Mr. Renault. When Garrett changed his mind, he'd set a course back to his room out of habit. So why not wait in the hall? He scanned the room, curious what led him here. The walkie-talkie sat lifelessly on the dresser. Books proving Julie's crime rested in the corner. He walked to the bed and tightened the sheets, then pulled the comforter to the head of the bed and folded the top back over itself.

There was more to his actions than finding a purpose. He was avoiding what was right in front of him. "Is something else troubling Marie?" he asked his pillow, as if it had any answers.

But the walkie-talkie did. "Find out in the gym. Ask her about kids. It'll leave you breathless."

Garrett leapt toward the dresser. He snatched the radio, holding the send button. "Find out what? Which kids?"

Static buzzed, crackling alongside the emergence of a second voice. An older, deeper male sang an unknown song with a country twang. The lyrics were too scattered to decipher.

Marie bounded into the room, patting her hands dry on her jeans. "I heard stomping. Everything okay?"

Garrett held the walkie-talkie up between them. "You can hear this right?"

She nodded, wide eyes asking if she was missing something.

"It's not weird?"

She shrugged up to her ears, looking around to emphasize where they were.

"Fair enough," he said. "Does the song make any sense?"

She crept forward, tilted her head in its direction.

"The voice sounds familiar, but I can't place it with the background noise. Change the channel."

He went up and down the nearest few. Silence reigned until he returned to the original channel. The singing faded into oblivion. He massaged the nape of his neck. "I thought I heard something before the singing."

"What?"

"Umm," he stalled. Should he follow the walkie-talkie's advice again? It served him well the first time, but the gym was an anathema for Marie. Derrick—Garrett still had to suppress making a fist when thinking of him—had said Marie would tell him why she avoided kids when she was ready. The walkie-talkie voice almost certainly alluded to that. Maybe it had to do with her younger brother who'd died in an accident. *Children are never to blame,* Iris had told him. Had Marie been watching him when a freak accident occurred? He shouldn't pry into that if so, but he had no way to know.

On the other hand, he might discover a clue to explain Mr. Renault's funny behavior and prevent a greater tragedy. Tipping the scales was the singing—a distraction to prevent him from learning more, suggesting its importance. He resolved to make one attempt and leave it at that. "I think the stress is getting to me. How about a workout? Didn't you say you wanted to try biking? Might get our minds off things."

She fidgeted with her fingers, and her tongue visibly worked the inside of her mouth. Garrett almost rescinded the idea completely. Then she sniffed a quick inhale that lifted her chest. "Indoor exercise, huh? Let's give it a try."

32. Crash

Despite Marie's initial enthusiasm about the gym, she stalled their approach to it in every way possible.

When they stripped to their underwear to change, Marie amped up her charm. Feigning indecision over which sports bra to wear, she tried several options. She claimed she needed better support, dawdling topless while searching for a replacement. Tension aching in Garrett's shoulders and core made the enticing spectacle hard to enjoy.

When they reached the landing between floors, she tapped the window, pointing out the permanent dusk had receded. She suggested running laps around the yard instead. He pulled her away, plagued by images of her stretched out bloody like Nia. He now felt a certainty that their safety depended on some concealed fact from Marie's past—not all of it, just a fragment. The potential for reopening the wound about her brother pained him enough as it was.

Last, at the foot of the stairs, she offered a meek rebuttal. "Dad probably needs a break. He'd also want to know about the walkie-talkie. Why don't we go ask him your question now?"

Temptation beset him at each attempt. He held strong, pressing onward to the walkie-talkie's proposed destination. But when stopped at the threshold of the gym, his calculating callousness gave way. Was her safety worth reliving her past? Only she could decide. "We don't have to work out."

She waged a mental war with the room. Garrett braced himself for an errant attack. Possession, madness, a twisting of reality, weights launching themselves through the air.

"It's fin. Fine." She wasn't prone to stuttering.

Was that more of his patented overthinking?

"I'm with you." He whistled the tune that Marie and Derrick used to signal safety to each other. One deep note, followed by three medium. Higher, higher, lower. He repeated the medium notes, gradually increasing the pitch until he slid back to the original note.

Marie's chin lifted, showing the faintest sign of comfort.

"If this is ever too much for you, we can leave it any time."

Marie nodded.

Garrett stepped into the room as if treading water of an unknown depth. Hands clasped at his waist, he wouldn't push her any harder than this. If she turned and fled then the walkie-talkie be damned, this wasn't meant to be.

She didn't run, though, and meandered toward the stationary bike. He pulled out weights from the out-of-place armoire he had to unlock and relock. Marie grasped the bike's handlebars, splitting her attention between it and the bench that Garrett surrounded with weights.

"Need any help?" he asked, then glanced at a pair of dumbbells in his hands. *I'm an idiot.* "I'm getting too many weights out, aren't I?"

"Yep." She giggled, but it sounded forced. "Could you help me move the bike closer to the entryway?"

"I got it." Relocating the bike gave him a nice warmup. "Good?"

"Yep. Don't wait on me though. I'll be a minute."

He placed his hands on her tank top strap and kissed her forehead. He normally expected her to reciprocate in some manner. Not today, not here. Garrett knew he was walking a fine line and resolved to watch for any signs she'd had enough. He sat on the bench and started his bicep curls. 60lbs rose to his shoulder, then fell to his waist. Too heavy from his time off. He swapped them for the 40lb weights. Marie was standing in the same place when he returned to the bench.

She finally hoisted herself up on the bike when he started his squats.

He laid down for chest presses by the time she began pedaling.

Julie checked in with a strange look on her face, equal parts approval and surprise. She raised her eyebrows at something that Marie mouthed, then went back in the direction of the library.

He neared the end of his deadlifts when she started hyperventilating. He dropped his weights. Hardwood cracked beneath the gym mat as he leapt next to her. He laid his hand across her back. "Are you okay?"

She stopped pedaling and gasped for air, practically breathless.

Find out in the gym. Ask her about kids. It'll leave you breathless, said the memory of the spirit. *Not now,* he countered.

He slid from touching her to embracing her, blanketing her like a shield. He rubbed her back, and her breathing recovered to an even tempo. He helped her down and returned the bike to its original position. In a dazed state, Marie found her way to the bench.

Trauma beyond imagination had occurred here. Was it her father? Had he been the cause of the younger brother's 'accident'? Garrett had promised himself he'd leave it alone, but how could he? Time wasn't on their side, and any atrocity she suffered wasn't her fault. Victims were victims, devoid of blame. And he trusted the incorporeal voice, trusted her breathlessness was a cue to prompt her. More importantly, he knew he could never bring her here again. After returning the final set of dumbbells to the armoire, he sat next to her, finding his courage. "Is this about kids?"

Abject horror consumed her. She didn't look as if she saw a ghost. That was too trivial. She looked as if she saw the devil himself. She sprang from the bench like it were a bed of coals, clutched the nearby bike for support. "You," she choked. "Knew?"

He reached for her, and she flinched.

You're trusting a random voice over your wife. "Sorry. You don't have to tell me anything."

She didn't answer for a while. Just crossed her arms, biting her nails. "If you already know, does this mean you forgive me?"

A strange mix of lament and confusion chaotically swirled throughout his body. He'd felt this way once before with her: when he proposed. She guarded a secret as big as living in a haunted house, and she hadn't trusted him enough to reveal it yet. He suspected that she selflessly blamed herself for her brother's death, always taking on too much. "Forgive you for what?"

"Then why? Why bring me here if you didn't know?" Panic infected her voice. He worried she'd hyperventilate again. "Why bring me here if you did?"

He wished for Julie's return, or anyone's arrival. He wanted an excuse to bury this conversation forever. Nobody came though, and tempered curiosity drove him forward. Pushed him into an unfailing commitment: he was done hiding things from her. He kept his voice low. "The walkie-talkie gave me a clue. Like something I needed to know happened to you here. Whatever it is, you can trust me."

"This isn't." She chewed her nails. "No, I can't. I mean I can trust you, of course I can. But this isn't about trust."

"Did your dad do something?"

She stiffened her slumped posture. "What? Why would you think that?"

"I've been hiding things from you about your family. I didn't think it was my place to tell you, but the secrets have been eating me up. Trust is cathartic, I suppose, so here it goes." Garrett inhaled with his palms turned to the ceiling. "Julie admitted to me that she burned that book we confronted her about. You know Claude was embezzling, but I should've told you as soon as I learned about it. Tommy also isn't blood-related. He's adopted. And Derrick"—his hands quaked as he struggled to get out this final truth—"isn't actually your cousin."

Marie's overwhelmed response suggested he'd revealed too much. She played with the stud earring on her left. Twirling it. Pinching it.

Here he was, thinking of himself again. Trust was cathartic, true, but its usage often weighed on the recipient. He had to explain why he'd said those things. "I think your dad's to blame."

Marie tugged on her ear with a jolt and yelped, wincing at the obvious pain.

"You can trust me. But." He gnawed his knuckle, torn between needing the truth and respecting her privacy. "If you don't feel comfortable telling me, that's okay. I'm still here. I love you." He held out in his hand in case she wished to take it.

She butted up against the bike, scanning between him and the far end of the bench. After a moment, her head and chest jutted forward, and she retched. "I'm sorry. I'm so sorry."

"You don't have anything to be sorry for. I love you."

Marie shook her head with the rhythm of an involuntary tic. Her lips quivered. She scrunched her eyes, tears streaming down her cheeks. Her back slid down the bike's frame, her legs nearly crumpling. Garrett rose to comfort her. She held up her hand to ward him away. A full minute of apologies poured from her, and he froze in a mid-squat until the well of sorrys dried up. Worry creased lines around her eyes. The head of the bench consumed the entirety of her attention, and an eerie silence pervaded the room.

When Marie next spoke, she affected the emotionless cadence of a robot and Garrett finally forced himself to sit. "Finn was my younger brother's name. He was six years old—Grady's age. I was ten. We were horsing around in here. The door was closed because we didn't want to get in trouble. We played adult by riding the bikes. I had to boost him up. Then we lifted a dumbbell together with all our might. We were about to leave when we sniffed something metallic. We peered at each other, trying to place the smell. As we did, this animalistic rage took over. I suddenly recalled every annoying thing Finn had ever done.

"I blamed him for Uncle Simon's death. Finn was born just weeks before, and my dad apologized when he first held him. He denied saying anything, and nobody else heard him, but I could tell something was wrong. Like he'd regretted Finn's birth. I lost rational thought and turned into an animal. My senses sharpened as I looked at my brother.

My *prey*. A similar rage burned in his eyes, and he snarled like a young wolf.

"We fought for I don't know how long. Nobody heard us. It was a month before the next Breach. The few spirits that came early were too weak to possess us or stifle the room's sound." She massaged the nape of her neck. "We've all been possessed before. This wasn't that. I wish it had been. I told myself after the fact I would've never strangled him. Except in that moment, I thought of nothing else. We tussled, and I fell on top of him on the bench. I squeezed his neck, dug my thumbs into his skin until he stopped scratching my arms. I kept at it for another minute. My instincts told me to ensure the kill. The smell of my dead brother turned sickly sweet. Once the scent finally faded, I screamed. Everybody in the house heard me then and followed my hysterical shrieks to the gym. One by one, they saw what I had done."

Dazed, Garrett responded by reconciling Marie's story with her personality. She was loving, forgiving, a spark of life on a dull night. He would've bet his life on her never harming another soul. He had in a manner, by agreeing to live here. The house was to blame, that was clear. It had made her do terrible things. But if this occurred outside of a Breach, then how? She admitted that no spirit or mekar controlled her actions.

That left one answer: Mr. Renault. "It's your dad's fault, isn't it? You're protecting him."

The accusation woke Marie from her haze. "What? No. I did this. I don't know what came over me, but it's my fault. I guess I was too weak, too jealous that I wasn't the baby of the family anymore."

Garrett jumped straight up, keeping his distance. "How are you," he controlled his voice. "Of all people, capable of something like that?"

"I don't know." She dabbed the corner of her eye. "I wish I did."

Then, he remembered the little clues. Derrick's slip about Marie's childhood trauma. Claude hinting at other compulsions in the family, and Julie's response that kids don't know better. Iris stating kids are never to blame. "Everyone hid this from me. Everyone lied." His suspicions, buried from when she'd first told him of her younger brother, burst out. "You told me it was an accident."

"I was ten. Everyone pretended a spirit did it. My dad made me repeat that I was innocent, but I never fully accepted that."

"You strangled your little brother here? On this bench?" Garrett pointed down, trying to ignore that he might've laid his head where a child was murdered. "I can't believe it."

She brought her hands to her face, squeezed it so the skin bunched under her cheekbones. "I'm sorry. Yes. I'm sorry. No, not *that* bench. But it 'appened, oh my God. If it wasn't for everyone supporting me, I don't know what I would've done. We would have never met, and I'm so glad we met." Her hand drifted toward Garrett then recoiled back to her cheek. "Ever since the day this, this, this," she stuttered. "This *thing* 'appened, I've never felt that way since. Something was lifted from me."

Marie's chin dipped. "We kept the room closed off for a couple years after. When we opened it up, we took down the door here and in every room without a backup exit. Everything in the gym got replaced. The floors, bench, bikes, weights. All of it. Everything except the memories. That place in the backyard, my personal space for Finn? It's not just a memorial. It's where I beg him for forgiveness."

And where you lied to your husband.

But Marie was hurting and in pain. She was opening up despite having every reason to hide the truth. He wanted to believe she wasn't a murderer, wanted to take her from this room and console her for as long as the spirits allowed. Wicked people didn't go out of their way to leave gifts for the deceased, but he deserved to know a truth like this well before today. He wanted no stone left unturned. "Wouldn't your mom have died in the following Breach?"

Her eyes widened, and she shook her head wildly. "No, no, no. Not you. You can't think that. Dad said I had nothing to do with it." A fresh set of tears poured forth.

"I don't think anything. I'm not exactly given the answers to do so, am I?" Doubt found a foothold in Garrett's psyche. He hoped for an explanation he could believe.

She fidgeted with her earring, then rubbed her limply hanging arm, and finally plucked her bottom lip, seeming to find no comfort with any of it. "It was the Breach after. She gave up. It wasn't because of Finn. It just 'appened. The ghosts got her. It would've 'appened anyway. Dad said so. Everyone agreed. She couldn't take the house anymore. It wasn't my fault."

"You're saying that a lot." His frustration leaked out. He'd always wanted a brother, and she killed hers. *It's not her fault.* Less of him believed that than before. *Why else lie earlier?* To cover up for someone else.

"Gare," she pleaded.

"You're right. It's not your fault. It's your dad's." It had to be.

"It's not. I'm telling you!"

"Well if the house isn't to blame then it's either you or him. And I just cannot believe—" He stopped. What if she was right? What if her father wasn't to blame? That left her, her alone. He'd married a murderer. Even if he survived this literal hell, he'd ruined his future. "I can't believe it's you."

Rapid thuds echoing from far away paused Marie's response. The distance closed, and the sound clarified. Furious footsteps echoed from the foyer, propelling themselves in their direction.

"What's going on?" Julie's raised voice gave away her approach. "I could hear you from the office, and it sure as hell doesn't sound like exercise." She stopped at the entryway and assessed the scene, quickly drawing her conclusion. She shot her finger at Garrett. "If you hurt her, you better hope the ghosts—"

"He knows," Marie interrupted.

Julie's jaw ratcheted open. Her tongue whipped from side to side as she processed. Animalistic facial features and the curl of her fingers gave her the look of a lioness prepared to defend her cub until with some difficulty, she reclaimed her composure. Her furious footsteps resumed, this time in a rush toward her sister, swallowing her in an embrace that pulled her in tight. "Oh, Marie."

Marie placed tentative hands on Julie's hips. "He thinks it's Dad."

A long pause. Julie's nose twitched. Garrett guessed the source of consternation before she confirmed it. "Well, what if it was?"

"What?" Marie pulled away.

"Not on purpose, of course." Julie defensively raised her hands.

"Dad didn't kill his brother. Dad didn't embezzle any money. Dad didn't burn books. He's the only one who's innocent." She heaved a shuddering sigh. "I can't be in this room anymore." She darted past Julie without looking back.

Julie watched her leave, then crossed her arms. She pulled her shoulders toward her back. Her throat pulsed, writhing as if from worms. She bit down on her lip, wincing as she drew blood. She wiped it away. "What is wrong with you? I trusted you to help us, not turn this fucking house into a shit show so the damned devils could have their way with us."

"Trust?" he scoffed. "This family doesn't deserve it."

Her eyes twitched. Her upper body—shoulders, chest, neck, and arms—crunched tight together. "If you need any help, you can go fuck yourself." She turned, fled in a fury that made her entrance seem docile, leaving Garrett alone in the room of murder and broken trust.

33. Basket Case

Never go to bed angry must have been the silliest romantic advice anyone ever uttered. Not only did it discount humans' inability to control their emotions, it lacked the practical means to eliminate said anger. Garrett and Marie could talk 'til the sun came up and likely just make things worse.

His anger extended far beyond her sin. It was the whole situation. Her family. Himself for rushing the relationship. In this state, his mind wasn't his own. Reclaiming it required time apart. Rather than follow that foolish adage, he slept separately from Marie. Not that he expected to sleep properly. He laid down, imagining hours of tossing and turning. Imagining his mind churning to make sense of the fact that his wife murdered her brother.

Yet he slipped into slumber with ease.

His mom split apart the darkness, speaking in full-on Mandarin. He knew a couple dozen words in the waking world, but here he was fluent.

"What did I tell you about marriage?" She lorded over him at his parents' kitchen table, placed at second base in a baseball diamond. In the dream, her short stature had transformed into a towering presence. Too tall to fit under the doorways of his childhood home.

Garrett responded in his mother's native tongue. "Find someone I trust who trusts me."

"And what did you do?"

Garrett twiddled his thumbs, shying away from her belittling stare. "That's what I did. I was just wrong."

"Were you?"

"Wasn't I?"

"This is what you've missed the past five Christmases for?"

"I've been gone less than two months."

"Look at me when we're talking." She grabbed his chin and yanked it up with an arm as long as a pool noodle. Angry tirades blistered from her lips, speaking a language Garrett once again didn't understand. He grimaced as he endured her yelling, each twitch moving them closer to the pitcher's mound. She stopped when all the table's legs stood on the raised earth.

Garrett's dad materialized in a chair across the table. A sixth sense suggested he was always there. Unlike Min Mueller's gigantic proportions, Tyler Mueller was no taller than his son. He spoke fluent German for the first time in his life, and Garrett understood him as easily as in the previous conversation. Mom resumed her admonition in muted fury.

"Garrett, I'm proud of you," Dad said. "You've done something brave in coming here and following your heart. You've taken these leaps your whole life, and they usually pan out. It's okay this one didn't. Your mom's worried. Come home. That's all we ask."

"How long has it been?" Garrett asked.

"So, so long," he drawled, suddenly tired and weak. His head, once full of thick black hair, thinned and grayed. His face wrinkled, skin sagging. His back gradually hunched. "Come back before it's too late." Teeth dropped out of his mouth with each word. He reached across the table in pursuit of rescue.

Garrett grabbed his forearm and held tight. Mom slumped to the ground, still as young as the last time he saw her. She broke down on the perfectly manicured grass of the outfield and bawled. "Why didn't he listen? Why didn't he come home?"

"Mom, I'm here. It hasn't been that long."

Over her continued wails, Garrett asked himself, "How has it been so long?"

The baseball field vanished, and with it, his mother and father. Unending darkness surrounded him. He brought his hands to his face and saw them clear as daylight. Not darkness then, but a void.

From a mile or more away, a colossal figure rose from the depths. The crown of its head was as big as Garrett's entire body. For a time, only the figure's thin hairline faced him. Unlike his father's withering scalp, the hair of this stranger glistened, manifesting its own source of light. The head tilted up and a bulbous, shirtless physique emerged from below. As the figure finished standing, the diaper and healthy fat of its owner left no doubt of what he saw.

"Dad-dy!" the baby cried.

Garrett pinched his cheeks, ran his hands through his hair. "Who are you?"

"Dad-dy!" The house-sized baby's arms shook in the air.

The child resembled him. He stepped toward the baby, but in the space of the void, drew no closer.

"I. Want. Out!" The child cried toward the heavens. Or toward hell. There was no up nor down in the void.

Garrett raised his hands, intending to calm. "It's okay," he cooed.

The tantrum subsided into giggling. The baby drew his arms in toward his chest. In one hand he now held a hand-woven hooded Moses basket.

"What do you have there?"

More giggling.

They repeated the exchange a half-dozen times, Garrett changing his inflections between stern, silly, and sonorous. Each attempt spurred the same result. Eventual progression came not from the giggling child, but from the basket. From within its woven walls, a hand grabbed the edge. A grown man pulled himself up on his side and cupped his lips as he shouted.

"Forgive her."

"Forgive who?" Garrett asked.

The old man shouted again. His words bounced against a barrier that materialized between them. Visible masses of sound collided with the invisible wall. The sonic wave rebounded and crashed against what served as the ground here. The baby and man crumpled too, like a coat falling from its hanger.

He was back on the baseball field. Dad sat across from him, healthy and whole once more.

"Son," Dad said. "What's happening? Your skin."

What was he talking about? Garrett's skin—

His skin was shriveling, worse than his dad's moments ago. Closer to a chemical reaction than rapid aging. Garrett tried to brush off the caustic source. His skin fizzed with no concern for his attempts.

An invisible presence peeled away at his skin.

"Son!"

Garrett flailed wildly against the unseen foe until sure he had fended off the assault. Yet when he brought his arms back to his chest, one had been reduced to muscle, tendon, and bone. The other's skin sliced and slipped off bit by bit. No physical pain struck his nerves, amplifying the torture. Pain would have taken his mind off the ghastly sight. Screams rattled his throat in a shrill cry, his uvula flung forward to the roof of his mouth.

"Hold on to me," Dad said. "Hold on."

He and his dad united over the table.

He woke huffing, his chest splattered with water.

His hand darted for the reading light. He punched the bedpost, groaned, and shook out his hand. With his other hand, he found the switch and illuminated the bed. He started to rest against the stiff drapes behind him and halted, twisting in expectation of finding nails or another object ready to pierce his flesh.

There was nothing besides a material identical to the house's window shades.

He eased himself against the drapes, locked and pulled so taut they may as well have been a wall, and brought his knees to his chest. Something in the room felt out of place. When he found the courage, he opened the drapery to examine the room.

The dresser was similar to the one in the room he shared with Marie, only with beveled edges and a darker coat of color. A Roman shade touched down to the windowsill, shielding him like his bed's canopy. His suitcase and backpack sat unassumingly in the corner. Nothing *looked* wrong. He shifted uncomfortably. His shirt bunched as he squirmed. In his fit, he realized what was out of place.

It was him. He covered his face, and pressing his wrists and his palms against his cheeks, dug the bristly ends of his beard into his skin.

He had to find a way out of here before it drove him mad or killed him.

34. Decisions

Outside the house's front door, Garrett sniffed at what passed for fresh air. Humidity moistened his nose hairs, warming his blood. Gloom darkened the mid-afternoon skies, a perfect encapsulation of the mood within the house.

He climbed the front steps and reentered the foyer. It didn't strike him until he'd walked inside that he never feared getting locked out. Absent ghosts should've led to celebration. Instead, Garrett focused on more sinister concerns—like Marie murdering her brother—as he wound his way up to the second story.

As his foot landed next to the antique clock, a door creaked open. Down the hall, Julie streaked toward him wearing the same clothes as the other day. He stepped to the side; she would've tumbled them both down the stairs if he hadn't. She saw him as she Saw most ghosts lately—not at all.

A moment before stepping down, she glared, as if suddenly realizing his presence. He dug his nails into his arm, holding his breath. Then she dismissed him and raced away. Her footsteps echoed in her descent.

That was the extent of their interaction. The extent of most interactions now. Balled fists, averted gazes, bit lips, and heavy sighs were all the same. Signs that screamed, *Leave me alone.* With Julie and the others, as well as between them.

Garrett trudged the remaining distance to his room. He scooted a dozen multicolored books from one side of his bed to the next and collapsed his rear onto the cleared space. He stared at his pants so long he could have counted the threads. Slowly, he veered his attention away from his clothes. The front of his unzipped backpack drooped from the wall to the floor. Near emptiness gave it a ragged shape. He'd removed everything except for a heavy coat, even taking out his precious laptop.

The nylon shell awaited supplies for his hike to Ajaccio. No, not Ajaccio. To the closest town without a relationship to the Renaults. Perhaps all the way to Alexandria, but the where could wait. He wasn't committed to leaving, not yet. He wasn't even sure he could. The Ring was out there, but the family's other lies called its power into doubt. The last time he passed through, Julie and Marie had goaded him into it, the sisters proving a point that seemed unnecessary.

Unless the point had been to deceive him. Electrical barriers could have produced the same effect. Tricked him into believing the futility of escape. If they meant to keep him here without him questioning them, psychology erected a more powerful wall than anything physical. Inconsistencies from books regarding the formation and mechanics of Hellspot barriers—the Ring seemed to be a personalized term—further validated his theory. It was clear that only the Renaults understood how *their* Ring worked.

Of course, these considerations only arose due to Marie's confession. He'd never imagined leaving her before. She could have remained silent, keeping him unaware. So why tell him?

The optimist's answer: she trusted him, or guilt overwhelmed her at the scene of the crime. The cynic's response: she was protecting her dad's graver sin.

Find someone I trust who trusts me. His mom's adage drove him to delve into his mind, finally allowing himself to parse the other night's dream. He'd ignored it yesterday out of suspicion that a Dreamer planted it. Whether true or not, data was data, and he needed every piece available.

If he dreamed it of his own accord, his parents urging him to return home made sense as a manifestation of his own desires. But if a Dreamer cooked it up, then they wanted him gone; they considered him a threat.

Then there was the baby who cried, *Dad-dy*. He guessed it symbolized a loss of family without Marie. Kids never excited her, and now he understood why. He wanted them though, wanted a loud and cheery house instead of a repeat of his tidy upbringing. They should have discussed it prior to marriage, but there hadn't been time.

That was the natural explanation.

If a Dreamer was responsible, it also called him to stay. To make amends with Marie to fulfill that desire. It didn't make sense that Dreamers wanted him to both stay and go though. Besides, could he ever trust her as a parent?

Finally, he considered the old man who shouted, *Forgive her*.

That seemed clear. Her referenced Marie. Perhaps the speaker was her grandfather, for all Garrett remembered of him from that one harrowing night. And wasn't it strange that he died right after Mr. Renault pronounced Garrett and Marie husband and wife?

Threads of coincidence tugged him into a mental whirlpool. He slapped his cheeks. The threads yanked back and he slapped himself harder. He couldn't link his wedding night to Maurice Renault's death with absolute certainty. What he could determine was whether to follow the old man's command. To forgive her.

Marie had easily done so after he'd groped her against her will. After he'd almost done worse. It was wrong, even if a ghost possessed him. She forgave him because he knew that wasn't really him. She even forgave Derrick, who inflicted much worse harm on his cousin.

Garrett shook his head, correcting cousin to sister. A twisted family for a twisted house. They deserved one another. He squeezed the comforter like a stress ball, pulling the fabric tight at the base of his fingers. He imagined twirling the blanket around like a savage hurricane, but that was all he allowed himself.

He sighed, released the comforter, and returned to the question: could he forgive Marie?

The answer was simple. If she acted of her own free will, then no.

Family was sacred. He longed for a big family. Longed for siblings to play with. Longed to share familial triumphs and tribulations with more than just his parents. Forgiving her necessitated an insurmountable mixture of jealousy and hate to have consumed her. Evidence from the texts piled on his bed suggested such a strong pull was far-fetched outside of a Breach.

Garrett wanted to lay the blame on Mr. Renault, whose guilt meant Marie's innocence. He directed his thoughts away from his dream, hoping his subconscious delivered an errant string of logic to validate his hopes. Marie's protection of her father made that difficult. She continued supporting him at every opportunity. Every action implicated her, and she made no defense against her crime.

In that moment of profound truth, he realized he had lost his trust in her.

Hollow emptiness replaced his organs and bones. Tension built by his grave analysis washed away in the wake of despondency. Hunched over on the bed, his skin hung loosely off his formless self. As the sensation of his heartbeat ceased, he entered a void similar to the one from his dream. Floated in space as empty as him. Time passed at an incalculable speed.

When he came to, he jolted back, wiping away a smattering of tears he never felt fall.

Should he investigate Mr. Renault or flee? The former called to him, the latter compelled him. Failing to escape still allowed him to investigate. But if investigating failed to prove Marie's innocence, he might lose his opportunity to flee. He may not even care about living at that point. A lengthier stay also gave Julie more opportunities to decipher why he'd borrowed books on Hellspot barriers. She'd learn he doubted the Ring's very existence.

The logic was clear: the longer he waited to leave, the lower his odds of success. Blood and oath be damned. If the Ring were a lie, then so were the threats resulting from abandoning the family. A successful flight would call into question every fact he'd learned.

The end of the world is at stake. That's what Marie had told him, though she'd conveniently left out killing her brother. Why trust any of it?

He grabbed the largest of the yellow-covered books and fanned the pages. He stopped on a section regarding the depth of Hellspot barriers. Seemed as good of a place as any to kill a few hours before the moon set and he dared his escape. Succeed or fail, he'd move forward. If he were to trust anyone in this house again, he'd build that foundation by verifying, for at least one time, they had told him the truth.

35. Flight

2 a.m.

Garrett's phone flashed the time as he shined its backlight on the nearby sunroom storage shelf. His free hand hovered over a box of energy bars. His backpack was slung to his side. He knew once he grabbed that first bar, he was committed.

At 2:02, he started taking supplies. Energy bars first, followed by bottled water, then other non-perishable food. Canned and dried meat, nuts, plastic fruit cups, and more. Alexandria was only a day away on foot, but he was past taking unnecessary risks. He scanned the other shelves for anything worthwhile. He smacked his head as he passed a can opener, then added it to his stash. Despite it all, he made sure to relock the containers when he finished with them.

After zipping up his bag, he peeked into the hall. Empty as his walk down here. He tiptoed toward the sunroom, intending to escape off the side of the house. No bedroom windows faced out there, and it was the least likely place to bury electrical wiring.

He entered the room with a methodical opening and closing of the door. As he walked by a wicker chair with a blue and white palm trees cushion, he clenched his straps. Garrett had sat here when the twins talked over his head about Marie's evil deed like he was an idiot. Sat here when Derrick tricked him into marrying his sister, with assertions of greater safer here than anywhere else in the world.

Another Renault lie.

But not everyone in the house was a Renault by blood. Garrett stalled near the backyard door. Should he invite Kelly? His hand itched to feel the comfort of twisting that metallic knob, but he owed her at least a passing thought. She was as innocent in this mess as him and upset enough to sequester herself. That didn't mean he could convince her to leave, or that he should try. She had married Claude years ago. They had a child, by birth or adoption making no difference. Kelly leaving her husband seemed as unlikely as enduring a fifty-mile hike with a toddler in tow. If he escaped, it was by himself or not at all. He opened the door, suppressing the voice that screamed not to leave her behind.

Patio lights brightened further as he stepped outside. He dashed into the yard, unmown grass cushioning his steps. His back hugged the limestone wall as he slid around to the house's side. A short fence divided the shadows near him from the dark grove on the other side. He squatted down and crept forward.

Sweat dampened his armpits. His heart thudded in his ear. Nausea rose to his throat. He reminded himself he wasn't leaving without just cause. A successful escape confirmed another lie, signifying uncountable more to come. Failing didn't exonerate Marie, but it narrowed the scope of her misdeeds. Distilled them down to one. A failed escape made forgiving his wife possible—he still thought of them as married, whatever that was worth.

Did she feel the same?

He ran his tongue around the inside of his mouth to spread the remaining moisture. He stepped onto the lowest board of the country fence and jumped over. He inspected the overgrown yard for snakes and other critters, a habit from hiking.

Settle down. Nothing's out there.

He still proceeded carefully, guessing at the Ring's diameter based on its location along the driveway. Trees occupied half of the space before him, forcing him to take a windy path. He snapped twigs off branches as he passed, carefully so as to limit the noise in the otherwise quiet night. He tossed them ahead every several steps, hoping they reacted with the barrier—if it existed—before he did.

Of course, he could turn back. He looked up and behind him. Leaving Marie was easier when he boiled it down to a calculation. A smart move after a series of rushed mistakes. But maybe this was the rushed decision?

Proof one way or the other is all you're looking for. Find the Ring and you can go back, with everyone none the wiser. Don't, and you can cut your losses. It's not like you haven't had your heart broken before.

He gritted his teeth and inched forward, tensing from head to toe with every step. Repeated it in a tiring rhythm: step, tense, relax. His veins pulsed beneath his forehead. Breathing became a chore.

Long hair brushed the back of his neck.

Garrett dropped his bundle of twigs and swatted behind him, striking low-hanging pine needles he'd absentmindedly passed by. Huffing, he snapped the branch off and threw it at the tree trunk. Exhausted by a physical challenge objectively easier than a light jog, he slowly recollected the twigs, then set his sights on a small clearing. Above that space, dull stars fought cloudy coverings to shine their light. Or was the Ring obfuscating them? Was it more like a dome? Perhaps a sphere wrapped around the earth underneath?

Doesn't matter. You're not flying or digging your way out. Keep moving.

His feet rejected the command. He stretched his arms out like a blind man in a foreign location, touching empty air. He waved twigs around and felt no resistance. After a moment, his brain explained his immobile feet: he was about the same distance from the house as his previous jolts.

He negotiated with himself to continue, eventually agreeing to move heel to toe as if walking a tightrope. Arms out, he tensed with each step, then twitching and recoiling every few after that. He took a break before forcing himself onward. Behind him, the house loomed like a terrible sleeping giant, the garage its faithful hound. How much of this until he decided the Ring was a sham?

Hours if necessary. He possessed more of those than lives. He wiped his forehead and sucked in a breath, inviting a confidence that never came. Each step was a battle. He broke off a new set of twigs and curled his fingers around them. Stopped every few steps to throw one. Trudge, trudge, trudge, throw.

Then, in an explosive burst, he dropped the sticks and leapt backward. He reacted to the impenetrable wall before pain lit up his nerves. Branding iron hot needles stabbed his knuckles, worked their way up his arm with machine gun speed. He groaned, stifling a worse cry that bulged in his throat.

Phantom needles weren't just piercing his skin. They were sprinting through his bloodstream, cutting him from the inside and racing to his chest to deliver a killing blow, slicing tendons and ligaments along the way. His blood cells equipped microscopic daggers and cut at his arterial walls to escape the invader. Pierced attacks came from within and without in every direction. He lost the strength to hold his cries at bay. He bit down on his arm, muffling his howl. Fell down to his knees, wrapping his arm around his neck. Lost himself in his survival.

He panted. His limbs convulsed. He swayed back and forth. Motion relieved enough pain to try to stand. He forced himself up, retched, and staggered toward the house. He'd rest once he reached the fence. After he put some distance between himself and the Ring.

He fixed his sights on a particular wooden post, lit up from the house like a heavenly beam. His periphery blurred in pursuit of his target. His eyes dried from holding his stare until an involuntary blink forced them shut. He struck something hard and fell backward.

He'd run into a tree. A tree he swore wasn't there seconds ago.

A force snatched his backpack, dragging him toward the Ring.

He whirled his head around. Nothing was there. *Nothing* was pulling him toward his doom. He dug his nails into the ground, clawed to keep himself immobile.

The force strengthened, tugging harder. Seconds separated him from death.

He slipped off the backpack and scampered forward. Endorphins pumped in a pathetic attempt to dull the Ring's searing, stabbing pain.

He made it five steps before the force slipped under his shirt's collar and hem and yanked him back.

Garrett stumbled, barely kept his footing. He trudged forward as if pulling a weighted sled through mud. Sweat sprung from his pores to douse the fire within. He jerked his shoulders forward, throwing off his attacker for a split second before it clamped down again. Little by little, he drew closer to the house. When he reached the country fence, he grabbed a high board. Splinters jabbed into his palm. A mere blip of recognition against the searing pain from within.

He tried hoisting himself up and over.

The force pulled the other way.

Garrett rose a couple inches and crashed to the earth but shed his counterweight in the process. His back struck the ground before his head, thick grass the length of his feet cushioning the fall. He bounced up, his thighs straining at the sudden jerk. He tried again to hurdle the fence, but his assailant returned.

He struggled for freedom, pushed himself up, twisted and thrashed. There was too much drag, the force too strong. He stopped struggling and planted his feet, tightening his grip. More splinters casually joined their friends under his skin, but worse were his sluggish muscles. Every limb burned every bit of strength to keep himself steady. Miraculously, the Ring's sharp pain had dulled to a dozen bee stings.

How long could he hold out? Twenty minutes tops. Should he shout? Hope for one of the Renaults to . . . what? Bat the ghosts off his back? The force tugging on him wanted to drag him through the Ring. Drag him to his death.

A second force tugged on the belt of his jeans. Twenty minutes down to ten. He had to act.

He let go of the fence almost, but not quite, all at once. He stumbled back but stayed upright as planned. He pulled his shirt off in the direction the force was dragging him. The collar went over his head, followed by the rest until only his arms remained in his sleeves, and he twisted free.

Resistance vanished.

His legs were already in motion.

He sprinted forward, teeth clenched, half-expecting the force to yank him down and break his leg in a strike against the wooden plank. Sweat dripped from his hair, blurring his vision. He wiped his face, never breaking stride. He leapt up, turned his body sideways, and pushed off the fence. He landed on the other side with enough momentum to dash to the sunroom. He pulled the handle back.

It moved a smidge.

He pulled, tugged, and yanked, rattling the door. Locked. The door was locked. He glanced back at the fence, costly and pointless given his assailant's invisibility. He grunted and dashed off again, running for the dining room door. The deadbolt clicked into place as he reached for the handle. He tapped on the glass panel.

"Hello?"

He bounced his head side to side and abandoned the entrance. Sped off around the side of the house, praying to a god he wasn't sure he believed in that he'd hear the door open. Unanswered prayers sapped his hope as he turned the corner of the house. He passed the tool shed as he picked his destination.

The front door made more noise and risked questions he didn't want to answer. But it gave him the straightest shot to his room and was closer. Between explaining and dying, the choice was easy.

Garrett turned the next corner and raced up the front porch steps, his stomach clenched in anticipation. He gripped the handle, depressed the thumb latch, and pushed. Resigned to the deadbolt barricading his entry, he already took a half step back and almost shut the door as he opened it. He wobbled, recovered, and sprung forward before the opposing forces trapped him outside. He glanced to the heavens in relief, then scoured at hell beneath. He wasn't alone in the foyer.

"Where's your shirt?" Julie stood in her typical position—arms crossed—with an unusual set of clothes. A tank top with thin straps and yoga pants clinging to her legs, her hair in a tight bun. Garrett didn't even think she owned workout clothes.

He looked in the direction of the gym. What was she up to? Exercise and Julie didn't mix.

"Are you going to answer me?" He was about to when she added, "What happened to your"—her head tilted—"fingers?"

The backside of his right hand's fingers had bubbled up a nasty shade of burned red. Garrett hid them behind his arm. He was still breathing hard. "They came after me. I got dragged through the yard."

Julie's scowl deepened. "I heard the commotion and changed in case I had to play rescue. You're an idiot for going out there, doubly so for going out alone. We warned you." Julie's eyes narrowed on his hand. She clenched her fist, raised it to eye level. Shot it forward and shook her finger at him. "You were going to leave her?" She scoffed. "Appalling. I can't believe I read you so wrong. I don't want you near Marie unless you're rescuing her from certain death. Do you understand me?"

As if this was his fault. As if he murdered his brother, burned books, embezzled from his family, and lusted after his sister. He clutched his jeans at his waist, his tongue itching to lash out. Then he glanced down, examined his shirtless torso, and the fight left him. His hands fell from their perch and drooped at his side. Surviving the attacking force had worn him down. Sapped his anger and left only shame.

"Are you going to tell anyone?"

"Unlike some, I'm capable of keeping a secret when it's for the greater good." She pressed her finger to her lips, as if deciding whether to leave her next words unsaid. "And I'm mature enough that in spite of all this, I still prefer you alive. You probably didn't realize this in your traitorous flight, but if ghosts are capable of dragging you, their cooperation is growing."

A memory stirred of Claude telling Garrett that multiple ghosts were needed to physically touch a living person. Until now, they had never been so coordinated. "Shouldn't we tell everyone?"

"Didn't I make myself clear? There is no we. I'll do it." She shook her head in an uncanny resemblance to Garrett's mother and stalked off to the library.

Garrett was alone again, with little more choice than to retreat to his room and dwell on Julie's remarks. He snuck up the stairs, balanced on the knife's edge between another ghostly assault and a second Renault discovering him. He hitched his step as he passed Marie's room. His confirmation of the Ring's deadly width stirred a faint desire to forgive.

With Julie's ultimatum, would he ever have that chance? He pushed himself forward. Avoiding Marie was for the best. His feelings on the matter were complicated enough. All of that could be sorted out after achieving the one goal everyone shared: survival.

36. Distractions

Variations of Garrett's dream from before his escape attempt played on nightly repeat. His parents lamented his time away as their skin peeled like lepers. The giant baby alternated screaming for Daddy with disconcerting giggles. Every morning of the several days that followed, Garrett woke earlier and earlier to the thin remnants of a burst water balloon. He sensed the two dream entities warred with one another, with him caught in the middle. The unnerving sentiment rendered it difficult for him to return to sleep. Meanwhile, the old man in the Moses basket never made another appearance.

He gave last night's dream the same passing interest as those previous and abandoned it. Dwelling on its meaning risked losing control. Nonsense begat madness, and he stayed borderline sane thanks to his sole friends of late: his books.

He dressed in jeans and a collared shirt and locked himself in the upstairs study. His research satisfied his bargain with Julie—her silence in exchange for his keeping away from Marie. He would've done the same anyway. He felt useful here. Safer too, given what he'd discovered his new family was capable of. He eyed a spacious corner before sitting. Sleeping here might get him even more work done. A consideration for later.

Piled on the desk were several books on two subjects: dream interpretations and historic Breaches with similar patterns as this one. So far, he'd discovered little, plagued by distractions worse than his dreams.

Voices whispered in the morning. Windows shattered in the afternoon. Walls quaked in the evening. The next day, everything returned to normal. Mekari and spirits attempted to lull him into complacency, to ignore the real strike when it came.

They'd have to try harder. His time playing the fool was at an end.

Garrett had moved on to texts about spirits manifesting sleep paralysis when a rhythmic set of knocks tapped the door, and an oval shadow slid under the door. He waited for the footsteps to wander away before standing. His hand no longer hurt to grip the handle. Skin singed by the Ring had mostly healed, leaving a pink, rough patch. He opened the door and bent down to pick up his prepared lunch. Reeled back after a closer inspection.

Worms the color of uncooked shrimp writhed on a tarnished copper plate. They curled around one another, squirming across the dish's entire surface.

What the hell, Marie?

He stepped into the hall to catch her, knowing he wouldn't. He'd timed his movements to avoid her, as much out of not wanting to face her as complying with Julie's demand. For whatever her reasons, Marie acted similarly, scurrying away each time she brought him lunch and dinner. He'd only nibbled at the first few plates, half-expecting poison while damning himself for his suspicion. But if she'd killed her brother, why not her husband too?

Yet as the meals filled his shrinking stomach again and again, no illness ever struck him. This garnered a small measure of trust—trap or no. Plus, the rewards outweighed the risk. Leaving the room to make food took too long, invited too many scenery changes that might twist his mind.

That same clarity struck him now. She wouldn't have fed him for days only to suddenly bring him worms. The house had tricked him again. He picked up the plate, eyes half on it as he set it onto a second chair. When he saw the food as food and his appetite returned, he'd eat.

Garrett dawdled at the window, his shaking hand rising to the Roman shade. He unlatched the lock that kept it taut and peeked behind, spotting Marie's tent and the bulge of the mattress she'd stuffed inside. Claude paced close by. He and his younger sister were the only two adults who seemed to spend time together anymore. What conspiratorial words passed between them?

He pulled back. The shade thwacked the window. He reengaged the lock and smacked his head in a trio of strikes. Blindly believing in the Renaults might brand him a fool, but he'd lose all hope casting blame for innocent companionship. To trust Marie again, he had to afford her some credit—especially given how she'd taken care of him.

But why did she have to murder her brother?

Shaking spread from his hand to his body. He forced himself to sit and stare at the book until his inner turmoil abated. Slowly, the words came into focus. He pushed through reading several chapters until his stomach grumbled as loud as a car engine. He peered at his companion chair.

The worms were gone. In their place sat a turkey sandwich and chips, on a paper plate and not a copper one. He opened a drawer and took out two bottles of water. After gulping the first, he snapped the seal on the second. He leaned over, snatched the food, and pushed the book away to eat his lunch. Toasted bread crisped between his teeth, its temperature and texture clashing. The sandwich had been previously warmed. In his wait to eat, it cooled to match the ambient air. He ate a couple of chips in between unsatisfying bites. All the while, the open book taunted him.

The current section regarded the collaboration between spirits. The six types of haunts rarely worked together, but like everything with this Breach, the information was outdated. The enemy had innovated. Mekari found a way to direct the spirits, to unify them in a historic manner. What benefit did obsolete facts bring to his survival?

Garrett stuffed the last of his meal into his mouth and slammed the book. Survival wasn't enough. He wanted his relationship with Marie back, when she wasn't a murderer. The old man in the Moses basket—

who Garrett once believed was Maurice Renault's ghost—had commanded him to forgive her. He wanted to. Wanted to admit to her he tried to run away. Forgiveness required more than wishing it though. Garrett needed a legitimate reason to explain Marie's heinous act.

Mr. Renault, of course. But how? Julie accused him of hiding part of the translation from Maurice's audio recording. Iris said his secret involved all of his kids. Garrett tried to remember why he woke up mistrusting Marie's father from that dream weeks ago. It had something to do with Claude, but how useful was that connection when heinous crimes tainted everyone?

Or was Mr. Renault relatively innocent? An adulterer, sure, but there were worse acts.

Like murdering your child brother.

Garrett's cheeks scrunched up, an inner mixture of frustration and sorrow confusing his facial muscles. He massaged his face back into a neutral state and stared at the closed book.

Chaotic energy swirled within, possessing him in a wholly natural manner as it yearned for release. He grimaced, then exploded in a fury. Shoved the sleeved book off the desk and flung its brightly colored companions to the floor. He gripped the edge of the desk, digging his nails into its solid block of wood. To forgive Marie, he needed to blame someone for her transgressions. If that someone wasn't Mr. Renault, then who?

He couldn't trust anyone, couldn't even trust his dreams. An aching pain splintered his fingers, pulling him back into complacency. He peeled his nails from the desk, staring at the fresh indentations. Focusing on the damage done and breathing carefully, he held his hands out in an apologetic gesture to the furniture.

I can't lose control. I've already lost so much.

37. Revelations

Silence throughout the room, throughout the entire house. Silence so thick, the pressure of it pounded Garrett's skull. Like diving to the bottom of the ocean.

It made the knock at the door sound like an atomic bomb.

He jumped up, painfully aware of his hunger. His stomach couldn't wait for Marie to walk her safe distance away. She delivered his meals erratically now, and he didn't dare leave to prepare them himself. He was so close to figuring it all out. He raced to the door, his legs resisting the movement. They'd grown lazy sitting in the contours of the study chair. He threw open the door, his eyes darting to the knocker's hands. They held nothing, and though the hands were female, they weren't Marie's.

Julie stepped back and covered her nose. The other hand hung limp at her waist, her arm in a sling. "Did you stop showering?"

"No time. Where's Marie? Where's breakfast?"

"Breakfast? It's almost dusk." She stretched her neck, peering over his shoulder. "Have you been sleeping here too?"

Blankets and sheets formed a makeshift sleeping bag at one end of the cramped study. He shrugged. "Get me food. I'm almost there."

"Get your own damn food. I'm here for my books."

"No," he growled.

"You brat. I don't have time for this. Let me in." She stepped forward.

Garrett slammed the door.

Wood rattled with the collision. A frustrated groan followed. "Congratulations, you've turned everyone against you. I'm getting in there, even if it means asking my asshole brother to break in."

"Just get me some food. All I need is a little more time and some food."

"What the hell are you talking about? Marie's brought you three meals every day. Answer the door when she knocks, and you'll—you know what, fuck you. I'll be back." She banged the door square in its center, howled in shrill anger, and stormed off. Silence devoured the footsteps within seconds.

He raised his eyebrows. Marie had been feeding him? That didn't make any sense. She set his food down with such regularity that the first time she was late, he checked the hall anyway to see if he missed her knock. He started checking several times a day the more meals she missed. Food only ever appeared following a knock.

Hopefully, Julie brought him something or told Marie. Otherwise, he guessed—

He flung his hands in the air. Think now. Food later.

Crumbled wads of paper littered the path to his desk. He plopped down, grabbed his latest work from between two stacks of books that towered at head height. A distilled list of key clues and suppositions.

Iris – Simon fertility problems. Derrick is Mr. R's son.

Marie – Mr. R regretted conceiving Finn but didn't have a choice.

Claude – More fertility probs.

Derrick – Corruption from a mekar, abated only by Nia's presence in his life.

Julie – Burned a book linking mekari and humans, then tore a page from a related one tied to fertility. Mr. R missed translations.

Metal clanged against metal above. Air conditioning rattled its morning ritual but sputtered at the end where it normally jangled. It sounded wrong, but his mind filed it away as unimportant in the face of his looming discovery. He was close, so very close.

Next to his note was Julie's scribbling regarding her grandfather's last day alive. Her best guess at translating the section her dad withheld. She hadn't noticed it missing, or she would've suspected him first.

Garrett zoned in on dialogue he'd read a thousand times.

Beta: I'm aware. It's my fault they're like that. How else could the family grow large enough to protect our Hellspot? Alpha: Silence. I said silence. Beta: They're strong though. They'll overcome it.

Garrett blanked, as he had so many times in the days (weeks?) since he'd secluded himself. His mind was like a vast stretch of space before the universe existed. And like the Big Bang, this time an answer materialized with a sudden burst of energy. "That's it!"

Excitement pressed against his bladder. He cinched the muscles in his groin, damming his pee from leaking out. The bathroom could wait—another silly, mundane concern like hunger in the face of a revelation. Laughter rattled his chest like a machine gun. His throat vibrated as the deep resonance escaped his mouth.

Fertility.

A deal with the devil.

Mr. Renault had doomed them all to give them life. Four tattoos on his face, in one of Garrett's forgotten dreams that now flared to life, hinted at this. A blast of discovery awakened the memory, instilling absolute confidence in his theory.

Why else would Julie burn a book and not remember the reason? Why else would Claude steal from the family he so clearly loved? Why else would Derrick assault his closest friend? His sister he knew as his cousin, but loved more than either relationship required?

Why else would Marie Renault murder her brother before she hit puberty?

Silence surrounded him, different than earlier. It pervaded the air, sickening the smell and lining the desk and walls with a hazy film. The silence was the culmination of a family's fall from grace, tumbling into the graveyard that awaited everyone in the end. Each putrid sniff reinforced the loneliness that had consumed him in this study. Of the loneliness that consumed the entire family. His family. He'd tried to run from them, but he belonged here.

Bound by blood and oath.

It all started thirty-something years ago, with Mr. Renault making an unholy deal. But that was history. Like one of his professors said, what have you done for me lately? What havoc had the spirits and mekari wreaked?

They'd splintered the family of their own accord, everyone retreating into themselves with selfish sights of survival. They were easy to manipulate for anyone that recognized their desires, fears, and relationships. Armed with that knowledge and appropriate talents, one only had to tip the correct domino. Start a cascade that buried the family before they realized there was no escape. Those dominoes were placed decades ago, the pieces standing sturdy until weeks ago when the first fell—Nia's murder.

She was the unsuspecting glue of the family. He'd once considered himself Dorothy here, in an idealized world of The Wizard of Oz. Marie, the Lion's heart. Julie, the Scarecrow's brains. Claude, the Tin Man's courage. If that were the case, then Derrick and Nia were the yellow brick road, and without Nia, there was no *them*. Once she died, Derrick lost himself, and an avalanche of catastrophe followed. The family lost their direction in an instant, never realizing how far they'd strayed off the path.

It explained the relative quiet of ghosts. Why meddle in human affairs when their own minds tormented them worse than any haunting? Garrett was sure he'd missed other revelations, but his new optimism prompted his first smile in days, perhaps weeks. He had answers.

"Marie, I forgive you. I hope you can forgive me too."

He rose and stretched legs sore from underuse, noticing the layers of grime and sweat caked on his sleeping arrangements. He chuckled at the turn of events. The end of his self-appointed prison time had arrived. He inhaled, crinkling his nose at the musk, finding sweetness in it all the same. He twisted from side to side, indulged a satisfying crack in his back.

The window shattered.

Warm air rushed the room. He bent down, eyes on his makeshift bed. Glass peppered the area between his lower back and calf. Half a dozen shards pierced his clothes before he reached his target. He slung his blanket over his shoulders, shielding him from a second salvo. Bundled the material so it covered his hands. Pain from the initial strike faded fast, as likely from adrenaline as the shallow wounds. The larger glass fragments had yet to slip by the shade and find him.

He bounded forward and swapped to holding the blanket with one hand. Grabbed hold of the door handle and pulled. It caught, resisted. The lock was disengaged. It felt like someone held the handle from the other side.

"Help!" He twisted and jerked the handle until the blanket fell from his shoulders, exposing him. He yanked his shield back up. Kicked the door's base, failing to budge it but reminding him of Claude's action-star performance. *Aim for just below the door handle.* Glass chips peppered his cloak, sprinkled the floor. A larger shard pierced through, gashing his upper arm. He cried out, fueling his next strike with panic and rage.

The door held sturdy. He scowled. Claude had kicked in and he was kicking out. Garrett dropped rear-first to the floor, the blanket padding his fall. He scurried backward, taking refuge underneath the desk. Smaller pebbles nicked his bare feet.

String zipped through metal behind him. The pull cord on the shade worked its way up, exposing him to the full brunt of the spectral assault. The shade slammed into the metal bar like the setting of a guillotine. But he'd had it locked. He was sure.

Ghosts and mekari don't care for rules.

The window cracked, split off into substantial-sounding segments. Shards already on the floor scratched their way to rising. A hundred pieces of glass, each the size of a stud earring, levitated in front of the door. Taunting him.

Think! They can't leave you alive. They know you know.

Taunts turned into strikes. The projectiles whistled toward him. Garrett tucked himself into a ball, kissing the floor, and yanked the blanket to cover his body. A minor hail storm struck his shield, failing to break through, and crackled against the floor. Other than ramming the door, there was only one other way out. Would the blanket absorb enough force if he jumped from the second floor?

Fabric tore behind him. Threads ripped. He shifted left as a knife's edge grazed his outer thigh. Glass the size of a chef's knife jammed into the floor point-first and then rattled to free itself. Garrett slapped down on its smooth top side, pinning it to the ground, and the shaking ceased.

Images of Maurice Renault's corpse, bludgeoned by his fall from this same height, warred with a pool of blood circling Nia.

The desk lurched, slid into him. Fastball-strength blunt force struck his arm and knee. Whistling pervaded his hearing, quieted only by sleet made of glass striking the desk.

Jumping was the only option. He'd lap the blanket over the window frame and hang off the edge before dropping down. He scampered out from his hiding spot. A bevy of levitating books greeted him, launching themselves straight at him.

Garrett dodged most, but the blunt edges assuredly bruised his calf and lower back.

With his head down, he strode toward the window before another strike came. He vaguely recalled those parachute jumpers from war documentaries his dad watched landing in a specialized roll. Hopefully his subconscious would fill in the blanks when he landed. He pulled the blanket to his chest.

Whistling came again, not from in the room but from outside of it.

"Garrett!" It was Marie. "Can you hear me? I slid my mattress over. It's safe to jump!"

He threw the blanket over the shallowest break in the glass. Considered his original plan. If she moved the mattress . . .

Scrapes and cuts slashed their way along his back. Cut his neck near his right shoulder. Blood dampened his grimy shirt. Piss ran its way from his groin to his lower wounds. He stopped thinking.

"Stand back!" Garrett hoisted himself up on the frame and hurtled himself out the window, spraying the outdoors with the few bits of glass that remained. Pinpricks pierced the blanket, scraping his palms. Down he fell, an eternity passing in a split second.

He landed feet first, dead center of the mattress, and crumpled to his side.

He was alive.

"You're bleeding!" Marie screamed.

He stood up, stumbled his way to the unmowed grass. His legs felt the burn of a hundred squats, but he could move. He could walk. She saved him, but if they didn't run that wouldn't matter. "We've got to go."

They grabbed each other's hands. He covered his side, where a gash flowed beyond the fibers of his shirt. He limped two steps toward the safety of the tent, and Marie left his grasp to wrap her arm around his waist and support his weight. They stopped short of her outdoor home, casting suspicion on the second floor. Whatever spirits attacked him hadn't followed.

Marie stroked his cheek. Garrett soaked up a sensation he'd missed so much, radiating a warmth that dulled his ubiquitous pain. She moved her hand down his neck, arm, back, and thigh. She wiped each of his wounds, blood staining her hand until it overtook her visible flesh. Finally, she brought her gentle touch to where Garrett was stanching his worst wound.

"I figured out something in the study," Garrett said. "Something you need to know." Pain crept back into his body. Each breath pricked and sliced his wounds anew. He controlled his grimace worse than he thought based on Marie's ensuing frown. "We've got to find everyone else though, so let's move while we talk."

"What are you talking about? We need to patch you up." Her voice was the sweet melody that Garrett had missed in the deafening silence of the study—his near tomb.

He caressed the back of her hand, lingering there, inviting her to join him with a glance. She completed the hand stack in full. Stronger together than apart. How he'd missed this union, bloody as it was. "I love you."

Her lips curled up, and her face softened. "I love you too." They froze in that moment until Garrett grimaced again, and Marie slipped out of his grasp. "One sec." She disappeared into her tent.

Blood tickled his cheek, wet his beard. Knees ached with a burning fire. A mixture of blood and urine had dampened his pants. Cramps racked his hands.

He wanted to crawl into the tent and curl up with her.

She came back holding a Harvard sweater. His sweater, before she permanently borrowed it midway through dating. "Had it in case that winter cold ever showed." She pressed it against his side. "You need it more."

He clutched the sweater against himself. They shared another moment before they both broke the silence, speaking simultaneously.

"Let's get you inside and bandaged," Marie said.

"Your brother. Finn. It wasn't your fault."

Her mouth hung open.

Find someone you trust, who trusts you.

"I was an ass," Garrett said. "I should've forgiven you as soon as you told me. I asked to carry more of your burden and at the first chance, I spurned you. I'm so sorry. I was scared. Lost. You couldn't have controlled yourself any more than when that Claimer possessed me in the kitchen."

Marie squeezed his hand. "Please. Stop." Every feature on her face drooped the faintest amount. She pushed against his lower back, guiding him toward the house. "We can talk about this later."

Garrett resisted. He squeezed his eyes shut. Stole a brief reprieve for the pain he caused his wife as he split open her old scar. As readily as she doled out forgiveness for others, she never found it for herself. "I know it hurts, but you need to hear this—everyone does. Can I tell you the rest while we walk?"

"If it'll keep you moving."

As Garrett hobbled alongside Marie, he revealed his suspicions, unsure whether Marie was listening or merely racking herself with guilt.

38. Rally

Marie hadn't heard a word Garrett said. Not the first time. He was rushing through it anyway. Fragments of the epiphany he almost died for were still organizing themselves in his head. He started over once they reached the sunroom. She interrupted him as they trudged down the hallway toward the breakfast nook.

"You're saying my dad," Marie stuttered, "made a deal with a mekar for fertility?"

"I know, but yeah. That's exactly what I'm saying." Garrett bellowed, hoping to draw the attention of the household. His painful limp slowed their advance. This would all go faster if the family came to them.

"My dad loves me. Why let me suffer if he knew all along?"

"I haven't figured that out yet."

"We'll ask him after we clean you up."

"It's not too bad." He lifted the Harvard sweater from his side. Blood stained its front but didn't soak through, the first three letters splotched with a truer crimson than the solid color surrounding them. Never mind that the shirt he wore was glued to his skin. "Plus, convincing everyone will be easier with visible proof that the mekari didn't want me relaying what I have to say."

"Bleeding on people isn't as convincing as you think. We'll clean you up, let you shower, and *then* we can round up the family."

Pain forced his lips to curl against his teeth. "We need to get this out. All of that can wait." He'd abandoned this family once. He owed them this.

Marie's eyes darted from wound to wound on his body. "Shush. We're almost there."

They stepped out from the arch of the breakfast nook, and Garrett walked face-first into a wire shelving unit. A box thudded onto the tile, and a bag that had been on top of it split open. Kernels of rice sprayed the floor. He whirled around, double-checking the hand he held was still his wife's.

Marie tilted her head at him. "Are you okay?"

"How'd we get here?" Rows of shelves stood behind them, with a line of freezers at the back of the room. The entryway peeked out into a hallway he thought he'd passed through going the other way.

"What do you mean?"

"We were walking toward the foyer, then I ran into this." He touched the shelf.

"Could be a friendly ghost or you bumped your head jumping out the window. Don't know, but this is exactly where I've been heading." Marie leaned over and flipped the light switch. Once, twice, half a dozen times. Near darkness consumed them. Sun rays bouncing off hallway walls provided their only light. "Power's out."

"Isn't there a backup generator?"

"Yeah, and the spirits shouldn't be able to . . ." To sabotage them. She needn't say it. "Stay where you are." Marie let go of him for the first time since she'd given him back his sweater. She crouched down and rifled through the middle shelf before moving on to the bottom.

"What are you doing?"

Marie came back up with an electric lamp and clicked it on.

"Right, good thinking. Let's get out of here."

"Umm."

"What is it?"

"Look." She pointed to the floor.

He leaned over to see between the shelves.

WAIT HERE, spelled the rice.

"All the more reason to go," Garrett said.

"No, this is good." Marie set the lamp on the shelf. "We're patching you up and washing out those wounds. Grab a couple bottles of water."

"I'm fine."

"Half your weight was on me by the time we got here. We're surrounded by medical supplies, and even the food is telling you to take a break."

"We don't have time." Blood trickled down his elbow. He cleaned it up with the dry side of his sweater and placed the sullied side back above his waist. Only three places really hurt—his side, his right shoulder, and his left calf.

Marie's hands writhed, erratically moving onto and off each other. "Time won't matter if you die, Garrett Mueller. You're not leaving me. I just got you back. This past month is the worst I've felt since . . ."

She grabbed the lamp and left him to sift through a nearby shelving unit. She fought back tears as she spoke. "You tell me I'm not to blame? I want to believe that. I want to believe that I don't have to be afraid around Grady or Tommy. Before you locked yourself away, you told me Derrick's my brother. That still hasn't set in. How long will this take? How can I ever know if it's true?" She shoved one box aside, searched through the next. "This Breach has ravaged my family. The time you spent in the study hit me as hard as losing my mom. But if you're right—despite some awfulness to it—I can see the silver lining. Having my own kids isn't something I've ever considered. If I get there one day, you better be standing next to me. So, we're not leaving this room until we've cleaned you up and wrapped you in gauze."

Garrett looked her up and down, really looked at her. Dirty tennis shoes. Headband slicking greasy hair to her scalp. Sunken eyes and an oversized tank top—had she lost weight? If so, it was his fault. He'd abandoned her. Left her for—

Dizziness forced him to grab the shelf for balance. He thought he had spent one, *maybe* two weeks in the study. "Did you say the past month?"

"Yeah, about. Christmas is right around the corner. You . . . didn't know?"

His mouth gaped open. Numbness encapsulated him, withering his insides. He felt as lost in this room as in the void of his dreams. Where had the time gone? With as little as he ate, how was he not thinner?

But he *was* thinner. He'd just not noticed until now. He lost more weight than Marie. Shapeless skin had eaten away at his hard muscles.

He was vaguely aware of Marie returning to his side, setting supplies on the shelf, then leaving again. He kept pressure on his wounds, feeling lightheaded. He ruminated on loss: his body, his mind, his time with Marie. Fading adrenaline and fatigue threatened to overwhelm him, slip him into the world of slumber.

"Okay," Marie said, suddenly standing in front of him with bottles of water. On the shelf at shoulder height, the lamp evenly illuminated both of them. Her voice revitalized Garrett, breathing new life into him as his epiphany had done in the study.

With a surge of emotions electrifying his body, he caressed her upper arm. "How are you so strong?"

She closed her eyes, absorbing his touch. Squeezed the water bottles tight to her chest. "You make me strong."

"Even after I ignored you?" Not to mention trying to abandon her. He wasn't ready to begin atoning for that.

"That wasn't you. It was the house."

He chuckled. It felt good, even as it splintered his side.

"What's so funny?"

"Happiness—a flash of it. It's been so long, I didn't know how else to react." He lifted the sweater. Blood now filled in the whites of HARVARD. "I guess I better get cleaned up."

"Yes." Her raised eyebrows added, *I told you so.* "Shirt off."

Garrett let his sweater fall to the floor and added his shirt on top of it. He took one of the waters and poured it over his largest wound. He used a second to wet a hand towel and clean up his other cuts—at least, the ones he felt.

Marie exchanged the remaining waters for gauze and hydrogen peroxide. He winced at the second item but nodded. As she doused his torso with antiseptic, he groaned. Burning multiplied the stabbing pain. Garrett dumped a third water on the white layers of solution after they stopped fizzing.

Water and antiseptics drizzled into a floor drain. He patted his side down with his towel and gave another nod. She wrapped two rolls of gauze around his lower torso. Then, she cut pieces of tape and made him hold them as she applied smaller dressings. She covered so much of him, he felt like she built him a makeshift shirt. It still hurt like hell, but he seemed to have avoided anything disastrous—thanks to Marie. Without her, he would've bled out shouting his revelations.

"Pants next." Marie smiled, even as her forehead creased in concern.

"Yes, ma'am." The impropriety of her request barely registered. Whatever she demanded, he'd obey. He slipped his pants to the floor, grabbed more water and doused his lower body.

Marie crouched down, covering her nose. Garrett knew he smelled disgusting, but his piss-soaked pants must've put her over the edge. She darted up when she finished, turned away, and took in a big breath.

"You're taking a shower," she said. "You're not convincing anyone of anything smelling like you've been rolling around in mud your whole life. I'll patch you up again, even better next time—once you smell like my old Gare."

Gare, he mused. *I've missed that.*

"You're the boss." He shimmied up his pants and gathered his shirt and sweater. "Put whatever you need on top of these."

Before she could act, the forgotten kernels of rice scratched the floor and shifted into a new arrangement.

TIMES UP, they spelled.

Footsteps struck just outside the supply room, louder and closer than made sense. As if the feet they belonged to had teleported past the hallway's adjoining rooms. Garrett and Marie inched closer, touching their shoes and forearms together.

"There you are." David Renault, in the flesh.

Air en route to Garrett's lungs caught in his throat.

David stepped deep into the room, too far in to block the exit. "You know where anyone else is?"

Garrett shook his head, resumed breathing. If he was right, and he was sure he was sans a few details, this man was responsible for Nia's death. Responsible for their whole situation. He wanted to shout, demand an explanation, but David Renault—*Mr.* Renault no more, he realized—was still a potential ally. Uncertainty stalled Garrett's response.

Marie held no such qualms. "Did you make a deal with a mekar to buy fertility?"

"What?" David glanced between the pair, lingering longer on Garrett. He smiled, but it didn't reach his eyes, eyes that blinked too often. "Where'd ya get that idea?"

"Doesn't matter. Is it true? Did I kill Finn because of some deal you made?" There wasn't an ounce of anger in her question. Only hurt and betrayal.

David rolled his shoulders, straightened his back. "I didn't make a deal with anyone." He scratched his cheek. Lying, or hiding something at minimum. Garrett recognized the signs from his corporate days. "Is there somethin' you wanna tell me?"

Marie prepared to respond, then gasped. Another pair of footsteps marched into sudden existence. Garrett clenched his fists. David backpedaled one shelf down the dimly lit storage room.

Claude strolled past the threshold, wearing dingier clothes than usual and holding a bundle at his waist. A bundle that accelerated Garrett's heartbeat as he raised it to his chest. "Found your backpack. Thing is ripped to hell. Got to be more careful dude, though I guess I'm a little late for that advice. What happened to you?"

Was this it? Had Claude figured why the backpack was beyond the fence? Garrett stumbled to answer. *Focus on the question at hand.* "Umm. I was in the study." Another hesitation. What if David wasn't on their side? How much was safe to say around him? And the backpack, what about the backpack? *Focus.* "The window shattered. Glass sprayed everywhere. Only reason I didn't break my legs jumping out was because Marie brought her mattress over."

"Glad you're safe. Been just me and her to keep each other company. You out of the study for good?"

"I am." He and Marie shared a look. He was committed to her, fully convinced she didn't kill her brother of her own accord.

"And are you planning to stay on the grounds the rest of the time?"

Garrett's blood froze.

He chomped down on his lower lip, panicking. He'd just reunited with Marie. This was happening too fast. What on earth possessed Claude to search out there? Overgrown grass obscured it from every angle along the fence line. Garrett had purposefully left it there rather than risk someone spotting him carrying it back inside. He'd clearly miscalculated.

"What do you mean?" Marie asked.

"Got some bad news," Claude said. "I think Garrett tried to run away. His backpack was near the edge of the Ring, filled with supplies for days. I also found one of his shirts out there, half torn up like the backpack itself. Guess the ghosts wanted to test the Ring with him too, see if they could escape early."

Garrett turned to Marie, steeling himself to admit the last bit of his hidden truths. This was his chance to come clean. Not out of earshot of David or Claude, not later, but now.

Only, her eyes never left Claude in the awkward moments that passed.

At last, she said, "Anything else?"

"What else is there to say? If you're cool with it, I'm cool with it. Just thought my little sis should know."

"Any good news?"

"Nope, none," Claude said. "Wish there was."

"That's what I thought." She advanced one cautious step, tugging Garrett with her. What was she doing? "Whoever you are, I caught you."

"Huh?" Claude said.

David tiptoed toward his son.

Garrett resisted the urge to slap his forehead.

"You're not Claude," Marie said. "From the first moment I could remember, Claude loved his good news, bad news. Didn't matter how serious or silly one or both were." Then, "Did you kill the power? Did you blow the backup generator too?"

Claude's mouth opened, emitting a cracked croaking. The backpack fell from his grip, thumped on the ground. He wavered, caught hold of the closest shelf. He fainted into his father's arms, rattling a dozen supply boxes but luckily not bringing them down with him.

"Great catch, Marie," David said.

Marie's whole upper body sank. "He's my brother. I should've noticed it earlier. We've been together every day for the past month. Looking back, he was a little too pessimistic, but I didn't see it. I wanted my brother. I wanted somebody."

"I'm sorry." Garrett rubbed her back, unsure if he deserved to touch her.

She leaned onto his bare shoulder, her head slumped. "It's not your fault. It's theirs. It's always theirs."

Memories from the weeks leading up to Marie's admission about the incident with her younger brother clicked in rapid succession.

Julie's laptop opening itself to Claude's embezzlement. A dying mekar compelling Claude to exhume his grandfather. Nia's murder driving Derrick mad. Circumstances forcing Kelly and Iris into full time parenting. A voice on a walkie-talkie tricking Garrett into pushing Marie into a joint workout. Each divided the house further and further until everyone was on their own.

The puzzle pieces snapped together, explained why the mekari and spirits didn't simply kill them in their fragile states. Possession was the answer. Why settle for spiritual freedom when corporeal freedom was available? That left one question: where did his father-in-law fit into this upheaval?

"That was their plan." Garrett grunted. "Split us up and possess us one by one."

"Think so," David said. "Tha's blown. Not much time before they attack in full." He laid his unconscious son's head on an unopened bag of rice. Crouching, he glanced at the kernels that had written messages to Garrett and Marie. Scattered, they no longer spelled anything. "We'll clean this up later. Slap Claude with some water and wake him up. You three needa find the others. Meet me in the sitting room in an hour. Hope Ah'm not too late."

"You're leaving?" Marie accused, then fell into a worrying tone. "Where are you going?"

"Can't. No time." More lies. "Ah'll see you in an hour." He fled the room before the possibility of a protest.

Garrett and Marie turned their attention to Claude. Properly waking someone caught as a Hider depended on the duration possessed. One minute of waiting per day possessed provided a smooth revival. Anything less risked confusion and hostility. That left the couple with time to burn, perhaps enough for Garrett to offer a satisfactory apology.

He rubbed the nape of his neck. Light sweat dampened his palm. "I'm sorry for trying to run away. I'm sorry I tried to leave you behind. I'm sorry I doubted you. You didn't have to tell me about your brother."

"Does that mean you for . . . for," she stuttered, "forgive me what I did?"

"Of course. It wasn't your fault. I knew you'd never—"

"Then I only need to know two things." Marie stuck her forefinger up. It quivered as much as her voice.

"Anything." Dryness in his mouth cut the last syllable short.

"Are you back for good?"

"Until the end."

"Too ominous." The corners of her lips ticked up. "Try again."

"Sorry. Yes, I'm back for good. Fully committed, whatever happens."

"Good." Her middle finger joined her first. "Second, did you pack any spare clothes in your backpack?"

"I did." His neck seized with tension.

"Good." Marie's eyes started to water. "Garrett, you forgave me for the most horrible act one could commit. How could I not do the same for you?"

"But you had no control. I did. I chose to leave you. I chose to believe you lied to me about the Ring. I chose to betray—"

She pressed her fingers to his lips. "It's the house. It's always the house. I forgive you unconditionally."

Garrett wrapped his hand around her fingers. Touching her here, her fingertips, her joints, the folds of her knuckles, all of it was bliss incarnate. He relaxed, the gravity of their situation granting him a brief respite. Both of them verged on tears as they stared at one another. Then, he remembered her second question.

"What was that about the clothes?"

"Oh, that. You reek. Clean up here and put on something fresh. Love's only so strong against that rank of a smell."

Garrett held his laughter until Marie gave in to hers. Together, they howled with joy until their lungs demanded they breathe, forcing the rare sound past its natural life span. When their laughter faded, they stared at Claude's motionless body. It might be their last laugh for a while.

39. The Gathering

It wasn't a real shower, but Garrett washed himself with hand soap and bottled water. Marie refused to play lookout, arguing she deserved a show after how he'd acted. He didn't argue, just slid behind the shelf with the most coverage. She whistled as he stripped. Oohed as he rushed through cleaning himself. Clapped as he dried himself with hand towels. Booed when he changed into his spare set of clothes. The impropriety of his public bathing, coupled with the anticipation of David Renault's meeting, refueled his adrenal supply, lacing it with what he imagined cocaine felt like.

His legs bounced as he and Marie shared a snack. She gave up trying to calm him after the third attempt. They woke Claude after enough time had passed. The trio spoke only the words necessary, and set out, quickly finding Julie in the library. Her sneer cemented her feelings about Garrett and Marie's reunion, but after hearing what happened in the storage room, she went along with helping to gather the others. The twins took upstairs, while the couple searched downstairs. They raced through the house as quickly as Garrett's injuries allowed. Now, everyone but Julie, Claude, and David sat or stood around the sitting room together.

Garrett and Marie shared the sofa. If anyone noticed or cared about the bulkiness underneath his shirt, they never asked. Derrick slumped in the far corner, between the wall and a decorative table cleared of its lamp and accoutrements. An exhausted Kelly dozed in a chair. Iris knitted methodically in the one adjacent. She had been the only one with the sense to check the breakers, reporting them an irreparable mess. Grady pondered a geometric puzzle on the floor while Tommy handed him pieces like a nurse assisting a surgeon.

Warmth seeped into the air. No power meant no AC, and December in Louisiana felt like July in Boston. A Roman shade covered the room's single window, blocking all but a trickle of sunlight. Battery-powered lanterns lit up the room surprisingly well though. Perhaps too well; frightened expressions bounced around the room as spirits beset the gathering.

Claimers clawed at their skin to dive inside. One breathed a chill down Garrett's neck, forcing him to relive his loss of control in the kitchen. He screamed at the top of his lungs, and Grady asked if he could help. Iris gave a sympathetic shake of her head.

Feeders amplified fears in random bouts. Kelly nearly fled the room. Derrick restrained her, enduring slaps and strikes until she apologized and settled.

Shifters forced them all to maintain skin-on-fabric touch with the room's aged furniture. Marie once needed Garrett and Kelly's reassurances that this was still Ajaccio, Louisiana and not Boston, Massachusetts.

She cried at the realization.

Deviants flung objects around the room. Children's toys made dangerous weapons, evidenced by the bump one of Grady's wooden triangles imprinted on Iris's forehead.

The room's inhabitants suffered the time between these strikes largely in silence. Talking led to hysterics that played right into their enemies' hands. Prompted questions like: did David send them here not to impart a revelation, but to deliver a killing blow? Garrett shared a glance with Iris and saw the same question written on her face. He had worn through the upholstery on his couch cushion and moved back to holding Marie. She was as limp as a corpse, until a thump like a dropped dumbbell pounded against the foyer stairs.

The thump came again and again. Descending toward them, a

reaper searching for a soul. Thump, thump, demanding investigation, inciting none. Garrett tensed, squeezing both a new spot on the couch and Marie, who grasped him just as firmly. The back of his knees dug into the seams of the cushion. His hamstrings and calves cramped. He winced and hesitantly stretched his legs out toward the long, leather ottoman. Thump, thump. A near-perfect pattern of repetitious advances. Nobody moved. One last thump echoed from the base of the stairs. A smooth sliding sound grazed the hardwood.

Garrett's vantage offered him first sight of who approached. "It's . . . Claude?" He didn't trust his eyes. "He's dragging Julie." And in place of her bulky pants, she wore the same leggings as the night she caught Garrett's failed flight attempt.

Tommy cheered for his dad, and Kelly bolted out of her seat. A few steps from her chair, her face contorted, and she froze at the edge of the room's ornamental rug. She curled her head into her chest, tugging at her dirty hair. Her fists came back with a few strands, then exploded open as her back stiffened. She slunk back to her seat, a disgusted sneer imprinted upon her.

What awful place had the spirits sent her?

Claude missed it. His back was turned to them, his arms awkwardly wrapped underneath Julie's armpits to avoid her sling. He stopped at the entryway of the sitting room. "Can someone move? She needs to lie down."

"What happened?" Garrett stood up and circled behind the couch, always keeping touch with the fabric or Marie.

"The Hider inside her got cocky," he grunted, sweat glistening on his neck and forehead. "It didn't realize there are things you don't try with a brother. She should reboot in twenty minutes." He hoisted Julie's entire body up and propped her on the couch, laying her head on Marie's lap, then stretched his arms. "Don't tell her I dragged her the whole way. She's mad heavy, like her bones turned to lead. Ghosts retaliating for spoiling their prize I guess, but she won't hear the reason in that."

Another Hider. One was chance. Two, in such a short time, all but confirmed Garrett's theory that ghosts sought possession over killing. Who else was not themselves? Who else might turn on them at a moment's notice? He saw the accusatory thoughts spread from person to person, save for the kids and the news bearer himself.

Claude's grin died at the dreary response. "Tough crowd. Something happen in here?"

"Yes," Iris said. "Where's David?"

Claude shrugged and sank to the floor, resting his back against the sofa arm. "Shouldn't be much longer. Julie and I were with him in Grandpa's room when I caught her Hider. He said he'd be down before she came to." Fidgeting fingers and furtive glances at his wife made it clear he wanted to check on her, but something kept him from acting.

"And what critical activity is consuming his time?" Iris asked.

"Reading. I think he translated more of Grandpa's notes. Said he was dotting his I's and crossing his—"

Derrick started hyperventilating. Clutched his neck as if choking.

Claude bolted up, his hand outstretched as he crept forward. Marie shifted in place, attention flitting between her unconscious sister and hysterical half-brother.

Hyperventilating turned into him beating his head against the wall, crying, "No, no, no."

"Daddy?" Grady abandoned his toys. Iris set her knitting aside and held his shoulder. A whispered word kept him from rising.

As Claude passed his wife, Derrick thrust his trembling hands out, signaling stop.

"Get back." His tongue slid along his top teeth, digging deep into their edges. He violently shuddered, then patted his Adam's Apple as he covered his groin. "I'm fine." He turned away and buried himself in the corner.

"That damned fool." Iris tucked her knitting needles and half-finished scarf next to her thigh. "What else is David hiding?"

"What do you mean *else?*" Claude backpedaled to the sofa.

"Nothing. Take a rest. You need it. We all do." Iris interlaced her fingers, reclined her head, and closed her eyes. Garrett didn't believe she'd actually sleep. He kept his attention on her, trying to signal his plans to publicize the secret about her son. Marie turned in Derrick's direction, assessing him in much the same manner. Iris might soon hate Garrett as much as David, but he and Marie had agreed. He'd reveal all of the family's secrets once David returned. He wouldn't risk giving him more time to prepare, more time to conjure another lie.

Claude looked around the room as he sat again, then honed in on his wife. "How about you, Kelly? Doing okay?"

She shrugged, with a hint of curl to her lips.

"Good to see you out of the room at last."

Her budding smile wilted. "Can we keep quiet until your dad gets here? We don't want to accidentally set someone off."

That finally zipped Claude's mouth shut.

Silent introspection pervaded the room until a spirit interrupted the peace yet again. Half of Grady's puzzle pieces levitated and flew at the couch. No one was seriously hurt, though Julie might find a couple of bruises to add to her sore armpits when she awoke. Iris forced the kids to store their toys inside the ottoman. To their credit, they sat quietly on the desolate floor, holding each other's hands. Marie studied them with newfound interest.

More time passed, and Garrett balanced frantic perusals of the room with mentally playing out the big reveal. Shouting always ensued, no matter how he and Marie phrased their words.

This time, a positive sign interrupted his thoughts: Julie stirring awake. With perfect timing, David made his entrance as she began to speak.

An uproar overtook the room, but David cut them off with a flat wave.

"In a few minutes, a mekar'll possess me. He's on our side, as much as a mekar can be. If he doesn't, a different mekar will, and my sins will persist. Ah've spent weeks researching, and the more time passes, the more it's clear this is the only way."

"What are you—" Marie started.

"Hush, ma chère fille, and we'll tell you everything."

40. A Simple Trade

"Is this safe for the kids to hear?" Kelly picked up Tommy and placed him in her lap. Her son reached for Grady, who gave him a high five. Both smiled, but their jovial expressions faded fast.

"Gonna have to be," David said. The white of his beard exacerbated his haggard look.

Iris held her grandson's shoulder, eyeing him as if considering removing him from the room. She ultimately gave David her attention, but her hand remained. Grady took on a somber presence, drawing from his father who slumped near the corner.

David scanned the room, fists curled at his waist. "I have a secret. Several of 'em, really. Julie and Garrett figured a few out, and y'all will know the rest soon." Julie groggily sat up on the couch at the mention of her name. "Ah'm sorry for lying. Couldn't risk saying anythin' until deciding to fully trust Lithyipur. You might recognize the name. He's the mekar my dad spoke with the night he died. He knows the deal I made, and what it entails. Dad did too, though he couldn't communicate it to anyone else. And that deal . . ." He clapped his fists, one on top of the other. He breathed in, looked to the ceiling, and readdressed his audience. "Sorry. I don't know what's gonna happen. This might be the last time that Ah'm me. I want to say more. I want to apologize. I want to earn your forgiveness. There's no time for any of that. I don't know how long Lithyipur can keep the threats at bay. Just know: it was horrible watching y'all suffer through the plights I caused.

"If I coulda told y'all sooner, I woulda. The problem is: another mekar, one far worse, woulda possessed me. Perhaps forever. And it wouldn't have fixed anythin'. Lithyipur comes with a solution, so I'm asking y'all to trust him as I did. Yeah, he's a mekar, but our interests align. He's our best shot." David surveyed his listeners, and Garrett swore he tensed up as his eyes fell on Marie. "At least consider what he has to say."

He took one more breath and pressed his knuckles into the corners of his eyes. He held them there long enough that he probably saw spots as he opened them back up. "My brother and I couldn't have children."

The admittance riled up everyone, but none more so than Derrick, who finally looked up. It seemed Garrett and Marie might not be the ones to reveal everything—or anything—after all.

"Something to do with these Hellspots," David said. "It's 'appened to others. Family lines died out, leading to the powers that be recruiting a new Overseer line. Mekari and spirits make use of this turnover to spring free. It's a mess for everybody, but especially the person who realizes they're the last of their bloodline. We coulda chanced adopting, but who knows what woulda 'appened with the precedents set?"

Sitting on the floor, Claude stiffened at that, pushing back into the couch's bottom half.

David continued without missing a beat. "Instead, I made a deal. Ah'd get my fertility, raise this amazing family." He gestured around the room. "In exchange, the mekar would take a portion from each child. Or in the case of anyone born after my second daughter, take all. Which is why Finn . . ." He cleared his throat, then rushed to continue. Claude must have told Kelly about his little brother based on her indifference. "I didn't know the exact price of this toll. It mighta made things worse if I did. How could I have kept that secret given what it forced y'all to do, 'specially Marie? And if I ever revealed this to anyone, my body was forfeit to this mekar. Though she called herself something different then, her true name's Tiliminia—the other mekar my dad spoke with before he died.

"I couldn't risk leaving y'all alone. Breaches are dangerous enough with a full house. Wha's more, running this place outside of a Breach still takes work. Julie's disciplined and dedicated, with all the right tools to succeed, but even she can't run it on her own. After this, unless I can get my body back, someone else'll have to stay. An issue for later, but I want you to understand. Since making that deal, Ah've lived every day in-between pride and regret. I love this family. I could talk all day about my pride, but Ah'm on borrowed time as is. Hope everyone can forgive me. Even if Ah'm not around to accept it. One more thing before I—"

His body convulsed. Claude and Derrick sprung toward their father. David's brief seizure ended before they reached him. He waved them off, and his expression grew harsh, just shy of a scowl.

"I am Lithyipur now," David's mouth said, speaking without the accent of the man whose body he inhabited, in a monotone more unsettling than any archetypal demon. "I secured David the longest duration of freedom I could muster. Tiliminia nearly collared him as it was." The anxious audience reacted faintly. Derrick and Claude stepped back, respectively to their corner and floor seat. Julie brought her knees up, guarding her sling-wrapped arm. Seated beside her, Marie grasped for Garrett's hand, the one that wasn't busy covering his vitals. "My kind is known for their avarice and deceit. It is prudent to mistrust me, but avail yourself to the viewpoint that I am the lesser evil. As a token of goodwill, I will postulate David's 'one more thing'. Maurice Renault has only recently passed on. He assisted here and there, as did I, though with reasons nobler than mine. An encounter with him, whether your soul slumbered or withered awake, likely was with him."

The old man in the basket. Garrett tilted his head in thought and almost missed Derrick, Kelly, and Marie doing likewise. They were all either bouncing their legs or chewing their nails. Iris was as stone-faced as ever.

"It is a matter that bears collective discussion. If desired, I will vacate the room. However, I must press upon you the more critical topic at hand. David's second contract—the one he negotiated with me."

When else had Maurice reached out to Garrett? In an earlier, forgotten dream? During bouts of unexpected calm? The walkie-talkies?

"Great," Julie spat. The voice of someone else speaking yanked Garrett's attention back to the sitting room. "So what? Dad paid his bank loan by borrowing from a loan shark?"

"I liken his act to refinancing a mortgage with better rates."

Claude scoffed. "I didn't know mekari had mortgages."

"We are not barbarians. We dwell in cities and communities like you. Unlike you, order reigns supreme throughout our civilization. A mere glimpse into your realm reveals the chaos humans sew and proliferate, beginning from when their seed sprouts, lasting beyond withered expiration. Our deceased are not so volatile in their first walk of what lays beyond, nor are they so easily corralled and coiled. Our legal loopholes make a mockery of all your laws combined, but I admit this order does not correlate with an idyllic society. Yet here we are, you relying on me." David's body—Lithyipur—stretched his arms and legs as if waking from a standing nap. How long would it take for his branding to mar David's body? Would it resemble the one on Maurice Renault's body the night of his death? "Now, my proposition. I will annul your sins, your curses, and any and all terms you wish to include in this wiping of this slate. In return, Marie will allow me to share some of myself with one who grows inside of her."

What?

All around the room, even the smallest motion froze in stasis. Sweat dampening Garrett's skin from the ambient air intensified, now trickled down his arm. He wasn't sure whether he or Marie clenched a tighter grip.

"Ah, it is a secret you guarded." He glanced at Marie and chuckled without mirth. "Forgive me. A secret withheld even from yourself. I suppose only a month has passed since conception. I humbly, and without any exchange necessary, offer you the first of your congratulations."

Marie shook her head, ran her fingers through her hair and pressed them against her scalp. "I can't. I can't have children. It's not safe. I can't. Not safe." Garrett slipped his hand onto her shoulder. The rest of him fell into a daze, nearing an out-of-body experience.

I'm going to be . . . a father?

"Again. In exchange for my demands, I will annul the contract that binds your family. As another gesture of goodwill, which requires no commitment to procure, I offer a taste of what awaits." Lithyipur closed his eyes, brought his arm to side, then made a flicking motion near his waist. He rolled his shoulders and was back to normal. "How do you feel?"

Derrick jolted. His lips quivered, then ratcheted open as shuddering breaths escaped. Beads of tears fell down his cheeks. "He's right." He slowly gestured at Marie. "I don't feel *that* way about her anymore. I can look at her. I love her, but I don't want—" He bent over and retched, covering his face. He roared as he shot back up standing. "If he's telling the truth, and you're"—he hummed—"pregnant, then do what you think is right."

He pressed his fingers to his lips, stalling his next words. "But Lithyipur is telling the truth, at least for me. I feel like me again, like when I was with Nia." He slid down the corner wall until his legs spread out across the floor. He cried freely and silently then, blotting away tears with his shirt.

I can have a family.

Marie patted Julie's back and rose from her seat. She walked over to her half-brother, crouched down, and slipped her arms around him. They held each other until Julie broke the touching moment with a grunt. They gave each other another good squeeze, then she stood up.

"Burning books and tearing out pages isn't an everyday occurrence for me," Julie said. "I doubt Claude is always thinking about embezzling or Marie about"—she glanced at the kids—"her issue. So, I'll trust Derrick." She swung her feet onto the floor and leaned forward. "What's your angle then? Marie is pregnant and you're going to what? Turn her child into a mekar? Are you asking us to raise Rosemary's Baby?"

A miracle or a curse? Both?

Kelly drew Tommy to her chest and covered his ears. He wiggled here and there but accepted his fate. Grady tried nibbling his thumb, and Iris kept pulling his arm back.

Lithyipur croaked an unnatural cackle. "Not a single soul will spot a difference. We are not the devils of your nightmares and religions. Mekari and humans resemble one another like two people born on opposite sides of the world. What's more, my baby's genetic composition will be comprised of two parts human to my one part mekar. I doubt even the human parents will distinguish the difference between either child." Another cackle, all throat. "Yes, either child. I appreciate the gift of empirically demonstrating why humans enjoy surprises so much. Twins are prevalent in your family, remember? I believe it is customary to congratulate the parents now."

Claude looked from Marie to Garrett, a grin on his face preluding a joke that he obviously thought better of. He respectfully bowed his head instead.

Garrett followed that bow back to his wife.

Fear spotted her hopeful face. Wrinkles and creases contended with her raised brows and wide-open eyes. He gestured toward her, abstaining from the conversation, his focus resting on her stomach. Those may be his children, but the implications weighed him down too much to feel his desires held any merit.

A mekar. A child with Marie. Impossible. Unreal.

"Why though?" Julie asked. "You only care about yourself."

"An incorrect assumption." Lithyipur opened his arms in an exaggerated flourish, seeming to relish his opportunity to wear human flesh. "Imagine you are an innocent thrust into prison. Not just thrust there, but born there. You have little chance of escape, and even if you do abscond, it is through the confines of a body with which you are barely compatible. Your only aspiration is to one day produce a child who will never witness the self-serving society that is your everything. We are not all evil. You know this. I would assist you because I desire a child in your world, and I *will* help my child."

The conversation veered into silence: an open opportunity for everyone to collect their thoughts.

"What's the process like?" Marie asked.

"A tad painful, but expedient. Akin to a sharp pinch."

"You're considering this?" Julie asked.

"I don't know," Marie said. "I'm trying to understand it all."

"What if he fooled Dad, and he's fooling you too? He might poison you. Kill you right before the ghosts and mekari turn up the heat again."

"Literally." Claude fanned his face.

"Not now." Julie snapped her fingers at him, keeping her attention on Marie. "We can figure out another solution. We know the problem for the first time in our lives. Let's fix this together."

"I don't know." Marie studied Derrick, who offered a wary smile. "What about Dad?"

"I don't know if we can save him," Julie said, "but we can't lose you too. *I* can't lose you."

Another lull, another opportunity to seize the conversation.

"Lithyipur, how do you know we'll"—Garrett winced—"keep the child?"

"You would endanger the fully human twin residing inside to murder an innocent babe? I should condemn you as monsters, but we view our offspring as vital instruments. You must not. Well, let us pretend you execute this act. Do so, and you void the contract. The cessation of your curses is predicated on the continued lifeblood of my progeny."

"But the original deal. How can you negate it?"

"As I explained, loopholes abound in our society."

The moments of quiet gained weight, pressing on Garrett's shoulders until shattered by talk.

"Hold on," Claude said. "One thing's bugging me. Dad said Uncle Simon was sterile too. Does that mean he agreed to the same deal? Or is Derrick"—he shifted around—"related in a different way?" His pitch raised with his eyebrows, focus settling on Iris.

She met his stare with such harshness that even Garrett turned away. She spoke like a politician issuing a decree. "You're all siblings. The few days I decide Jesus is worth speaking to, I praise him for Derrick. If y'all aren't damned fools, you should do the same. The rest is history. Don't matter." She paused, drawing in a loud breath to show she wasn't finished, then pointed her acrylic needle at Lithyipur. "Give the mekar what he wants."

"You can't be serious," Julie said. Incensed as she was, she invited more attention than Iris's stoic coldness. "Knowingly unleashing a mekar into the world is wrong by every use of the word."

Iris dismissed the concern with a wave. "Who knows how many mekari live in the world? Couple dozen I'd guess. You know damn well Breaches ain't sealed tight, and they can live a time without a body."

"That's different than—"

"This a simple, simple trade. Don't over-complicate it. You four get your life back. We get an ally against an army of demons and the dead. He might be the only reason we live at all. And if anyone is capable of molding a mekar-blooded baby into a sweet child, it's Marie."

Claude chuckled. "Aunt Iris is right about that. But this is up to Marie as far as I'm concerned."

If they rejected Lithyipur's offer, not only would they be on their own, but Marie might lose the children growing inside of her. There was a certain mysticism to their conception. Miraculous life granted on a Hellspot could be taken away just as suddenly.

I want this. I want her to want this. We can do it together.

Yet his feelings mirrored Claude's words. Only Marie was fit to make this decision. From across the room, he smiled at her, his face-up palm abandoning his role in the decision.

"Oh no," Marie said. "You're not getting off that easy. This is your child too. What do you think?"

"It's like your Aunt said." Garrett kept his touch with the couch as he stepped around it and toward Marie. She left her place at Derrick's side to meet him halfway. "You'd be a great mother, whatever the child's bloodline. I have full faith in your ability to raise a family. I always have." Their sights locked, the couple reached one another and melded into their hand stack. He waited with bated breath for her response. For a moment, the only sound in the room was him rubbing his thumb across the back of her hand.

"Then we do it." She nodded so forcefully, she half-bowed. "We'll raise the hell out of this kid. Nurture beats nature anytime, and at least their paternal side has good, uncorrupted genes."

Grady, who had sat quietly this whole time, clapped his hands. Derrick snorted and left his corner to pick up his child, who clapped even louder. Derrick kissed him on the forehead and stifled the claps by holding his boy's hands within one of his. Even Iris smiled for a moment, though Garrett might have imagined it.

Lithyipur prepared to speak, but Marie wasn't done yet.

"Will you give Dad back his body?"

"My soul bears no desire to live trapped in this shell," Lithyipur said. "It is a fascinating venture, but for an eternity? A prison by another name. No, the only mekar who will depart in a human body is my child. Once it is safe to do so, I will relinquish control of your father's form."

"Alright, then." Marie straightened her posture. "Tell me what to do."

"Excellent. Such a blessing to have dispatched of the easy part."

"Easy part?" She caressed her stomach.

"Yes. Have you dismissed the notion that you still need to survive?"

41. Preparation

Lithyipur and Marie stood in the open doorway between the foyer and sitting room. She lifted her shirt halfway. He extended his arm and poked her bare stomach. "Not bad?" he asked.

Garrett shuddered.

"Not bad." Marie was tapping her foot on the floor and fidgeting with her shorts.

"The more you move, the longer this takes."

Marie nodded, biting her lip. A balled fist replaced her twitching. She tightened it until only a trace of pink skin remained.

Garrett hovered nearby, waiting for the all-clear to hold her. Touching her during—whatever Lithyipur was doing—risked the health of Marie and the unborn babies alike. The mekar explained the process in detail before beginning, but believing even half of what he said tested Garrett's faith. His eyes dried from barely blinking before he heard the magic words.

"We are finished." Lithyipur stepped back.

Garrett slid over and reached for Marie. He lost the fight for her notice. She cradled her stomach like a woman near birth. He settled for wrapping his arm around her lower back. She lost herself in her own world, and he vaguely remained cognizant of the one around him. *A father*, he mused. *Not just a father. A father of a supernatural child whose distant family wants to murder us.*

"Now, you should all begin preparation." Lithyipur moved past the couple into the center of the room. Garrett turned around, taking a compliant Marie with him. Everyone save Julie sat on the couches and chairs. "What I suggest—"

"I'll take care of it." Julie stood guarding her injured arm. "As long as I can See. You can fix it, can't you?"

Lithyipur tilted his head. "Why would you believe that?"

Julie sneered. "Do I have to spell this out?"

"It seems so, if you wish for me to understand that which you ask."

"As long as there are multiple mekari in this room, I can't See. My Dad"—she pointed at Lithyipur—"can't Feel."

"I had no idea." Apparently, the mekari weren't listening too hard to their conversations after all.

Julie's mouth hung open for a moment. She sealed it with a huff before starting again. "Fine. All I care is that you send some of your friends away, long enough so that I know what we're dealing with."

"Friends?"

"The other mekari."

"Oh, them?" Lithyipur studied Julie like a complex math problem. She held his gaze. "None of us are friends. We are more business associates. I am no sorcerer—I cannot control them. My talents do not lie in magic but in manipulation." He grinned wide as the ensuing commotion broke out.

Cries and mutterings of "Manipulated", "You!", and "Fools" burst forth from different sources.

Garrett started to join them. Stopped at catching Iris's ambivalent response and a sudden worry of jarring Marie.

The mekar held his forefinger up, tutting. "Yes, I manipulated you, but I uttered no falsehoods. You have nothing to fear from me. Besides, the contract is sealed. You have no choice but to trust me. Maurice Renault has passed on. David broke his deal with Tiliminia, sacrificing himself. I am your only ally. If not for me working behind the scenes, you would not have lived this long. As is, I estimate one hour before the ghosts and mekari fully assemble, and the assault commences. I will not alarm you with the numbers. They will come at you with everything. A relentless strike that will last until the Breach's dismissal."

"That'll take weeks," Claude said.

Garrett rubbed Marie's back with one hand and flexed his fingers with the other.

"Yes, weeks," Lithyipur said. "With limited time to prepare, so do not interrupt. Detach the double glass doors to the foyer. Take them outside and throw them across the Breach line. I am amazed you keep anything breakable in this house at all."

"Should we board up the windows?" Claude asked.

"Do. Not. Interrupt." Lithyipur stared at Claude until he defensively raised his hands and leaned against the couch's arm. "Board up the windows, and you must defend against glass and nails alike. So, no. I will manage the responsibility of the windows. Once the doors are removed, strip the dining room hutch and bring it here to block the foyer exit. Ghosts may knock it over, but its width will cover the space, and its weight will provide ample time to react before it falls. Procure as much food as you can now. Stock bags upon bags. Separate dense objects like cans and deposit those in the dining room. Hold out and make the enemy work for every inch. That is the game we play." He scanned around. "You did this room mostly right, at least. Nothing loose on the furniture. No paintings. Logs in the fireplace. Light them as soon as you complete the other tasks. That will offer a place to act as a sanctuary."

"Why don't we sit tight?" Garrett asked, not missing that Lithyipur equated their defense to a game. "Won't they pick us off while we're prepping?"

Lithyipur sighed with a demonic rumble. He clearly tired of his audience. "They do not adapt well. The plan is simple. Ram you in full force once they've assembled. There are no tactics, no concerns, no stratagems. An army of the dead against ten frail bags of flesh, two of whom drain vital attentions by their existence."

"Is he talking about me, Nana?" Grady asked.

"Don't listen to him," Iris said. "He's speaking to the adults."

"Yes," Lithyipur said. "And they best heed my advice."

"You keep saying *you*," Kelly said.

"What do you mean?" Marie's possessed father asked.

"Everything from your perspective is you, not we. You're not on our side. You're not with us at all. How can we trust you?"

"Again, the child we share bonds us." He gestured at Marie, who clenched her arms below her navel. "You have a fair point though. I am for me and my child alone. I will work harder to save Marie than the rest of you, but the more of you that live the better the chance she survives. That said, I am not so enamored by my offspring that I will sacrifice myself for him, her, or any of you. What point is there in bearing a child if you do not live to watch them grow?" He clapped, cracking the air like a gunshot. "Now you know the precise extent of my trustworthiness. You can calculate my betrayal. Unlike that of the man whose body I inhabit."

"Bastard," Julie said.

Claude tapped her shin, then stood from the floor. "Come on, let's get the doors off."

She gestured wildly at her sling.

"We don't have a lot of options, do we? Just put your legs into it."

Julie shook her head, first at her brother, then Lithyipur. She rolled her eyes for good measure, then joined Claude.

Garrett rejected taking Marie on his food run. She was recovering, still in a daze. He wasn't sure whether from the recent discovery of her pregnancy or Lithyipur's ritual. He fared only a tad better. Impending parenthood required more processing time than a scant half-hour, and his wounds ached in full force. Following Lithyipur's advice at least gave him an avenue to direct his energy, even if it invited danger by splitting up.

Derrick's approach simplified the dilemma. "Garrett, want to help me with the food?"

Garrett clenched his jaw. Despite clear knowledge that Derrick wasn't responsible for his attack on Marie, Garrett's mistrust lingered.

Only time together would heal that. He assured himself that's why he agreed, not because he feared leaving Derrick with Marie. "Sure. Where do you keep your bags?"

"I'll show you." Derrick walked over.

"Very good," Lithyipur said. "One more topic of note. I am fairly confident another of you is possessed with . . . what do you call them? The ghosts who act like you instead of themselves?"

"A Hider," Claude said.

"Yes, an appropriate designation. If there is any plan for the forthcoming attack, it is to subjugate your physical forms. Once enough Hiders claimed you, they would open the gates from within, so to speak."

"We figured that already, more or less. Any idea who it is?"

"I'm not sure there is only one. And it might be none. My supposition originates from the auras I detect. Or rather, those I do not detect from the hostile mass gathering. You must discover who it is. I advise you to begin preparations though. There is already a high probability that all of you will perish in not so short a time."

"Great pep talk," Claude said. "Word of advice: don't get into motivational speaking." He motioned from Julie to the dining room. They marched off, presumably for a drill to take down the doors.

Derrick went off in the other direction, toward the foyer. Garrett kissed the cheek of a near-comatose Marie, and glanced at Kelly, who gave an *I'll watch her* look. Then he jogged up to his brother-in-law's side.

On their march to raid the sunroom, and subsequent return, Garrett studied Derrick's every move. Hung on his every word. His brother-in-law had played a pivotal role in convincing his family to agree to Lithyipur's proposal. What if that was a ruse?

But although Hiders wove decent lies, he cleared himself as well as anyone. In the weeks since his attack on Marie, he'd passed the time by meditating in isolation. He admitted his regret, his lust. Detailed their mixture into a caustic concoction that plagued his waking hours and tormented his sleeping ones. He truly was a victim in the atrocity with Marie. Sympathy nudged out over Garrett's suspicions and pointed his doubt in a new direction.

Himself.

42. Finale

A barren sitting room greeted Garrett and Derrick on their return. The ottoman, end tables, and decorations were gone. Only the oversized chairs, couch, and rug remained, with the addition of the flat-bottomed dining room hutch next to the doorless foyer entrance. A shade fluttered in a warm breeze, its accompanying window taken out from the center of the wood-accented wall. Everyone looked as if they waited for a funeral service to begin.

Everyone except Claude, who raised a disposable cup. Purple stained his lips. "Right on time. Ol' Lithy expects the show to start any moment. Set the bags down and take a seat. I'll get the hutch." He proffered his drink to his wife. "Mind holding this?"

Kelly accepted the cup. "I can't believe you're drinking."

"Takes the edge off."

"What a surprise." But she gave the hint of a grin and sipped his wine.

"I knew you'd fold." He traded places with Derrick and Garrett, then pushed the hutch into place. Wood slid against wood, sounding distant in the echoes of the cavernous room. The hutch's profile covered the foyer entrance as if built for that purpose.

"Want these anywhere in particular?" Derrick asked. He adjusted a backpack hanging off his shoulder. Garrett doubled up the strap of a duffel bag slipping his grasp. They had six bags of supplies between them, minus the two with canned food they placed in the dining room.

Lithyipur stood on the edge of the rug, the fireplace crackling behind him. "Place half near me. Divide what remains between the two doorways."

They did as instructed, splitting the supplies and taking their places around the room. Derrick hunkered down near the locked double doors to the dining room, crouched and holding tight onto a backpack and a duffel bag. Claude clamped his feet over the straps of the bag placed next to the hutch, his cracks of worry starting to show.

Garrett joined Marie on the couch and wrapped his arm around her, her damp shirt immediately clinging to him. She pursed her lips, and apprehension consumed him. Where would the first strike come from? The doors? The walls?

Himself?

If a Hider lived within him without his knowledge, how would he know for sure until it was too late? *Thinking I'm a Hider probably means I'm not one, right? Like how a crazy person never thinks they're crazy.* He still contemplated pulling away from Marie. She needed time to react in case he turned.

Blunt strikes started hammering the hutch from the foyer side. The wood jutted forward on its right side, swinging the makeshift door open. Claude pushed it back flush against the wall.

The locked handles of the dining room doors rattled. Derrick clamped onto them.

Garrett clutched Marie tighter. His recent injuries throbbed in response. She clasped his free hand between both of hers and bounced her knees.

Pounding intensified and multiplied. Another intruder banged against the wall for entry.

This doesn't make sense, he realized. *They're ghosts. They could just—*

An invisible force lifted the couch and Garrett like the ascent of a roller coaster. Before he could leap off with Marie, the whole couch flipped over, wrenching him from her. His head went horizontal to his waist, then flew toward the floor. His body turned to the side, and his shoulder collided with the rug, bearing the brunt of his fall. The base of the couch struck his heels and settled onto the balls of his feet. He yowled, nerves signaling cut circulation to his toes. His head swam in a murky daze.

Screaming followed. Masculine first, followed by higher-pitched cries, both muffled by the couch on top of him. Children bawled in an undercurrent of the adult uproar. All of it sounded more distant than made sense, as if his mind rejected the situation and guided him into a dreamlike state.

Two groans snapped Garrett back into the moment. *Marie. Julie.*

He pushed himself up, resisting the couch's weight. He held firm for a moment before falling back to the ground. He landed straight onto his stomach, knocking the wind from him. The pinch on his toes tightened, numbing them. He tried to rise again, this time feeling a lighter load buoyed by help from his sides. Julie strained with her one good arm. Marie's face was bright red, but she seemed no worse for wear. He surged up, and together the three of them thrust the couch off of them. They caught it before it flipped over, then eased it back onto the floor. Garrett's toes ached as feeling rushed back into them.

Claude was covering his right eye. Blood oozed down his cheek. Cries of agony raged from his mouth in repeat fashion. Gasping. Wailing. Howling. His free arm convulsed at his side. Next to him, Kelly lay unconscious, sprawled across her stuffed chair.

"Claude!" Marie abandoned Garrett for her brother. "What 'appened?"

Claude's head snapped toward his wife's lap. A crimson-stained pocketknife blended into her floral shirt.

Julie rushed at her twin brother. "Leave her alone, demon!"

"Mom?" Marie reached for her sister as she flew by.

Julie crashed into Claude. The twins tumbled to the floor. Blood spurted up into her face. He scampered back, placing his hand back over the red well that was his eye.

Dread immobilized Garrett. *Sometimes the batter has to wait on his pitch. Watch it all play out, that's the way.*

Lithyipur wrenched Julie up by her waist. She snarled, writhing in his grasp.

"Let me go, Dad!"

He slapped her hard enough to force her head over her shoulder. "I am not your father, and that is not a demon." As her writhing subsided, he released her.

Julie raised her hand to her cheek.

Claude continued shuffling away, stopping as his head struck a dining room door. He sat up straight against it and tore off his top, then wrapped his face with it. A trail of blood marked his retreat from the sofa chair.

In the corner behind Garrett, Iris whispered soothing words to two sobbing children.

Derrick had traded places with Claude. He now braced himself against the hutch. The antique wood clamored for freedom, putting its weight on its front side and threatening to topple over. Lithyipur left Julie's side to help Derrick press the furniture back into place.

Claude shook his head, focusing on Kelly's chair.

Garrett wrapped his arms defensively around his torso. His heart-beat was practically a blunt weapon against his forearm. Blood seeped through his side bandage. *Move and die. Stand still and survive.*

"Mom." Marie brushed Julie's arm, who whipped around with nails ready to claw.

Julie's hand fell to her side as she mouthed, *Mom?*

"I'm sorry for Finn. I didn't mean it. It wasn't my fault, was it?"

"I'm not . . ." Julie's face contorted into an angry mask of demonic proportions. "Marie, it's Julie. A Shifter's messing with your head."

"Julie's okay, Mom. She's strong. Did you know I'm pregnant?"

"I'm not Mom!" Julie's eyes bulged as she noticed Claude. She wrenched free from her sister, ran, and slid knee-first onto tacky ground beside him. She fell forward onto the palm of her good arm, shrieking. "I'm sorry."

Battered strikes wore down both the dining room doors, a storm intensifying into a hurricane. Inside panels bulged with each attempt at entry. Slivers broke from the solid wood, flew halfway toward the floor, then halted mid-air.

Terror struck Garrett anew. Immobilizing, unassailable terror. They'd cleared the room of projectiles, but the spirits found ways to smith weapons. Where would they aim? Surely, not at him. Nobody saw him. He was a ghost among ghosts, safe from the carnage. He could survive—as long as he stayed still.

A sliver from the damaged doors shot right and stabbed Derrick in the arm. He yelped, jerked it free.

"Toss it in the fire." Lithyipur slowly lost ground in his battle over the hutch. He squatted to better press his weight against it. "Incinerate their weapons. I'll handle this."

Derrick sprinted past a stunned Marie once again cradling her flat stomach. He threw the splinter into the fire and raced to add more tinder as fast as pieces came off the doors.

"Grady!" Iris shouted. "Tommy! Get back here."

"No, Nana," Grady said. "Your eyes are white."

"That's because they took my sight. I can't see you, so I can't protect you unless you get here *right now*." Her hands smacked the floor in a searching pattern. The boys stayed silent, keeping their distance.

"Julie." Lithyipur rolled his ankle as he readjusted to another surge, then groaned. Julie continued babying Claude, ignoring the mekar's words. He sneered at her. "Claude's in shock from Kelly stabbing him. It will pass. You must wake Garrett and Marie."

Stay away. Stay away. Stay away.

With hesitation, then a sisterly hug for her stunned brother, Julie pulled herself away and stood up. She stumbled back to the center of the room. Sweet relief washed over Garrett as she winced her way to her sister instead of him.

"You're bleeding." Marie pointed at Julie's knee. "I can get Julie to help with that."

"*I'm* Julie!" Julie clutched her sister's arm. Shaking her head, she enunciated, "I'm. Not. Mom." She squeezed, then loosened her grip. "I need my sister back. I need Marie. You've got to snap out of this. We don't have time."

A circular plate rolled through a slight opening between the hutch and foyer. Lithyipur was focusing on the sisters and the battering ram striking the dining room doors. He didn't notice the thin dish moving past his feet. Nor the dinner set. A spoon, fork, and knife glided in a line. Locks on cabinets and doors had kept the Renaults safe from errant projectiles for generations, but mekari and ghosts finally found the dexterity and intelligence to crack them.

The hutch's topmost shelf creaked, then cracked as it split free from the brackets holding it in place. The shelf, plate, and silverware hovered between knee and head height for a moment, as if scanning the area for their target. Then everything launched in Julie's direction. Nobody else could warn her.

Garrett yearned to, but as long as he sat perfectly still, he would stay safe. It had worked so far. Meanwhile, he'd let everyone else die. Could he live with himself? His breathing grew ever more labored.

Projectiles zipped toward Julie's blind side.

The shelf reached her first but never struck. It instead stopped inches from her back and rotated onto its flat side. The plate collided with it, shattering glass into a hundred tiny shards. Julie turned wide-eyed at the sound. Then the shelf swooped low, catching the sharp ends of the knife and fork. The spoon bounced off.

Julie jerked and stepped back with Marie at each subsequent collision. Derrick ran over to the sisters as the spoon hit the floor. He pumped his older sister's shoulder and gave a look that must've asked if she was okay. She nodded right after, and in an instant, he was moving toward the shattered glass plate.

Glass vibrated below him, stopping his advance. Plate shards levitated nearly an inch before their assault was again halted. The shelf slammed down, covering them and skittering the fork and knife along the floorboards. Derrick removed his sweat-soaked pullover and swept up the errant silverware and remaining glass.

"Seems one ghost relishes your existence." Lithyipur readjusted to close the hutch gap.

"Billy." Julie was breathing hard, still holding Marie's hand. "It must be."

"You named him? How quaint."

The flash of a smile fled her lips. She peered at Garrett, snapping her fingers in his direction. He kept his expression frozen. Her snapping fingers balled into a fist that she released with a sigh. She turned her attention back to Marie, who blinked with an otherwise blank expression.

Derrick ran back and forth between the center of the room, casting anything loose into the fire. All except the animated shelf, which he left alone other than to clean up the glass underneath.

Claude sat motionless, save for the occasional shudder and otherwise faint rise and fall of his chest. His hand remained pressed against the makeshift bandage covering his face.

Lithyipur struggled to barricade the foyer as ghosts clamored for entry with changing tactics. Try as he might, weaponized place settings made their way into the room. He shifted so that most of his body pressed against the hutch but freed one arm to intercept the latest projectiles. He grabbed two plates as they sauntered into the room. Handed them to Derrick whenever he dashed close by. One shattered at his feet. Flecks of glass buried themselves in his calf. He grimaced but otherwise stoically bore the wounds.

Iris cooed at the children, failing to calm their hysterical fits.

Garrett continued to watch and listen. He was no help, and he was safe standing still. He repeated the false lines over and over, unable to escape their allure.

Marie's face wrinkled with lines of confusion. Her lips trembled to speak. She scanned the room, then glanced at her stomach. Creases of terror replaced her confused stare. "Julie? What . . . what 'appened?"

Julie wrapped her good arm around Marie, held her tight for a firm and fast hug. "A Shifter or Dreamer got to you, but you're back, and I need you. I'm going to help Claude. You need to wake up your husband. His feet have been glued to the floor since we pushed that couch off us."

"Couch?" Marie tilted her head, then seemed to remember the past few minutes. She broke free from Julie and cut around the fallen piece of furniture.

Garrett bit his lip, clenched his torso tighter.

Julie, wincing, knelt on the floor next to Claude.

Marie peeled Garrett's hands free and sandwiched them between her own. "I need you, Gare. Stronger together than apart, remember?"

He did, but why bother? Moving made him a target. He was safe here. Except he wasn't. Shame bellowed like the fires of a forge within him.

"Please, please, please." She kissed his cheek. His forehead. His hand.

At least she was safe at the moment. That was good. Comforting thoughts served him better than death-defying action.

Derrick tossed more splinters into the fire, then prepared for another sweep of the room. Sweat-drenched clothes clung fiercely to him, leaving little of his body underneath to the imagination. As he planted one foot on the rug, he suddenly stopped and turned back. Mesmerized by the flickering flames, he slowly crouched forward. He reached out, nearly touching a burning log before reeling back.

Ghosts wouldn't touch the fire.

But a possessed human would.

"Hey, hey, hey," Garrett shouted, finally breaking free from the Feeder's paralyzing fear. He slipped Marie's gentle hold and approached

Derrick from the long way around the couch. He pried the knife from Kelly's sleeping grasp—just in case things turned out—and closed it before pocketing it. He tiptoed to the fireplace, a calming hand leading the way. "Derrick, stop."

Derrick shot up, staring in bewilderment until Garrett was in arm's reach. Then he punched him square in the face, casting him to the floor. The back of his head cracked against wood, and a nightmare overtook his consciousness.

43. A Fickle Thing

Ghosts. Goblins. Dancing on his grave.

Ghosts. Goblins. Dancing on his grave.

What's going on? Garrett walked the other direction, entering the same scene. Black skies, dirt stretching to the horizon. An unlabeled tombstone sticking up from the ground. No trees or other plants. And . . .

Ghosts. Goblins. Dancing on his grave.

This doesn't make sense. I know *it doesn't make sense. I'm dreaming.* He pinched himself. Blinked hard.

Ghosts. Goblins. Dancing on his grave.

Garrett threw his arms to the side, opening up his chest, and roared at the sky. He screamed until his lungs burned, and his bare knees slumped to the earth.

Ghosts. Goblins. Dancing on his grave.

I have to get out. I have to get to the others. He prostrated himself before the lone tombstone. He beat his forehead against the dirt, trying to wake up, and instead buried his head in the freshly laid plot. Reptilian cackling and discordant whistling yanked him back out. There they were.

Ghosts. Goblins. Dancing on his grave.

He pulled out his hair in small clumps.

"Do your efforts work as intended?" a gravelly female whispered into his ear.

Garrett whirled around, slamming his rear onto the dirt where he'd beaten his head. He scampered back a few feet. Dirt sifted over his hands, embedded granules underneath his nails.

The speaker was barely in view. A shimmering brown silhouette too distant for the nearby voice that spoke to him, yet he knew it as hers when she spoke again. "Are you enjoying your glimpse of the future?"

"What do you want?" Garrett asked. The pitter-patter of goblin feet behind him sounded closer than ever. Ghosts breathed winter frost onto his neck. He didn't dare turn to face them. His greatest threat lay straight ahead.

"To make a deal." Not an inch of her silhouette moved.

He willed himself to stand. "Let me out of here."

"That's what *you* want. We're here to discuss what *I* want, which is simple. I want your body. I should've had David's until that traitor stole it, but yours is an improvement."

"So what? I won't wake unless I agree? I'd rather live out this nightmare than give you my body."

"I imagine so. Fortunately for you, more lies on the table. I'll cease the attacks. Your family goes free. Lives, at least until the next Breach. It's your life or everyone's. Unless you believe you can hold out for another few weeks."

A few weeks? The chaos of the room took place in the span of a few minutes. Ghosts eventually tired but not as fast as the living. Even if everyone survived the opening salvo, how long could they keep it up?

"How will you stop the attacks?" he asked. "How do I know you're even capable of it? Aren't the ghosts and mekari fighting to escape just as you are?"

"Do you know who I am?"

It was obvious. "Tiliminia."

"Good. The others will listen to me because this arrangement was my idea from the start. If I order it, it will be done. And I'll keep my word because frankly, it's in my best interest not to flood your world with spirits and mekari. I'd risk losing a good thing. As a gesture of goodwill, I'll cease the attacks when you wake up."

These mekari love their gestures of goodwill.

"We do, indeed."

Garrett scoured his scalp, searching for the sieve that leaked his thoughts.

Tiliminia laughed, inhuman teeth flashing a vile yellow. A crimson corona outlined her silhouette. Scents of burning chemicals and smoke wafted in Garrett's direction. "You have an hour to consider my proposition."

"An hour?" He'd needed months before he quit his job to pursue an MBA.

"An hour. The process is simple. When you realize you have no choice, you will open yourself to possession. Take down the walls that keep me out, and I shall be first in line."

"What will you do with Marie?"

"Nothing. She can live her own life."

"As a single mom?"

"An improved position over the one where you allow these attacks to continue."

"You can't expect me to tru—"

"One hour. If you tell anyone, my proposition is retracted. I have no desire to worry about someone stabbing me while I sleep. Now, prepare to wake."

Blackness exploded in totality before him. Sounds of ghosts and goblins halted. It was like a movie turned off mid-reel. He closed his eyes. Maybe things weren't as bad off as he'd left them. He'd survived some length of time while unconscious. If the Renaults had fought for two hours and beat the enemy back, there was a chance they could last the remaining weeks. With luck, the Breach might even end early. Theories from Overseers suggested an attack of this magnitude may prematurely close a Breach.

What's more, death was preferable to life as a backstage guest inside his own body.

Was that too selfish a thought? After all, this whole experience proved the existence of an afterlife. Death wasn't the end, for him or anyone else in the house. Letting loose a mekar with his identity threatened to wreak more havoc than releasing a host of incorporeal beings into the world.

This was an impossible choice.

He sat still, waiting to wake. After a moment, he laughed. A bitter, cold laugh reminiscent of Tiliminia's. He held more control over his life than ever, and he didn't want it.

He opened his eyes, hoping for a reprieve from complete darkness, if not from this perversion of sleep.

Emptiness surrounded him. He lost sense of floating or sitting altogether.

He closed his eyes.

Opened them.

Let this end.

Closed them. Opened them.

WAKE UP!

Closed. Opened.

Then he saw.

Not the room where a possessed fist had knocked him down. He instead lay in bed in his Boston apartment. Marie slept soundly beside him. Both wore a shirt and underwear, carefree in his home. He shook her but couldn't wake her, no matter the force.

"Nice place," a stranger said. "Sad I won't get to see it in person."

David Renault stood at the foot of the bed.

Garrett shielded Marie with his body. "Wha—"

"Shh. Not much time. Take the deal. Lithyipur's aware of it. He's got a plan. But don't speak of it when you wake or Tiliminia will know." Like Garrett's last dream involving David, there was no accent.

"How do I know you're not Tiliminia trying to trick me?" Garrett asked.

"My spirit's in limbo while Lithyipur's in my body. We've worked out a plan. All you need to do is remember this: a golden sun sets brightest over the coldest lake."

He scratched a beard that wasn't there. Smoothly shaved skin brushed against his nails. David's appearance confused him as much as the bizarre phrase. "What?"

"Say it. A golden sun sets brightest over the coldest lake."

Garrett repeated the phrase. What did he have to lose? Back and forth they went a dozen times until with a blink, he shuddered awake.

Hardwood braced against his back. His shoes rested comfortably on the end of the rug. He stared at copper ringlets inlaid in the beveled plaster ceiling of the sitting room. A voice to his left snapped him from his daze.

"Welcome back," David whispered. "You have not missed much." Not David. Lithyipur. The monotone gave it away before the neutral accent.

"Where's Marie?" Fatigue racked Garrett, weakening his voice as much as his limbs. He wasn't sure Lithyipur heard him.

"She is well." Lithyipur knelt, bringing his face inches from Garrett's. "Everyone is still alive. A few worse for the wear. I am assisting in rousing everyone. Only Iris remains in slumber. Someone will get ice for your eye. In the meantime, a golden sun sets brightest over the coldest lake."

"Huh?"

"He wakes!" Lithyipur stood, patted his knees, and stepped out of reach.

Footsteps pounded against the floor, reverberating in his back. Marie sat down with him, held his cheeks, and kissed his lips with a tight hold that seemed to last as long as his dream. She set to redressing his wounds once they pulled apart.

The second message had come from Lithyipur, if not David himself. What if Tiliminia's message had been his too? A clever ploy to trick him. What was he going to do?

He had an hour to decide.

44. Control

"Why did they stop?" Marie doled out energy bars around the room, giving the last two to Garrett before squeezing in beside him. They crammed themselves in the chair occupied by Kelly before the attack.

As an automatic reflex, he wrapped himself around her, but her warmth felt distant, as though separated by invisible layers. Pain, too, registered as a faint annoyance, his bandaged skin pulsating under his clothes. The room's whole conversation seemed to take place miles away.

A single thought diminished the entirety of his senses.

Can I trust Lithyipur?

"I don't think they're in a rush." Derrick, wearing a fresh set of clothes, leaned on the wall near the fireplace. Grady clung to his side. "They can turn us against each other on a whim. Sorry for that shiner, Garrett."

After noticing the room was waiting for his reaction, he offered a forgiving nod.

"It's not like we'll last long losing our senses, losing our minds. Speaking of, how's the eye, Claude?"

"Painkillers are mankind's greatest invention." He gave a long, low sigh. "But I think it's a goner, and it still hurts if I use my good eye. You'll excuse me if it looks like I'm taking a nap." Claude sat upright on the couch, one eye closed, the other covered by layers of bloody gauze taped to him. He bit into his square of congealed oats, sugar, and protein. Kelly sat next to him, with Tommy in her lap. She rubbed Claude's thigh and whispered into his ear with an apologetic look. After a pensive moment, he half-smiled and held her hand.

How can inviting a second possession be the right answer?

"Claimers and Hiders might seek another way in." Julie paced in front of the dining room doors. The heavy-duty lock held, as did the bolt up top, but chunks as large as a square inch were knocked out of the wood. "That's where they did the most damage. They've been resting for weeks, so it's not a matter of fatigue. They've gone somewhere to regroup."

"Are you sure they're gone?" Derrick asked.

"Yes. I See Billy bouncing in place, and no other spirits." Julie pointed to her left, at the corner nearest Lithyipur. Her pointing turned into a dismissive wave. "Yes, yes you did well. Thank you." She snorted. "He's proud of his heroics."

"As he should be." Lithyipur spoke slowly and crossed his arms, subjugating the conversation with an aura of control. Behind him, half the hutch's cabinet doors and both its shelves were missing. The framing held strong for now. "You will want a plan sorted out by the time Iris wakes." His gaze lingered on Garrett a little longer than the rest.

What benefits Lithyipur the most?

"She'll want to give her input." Derrick tilted his head at his mother, asleep in her favorite chair.

"I mean no disrespect," Lithyipur said, "but she exudes an air that would rather judge a plan than present one. She will have a say though. Now, this remains the safest room in the house, so I suggest we stay here. The fireplace should last until morning, especially once the hutch has worn out its other uses. Despite the risks, I regret not boarding up the entry points as Claude suggested. No time for that now."

"We can reinforce the frame of the dining room doors," Derrick said. "Take some pressure off the handle. We only need a few boards."

"Do it. Give me the hammer when you finish. I will ensure the nails stay in place."

Derrick whispered with Grady. They exchanged smiles and wriggling eyebrows, then hugged. "Y'all keep at it. I'll be back in a sec." He jumped up and jogged into the dining room. Grady positioned himself near Iris's unconscious body.

Julie stopped pacing and stomped the floor. "We're going to give a mekar the only weapon in the room?"

"If I have not earned your trust by now," Lithyipur said, "it is already too late, and your work is for naught." He snuck another glance Garrett's way.

Marie's pregnant. One baby with mekarian blood. Lithyipur might want to raise his kid after all, and what body is better than the father's?

"I don't trust you," Julie said, "but I'll be blind when they return. Not much choice, I guess."

Lithyipur grinned. "That leaves two entry points. If two people cover the foyer and two the window, three adults can remain to watch the children and feed the fire with any debris. Claude is faring better than expected, but our position improves if he rests until he has stanched the bleeding. That actually leaves one for debris, and one for the children. There is no allotted room for error."

A coded message? It doesn't matter. You know what he wants. Is it worth the risk?

"I can help." Grady plucked at the fabric of the chair's arm. "I'll watch Tommy."

That puts them both in danger.

Faces around the room mirrored his concern.

Lithyipur stretched his neck to one side, then the next. "Only if your father accepts this proposition."

"I can do it." The boy's hands shifted until he folded his arms, his elbow still in contact with the chair.

Marie leaned over Garrett, propping her elbows on the armrest. The length of her body stretched before him. "I believe in you."

"Thanks, Aunt Marie." He stiffened his back, though his shoulders still slumped.

"You got it." Marie slid back into her tight spot, kissed Garrett on the lips as if nothing was wrong. He kissed back, automatically again, not feeling a thing but frayed nerves. He didn't see if she noticed, his attention occupied by Lithyipur and Julie retaking the stage.

"Food and sleep are the other issues." Julie leaned against Iris's chair at an arm's length from Grady. Her aunt twitched and then returned to peace. "Real food, not just energy bars, and real sleep. We can empty out the ottoman and bring it back to barricade the dining room. Grab a couple sleeping bags, and put them in the center, in sight of everyone. The more I think about it, the more we need Grady." She swiveled her head toward him. "I'm glad you're tough, but if your dad allows it, you still have to come to us if you need help. Bravery only does so much, okay?"

Grady nodded, but facial tics muddied his messaging.

"As for food. We'll have to make runs in pairs. Can we expect more lulls like this, mekar?"

Lithyipur didn't react to her tone. "I doubt it, but I cannot know for sure as long as I inhabit this body." His eye twitched as he met Garrett's gaze. Small and imperceptible, if one wasn't watching for it. "I sense their presence," he explained, "but I cannot communicate with any of them."

He's watching his words, deceiving someone. There were only two answers. *Either me or Tiliminia.*

Measured footfalls echoed from behind. Garrett panicked that his hour had ended early. In his frantic turning, he nearly headbutted Marie, who stroked his arm in response. Derrick entered the room a moment later. He held a hammer, plus boards under each arm. A square shape—presumably a box of nails—bulged in his pant pocket.

"Just me," he said. "Y'all look like you've seen a ghost."

"You lose one eye." Claude opened his good eye, winced, and shut it. "And someone thinks it's okay to steal the role of family funny man." Kelly squeezed his hand and whispered again to him. He mouthed something that relaxed her shoulders.

The room continued to discuss preparations. They assigned roles with backups depending on how the next attack went. Everyone did their part. Bore their weight to help the others. Garrett needed to do the same, but giving up his body? Was that the only answer? The prospect almost short-circuited him. He recovered by seeking an answer: a sign beyond an encoded message. Scanning his memories, he waded through painful moments over the past two months. Words spoken by David, Marie, and other Renaults. Maurice Renault sneaking into his dreams and guiding him. Nia's last moments. None of it helped, he realized, because he sought answers to the wrong questions.

"Want to help me with the rug?" Marie asked.

It was to be hung somewhere, but Garrett couldn't recall the details. "Can you ask Julie? I'm still a little dazed. Give me a minute, and I'll help with the next thing."

Marie's lips swept to the side. She froze in this pensive state. Had she read his thoughts? As he clenched his stomach and jammed his tongue against his teeth, she kissed his forehead and left. He breathed slowly, staying careful to keep quiet and not draw notice.

A new set of questions stirred. Did Lithyipur really care about his child inside of Marie? And was he better suited to help them from inside a human body or living on the mekari plane? How could Garrett know either answer for sure? Even Julie didn't understand the mind of a mekar.

Were Lithyipur and Tiliminia diametrically opposed?

David's translation from the night Maurice died indicated a certain friendliness between the former family patriarch and Lithyipur. Marie and Derrick even viewed him as a potential ally at the time. Garrett also believed that Tiliminia had instructed a Dreamer to put the idea of Claude and David's betrayals in his head.

Her whole plan had been to sow division in the house. Perhaps, in part, to force David to admit his crime and open himself up to Tiliminia. Ultimately, that left two options. Either Lithyipur had a way to get Tiliminia out of David, or Lithyipur and Tiliminia plotted together.

How could he know the truth? Garrett gnawed on the fat of his index finger. His right leg bounced. He quieted it by tapping his toes instead. He wanted to believe Lithyipur. Knew the chance of them all surviving repeated attacks otherwise neared zero. And logic suggested the mekar had told the truth. Spreading his seed on Earth seemed a victory in and of itself.

Derrick was finishing boarding up the dining room, time ticking with each strike of the hammer.

Garrett had to try this. He waited to stand until Marie absorbed herself in her project. He knew seeing her face or hearing her question him would render his task impossible. He snuck toward Lithyipur and gave him a well-understood nod that was returned in kind.

Garrett propped up five fingers on his shoulder that only the mekar could see. One by one, he curled them into his palm. When he reached the count of zero and formed a fist, he opened himself up.

He floated in the current of life like a leaf on a river.

It lasted a scant moment. A force drove him down, pushed him into the role of spectator within his own body. Lithyipur's thoughts merged with his own.

You made the right choice. Unfortunately, you're not going to like it.

45. Atonement

Iris woke with a start. She sat bolt upright, locked onto David. She called out his name. Grady inched toward his grandmother, stopping short of touching her. She ignored him, as did everyone else, who halted their tasks to inspect the commotion.

David Renault's face contorted into harsh lines of anger and hate. "Good work, Lithyipur."

Tiliminia, Garrett realized, from deep within his own body.

Yes, confirmed Lithyipur.

"Indeed." Lithyipur, controlling Garrett's limbs like a marionette, reached into his pocket. Withdrew the knife inside. He flipped it open with deft experience, but it wasn't until the first blow landed that Garrett understood Lithyipur's plans.

Stabs bore into David's body like the assassination of Julius Caesar. Tiliminia stumbled back, slammed against the ravaged hutch. Screaming of various pitches filled the air, but only Marie's pierced the chaos.

"Gare, no!" Tears lay audible in her plea.

Tiliminia slumped to the floor. Lithyipur swooped down like a hawk, continuing his attack as if the wounds may seal at any moment.

"How?" Blood sputtered from Tiliminia's—David's—lips. "We made a deal."

Those words only intensified the assault, until the combined strength of David's children dragged Lithyipur from the scene. By then, he didn't resist. His work done, he allowed Julie to take the knife. David's head lolled lifelessly to the side. Though Garrett controlled nothing, he felt a soreness from the grip.

"Where did he get this?" Julie closed the blade after a brief inspection. She stared aimlessly in a manner Garrett had never seen: dumbfounded.

Marie collapsed over her father, wailing.

Claude stood over her, covering his gauze-wrapped eye. "From Kelly. Same one that went through my eye." He covered his good eye as his voice cracked. "Dad . . ."

Derrick nibbled his thumbnail as he held onto *Lithyipur*'s shirt collar—if Garrett didn't own his body, he didn't own his clothes. The mekar tilted his head back to indicate he'd sit a safe distance away. Derrick released the shirt with a push that stumbled Lithyipur to his destination. As if realizing the body's true owner, he placed his palms together in an apology.

Lithyipur waved him away, sat cross-legged on the floor next to the far end of the couch, barely in view of the murder scene. "My obligation to you all requires that I grant an explanation." *And I'm going to need your body a moment longer.* Garrett felt cramped, as though stuck in a coffin.

Julie had just knelt next to Marie. "Lithyipur?"

"What are you doing?" Marie screamed. "Help me with Dad!"

"It's too late for him." Julie's yoga pants drank up David's blood, saturating them.

"We have to try." Marie used her body, hands, and arms in a futile effort to stanch her father's wounds.

Grady and Tommy's sobs sailed from the room's corner. Garrett assumed Iris was with them, but Lithyipur never checked.

Derrick sidestepped to where Marie draped herself over her father. Did he think of him as his father too—or still an uncle? Either way, he crouched down and rubbed her back, coaxing her away from the lifeless body. She leapt into Derrick's embrace, and the two toppled to the floor. Bright red soiled her skin and clothes above the waist, as if *she*'d been stabbed. Her crying didn't bother Lithyipur in the slightest, and Garrett had no control over his heart to make it ache.

"As I was saying." Lithyipur straightened Garrett's back. "An explanation. Tiliminia had to die to ensure your safety. That necessitated trapping her in the body she so desperately craved."

"How do you know Tiliminia didn't escape? You jump bodies well enough." Julie fidgeted with the knife and locked onto Garrett's body like she was considering filling him with holes as Lithyipur had done to her father.

What about the deal she mentioned? Garrett asked.

You humans are not the most patient creatures. Lithyipur raised his forefinger, commanding silence in a way Garrett was incapable of with his own body. "Patience, please. I assume you would prefer Garrett's company to mine, but once I depart, you will not hear from me for some time. Unless one of you inherits your grandfather's talent and learns our languages."

"We're," Claude's voice hitched, "listening." Except for his mouth, he was covering every inch of his face. The volume of Derrick and Marie's crying upstaged whatever grief their brother put forth.

"Tiliminia negotiated a particular deal with David, binding her to him when he broke their arrangement by speaking of it. I interrupted that when I possessed him, but David and I had no such deal. He simply opened himself up—like Garrett did—and no human body is big enough to hold two mekari. I snuck in like a thief, able to leave just as quickly. My departure created the vacuum that drew her in, a prison she desired until the moment I betrayed her. Her backup plan contrived to trade your safety for permanent control of Garrett. The two spoke while he lay unconscious. I dispatched David to spy on the arrangement and devise our own play."

"That damned fool," Iris snapped, confirming her place near the kids.

"I then spoke with Tiliminia. Proposed a deal to her where she determined the safety nets. It involves a plethora of mekarian legal jargon, but the effect is that I can only pass beyond an Earthly Hellspot while Tiliminia lives. Obviously, I have expunged that possibility. What Tiliminia did not count on was how little that freedom concerned me. She did not believe I would sacrifice the chance to walk your world, child or no, and she died for it. The challenge lay in convincing Garrett, who rightfully mistrusted me. Whether he made the correct decision is for you all to decide, though I doubt you would have lived past tomorrow otherwise."

Lithyipur inspected his hands—Garrett's hands—as if seeing them for the first time. He brushed stiff blood off his palm and snorted. "Some lingering ghosts will continue haunting you until the Breach closes, but they should not pose any serious threat. As for the mekari who followed Tiliminia, I will render them docile."

More loopholes? Garrett asked. He felt Lithyipur hiding something, as if protecting the Renaults from his fellow mekari was less a favor, and more an inevitability. What *had* drawn so many mekari to one place? Surely, it wasn't just the curse.

"More loopholes," Lithyipur confirmed aloud. He opted not to elaborate, pushing Garrett's lips into a grin.

"Why should we believe any of this?" Julie fidgeted with the knife.

"Ask her." Lithyipur pointed at Iris. "Take care of my child. I look forward to seeing him in a few years." An icy threat lined his voice. "Garrett will return to you shortly."

About Marie's curse, thought Lithyipur. *It is lifted, but the burden her father placed on her will never lighten. If she ever doubts herself as a mother because of the harm she inflicted upon her younger brother, tell her that her cursed behavior didn't extend to all children. Only would-be younger siblings. Your sweet Marie was the gatekeeper that kept her father's progeny trimmed.*

Is that true? Why only tell me? Why would I wait to tell Marie?

A response never came.

Lithyipur's departure felt like the aftereffects of vomiting up contaminated food. It sapped Garrett's energy in exchange for a sensation of wholeness. He snaked his soul back into control of his body, sprinting through a labyrinth that ran in one direction. Vague awareness of a discussion took place around him. His hearing fought to reconnect with his mind and provide more than muffled words. His sight dimly registered faint shapes, and the smell of sweat-filled air slowly intensified. When he regained his senses, he gasped as if rising from several minutes underwater.

"I guess you're back." Julie crouched beside Garrett's supine form, no longer holding the murder weapon. A pair of thin legs stood behind her. Marie sniffed erratically as her sister spoke. Shame kept Garrett from facing her, regardless of whether she blamed him. "David spoke with Iris in her dreams as well. She corroborated Lithyipur's story. Told us that this was Dad's choice. He knew he was going to die but saw no other way to save us. I don't know if I believe it all, but I checked the foyer. I can See ghosts like it's a normal Breach, which matches his promise to drive away the mekari. The ghosts are in disarray, like chickens without heads." She sighed, stood up, and faced away. "Yes, except you, Billy."

"Gare." Marie waited a moment, spoke again with a tinge of forcefulness. "Gare, look at me."

Garrett closed his eyes, tilted his head up, and took a deep breath. Only at the end of his exhale did he open them. Lithyipur's final revelation tortured him, but not as much as the blood on his hands.

"Did you know Dad would die?"

"No." He reflexively lifted his arm to comfort Marie. It never reached her, instead shaking a foot above his chest. "I'm so sorry. I thought Lithyipur had a plan for Tiliminia, but I never expected this."

Marie, silent, tormented him with her sad eyes. She occasionally glanced at her father, her fingers twitching on her thigh each time she did. A long tablecloth shrouded him.

"We have a plan at least." Claude now sat on the couch. Kelly was missing. So too were Iris and the children. Muffled juvenile crying one room over gave away their location.

Standing between Claude and Marie, Derrick rubbed his eyes. "What do we do with Uncle Dav—with Dad—with David's body?" His defeated cadence mirrored that of his siblings.

"We have to bury him," Julie said.

"Is that safe?"

"Does it matter?" Claude asked. "It's Dad, and the kids have seen enough without his corpse living in the room."

"Then we all go together," Derrick said.

"Not me," Julie said.

"What do you mean?"

"I'm too mad at him to say goodbye the right way. I'll sort out my feelings after the Breach."

"But Julie." Marie's shoulders slumped, and her arms went limp beside her.

"Stop it. I'll clean up here while y'all take care of business. We don't want to stare at dried blood in this room for however many weeks remain. Garrett and his two good arms can help me."

"Is that a good idea?" Claude asked.

"Why? Because the last thing he did was stab Dad? Either we buy into everything Lithyipur said or none of it. I don't trust Garrett, but I'm not worried about him attacking me. Besides, I still have the knife." She patted a small bulge in her leggings' pocket.

Marie started to say something. To defend Garrett, perhaps. She cleared her throat instead. He understood. He deserved what came his way.

"Good. We'll reconvene after the burial and decide how to handle the Breach moving forward. Marie, can you get a body bag from storage?"

In response, she swayed back and forth, then walked to where her father lay. She crouched on a dry patch of floor near his face and pulled the tablecloth down to his neck. Her sobs started like snorts, then evolved into heaping shudders.

Garrett pushed himself up so fast that dizziness kept him from rising to his feet. He pressed his hands against the floor for balance. Derrick crept up behind Marie, delicately stretching his hand out. Before he reached her, she stopped crying with a sharp inhale.

Marie wiped her cheeks and nose, snot trailing on the back of her hand, then lifted her shoulder in her father's direction. "I'll carry him with Derk."

"Are you sure?" Julie asked.

"I said I'd do it."

"I'd like to help too," Garrett said.

Julie scoffed. "You can't be serious."

"I owe him that much. I'll be back here as soon as we set him down. You don't need to worry about cleaning anything either. My mess, my responsibility." He assumed the family kept supplies for getting blood out of hardwood, but even then, he knew cleanup would last hours.

"I think," Marie said, "that sounds good." She stood up straight, with a stiffer confidence than usual. She walked over and reached to help him up. Derrick jogged to his other side. Together they hoisted him up, though it was Derrick who supported him once on his feet. "I'll be right back with the . . . bag."

She scooted the shelfless hutch, then disappeared into the foyer.

"I need to check on Tommy." Claude meandered toward the dining room. His hand hovered over the door handle a moment before he turned it open. "Hope he's not too afraid of old gauze face here."

"Daddy!" Tommy yelled.

"Hey kiddo."

Julie rubbed her forehead. "Things will be different now." Before Garrett or Derrick could respond, she fled into the dining room as well.

Garrett's thumb grazed his lip.

"Can you forgive me?" he whispered to himself before speaking louder. "Do you think she'll forgive me?"

"Julie?" Derrick smiled.

"I mean Marie."

Derrick's smile vanished behind a rigid face. "Yeah, I knew who you meant. I told you a long time ago—we're all on the same side. Julie *is* right though. Things will be different now."

EPILOGUE

"Julie!" Marie shouted from the house foyer. She wore a loose-fitting long-sleeved shirt, hiding that she was starting to show underneath. "We're going to the doctor."

"Stay safe," her sister called from the library.

Holding hands, the couple meandered into the sitting room. It looked as it had before the Breach. Reupholstered furniture. Fresh staining on the walls. Doors back on their hinges. He'd witnessed first-hand how little concern the Renaults held for finances. Despite harsh winter conditions that struck the surrounding areas, repairs started the week after the Ring fell. It had made Garrett's decision easier. Now he just needed to tell Marie.

"What do you think she's reading?" he asked.

"Probably how to tell if a child's part mekar from an ultrasound."

"Not a revenge spell?"

Marie rubbed his arm as they continued from the dining room into the kitchen. "She'll forgive you. Eventually."

Garrett nodded, not wanting to argue and upset her. Julie had yet to absolve him or her father for their parts in David's death. Since only she, him, and Marie had occupied the house for the past month, he started to wonder what she did with all the time not speaking to him.

A worry for another time. Today was a happy day.

He led Marie into the garage. Their hands fell apart only once they reached the sedan. The same one that brought him to this house several months prior. They hopped in, and Garrett pressed the garage button.

No sooner had the chain brought up the door did Marie ask, "Would you mind getting me a snack?"

Garrett pulled out an energy bar from his pocket and handed it over. "Got you covered."

"Schwaz!" She tore into the wrapper. Ate it so fast that Garrett waited to start the car in case she needed a second. As she chewed the last bite, she gave a thumbs up, and he started the engine. They rolled out onto the driveway, closing the garage door behind as they circled around the estate's wide driveway. Then they were off to Alexandria.

Marie wanted to use a doctor closer to Ajaccio, but Garrett held steadfast against that one point. The pregnancy might turn complicated, and he wanted a city doctor to take care of her. They drove to the tune of pop music similar to what they played in the Northeast. Only difference was a bit of country added to the mix, something he immediately took a liking to.

They talked about silly things, ebbing in and out of silence. During one bout of quiet, Garrett decided to tell her his decision. Apparently, Marie needed to share her own news.

Simultaneously, they said, "I have something to tell you."

After sharing an awkward chuckle, Garrett prompted her to go first. A couple more minutes to strengthen his resolve wouldn't hurt.

"Okay." She intertwined her fingers and tapped her thumbs together. "First, let me say that I don't want this, but I think it's only fair." She took a breath. "You should go back to Harvard in the fall. I've got Julie to look after me, and Derrick might be moving back to Louisiana. It's not fair to force you to live out the rest of your life in a haunted house."

Garrett started with a snort, then laughed so hard he veered onto the rough grooves of the shoulder before correcting.

"You okay?" Marie asked.

"I'm fine. It's just—I knew this was going to happen."

"I don't want you to go. I love you. You know that, right?"

"I do. That's what worries me about what I need to say. I officially dropped out of Harvard. I'll start sending applications to online MBA programs next week. Should give me plenty of time to start in the fall. It's not Harvard," he rolled the 'r', "but at least we'll stay together."

"No!" Marie swiped her finger across the open air. "You can't give up on your future because of me. You had everything planned out."

Garrett's mother had told him many times to find someone he trusted, who trusted him. After the ordeal suffered with Marie, he knew no one could compare—not that his binding by oath offered much of an alternative. The experience made their wedding vows seem like a childish promise by comparison. "I'm not giving up anything. You're my future."

"What are you gonna do for work?"

"I'll find something remote. Worst case, I take on contracts or consult. I might not always be home, but at least my home will be with you."

"What will your parents think?"

"I'll wait to tell them until after next weekend. Meeting you will make the news easier to digest." He wanted this conversation over. The longer it lasted, the longer it stretched out Marie's guilt. "Plus, we're technically living rent and board free so money's no problem. The extra time off will help us plan our big showy wedding. And this is what I want. It is."

Marie's expression flickered between a smile and a frown, eventually settling into a set of pursed lips. "If you say so."

Over the course of the remaining car ride, her demeanor gradually shifted to effervescence. She serenaded him with more of the radio's pop songs. He caught her glancing his way, trying to hide how happy his decision had made her. She might try to talk him out of it again, but by the time they reached the gynecologist's office, she practically skipped alongside him.

His insides knotted as they had off and on since David's death. He held tight to his other secret—the one Lithyipur had revealed about the specifics of Marie's former curse. He worried that telling her may do more harm than good and that it was all a lie anyway. Most of all, he worried telling her earlier than Lithyipur wished would somehow break the mekarian contract that kept her and her siblings' curses in check. He pushed the guilt down as he always did—by bringing her hand up for a quick kiss. Her ensuing smile calmed his inner turmoil.

They checked in at the front desk, and a nurse directed them to a patient room. The pristine walls and extravagant decor fit a high-end jewelry store. The nurse took Marie's vitals, asked her some cursory questions, then left them alone. They waited several minutes for the doctor to show. Marie sat on the exam table in the center of the room while Garrett stood beside her. The ultrasound machine was set up nearby.

A knock came at the door, followed by the entry of Dr. Khatun. He had dark skin, a dad bod, and rectangular glasses. Nobody within a two-hour drive came better recommended, especially for twins. He set Marie's chart on the counter and extended a hand from the sleeve of his lab coat. He shook Marie's hand first, then gave the same gentle handshake to Garrett. They exchanged short pleasantries, then he dove right in.

"I know you're eager to learn the genders, but it's possible I won't be able to tell today. I don't want to get your hopes up." He put on a pair of sterile gloves.

"Yep," Garrett said. "You told us last time."

"You'd be amazed how many parents don't listen." Dr. Khatun angled Marie's seat back. Asked her to pull her shirt up to her chest. He wheeled the ultrasound monitor close to him and applied gel to the attached wand. He rubbed the head of it over her stomach, moving it all around until a grainy image of two fetuses showed on the screen. Garrett and Marie's hands crept onto one another while waiting for him to speak. "Congratulations," he said at last. "One boy and one girl."

"No horns or anything?" Garrett joked, half-serious. Marie narrowed her eyes at him.

"You'd also be amazed how many parents ask that," Dr. Khatun said. "No horns, just two normal-looking babies. Everything looks good. Did you have any questions?"

Garrett and Marie glanced at one another, then shook their heads. What they needed to know, he couldn't help with.

"This will help get that sticky gel off." Dr. Khatun handed Marie a washcloth and readjusted her seat forward. "Your next check-up should be in a month. You'll need some blood work done before then. I want to check your hormone levels and make sure everything looks as healthy as last time. There's a lab down the street if you've got the time for it now. Otherwise, the front desk can provide a list of locations." After tossing his gloves in the trash, he picked up Marie's chart. His eyes stuck to a particular line. "I did have a question for you, actually."

"What's that?" Marie cleaned off her stomach and pulled down her shirt.

"Did you know people say you live in a haunted house?"

Marie smiled. "It's a hard rumor to avoid. Lived with it my whole life."

"So, no truth to it?"

Marie shook her head convincingly. "Why do you ask?"

"I love ghost stories. One of those late-blooming fascinations. I even convinced my wife to stay in a haunted hotel in Austin once. I came across your house browsing the Internet a week or so ago and recognized the street address here." He tapped Marie's chart. "I'm glad it's not haunted. Raising twins is challenging enough. You'd probably need a third parent if ghosts were in the picture."

Garrett gulped. His stomach clenched, the innocuous statement clamping tight around his gut. He realized he was squeezing Marie's hand as it went limp. He let go, and she massaged her palm.

"I'm sorry," the doctor said. "Did I say something?"

"No," Marie said. When he seemed to be waiting for a follow-up, she added, "I think the whole twins thing is setting in."

"It's a lot to take in, but you two are great together. You'll be okay." He winked, gave another round of handshakes, and turned to leave. As he opened the door, Garrett spotted a tattoo on his neck. Three cramped parallel lines about half an inch long.

"Dr. Khatun, what's that behind your ear?"

The doctor touched the spot. He stood halfway between the hallway and their room. "You've got good eyes. It's a bad decision from a long time ago. I thought about getting it removed, but it's so small, and hardly anyone notices. Those who do usually think it's a birthmark. I use it as a reminder to always think things through. Call if you have any questions or experience any strange discomforts. Congrats again on the boy and girl."

On Garrett's right shoulder was a small chevron about the same width as Dr. Khatun's tattoo. He first noticed it a week after the final assault that cost David Renault his life and Claude his eye. He assumed it a scar at first, but while his wounds from the window shards changed shapes as they healed, the chevron stayed a constant. That left Lithyipur's branding as the likely cause. Julie reassured him inactive mekarian brandings faded with time. He had mostly put it out of his mind. If Dr. Khatun's three lines signified a previous—or worse, current—mekar possession . . .

A coincidence, nothing else. Marie's tainted pregnancy pushed his apprehension into overdrive. This wasn't the first time, and it wouldn't be the last.

"What are you thinking about?" Marie asked.

The doctor was long gone, the door closed to their private room. Marie had enough on her plate without mentioning everything that set Garrett's nerves on edge. If he noticed anything else strange, that's when he'd tell her his worries.

"Nothing. Just can't believe we're going to be parents. You good to go?"

"Yep." She smiled, though it didn't reach her eyes.

Garrett thought he caught a whiff of disappointment in her voice too. Did she not buy Dr. Khatun's story either? Did . . .

Apprehension went into overdrive yet again. They needed to get away for a vacation before the twins came. Typical parental fears paled against the knowledge that he would raise a child of mekarian descent.

And it would drive him mad if he let it.

A bleaker world awaits. The next book in the Virulent Nightmare Origins quartet is due in 2025.

Subscribe to my newsletter at cjweiss.com for announcements and updates.

Terms of Secrets Gnaw at the Flesh

My recommendation is to only reference these terms once you're deeper into the story, and only as needed.

Breach – A sporadic occurrence on a Hellspot that allows the inhabitants of the physical world, spirit world, and mekarian world to all travel within the same confined area.

Blood or Oath – Related to a family of Overseers through genetic lineage or by marriage, respectively.

Catching a lie – Pointing out a behavior that is uniformly uncharacteristic of an individual possessed by a Hider in order to oust the spirit.

Haunt – The method in which a spirit interacts with the physical world. Further categorized in the following Haunts section.

Hellspot – One of twelve locations on Earth where spirits and mekari can move from their plane of existence to the physical world via a Breach.

Mekar (pl. mekari) – An immorally inclined, humanlike species living on another plane of existence. They generally seek entry through a Breach in order to terrorize and inflict suffering or as a means to consolidate power in their world.

Overseer – A family member tied by blood or oath to protect a Hellspot during a Breach. As long as a single Overseer guarding a particular Breach lives, mekari and spirits are unable to pass farther into the physical world in all but the rarest cases.

Spirit – Ghosts as traditionally defined, with the exception that Overseers categorize them with more specificity in how they haunt living humans. Their tenuous relationship with the physical world makes any given haunt short-lived.

The Ring – An invisible, impassable enclosure that forms around a Hellspot shortly before a Breach, turning impassible upon the Breach's full emergence. The term is specific to the Renault family.

Haunts

Aware – Semi-civilized and usually non-aggressive. Typically encountered outside of a Hellspot. All spirits are Unaware or Aware and, if capable of affecting the physical world, do so as one of the types listed below.

Claimer – Forcefully possesses people for short durations. Latches onto specific emotions which determines how the possessed individual acts.

Deviant – Moves objects in the physical world. Heavier objects are more difficult to handle, but anything without sufficient resistance may be thrown, pushed, pulled, or otherwise forcefully relocated. Objects in direct touch with humans typically require multiple Deviants to affect.

Dreamers – Twists dreams in order to frighten, deceive, or weaken one's willpower. Can sometimes leave physical marks.

Feeder – Feeds on doubts and emotions, multiplying the strength of a person's negative feelings.

Hider – Gradually possesses people, slowly affecting mannerisms and behaviors until the effects are permanent, or they are caught in a lie.

Shifter – Alters the perceived reality around a person or area, which may include any given sensory element.

ACKNOWLEDGMENTS

There is no good book written without the help of early beta readers. Thank you to Rachel, Mike, Sara, Mark, Khushi, Britt, Rick, M.W., Paul, Vicki, Wes, Liberty, Lavanya, and Maddy. With your input, *Secrets Gnaw at the Flesh* became the best version of itself.

I must also give thanks to anyone who picked up this book—whether borrowed from a library or purchased from a bookstore. Your support is the reason I continue to write. As much as I love my stories, they mean little without others to share them with.

As this is the acknowledgments section, I must also acknowledge that if it wasn't for Baldur's Gate 3, this book would have come out a week sooner.

ABOUT THE AUTHOR

C.J. Weiss lives in Austin, TX with his wife, Rachel, and their two cats. In addition to *Secrets Gnaw at the Flesh*, he's the author of *A Broken Clock Never Boils*. Aside from reading and writing, he loves hiking, board games, video games, traveling, and peanut butter.

Follow him at cjweiss.com.

www.ingramcontent.com/pod-product-compliance
Lightning Source LLC
Chambersburg PA
CBHW031955150726
47990CB00005B/1715